MULTIPLE MOTIVES

A Kate Huntington Mystery

Kassandra Lamb

MULTIPLE MOTIVES
A Kate Huntington Mystery

Published in the United States of America by **misterio press**,
a Florida limited liability company
www.misteriopress.com

~~~~~~~~~

Cover art by Martina Dalton

Interior design by Debora Lewis arenapublishing.org

~~~~~~~~~

ISBN 13: 978-0-9913208-4-4 (misterio press LLC)

ISBN 10: 0991320840

To Angi –
without whose friendship, encouragement, feedback,
and willingness to read the manuscripts multiple times,
this series never would have happened.
And to all the wonderful people who read and critiqued
this book and helped me make it better.

PROLOGUE

The vehicle cruised sedately down the street.

Don't want to be getting a speeding ticket and draw attention to ourselves, now do we?

The driver of the vehicle pulled into a parking place near the intersection. The target had crossed here the day before, striding briskly along the crosswalk like she owned the world.

Rage surged, threatening to explode.

It starts today. With her!

The rage subsided, temporarily appeased.

The numbers on the sign above the bank building rolled over from 11:56 to 11:57. She didn't always go out to lunch, but that was okay.

If not now, then later. Either way, it starts today.

CHAPTER ONE

Kate ushered her last client of the morning to the door, then dug her insulated lunch bag out of her drawer and flopped down in her chair. Sighing, she put her feet up on the corner of the desk.

It had been a long morning, and a bit of a roller coaster ride. She'd gone from convincing a severely depressed new mother that suicide was not her best option to giving dating advice to a woman almost twice her age. The well-to-do widow had desperately wanted to believe the white-haired Romeo at her senior center, who claimed he lay awake every night thinking about her. Kate had gently suggested a swollen prostate was the more likely explanation for his insomnia. The woman had laughed and promised to go slow.

And then there was the client who'd just left–a fragile young woman who was starting to realize her lousy self-esteem was not because she was truly worthless but because she'd been told she was her entire life, first by her parents and then by a string of abusive boyfriends. Kate hoped she'd shored up the woman's shaky psyche sufficiently that she'd make it through the week without an emergency phone call.

Excitement bubbled in her chest as she popped the lids off containers of raw veggies and low-fat dressing. She looked at the rabbit food skeptically, not at all sure it would stave off her hunger until this evening, when she and Eddie were heading to their favorite restaurant in Towson to celebrate their anniversary.

Client hours on Tuesdays normally extended well into the evening, but today she'd rearranged her schedule and Sally, her boss, was covering emergency calls for her.

So I can turn the damned cell phone off. The only person she wanted to talk to this evening would be the man across the table from her.

Kate blew an errant dark curl out of her eyes as she wondered again if she was going to look like a fool in the slinky black dress she'd bought on a whim. At thirty-eight, her broad shoulders and a good metabolism still kept her looking trim in tailored office clothes or the jeans and loose shirts she wore around the house. But there were some lumps and sags that hadn't been there in her younger years, when she'd taken her ability to wear black slinky dresses for granted.

She popped a baby carrot in her mouth and let her mind wander.

Ten years ago today, Kathleen Nora O'Donnell had married Edward James Huntington, Jr. in an Episcopal church–a failed attempt at compromise that had satisfied neither set of parents. "Catholic Lite. Same rituals, half the guilt," Eddie had quipped at the rehearsal dinner. Kate was the only one who'd laughed.

Her Irish-American parents, warm loving people by nature, had quickly forgiven Eddie his Protestant roots and adopted him into the large O'Donnell clan. But Kate suspected her mother-in-law would never completely forgive her for stealing her only child. Especially since said child allowed his wife to call him Eddie, a nickname that previously only his mother had used.

Despite the subtle tensions in Kate's relationship with her mother-in-law, the marriage had flourished. Of course there'd been some bumps in the road along the way. Most of the time though, Kate felt like pinching herself to make sure she wasn't dreaming. Eddie was a kind, thoughtful man, with a delightful sense of humor.

Not to mention, he's not hard to look at and he's good in bed.

Bed reminded her of the only significant dark cloud in their lives. No babies. Seven years ago, they'd stopped using birth control and allowed nature to take its course. Mother Nature had not cooperated, and time was running out on them.

Speaking of time…

She glanced at the clock on her office wall, then dropped her feet to the floor. She had four more clients to see before she could go home and squirm into that black dress.

~~~~~~~~

Walking hand-in-hand with Eddie up the dark sidewalk to their front porch, Kate was no longer feeling the least bit self-conscious about her dress. A bit fuzzy-headed from wine, she stumbled on a crack.

Eddie deftly caught her before she could fall. He wrapped strong arms around her and held her against his lanky frame. Several minutes of some serious kissing left Kate even more light-headed.

She gently broke away. "We'd better take this inside before we scandalize the neighbors," she whispered, her voice husky.

In the living room, she kicked off her pumps and, out of habit, picked up the phone to check their voicemail. Her mood abruptly sobered when she heard incoherent words interspersed with stifled sobs.

Dear God, not a client emergency. Had the answering service screwed up and patched the call through to her instead of Sally?

She punched the button to replay the message. Fear twisted in her gut when she recognized the voice. She could only make out a few words but the ones she caught made the blood drain from her face.

She turned to Eddie. He froze in the act of pulling off his tie.

"It's Rob and he's sobbing." She faltered, struggling not to cry herself. "I think something's happened to Liz. They're at St. Joseph's Hospital."

Eddie was already headed back toward the front door. "Grab some comfortable shoes. I'll start the car."

As her husband drove through the dark streets as fast as he dared, Kate worried about her friend sitting scared and alone in a hospital waiting area. She imagined his tall frame slumped over, broad shoulders drooping, his face pale under salt and pepper hair. She prayed that whatever had happened to Liz wasn't life threatening. Rob adored his wife. Kate wasn't sure he'd survive losing her.

Rob Franklin's law firm was right down the hall from the counseling center where Kate worked, and they'd consulted on many mutual cases through the years. Most had involved someone trying to get out of a destructive marriage, although they'd referred clients to each other for other reasons as well. She'd found Rob to be a formidable advocate for her clients. In his personal life, he was almost as easy-going as Eddie, but when the chips were down he had a backbone made of steel. On several occasions, she'd watched him rip holes in hostile witnesses in the courtroom.

It was not surprising to her that their work relationship had evolved into a friendship. He was a bright man, with a sharp wit and an intuitive grasp of what made people tick. Nor was it surprising that once they'd started socializing outside the office, they'd become friends with each other's spouses as well. She and Eddie couldn't help but love Rob's wife, whose vivacious and feisty personality seemed too large for her petite body.

Kate's throat tightened. She blinked back the sting of tears. *Dear God, let Liz be okay.*

Eddie spun the car into the hospital's parking lot. She jumped out before he'd come to a complete stop.

In the surgical unit's waiting area, Rob's broad face was even more washed out than Kate had imagined. He started to apologize for disrupting their anniversary, but Kate cut him short. "No, no, dear, that's okay. I'm so sorry we didn't come sooner. Our phones were off."

Rob was shaking as he filled them in. Liz had been run down by a hit-and-run driver while crossing the street after work. All the doctor had said, before whisking her into surgery, was that she had several broken bones and internal bleeding.

Rob hadn't phoned his daughters yet. Shelley was away at college in Maine, and Samantha was studying at a friend's house. "It would just upset them. And by the time Shelley could get here, Liz will either...." His voice trailed off.

Be out of the woods or dead, Kate finished the grim thought in her head.

She mentally put herself in Shelley's shoes. The Franklins' eldest was a blend of her parents, but she had enough of her mother in her that Kate knew she'd be furious with her father for keeping her in the dark.

Kate shared her thoughts with Rob. He nodded in response. After refusing her offer to make the call for him, he shuffled down the hall to find someplace that was not plastered with signs prohibiting cell phones.

Eddie went off in search of coffee for all of them.

Kate sat down on an ugly beige couch to wait. She laid her head back against the wall and took in a couple ragged breaths, trying to loosen the knot in her stomach.

She was snorkeling with Eddie in the Bahamas on their honeymoon, holding hands under water. Awestruck, they watched the brightly colored tropical fish swim around them.

She woke, disoriented, to find Rob's bulk squeezed in beside her on the small couch. He clung to one of her hands. Praying she hadn't been snoring, she discreetly checked her chin for drool with her other hand.

"Sorry. I didn't mean to wake you. I just needed to…"

"… hold onto something," Kate finished, her heart aching for him.

He nodded. Tears pooled in his eyes.

Eddie came through the double doors down the corridor, balancing three steaming vending-machine cups in his hands. "Who wants bad coffee?" he asked as he approached them.

Kate squeezed Rob's hand, then released it to take one of the cups.

Rob turned his head away. He swiped his shirtsleeve across his wet face, then blew his nose into an already soggy handkerchief. When he took the proffered coffee cup from Eddie, it was now wrapped in a fresh man's handkerchief.

Kate's eyes stung at the sweet gesture. She took a sip of coffee. It truly was awful. She set the cup down on the table beside the couch.

Eddie touched her shoulder and whispered, "Walk with me for a minute."

Rob hadn't seemed to hear him. His face was turned away again. Kate thought she heard a sniffle.

They walked down the hall. Once out of Rob's earshot, Eddie slowed his pace. "I'm wondering if I should go home," he said in a low voice.

She stopped walking. Had she heard him correctly?

"Not that I want to," he quickly added. "But you two are closer, and a man can open up more readily to a woman than to another man. You know what I mean?"

"That I might be more comfort to him without you here," she said.

"Yeah. I have an early meeting tomorrow morning. You can give him that as an excuse. Unless you think I should stay?" Eddie now sounded uncertain.

"No, I think you're right. I'll drive him home later and call a cab from his house." Kate reached up and pecked her husband on the cheek. "You know, for an accountant, you're a pretty darn good psychologist."

He gave her a brief smile. "Call if you need me, and I'll be back here in ten minutes. Call anyway as soon as you know anything… if, when Liz…." His Adam's apple bobbed as he swallowed hard.

He gathered her into his arms. They clung to each other for a moment. Then he let go and turned toward the doors at the end of the hall.

Kate walked back to the couch. "Eddie's going to head home. He's got a big meeting early–"

Rob's gaze moved from her face to something behind her. His eyes went wide and he jumped up.

Kate turned to follow his stare. Eddie had frozen in mid-step. Beyond him, a doctor, wearing O.R. scrubs, had come through the doors. His mouth was set in a grim line, his skin gray with exhaustion.

She turned back to Rob just as the cup slipped from his hand, spilling bad coffee over their shoes. He swayed on his feet. His face had gone slack. She grabbed for him, and they tumbled backward onto the couch.

The doctor rushed forward, running into Eddie and knocking the cup from his hand. More coffee hit the floor. They both raced toward her, colliding again just before reaching the couch.

A bubble of hysterical laughter threatened to erupt from Kate's throat, even as her eyes stung with tears. Rob's inert body was pinning her to the couch. She struggled with one hand to pull her uncooperative black dress into some semblance of modesty.

"I'm sorry," the doctor said.

Horror washed over her. It must have shown on her face.

"No, no, that's not what I meant," the doctor quickly reassured her. "Mrs. Franklin is stable. I'm sorry I scared you. I probably looked like the Grim Reaper coming through those doors. My mind was on another case from earlier that didn't turn out so well."

A rush of relief. The bubble of laughter broke loose.

～～～～～～

Rob opened his eyes in an alternate universe. The doctor had come to tell him his Lizzie was dead, and Kate was lying underneath him and *laughing*.

He twisted around to look at her face.

Kate's giggles came to an abrupt end. "It's okay! Liz is stable. Now get off me, you big oaf."

He stared up at Ed and the doctor as he tried to process her words. Ed was grinning.

"She's really okay?"

The doctor nodded.

The ten-ton weight lifted from his chest. Scrambling to his feet, he reached down to help Kate up.

"We successfully stopped the internal bleeding," the doctor said, "and she's been given a blood transfusion. No other signs of internal injuries. The femur in her right thigh was fractured. A clean break. We've attached a metal plate to the side of the bone to stabilize it until it heals." He shook his head. "Her left ankle didn't fare quite so well. It looks like it twisted under her as she fell."

He explained that an orthopedic specialist had been called in and had put several pins and wires in the ankle. "The good news is her leg twisting under her probably saved her from serious head injury by slowing the momentum of her fall. She's moderately concussed, but it could've been a lot worse. From the nature of her injuries it looks like she bounced off the bumper or fender. If she'd been hit more squarely by the front of the vehicle...."

Rob felt the blood drain out of his face. His knees threatened to give out on him again. Both Kate and Ed reached out to steady him.

The doctor gave him an apologetic look. "She'll be our guest for a few days, but I have every reason to believe she'll be fine in due course."

"Sounds like she'll be an airport security person's nightmare from now on," Kate said with a small grin.

The doctor returned her smile, but it didn't reach his eyes. "We'll remove the plate in her thigh when the bone is healed, but, yeah, the hardware in her ankle will be permanent."

Ed offered to give blood to replace some of what had been used from the hospital's blood bank. The doctor sent him to the nurses' station to set up an appointment.

Rob reached out to shake the doctor's hand. "Thank..." His voice caught in his throat. "Thank you," he finally managed to whisper.

"At least this case has a happy ending," the doctor said, but he didn't look happy.

Kate's face morphed into the expression Rob thought of as her *therapist look*–one part sympathy, one part attentiveness. His mouth formed its first genuine smile of the evening.

She just can't help herself.

Her expression had the desired effect. The doctor shook his head. "Let's just say that kids on skateboards and teenaged drivers on cell phones are a very bad combination."

"Oh, no!" Horror joined the sympathy on Kate's face. She reached out and rested her hand lightly on the doctor's arm. "That's got to be as rough as it gets."

He patted her hand. "I'm glad I get to end my shift on a good note, and next time I'll take better care to adjust my expression before coming through those doors." Turning to Rob, he added, "Your wife should be coming out of recovery soon."

After the doctor left, Ed shook Rob's hand.

Kate gave him a hug. "I'll touch base with you tomorrow to see how Liz is doing."

As they walked away, Rob overheard Ed say, "I'd hoped for a little excitement this evening, but this wasn't exactly the *type* of excitement I had in mind."

Rob stifled a chuckle as Kate shot her husband a devilish grin.

CHAPTER TWO

Kate woke to the smell of coffee floating down the hall from the kitchen. She took a deep breath. Her smile faded as she realized the fragrance was faint. Eddie was long gone. One of the many things she disliked about tax season was eating breakfast alone, and all too often dinner as well.

Wednesdays were half days, in exchange for working until noon on Saturdays. But in Kate's mind, a weekday afternoon off didn't compensate for losing a quarter of her weekend with Eddie. The only time she really didn't mind was this time of year, when he worked seven days a week.

It turned out to be a hectic morning. Two clients called with mid-week crises while she was in her first session. Sandwiching return calls between her other sessions was challenging.

Finally, she was gathering her things to leave at twelve-twenty when the counseling center's receptionist stuck her head in the open doorway. "Hey, Kate," Pauline said. "Rob's wife's accident is on the news."

Kate hurried out to the reception area. On the television, a toothy anchorwoman was describing Liz's accident as the lead-in to a story about the rising number of hit-and-runs in the area. "Mrs. Franklin is one of the lucky ones," the woman concluded. "She's in stable condition at St. Joseph's Hospital."

On the off chance that Rob was in his office, Kate walked down the hall to the law firm of Stockton, Bennett and Franklin. He was there, stuffing papers into his briefcase.

"Hey, they just reported about Liz's hit-and-run on the noon news," she told him. "How's she doing?"

Rob glanced up. "Not too bad, all things considered. She's been conscious but woozy most of the morning. She even cracked a feeble joke about vampires when the nurse took some blood for tests. I'm gathering up some things so I can work at the hospital when she's napping. Then I've got to swing out to the airport and pick Shelley up."

"Do you think Liz is up for more company? I thought I'd stop by on my way home. But I don't want to tire her."

"She'd love to see you, but you probably do need to keep it brief. She fades in and out. And I should warn you. She looks like a woman who's had an argument with a truck. She's pretty scraped up and bruised."

Kate's mouth fell open. "She was hit by a *truck?*"

Rob had finished packing his briefcase. He flopped down in his desk chair with a sigh. "Maybe. There were several witnesses, but their stories conflict."

"Ah, the foibles of human memory."

"One witness was sure it was a red van. Another thought it was a brown truck. The third agreed it was a larger vehicle but wasn't at all sure what color it was. None of them got the license number, unfortunately. One lady said she tried to, but the license plate was so dirty she had a hard time reading it. She was only able to make out an R before the jackass took off!"

Anger at the guy who'd almost killed his wife wasn't far beneath the surface. Kate couldn't blame him one bit.

"It all happened fast. Liz stepped off the curb at the same time this clown sped up to beat the light. Then he kept on going after he hit her."

Her own anger surged in her chest. "There are way too many crazies out there on the road."

The corner of Rob's mouth quirked up. "You're falling down on the job, lady. You're supposed to be making them all sane."

She snorted. "Yeah, right. Ever heard of the proverbial drop in the bucket?"

His expression sobered. "Actually this guy may be crazier than most. One witness swore he did it on purpose. She said the guy seemed to aim right for Liz."

"Oh, no! We're in big trouble if drivers are starting to intentionally aim for pedestrians."

"Yeah, makes me want to pack up the family and move to, I don't know... maybe a forty-acre farm, with an electrified fence around it."

Kate snorted again. "Somehow I don't see you in denim overalls and a John Deere cap." Crisply pressed Dockers and a golf shirt were Rob's idea of casual wear.

He chuckled, then said, "Seriously, between the traffic and pollution and the Type A crazies, Towson just isn't what it used to be."

"It's certainly a lot more crowded," she conceded. "Hey, how about bringing the girls by the house later for a quick visit, after you've been to the hospital? I haven't seen Shelley in eons."

"Yeah, once the brats morph into teenagers, they don't want to hang out with their old fogey parents and their friends anymore."

"Hey, Bub, watch who you're calling an old fogey." Kate punched him lightly on the arm. "You may be one, but your friends are still in their prime."

~~~~~~~~~

The next afternoon, Kate was between her last two sessions when Pauline waved her over to the reception desk and handed her a message slip. A business card was stapled to it. "This guy came in a little after three." The receptionist dropped her voice so the clients in the waiting area couldn't hear her. "Had a heck of a time convincing him that one does *not* interrupt a therapy session. I told him unless he was here to report that the building was on fire, he'd just have to wait. He opted to leave a message instead."

Kate read the message. *Call Detective Phillips, Baltimore Co. Police.* Anxiety fluttered in her chest. Had something happened to one of her clients? She asked her next client to wait a few minutes and hurried into her office to make the call.

"Thank you for calling, Mrs. Huntington. I'm investigating Elizabeth Franklin's hit-and-run. I understand you're good friends with the Franklins. Could you tell me if Mrs. Franklin has any enemies?"

"Not that I know of. Why do you ask?"

"From some of the eyewitness accounts, it's possible the driver hit her intentionally," Detective Phillips replied. "We're investigating the incident as a possible assault. What about Mr. Franklin? Do you know if perhaps he's, as they say, engaged in some indiscretion? Maybe there's a jealous girlfriend out there."

Kate's temper flared. She reined it in. "No, Rob and Liz are madly in love and neither has engaged in any indiscretions."

"Oh, come on, Mrs. Huntington, they've been married a long time. Nobody's still *madly* in love after a couple decades of staring at each other over the breakfast table. If there's any sour note in their relationship, I need to know about it. Sometimes spouses decide that a little accident would be cheaper than divorce."

Self-control suddenly seemed over-rated. "That's a despicable thing to say. Rob would never harm his wife."

"Well, maybe you don't know him as well as you think you do."

Kate gritted her teeth. "De-tec-tive," she enunciated each syllable, "Rob Franklin is my closest friend and I *know* he is not having an affair. I have a client waiting, so goodbye, sir!" She punched the end button on her phone and longed for the days when you could slam a receiver down in the cradle and give the obnoxious person on the other end a headache.

Kate took several deep breaths to calm herself. She needed to get to her waiting client.

An hour later, she ushered her client out the door, then called Eddie at his office. She was so pissed she could hardly get the words out as she told him about her conversation with the police detective.

"Not good," he said, when she finally wound down. "You need to tell Rob about this."

"You're right." Kate looked at her watch. Quarter after five. "I'll track him down. Love you. See you tonight."

She punched in Rob's office number and drummed fingers on her desk as the phone rang in her ear.

His administrative assistant picked up. "Mr. Franklin's office."

"Hi, Fran. Is he there, or is he over at the hospital?"

"He just got back here a few minutes ago. He has a deposition we weren't able to reschedule, at five-thirty."

"I need to talk to him. I'll be right there."

Kate rushed out of the center and down the hall to Rob's law firm. She waved at Fran as she swept past her desk, then tapped on Rob's half-open door.

"Come in."

She closed the door behind her. He sat at his desk, looking over some papers in an open file folder.

"You're never going to believe the conversation I had earlier with the biggest jerk in the world." In an irate voice, she summarized the phone call with Detective Phillips.

Rob sat back in his chair and looked pointedly at her fists clenched at her sides. "Calm down, Kate. He's just doing his job."

She willed her fingers to uncurl. "Easy for you to say. You weren't talking to the…" Several words came to mind that she didn't normally say out loud. She settled on "jackass."

"Oh, he's questioned me twice already, and I'm sure he'll be back around again. Once he's finished his fishing expedition with my colleagues and friends." Rob's voice was grim. "The spouse is always the first suspect in a murder or attempted murder."

Kate stared at him. The word *murder* had rendered her temporarily speechless, a rare experience for her.

After a long pause, she said, "Well, considering the possibility that you were behind Liz's accident–or non-accident if indeed it was intentional–that's one thing. But it sounded to me like he'd already proposed marriage to the theory and was about to waltz it down the aisle."

~~~~~~~~

Friday at noon, Kate sat back in her desk chair with a sigh. It had been a tough morning, topping off a bad week. "TGIF," she muttered. Taking a bite from her ham sandwich, she mulled over the session she'd just had with Cheryl Crofton, a pregnant, domestic violence survivor. Cheryl's estranged husband had gotten his hands on her phone number. Thank God he still didn't know her new address.

He'd called her the previous weekend, and of course they'd argued. Now that Cheryl felt relatively safe from her abusive spouse, her anger was surfacing. An all too common reaction, as Kate knew. Cheryl had ended the conversation by informing him he now had to talk to her lawyer, Robert Franklin, instead of to her.

"Has he threatened you?" Kate had asked.

"No, not really. He just keeps sayin' he's gonna make me come home."

"I don't want to frighten you, but sometimes after the woman leaves, a wife-batterer becomes more violent. I suggest you get your phone number changed. If you tell the phone company someone's harassing you, they might change it for free."

"Oh, don't worry. I'm not scared. I bought a gun and a friend of mine's teachin' me how to use it. I'm never gonna let *nobody* intimidate me again."

Kate had reservations about Cheryl as a gun-toting mama but she'd kept them to herself. She didn't want to undermine her client's newfound assertiveness, and the threat of a spurned wife-batterer turning deadly was real. At least she was getting lessons on the gun's proper use, which hopefully would include safety instructions.

Kate chomped down on the dill pickle spear the deli had delivered along with her sandwich. As she chewed, her mind turned to her first session that morning. Multiple personalities–or dissociative identity disorder as it was now called–was more common in women, but Jim Lincoln was the second man with the disorder whom Kate had treated in her twelve-year career as a psychotherapist.

Jim was quiet and shy by nature. In addition to the D.I.D.–which was tough enough to treat–he was still confused about his sexual orientation at age twenty-nine. He'd grown up in rural western Maryland, in the foothills of the Appalachians. His seductive mother had fondled him as a child and eventually moved on to even more inappropriate sexual behaviors. Meanwhile his homophobic father had beaten him on a regular basis. At age four, his father started taking him to Ku Klux Klan meetings to "teach him how to be a man." His first alter personality developed at that time–Steve, who was now an ultra-macho, heterosexual fifteen-year-old.

Other alters had joined the ranks through the years to help the sensitive boy cope. One was a little girl named Lilly who came out whenever Jim wanted to play dolls with the neighborhood girls instead of baseball with the boys. This made it okay and warded off his fear of his father's wrath. After all, it wasn't Jim who was playing with dolls; it was this female, Lilly.

Lilly had come out toward the end of today's session. She'd then been resistant to giving up control of the shared body so Jim could get home safely. Lilly, at age six, did not know how to drive a car.

Kate let out a sigh and took another bite of her sandwich. There was a soft knock on her slightly ajar door. Expecting Pauline with phone messages, she mumbled, "Come in," around ham and cheese.

Rob's head appeared instead. "We're headed for the airport but Shelley wanted to say good-bye." He ushered his daughter into the office.

Swallowing quickly, Kate jumped up to give the young woman a hug. "Sweetheart, getting to see you was the only good part of this lousy week." She stepped back, her hands still on the nineteen-year-old's shoulders. "I can't believe how grown up you are now. And you look so much like your mother."

After a few minutes of chitchat, they said their farewells. Kate settled back down in her chair. She picked up her sandwich and took a bite.

Two loud cracks, followed by screams. Kate almost choked on her food. She bolted out of her chair and across her office. It sounded like the screams were coming from the street in front of the building. Heart in her throat, she ran through the center's outer office and down the central stairs to the first floor.

She reached the lobby at the same time as the building's security guard. He motioned for her to stay back. Drawing his gun, he cautiously eased one of the glass doors open.

The door was yanked out of his hand. Rob barreled through, his daughter in his arms. He flattened his back against the lobby wall. Shelley's feet slid to the floor. She stood trembling in her father's arms.

Kate raced over to them. "Oh my God! Is she hurt?"

"I don't think so." Rob's voice was shaky. "Are you hurt, baby?"

Shelley shook her head and burst into tears.

He held his sobbing daughter tightly, his cheek pressed against the top of her head. "One shot hit right beside her. It got one of the flower pots."

Kate leaned over and peeked through the glass door. The large pot of geraniums to the left of the door was intact. Dirt, chunks of terra cotta clay, and mangled flowers were scattered on the sidewalk where its mate used to be.

There were two shots.

Her hand flew to her chest. A young man, in biking helmet, shorts and T-shirt, was crumpled on the sidewalk near the curb. He moaned and clutched his bleeding leg. His bike lay abandoned in the road.

An older couple had already come to his aid. The man pressed a clean handkerchief against the wound while his wife draped her sweater around the biker's shoulders.

The security guard came back through the other door. "Police and ambulance are on the way," he announced. "Is the girl hurt?"

Rob shook his head, then looked at Kate. His expression said, *I can't take much more of this.*

Kate wrapped her arms around the big man and his daughter. They were both trembling. "Sh-sh-sh, it's okay," she whispered. "Sh-sh, it's over now."

She hoped she was right.

CHAPTER THREE

On Sunday, Eddie had just gotten home from a day of tax forms and stressed-out clients. He was pulling off his tie as he walked through the living room. The phone rang. He picked up the receiver and said, "Hi, Rob."

Kate hustled into the kitchen to grab the other phone from its base.

"The doctors feel Liz is recovering well," Rob was saying as she picked up. "But I didn't tell her about the shooting yet. I'll wait until she's a little stronger. Shelley ended up staying through this morning. She was pretty shaken Friday night, but she seems fine now. After a weekend of fighting with her sister, she was quite ready to go back to school."

"Ah, the resiliency of kids," Eddie said.

Kate pursed her lips. One of her pet peeves was adults assuming kids were more resilient than they were. "I don't know," she said into the phone. "I wonder sometimes if they figure they don't have any other choice. Kids cope because they have to."

"Well, she seems to be coping better than I am," Rob said. "I have a wife in the hospital, just spent the weekend in a teenage war zone, and Samantha is now pouting in her room because I told her, no, she could *not* wear a leather halter top and miniskirt to her school dance."

Kate opened her mouth, then thought better of it. Now probably wasn't the best time to point out that his daughters might not be coping as well as they seemed to be.

"Hmm, maybe we should rethink this baby idea, love," Eddie said.

"Don't worry, they only stay rebellious teenagers for a few years, although it feels like a decade or two," Rob said with a chuckle in his voice.

Kate decided a change of subject was in order. "What have the police come up with on the shooting?"

"They haven't a clue. After all, drive-bys aren't exactly commonplace outside of the city. By the time people figured out what was going on, the shooter was long gone. The police don't think he was aiming for anyone in particular. Just some crazy who thought it would be fun to take pot shots at people."

"Some crazy who's seen one too many violent movies," Kate said. "I was going to stop by the hospital after work tomorrow. You going to be there?"

"Yeah, see you then." Rob signed off.

"Geez," Kate said as Eddie walked into the kitchen. "Talk about adjusting because you have to. We sounded like all this is normal. Calmly discussing drive-bys in suburbia and visiting friends who've been run over by trucks."

Her mind flashed to the haunted look on Rob's face two days ago. She wondered if any of the Franklins were doing quite as well as they seemed to be.

~~~~~~~~~

On Tuesday, Kate was anticipating a long but relatively easy day. She had late office hours this evening, but the only tough session was likely to be Jim Lincoln's. With D.I.D. clients, there was no such thing as an easy session.

It was even harder than she'd feared. Steve, the macho alter, came out and flirted quite blatantly with her. Sidestepping the come-ons without being outright rejecting was tricky.

By the time Cheryl Crofton, her last client of the evening, arrived, Kate was beginning to drag.

Cheryl was in a good mood, almost manic. "I don't think I'll need to change my phone number. Frank called again. I told him you said to change it, but he said," she puffed up her chest and said in a deep voice, "'Don't bother. You won't be hearing from me for awhile.'" Then she gave a little laugh.

"What do you think that means?" Kate asked.

"I don't know. And I'm not sure I care. As long as he stays away from me."

Kate was pleased by that response. The woman seemed to be truly letting go of her husband, a process that was often a lot longer and harder than one might expect, even when the man was abusive.

Toward the end of the session, Cheryl started discussing her legal case. Whenever she said Rob's name, her voice softened and a wisp of a smile floated across her face.

Uh, oh. She's falling for the white knight.

Kate decided not to address the issue tonight, however, since they were running out of time. Instead, she brought the conversation back to the woman's concerns about her finances.

As the session was winding down, Cheryl abruptly changed the subject. "Hey, did I show you my new shoes?" Her voice had a manic edge to it again. She held up one foot encased in a strappy black sandal with a very high heel. "Ten bucks at Walmart. Doncha love a bargain!"

"How do you walk in those things, especially pregnant?" Kate asked. Cheryl was not a small woman.

"It ain't easy. But it's worth it. They make me feel sexy."

The shoes were somewhat incompatible with the rest of her casual attire–a loose top over a denim skirt–but Kate had to admit they did show off the woman's muscular calves. She chuckled. "I hate to tell you what we called those when I was in high school."

"Ho shoes," Cheryl replied, and they both laughed. Almost out of time, Kate decided to let the session end on that light note.

Kate was writing notes in Cheryl's file–the woman's mood was a bit strange tonight–when Rob knocked lightly on her half-opened door.

"Hey, what are you doing here so late?" she asked.

"Meeting with a client. I went over to the hospital for awhile at lunchtime. Liz said not to bother coming by this evening." He sounded tired.

"So how are you doing?" Kate asked, as she put the file in her cabinet, then locked it.

He flopped onto the loveseat in the corner of her office. "Okay, I guess." His bleak tone said the opposite.

Her own fatigue temporarily forgotten, Kate sat down in her desk chair and turned it toward him. She tried not to let her worry show on her face. A comfortable silence settled around them.

Rob sighed. "What a week it's been." He was quiet again for a moment. Then in a voice so low she could barely hear him, he said, "My God, Kate, when I think about what could've happened. I… I could've lost both of them." His voice broke on a sob.

She moved quickly across the room and crammed herself in next to him on the loveseat, wrapping her arms around him as best she could. Rob dropped his head onto her shoulder. His broad back was shaking. "That didn't happen," she whispered in his ear. "They're both okay."

After a moment the shaking stopped. Kate was wondering how they would extricate themselves from this scenario with Rob's ego relatively intact, when a noise outside her open door provided an opportune distraction. She struggled up from the loveseat to investigate, while Rob searched his pockets for a handkerchief.

There was no one in the waiting area. Were those heels clicking in the hallway? She walked to the center's outer door, opened it, and looked in both directions. The hallway was empty.

Must be imagining things.

Every time the nearby kitchen door opened, the fragrant combination of hot grease and Old Bay seasoning wafted in Kate's direction. Her stomach growled. She closed her eyes and savored the anticipation of the crab cake she would soon be eating.

She jumped a little when a man plopped down across from her in the booth. His gray T-shirt said *I may be ugly but you're….* Fortunately, the last word was covered up by the top of a large grease-splattered apron.

"How ya doin', sweet pea?" The twinkle in his blue eyes belied his gruff tone.

Kate smiled at the man who'd angrily called her a big, dumb sweet potato after she'd accidentally knocked his sweet potato fries out of his hand at the Maryland State Fair. He was seven and she was five at the time. Somewhere in their teens, the childish taunt had morphed into the shortened endearment, *sweet pea.*

"I'm good now, Mac, but it's been one hell of a week."

He nodded. "Ain't been to the hospital since Sunday. How's Liz doin'?"

"She's fine. Rob called this morning and said she's coming home tomorrow."

"Good," Mac said, then shook his head. "World's goin' to hell in a handbasket." He crossed himself dramatically.

Kate chuckled at the old-fashioned saying–his late mother's favorite line–and at his exaggerated piety. Mathias McKenzie Reilly was one-eighth Greek Orthodox and seven-eighths Irish Catholic. His mother had named her only child after his maternal grandfather, while his father had taught him the importance of a good pub.

When Mac's parents had died in a car accident five years ago, he'd taken over the corner bar they'd operated for decades and turned it into a full-blown restaurant. Mac's Place offered an eclectic blend of Greek cuisine, Irish bonhomie and the Chesapeake Bay region's passion for seafood. Most Wednesdays, when Kate got off early, she and Rob met here for lunch.

Mac wasn't exactly your typical restauranteur. He was only forty but his weathered skin and gruff manner made him seem older. His scruffy appearance was in sharp contrast to his military-style buzz cut, a leftover from the decade he'd spent in the Army. He was short and wiry, the only fat on his body the beginnings of a paunch that indicated he shared his father's love of beer.

Rob appeared next to the booth. "You trying to horn in on my date, Mac?"

Mac grinned at him as he slid out of the bench. "What'll it be, folks?"

Kate had no need to consult a menu. "Crab cake sandwich and a Greek salad."

"Same for me, but with fries. Did Kate tell you Liz is coming home tomorrow?" Rob's tone was downright exuberant.

Mac flashed him another grin. "Yup. Give her a peck on the cheek for me." He headed for the kitchen to place their orders.

Kate was relieved to see Rob in better spirits today. "How's Liz going to manage? Can she get around yet?"

He sobered slightly. "Actually, no. She'll be in a wheelchair for at least a month. I've hired a home health aide to stay with her during the day, and take her to her physical therapy sessions."

They discussed mutual cases until their food arrived. Rob stole the pickle slices off her plate to add to his own. She swiped one of his seasoned fries, lightly sprinkled with Old Bay seasoning. While they ate, she regaled him with stories of the staff meeting that morning at the counseling center. It had been established in the early 1970's with the moniker of Victim Services of Maryland. Now the staff was trying to come up with a catchier name–one that would get away from the connotations of a *victim* as weak and helpless. The term had long since been replaced in the trauma recovery field by *survivor*.

When the check arrived, Rob pulled a twenty-dollar bill out of his wallet to match the one Kate put on the table. She hid a smile. He'd finally stopped arguing about splitting the check.

"My favorite suggestion," she picked up the conversation again as they headed for the door, "was Violence Recovery Unlimited. And then someone got totally silly and suggested that since we're primarily in the business of helping people find the guts to stand up for themselves, how about Guts R Us."

Their chuckles were abruptly cut off when they reached her car parked in front of the restaurant. The right front tire was flat.

Holy crap! Kate felt her mood deflate as well.

They stood at a loss for a moment, long enough to catch Mac's attention through the big plate-glass window of the restaurant. He came outside, and the two men argued good-naturedly about who was going to change the tire. Mac won when he pointed out that Rob would ruin his expensive suit, while he had a change of clothes stashed in his office for those occasions when a kitchen mishap dumped grease or other unmentionables on him.

Their friendly banter cheered Kate up some. She grinned at Mac's back. Since he considered T-shirts with obnoxious sayings on them as appropriate work attire, she figured the unmentionables would have to be pretty bad before he'd change his clothes.

Rob was razzing him about the proper way to change a tire when both men suddenly grew quiet.

"What? What's wrong?" Their backs were blocking her view of the tire.

Rob crouched down to get a closer look. "Shit! Your tire's been slashed, Kate."

~~~~~~~~~

She was still a bit shook that evening as she told Eddie about the mutilated tire. They were getting ready for bed, dropping jewelry, change and wallets onto their respective bureau tops. "You know, I'm beginning to think Rob has a point," she said. "Friendly suburban Towson isn't feeling so friendly anymore."

"Oh, come on, this has got to be some weird aberration." Eddie tossed his undershirt in the general direction of the hamper. "Normally, this is a quiet enough region of the world, except when the university students are partying."

He steered her toward the bed. "Look, things are crazy the rest of this week, but next week you take my car one day. I'll take yours to the tire store on my lunch hour. Get you a new tire."

She snorted. "What lunch hour? It's tax season."

"Have you lost track of time in all the chaos lately? Next Monday is April fifteenth."

"Oh, yeah. That's right." She smiled.

I'm getting my husband back!

Eddie put his arms around her waist from behind and pulled her against the warmth of his bare chest. "You've had a stressful time lately. The least I can do is take care of your tire for you." He kissed the nape of her neck, sending a delightful shiver down her spine. "Have I told you lately that you look particularly fetching in that nightgown?"

She laughed out loud. "Now I get it." Grabbing a pillow off the bed, she turned in his arms and gently smacked him with it. "You're not just trying to be nice, you're trying to get laid!"

"Is it working?" He wiggled his eyebrows and gave her the most lascivious grin she'd ever seen. "You also look quite fetching *out of* that nightgown, my love."

He let go of her and dove into bed. Giggling, Kate slid under the sheet. She cuddled close to his lean body, and indeed the nightgown did not stay on for long.

CHAPTER FOUR

Tuesday morning, Kate was slurping down a second cup of coffee at the kitchen table. Despite her fuzzy head, she was feeling quite happy that another tax season was behind them.

She'd had her last lonely weekend for awhile. At least she'd put the time to good use and had gotten all the peeling paint scraped off the front porch. Many of the floorboards were squeaky, which meant someone would have to crawl under the porch and shore up the supports. With a shot of malicious glee she wasn't totally proud of, but also wasn't totally ashamed of, she'd opted to leave that nasty task for Eddie.

When he'd finally gotten home last night, they'd celebrated with a late supper. He'd grilled steaks and they'd shared a bottle of their favorite wine.

Fortunately, she didn't have to be at work until eleven this morning, but she wasn't sure how she was going to get through the long day on too little sleep. With some relief, she realized that Cheryl Crofton was her last client tonight. She'd been doing so well lately that Kate was considering cutting their sessions back to every other week.

By the middle of their session that evening, Kate had mentally tabled that idea. Cheryl's demeanor had abruptly changed. Her face a mask of rage, her voice had become an aggressive growl as she described what she'd like to do to her soon-to-be-ex in retaliation for the abuse she'd suffered at his hands.

Kate was finding the big woman rather scary when she was this angry. Keeping her voice calm, she pointed out that it was natural for pent-up anger to surface, now that Cheryl felt safe.

The client continued to rant for a few more minutes.

"Frank isn't worth going to jail for," Kate finally said, her voice a bit sharper now. "And you don't want to stoop to his level, do you?"

After a beat, Cheryl's face relaxed. In a more normal voice, she said, "Nah, you're right. Living well is the best revenge."

Engaging in some end-of-session chitchat, Kate escorted her client to the door of her office. As the young woman started to walk away, the sound of her high heels triggered a memory. "Cheryl, wait. Did you come back to my office last week? I thought I heard someone in the waiting area."

"Yes, actually, I did. I, uh... couldn't find my keys." She was avoiding eye contact. "I thought maybe I'd left them in your office, but then I heard Rob's voice. I, uh, didn't want to disturb you, like if you were in a meeting or something."

Cheryl was now examining the pattern in the fake-wood flooring. "So I just left," she finished lamely.

From her embarrassment, Kate suspected the woman had seen her comforting Rob and had misinterpreted it as a romantic encounter. She considered setting the record straight, but decided she'd sound like she was protesting too much. Instead she gently said, "You could've knocked. Our meeting wasn't so important that we couldn't have helped you find your keys."

"Oh, that's okay, I found them. They were in the bottom of my purse all along."

"Well, you take care now, and take care of the little one, too." Kate pointed to Cheryl's slightly rounded belly, under her loose top. "When are you due, five more months, right?"

"Yeah, and I can't wait." The young woman grinned, apparently happy to be back on safe ground. "This little tub of lard's already startin' to weigh me down. I think I'm gonna name him Tubbo."

"Don't you dare. You'll scar his psyche for life, and it might be a girl, you know. Let's not be sexist."

"OK, then I'll call her Tubbette," Cheryl cheerfully threw over her shoulder as she walked away.

Kate breathed a small sigh of relief. The silly banter had served to restore the balance in their relationship.

~~~~~~~~

On Wednesday, Kate was feeling drowsy as she waited for Rob at Mac's Place. She still hadn't completely recovered from staying up late Monday to celebrate the end of tax season. Maybe she would take a nap this afternoon.

Eyes drooping, she startled a bit when Rob slid into the booth across from her.

"I didn't see your car out front," he said.

"I've got Eddie's Saturn. He took my car today so he could go by that discount place near his office at lunchtime. If they've got a good sale going he said he might replace all four tires and be done with it. So, how are you? And how's Liz?"

Rob caught her up on the Franklin household's adjustments to Liz's temporary semi-invalid status. Then they discussed mutual cases for awhile, including Cheryl's. Rob had filed for a hearing to try to get her alimony. The courts, unfortunately, were backed up even more than usual and he hadn't been able to get her case on the docket until July.

Kate shook her head. "She's a waitress with minimal benefits. Will you be able to get her alimony? She's worried about her finances around the time the baby's born." Kate was worried too. Rob was handling the case *pro bono* and the counseling center had a sliding scale that went all the way down to a dollar a session, but still the woman had to eat and pay the rent. Financial stress might weaken her resolve to go through with the divorce.

"It's not a given," Rob said. "Especially since her husband doesn't make a whole lot more than she does. The fact that she won't be able to work for several weeks is my strongest argument. She'll definitely get child support, but I can't file for that until after the baby's born."

As they ate, their conversation meandered through other subjects, professional and personal. They were waiting for the check when a man approached their table. He was a bit stocky, slightly shorter than average, and wearing an inexpensive business suit. There was an air of self-importance in his body language.

"Mrs. Huntington?" he asked.

Kate nodded.

"I'm Detective Phillips. We spoke on the phone two weeks ago."

Kate felt her face tighten. "Yes, I remember."

"Your receptionist said I'd find you here, *lunching* with Mr. Franklin."

Kate narrowed her eyes at him. "What is it you want, Detective?"

Phillips was staring intently at her, but his voice softened as he said, "I'm afraid I have some bad news, about your husband."

Icy fingers wrapped around her heart. She stood up, then grabbed for the edge of the table as her knees threatened to give out on her. "What? What about my husband?"

Rob also jumped up, alarm on his face.

Phillips looked uncomfortable. "Maybe we should go somewhere private, Mrs. Huntington."

"Tell me, damn you!" Blood pounded in her ears. "Tell me what's happened to my husband!"

"Um, I'm afraid…." Phillips cleared his throat. "I'm afraid, Mrs. Huntington, that your husband's been killed."

The room spun. She felt Rob's hands on her arms, holding her up. Then the world went black.

Kate woke up on a small couch in the restaurant's office. In a fog, she focused on the strange image of Mac wringing his hands in the doorway. Rob and another man were arguing. Rob was yelling, "How dare you tell her like that, in the middle of a crowded restaurant."

Tell me what?

Curiosity shifted to resistance. She didn't want to remember. She wanted to make the man tell her it wasn't true.

The arguing stopped when she sat up. Her head felt strange. Rob sat down beside her and put his arm around her shoulders.

"How are you doing, Kate?" He sounded choked up.

Did something else happen to Liz? she wondered numbly.

"How touching," the other guy said.

Rob ignored him but Mac stepped forward. "Get the hell outta my office," he growled at the man. The guy didn't leave but he did step back to the doorway.

Thinking about what might have happened to Liz was opening cracks in the numbness. Kate sensed some horrible truth was lurking, about to overwhelm her.

"I can't think about Liz."

"What did you say, dear?" Rob asked.

She hadn't realized she'd said the words out loud. Again she whispered, "I can't think about Liz."

Then she lifted her tear-stained face to him. "Rob, I can't! I just can't think about Liz."

The dam inside her chest broke. She started sobbing as she rocked back and forth on the couch.

Rob wrapped his arms tightly around her and rocked with her. "It's okay, sweetheart. You don't have to think about anything right now."

～～～～～

They'd forgotten that Detective Phillips existed.

He was taking it all in, especially the endearments–*dear* and *sweetheart.* This wasn't a man comforting a grieving friend. He was looking at two lovers, who'd plotted to kill their spouses.

I can't think about Liz.

Sure sounded like guilt to him. Then again, her grief seemed genuine. She couldn't be that good an actress. But she wouldn't be the first woman who murdered her husband, then realized with horror that she still cared for him.

Phillips slipped out of the room. Better not let them see the grin spreading across his face. Now that he knew what had happened, all he had to do was prove it.

He leaned against the wall in the back hallway of the restaurant and waited.

A few minutes later, Franklin led Mrs. Huntington down the hall. Phillips straightened and opened his mouth.

Franklin cut him off. "I'm taking Mrs. Huntington home–"

"Her husband's been murdered. I have to question her."

"I'm taking her home now." Franklin's tone was curt. "You may question her later, at her house. Call first." He half led, half carried the stumbling woman out the back door of the restaurant.

The scruffy little guy, the restaurant owner, held the door for them. He patted Mrs. Huntington on the shoulder as they went past.

～～～～～

Rob helped Kate into the passenger seat of his car. He was still trying to figure out what the hell Liz had to do with any of this. But now was not the time for questions.

He went around to the driver's side and got in. He was buckling the seatbelt around her when Kate turned to him, wide-eyed. "Murdered?"

Rob's chest tightened. His eyes stung. For a moment he wasn't sure he could hold it together.

Before he'd started yelling at Phillips, the detective had told him that Ed's car had blown up, with Ed in it. But Kate wasn't ready to deal with that gruesome image, or the thought of Ed's last moments alive.

He was barely dealing with it himself.

"We'll find out the details later, sweetheart. Right now, I'm taking you home."

Detective Phillips didn't call first before showing up at Kate's door an hour later. He had a female uniformed officer in tow. Rob begrudgingly let them in.

The uniform's nametag read *Hernandez*. "I'm sorry for your loss, ma'am," she said to Kate, who sat mutely on the sofa clutching her stomach.

The young woman gave Rob a slight nod, sympathy in her brown eyes. She took out a small notepad and stood unobtrusively in a corner.

Rob sat down beside Kate and put his arm around her shoulders. He waved Phillips toward an armchair.

During the last hour, the detective seemed to have dredged up a modicum of humanity. Leaving out most of the graphic details, he told them what had happened. Ed had left his office at eleven-ten, gone to the parking garage nearby, started his car, and it had exploded. A passerby called 911, but by the time the fire engines arrived, the car had been completely engulfed in flames.

"He was probably gone as soon as the explosion occurred," Phillips said in a voice that sounded almost sympathetic. "He never knew what happened, never felt any pain."

Rob knew damn well that probably wasn't true. But he had to give Phillips credit for the kind lie. It was what loved ones would worry about. Did the person suffer? Did they have time to know they were dying?

Kate was shaking. He tightened his arm around her.

The detective said, "Mrs. Huntington, I need to speak with you alone."

She turned to Rob, horror on her face.

"I'm the family attorney, Detective," he said in the firm tone he used in court. "I'm not leaving the room."

Phillips narrowed his eyes at him, but then he shrugged. "Mrs. Huntington, do you know why your husband left his office at that time? It was a bit early for lunch."

"He was going to get tires," Kate choked out. Fresh tears streamed down her cheeks.

"He was probably going to buy the tires, then go get lunch while they were being mounted," Rob said.

"I wasn't asking you, Mr. Franklin."

Rob's jaw tightened. "Too bad, 'cause I answered. The woman just lost her husband and you want a dissertation from her?"

Phillips didn't respond right away. Then he asked, "Who else, besides Mr. Franklin here, might want your husband dead?"

Red hot rage exploded in Rob's chest. Fists clenched, he jumped to his feet. "How dare you, you son of a bitch! Ed was my friend…." His voice broke. He struggled to suppress the sob threatening to escape his throat.

Kate reached out toward him. Rob took her hand, not sure who was comforting who at the moment.

Phillips stood and made a mock bow in his direction. "I'll rephrase the question, Counselor. Mrs. Huntington, did your husband have any enemies?"

Rob turned his back on the detective and lowered himself down beside Kate again.

After a brief pause, she said, "No. Eddie's a very sweet man."

"Perhaps at work? Everybody makes at least some enemies at work, office politics and all." Phillips also resumed his seat.

"He's an accountant," she said. "Accountants lead very boring lives, at least at work."

Pain stabbed Rob's heart. She was using the present tense.

"Maybe he was embezzling?" Phillips asked.

Kate just frowned at him, her eyes narrowed.

Rob took a deep breath to calm himself, then said, "Since he's co-owner of the firm, he'd be stealing from himself."

An awkward silence. Then the detective asked more questions. How did Ed and his partner get along? What were his habits? Did he come home on time? Could he have been having an affair?

Kate glared at him. "You've got to be kidding, Detective."

"I have to ask," Phillips said to her as he gave Rob a defiant look.

Ignoring the detective, Rob turned to Kate. He cupped his hand around the side of her face and swiped the tears from her cheek with his thumb. What he'd give to spare her the next few moments.

Quietly, he said, "Detective, it wasn't Ed's car. It was Kate's."

She clutched her stomach and sobbed. He pulled her against him. Tucking her head under his chin, he stroked her hair.

"Who would want you dead, Mrs. Huntington?" Phillips asked.

She shook her head against Rob's chest.

"I think that's enough for now, Detective." He wrapped his arms more tightly around her. "Sh, sh. It's okay, dear. It's okay," he whispered into her hair.

Kate sobbed against his shirt for a couple minutes. Then she pulled back and looked up at him, her eyes full of pain.

He shook his head slightly.

What a dumb thing to say. Of course it's not okay.

CHAPTER FIVE

For Kate, the next few days went by in a numb fog, punctuated by moments of excruciating reality.

At Liz's insistence, she'd spent the first night in the Franklins' guest bedroom, staring at the ceiling. Rob had borrowed her cell phone and called her family. Then he'd tracked down Eddie's parents, who were traveling in Europe.

Kate was relieved she hadn't had to tell the Huntingtons that their only child was dead. Then she'd felt guilty for feeling relieved.

The next morning, Rob drove her home. He promised to come back once he'd taken care of a few essentials at his office and cleared his schedule for the rest of the day.

"You gonna be okay for a little while?" he asked, ambivalence in his voice. "Your family should start showing up soon."

She nodded. "I need to take a shower." She couldn't think of anything else to say. She'd be alive when he got back. She wasn't the suicidal type. But that was the highest level of okay she thought she could manage today.

She sat down on her living room sofa, thinking she'd get up in a moment and change out of yesterday's clothes. She was still sitting there a half hour later when the doorbell rang.

It was her oldest brother and his wife, Phyllis, who lived in Silver Spring near Washington, D.C. Unfortunately, Kate wasn't very close to them. She and Michael were six years apart and had little in common.

Phyllis headed for the kitchen to make coffee while Michael stood around looking uncomfortable. When his wife suggested he go pick up the incoming family members at the airport, he hustled out the door.

Miraculously, Kate's younger sister, Mary, was the next to arrive. She'd left her husband in charge of their nine and seven-year-old girls and had camped out at the San Francisco airport the night before until she could get on a red-eye. Michael dropped her off, then turned around to go back to Baltimore-Washington International Airport to get their parents and brother, Jack, due in from Florida and Chicago respectively over the next couple hours.

Kate and Mary were only twenty months apart. Mary was an inch or two shorter, with a slightly more hourglass figure and a tinge of red in her dark curly hair, but her blue eyes matched her older sister's.

Kate was much closer to her sister than to her brothers. The sight of her unleashed a round of tears. Mary sat down on the sofa and wrapped her in her arms. They hugged, rocking back and forth, until the surge of pain passed and the numbness returned.

Then Kate watched as her baby sister quietly took charge. Arrangements were made with Phyllis for the rest of the family to stay with them in Silver Spring. Then Mary carried her own suitcase up the stairs to the guest bedroom.

~~~~~~~~~

Rob put the car in park. Leaning his forehead on the steering wheel, he groped blindly for Liz's hand. "I almost said to sit tight while I got Ed to help with the wheelchair," he choked out. They clung to each other for a minute. Then Rob carried first the empty wheelchair, then his wife, up the porch steps.

Inside, he transferred Liz from the wheelchair to the sofa next to Kate. He carefully lifted his wife's legs onto an ottoman. Liz took Kate's hand.

The streaked makeup and disheveled hair told Rob the shower had never happened, but Kate was wearing fresh clothes. Mary's doing, no doubt.

Kate's parents and Jack arrived. Mac showed up a few minutes later. He was unusually quiet. After patting Kate awkwardly on the shoulder, he took off with Michael and Jack for the closest bar.

Rob declined the invitation to join them. Sitting in the armchair across from Kate and Liz, he stared sightlessly at the rug, and grieved for his friend.

~~~~~~~~~

The second day after Eddie's death, the roller coaster of emotions was worse. Kate retreated into the numbing fog, wrapping it around her like a thick blanket whenever the pain threatened to overwhelm her.

Phyllis brought Jack and their parents over in the morning. Michael had gone to work, for which Kate was grateful. One less person milling around trying to figure out what to say to her. Having her family here was good, made it more bearable. But Kate had no desire to talk to anyone.

Bridget O'Donnell, a shy woman by nature, seemed to understand. She sat quietly beside her daughter most of the day. Kate's father sat in the armchair across from them, eyes red-rimmed, big hands on his knees. "Kin I get ya anythin', lass?" he would ask periodically, his slight Irish brogue thickened by emotion.

Not trusting her voice, she shook her head.

Throughout the day, her mind kept going back to the evening of their anniversary. Tears slid down her cheeks as she relived the conversation over dinner. As usual, they'd talked about the renovations they were making on their old house. Having turned the small dark rooms of the first two floors into the bright, airy living spaces they preferred, they'd wondered what to tackle next. The tiny rooms under the eaves on the third floor or the front porch?

They'd decided on the porch. A friendly debate had ensued regarding how to furnish it once it was scraped, sanded and repainted. Kate had voted for wicker rockers.

"I don't know," Eddie had said. "I like those wooden chairs that you can never get out of because the seat's so low and the back tilts way back."

"I think you're talking about Adirondack chairs."

"Why the heck are they called that?"

"I have no clue," Kate had admitted with a laugh.

Eddie had then brought up their other most common topic of conversation. "Of course, if you do happen to get pregnant soon, we'll need to think about where to put a nursery." They'd rehashed the possibility of fertility treatments for a few minutes before dropping the subject for lighter conversation over dessert.

She couldn't get the image out of her head of Eddie licking the last of the chocolate mousse off his spoon and pretending to swoon.

The idea that she would never see him sitting across the table again, that he would never again reach over to hold her hand, was unfathomable.

But there would be no more anniversaries, and no babies with Eddie's sweet smile.

Kate swiped at her wet cheeks with the back of her hand and struggled to wrap the blanket of fog around her once more.

Midday, the phone rang. Mary answered it and was informed that the coroner's office was releasing the body. She contacted a funeral home and plans were made for a viewing and memorial service.

Actually *viewing* was a misnomer. What little was left of poor Ed would be cremated.

The funeral director asked, in a solemn voice, what the loved ones wished to do with the ashes. Trying to ignore the ache in her chest, Mary passed the question on to her sister.

It was apparently one decision too many. Kate mutely shook her head.

Mary said into the phone, "Just put them in a nice but not too expensive urn."

Ed's parents arrived that afternoon. Michael had left work early to meet their flight at Dulles airport in Washington.

They were in their mid-sixties and, unlike the elder O'Donnells, they'd managed to avoid gaining weight as they'd aged. Slender, silver-haired and well dressed, they were an advertisement for the benefits of membership in the upper middle class—until one noticed the shell-shocked look in their eyes and the gray tinge under the tans they'd so recently been nurturing in the south of France.

Mary quickly assessed the situation. "You must be exhausted," she murmured and gently took each of them by an elbow to guide them up the stairs to the guest room. She shot a meaningful look at Michael and then at their bags. He took the hint and followed with the luggage, placing it against the wall inside the bedroom door and then fleeing.

"Give me a moment," Mary said. She gathered her own things and transferred them to the study on the first floor.

When she returned to the guest bedroom, Ed, Sr. was slouched in the armchair in the corner, staring at his knees. His wife was still standing where Mary had let go of her arm, a glazed look in her eye.

Mary pulled fresh sheets for the queen-sized bed from the chest of drawers. Stripping the old ones off and tossing them on the floor, she started to shake out the fitted sheet. Mrs. Huntington suddenly reached out to grab one edge of it. Silently, she helped Mary make up the bed.

Not sure if they had ever stayed at Kate and Ed's house before, Mary pointed across the room. "Bathroom's through there."

Edith Huntington gave Mary a feeble smile that came nowhere near her eyes. Her voice shook as she said, "Thank you." She shuffled in the direction of the indicated bathroom.

Mary picked up the discarded sheets and left the room, gently closing the door.

~~~~~~~~~~

Looking back on it later, Kate wasn't real sure how she'd made it through that evening and the next day. Her father and Mac, with the ready assistance of Jack–and Michael, once he'd had a couple beers to loosen him up–had turned the evening viewing into an old-fashioned Irish wake. Mac snuck several six-packs of Guinness in. Whenever those got low, more miraculously appeared, no doubt from a cooler in his truck.

The O'Donnells and Franklins gravitated to one side of the funeral home, while the Huntingtons and their friends stood around on the other side. Some of Ed, Sr.'s and Edith's friends shot judgmental looks across the room, when laughter periodically erupted.

Mary and Phyllis made the effort to wander back and forth, attempting to give the impression it was one big, not-so-happy family. Kate, however, couldn't drum up the energy to go over to her in-laws. She felt bad that they'd lost their only son, but she needed the warmth of her family.

They sat in a loose circle, sipping beer and telling stories about Eddie–his humor, his easy-going smile and how he was always ready to help with whatever needed doing. Jack repeated a joke Eddie had told him. During a lull in the conversation, Michael said softly, "When we lost the baby…" He choked on a suppressed sob. Three years ago, Phyllis had unexpectedly found herself pregnant, long after they'd thought they were done with having children. The baby had been born premature and had lived only two days.

Michael looked around, making sure his wife was out of earshot. "Everybody was focused on helping Phyllis, myself included," he said so quietly they had to strain to hear him. "But Ed thought to take me aside and ask how I was doing." He swiped at his face with the sleeve of his shirt.

There was a long pause while everyone struggled with their grief. Then Rob told the story of how Ed had helped him sort out the estate of one of his clients, and had refused to take any fee for his services from the widow.

Lying in bed that night, Kate thought about how Eddie's helpful nature had gotten him killed. She could have easily taken the car to get the tire replaced. She'd had that afternoon off. But Eddie had insisted, pointing out that the tire store was right up the street from his office.

Irrational anger exploded in her chest. *Why did he have to be so damned nice?*

In the next instant, anger was banished by a knife of guilt twisting in her gut. She was the one who was supposed to be dead, not him. Kate wished with all her heart that she were.

CHAPTER SIX

Kate sat on a bench in the soft May sunshine, picking at the carryout crab cake she'd bought and watching the people bustling along the sidewalks of the Inner Harbor in Baltimore City. It was the first Wednesday after her return to work, and the five-week anniversary of Eddie's death.

Rob was in court that afternoon, which was just as well. Considering how the last one had ended, she wasn't ready yet to resume their weekly lunches.

Unable to face the long afternoon and evening in her lonely house, Kate had decided to come downtown for a change of scenery and some people watching.

Her boss Sally had encouraged her to take off as much time as she needed, but Kate had been going crazy sitting at home. She was better off working. Each day she was able to put aside her feelings for awhile as she focused on other people's problems.

Closing her eyes, she lifted her face to the sun. As it all too often did, her mind wandered back to Eddie's memorial service. She wasn't sure if it had been better or worse that there'd been no corpse to view or put in the ground. Theoretically, she understood the psychological purpose of such burial practices. Seeing the body, watching the casket being lowered into the ground–these things helped loved ones break out of their denial so they could let their grief out.

But knowing the theory and living the reality were two different things. At the time, she'd been grateful for the numbness she had felt most of that day.

When her in-laws left the next morning, she'd moved upstairs to the guest room, unable to deal with another night in that empty king-sized bed. And three weeks ago, Rob had helped her pick out a new car, after she'd admitted to herself she would never be able to drive

Eddie's Saturn. The interior would smell like him, and she wasn't ready to face the little things one leaves in one's car–his umbrella and gym bag, the power bar wrappers scattered on the floor. She hadn't traded the car in, however. She wasn't ready to part with it. It was parked in the dilapidated garage behind the house.

There were a lot of things she wasn't ready to face yet. But she was letting the grief out, in the privacy of her backyard surrounded by pine trees as tall as the three-story house. She'd bought an Adirondack chair–Google having informed her they were named after the mountain chain in New England where they had originated. Each evening, she sat in it under the trees and just let herself feel.

Tears would stream down her cheeks as she recalled the things she and Eddie had done together. Sometimes a sob would escape. Occasionally she'd chuckle out loud at some joke he'd told her. The neighbors, overhearing these odd noises, probably thought she was nuts, but she knew it was what she needed to do.

Lately she'd started talking to Eddie in her head and imagining what he would say back. It was comforting, as if he were still there with her in a way. She'd decided not to tell anyone about these imaginary conversations however, not even Rob.

Having finished her crab cake, Kate strolled back toward the parking garage on Light Street where she'd parked her new Prius.

Her thoughts turned to the investigation into Eddie's murder, which seemed to be going nowhere fast. Detective Phillips had been back several times, repeating the same questions as if she might start giving him different answers. Most of those times, Officer Hernandez had been along, writing the same old answers in her notepad. At some point, Phillips would ask, with that smirky tone Kate had grown to hate, if she had seen her *friend* Mr. Franklin lately.

When she turned the tables and asked about the investigation, she got the typical stonewall answers. "The investigation is ongoing. We are following all leads."

The second time the detective and his shadow had returned had been two days after the memorial service. Kate knew Rob would be angry with her for not calling him, but she hadn't been able to dredge up the energy to make the call. And she definitely had no desire to sit around making small talk with the obnoxious policeman while they waited for Rob to shake free of his other duties to join them.

Besides, Phillips hadn't asked her anything she hadn't already answered. When he'd requested the use of her bathroom, she assumed he wanted to snoop around. Normally such an intrusion would have pissed her off, but that day she was too depressed to care. Once he was out of the room, she'd begged Officer Hernandez to tell her what was going on in the investigation.

The young woman hesitated, then said, "Not much to tell, ma'am. Perp didn't give us much to go on. Homemade pipe bomb. Not that hard to make. Anyone can find out how on the Internet. If there's anything you can think of that you haven't already told us, it might help."

Kate searched her brain again for anything she could offer, and indeed a new idea occurred to her. She'd told them that she had no enemies, but maybe that wasn't true.

When Phillips returned to the room, Kate said, "Detective, I don't know of any personal enemies. But in the work I do, not everyone is happy with me at the end of the day. There are some spouses and abusive parents out there who think I'm the devil incarnate because I helped their mate or grown child stand up to them. Not to mention I've reported a few child abusers through the years, some of whom have ended up in jail."

Phillips nodded to Officer Hernandez and she poised pen over notepad. "And what are the names of these people who might be mad enough to do you harm?"

At that moment, Kate had realized this could go no further. She could give him the names of the abusers she'd reported–that information was already available to him. But she couldn't break confidentiality and give out details about clients' cases, on the off chance that someone connected to them might have decided to take revenge against her.

She was ethically and legally required to keep clients' names and any information about them to herself. Even if she strongly suspected someone connected to a client was Eddie's murderer, technically she should get the client's permission before revealing details about the case to the police. Otherwise, she'd risk losing her psychotherapy license.

Although if she actually knew who the killer was, she'd tell the police in a heartbeat and her license be damned.

The ding of the parking garage elevator broke into her reverie. As she stepped off the elevator, she double-checked the aisle number she'd scribbled on the time-stamped ticket.

Three cars away, her steps faltered. She stared dumbfounded at her new Prius. The back window and one of the taillights were shattered.

Assuming it was random vandalism, kids busting out car windows, she looked around. The cars near hers were intact. Confused, her mind searched for some other logical explanation for the damage, as if expecting to see a blown-down tree in the middle of a cement-and-steel parking garage.

She approached her car. The back seat was covered with tiny shards of glass. She looked up at the sound of a car door slamming. A young couple was getting out of a red sports car in the next aisle.

With a jolt, she realized that whoever did this could still be nearby. The young couple's presence might be the only thing preventing an attack on her. Heart pounding, she almost dropped her keys as she struggled to unlock the door. She scrambled into the driver's seat, started the car and raced through the garage.

At the cashier's booth, she stomped on the brakes and threw the ticket along with a twenty-dollar bill at the attendant. Without waiting for change, she shot out into the street, barely missing a car that swerved into the next lane to avoid her.

A few blocks away, the after-shocks hit her. She was trembling so badly she had to pull over to the curb. Too late, she realized she should have been concerned about another car bomb. But she'd felt so vulnerable in the parking garage, all she could think about was getting out of there.

Digging her phone out of her purse, she tried to call Rob's cell. Shaky fingers hit the wrong numbers. She had to start again. It went straight to voicemail. He must still be in court.

"Hi, it's me. Somebody broke my window. In my car. Actually the whole back window." Realizing how inane this message was sounding, she ended with, "Call me when you get a chance."

Knuckles rapped against her side window. She jumped, hitting her head on the ceiling of the car.

A thirty-something Baltimore City police officer was standing there, a combination of concern and suspicion on his brown face. She realized she'd pulled into and was blocking a bus-stop area. She lowered the window.

The officer asked for her license, then got a better look at her pale face. "Are you all right, lady?"

Halfway through an incoherent attempt at an explanation, Kate gave up and asked the officer to contact Detective Phillips in Baltimore County and ask him to meet her at her house.

The officer nodded, his eyes still worried. "I'm sorry, ma'am, but I've got to give you an inspection notice on that busted taillight. You've got thirty days to get the repairs done. I'll give you the number of the vandalism report, for your insurance company."

While he went back to his cruiser to write the inspection notice, Kate took several deep breaths in an attempt to calm herself. By the time the officer returned and handed her the notice, she was able to shift the car into gear and steer carefully back into traffic.

Rob returned Kate's call as he was walking across the courthouse parking lot. She was telling him what had happened to her car when he heard her doorbell ring in the background.

"Hold on," Kate said. "Someone's at the door." His lawyer instincts kicked in when he heard her say, "Detective Phillips. Wow, the officer actually called you."

Shit!

"Don't say anything, Kate! I'll be there in ten minutes."

When he arrived, Kate and Phillips were already in full-blown argument. The detective kept referring to her "little stalker story." She was waving the inspection notice in his face.

In response to the detective's what-does-that-prove shrug, Kate said, "Go to the garage. You'll see the glass there."

"Where were you parked?"

She froze.

Rob realized she didn't remember. Under the best of circumstances, it was the kind of information one only committed to memory temporarily.

"I'm not sure," she said.

Phillips smirked. "How convenient."

"Look, *Detective*, when are you going to give up your little pet theory and actually start *doing* some detecting?"

They had a staring match for several seconds, then the detective said in a flat voice, "If I can find a uniform with nothing better to do, I'll send him down to look around that garage."

Phillips turned to Rob. "Ah, and here is the knight in shining armor, always ready to rescue damsel Huntington when she's in distress."

Rob fought the urge to bust the man in his chops. He clenched his fists and ground his teeth. "Phillips, I think you need to leave now before one officer of the court is forced to deck another."

Phillips smirked at him, but there was a flash of fear in his eyes. Rob was half a foot taller and at least thirty pounds heavier. The detective gave an elaborate shrug and headed for the front door.

Once the jackass was out the door, Rob turned to Kate. "I don't want you talking to him again without me present." He realized too late how sharp his voice sounded.

Kate arched an eyebrow at him, a silent reminder of something she'd pointed out to him before. When he was fresh from the courtroom, he tended to be a lot more adversarial than usual.

He huffed out air. Softening his tone, he said, "Look, I'm not going macho on you here. I'm talking as your lawyer. This guy seriously believes we're having an affair and we're trying to get rid of our spouses. He even checked out my alibi for when Liz was hit. Fortunately, I was in a settlement conference with four other people at the time."

Anger surged again in his chest. "Then he asked if I'd hired a hit man. I've never wanted to physically harm another human being in my entire life, but I want to put my hands around that detective's neck and squeeze 'til his eyes bulge!"

Kate patted his arm. "Whoa, Tiger. Actually a little macho protectiveness feels good to me right about now, but let's not get ourselves thrown in jail for assaulting police officers. And what happened to the he's-just-doing-his-job attitude?"

There was an irritating twinkle in her eye as one corner of her mouth quirked up.

"Humph," he snorted. "In my line of work, I've rubbed elbows with a fair number of police officers. Most are intelligent and dedicated, but I've encountered ones like Phillips before. Ambitious, not overly bright and dedicated only to number one." He pointed his thumb at his chest. "Their goal is to close cases quickly so they look good, and to hell with whether or not they have the right suspect."

He decided not to tell Kate that Phillips had also searched his house and garage, no doubt looking for signs of bomb-making. He'd granted permission for the search since he had nothing to hide. But when Phillips had wanted to search Kate's house, Rob had told him to get a warrant.

Which the jackass had been unable to do. The judge had been unimpressed when the only probable cause Phillips could offer for intruding on a grieving widow was the fact that a male friend had hugged her and called her *dear* right after she'd learned of her husband's murder.

Rob ground his teeth one last time, then changed the subject. "Okay, if you're going to let me take care of you some, get me the phone book so I can find a glass repair shop." He was much less concerned about the taillight than he was about someone crawling into her car through that back window. "Then I'll follow you over to drop the car off."

"My hero!" Kate gave him a mock simpering smile and fluttered her eyelashes.

"Milady," Rob said, taking off an imaginary hat and bowing deeply.

With a snort, Kate went off to find the phone book, shaking her head at his silliness even though she'd started it.

Okay, sense of humor's coming back. She'll make it. He smiled to himself.

The smile faded at the next thought. *If nobody kills her, that is.*

CHAPTER SEVEN

Thursday evening, Mary called her sister.

"Wow, you are psychic, girl!" Kate said. "How'd you know I needed to hear your voice?"

"Don't know about psychic, but I was thinking I'd fly east this weekend and visit. Maybe stay a week and get together with some old friends." Mary tried to sound nonchalant, but she was worried about Kate. She could only begin to imagine what her sister was going through. The thought of losing her own husband was unbearable.

Pete, the sweetie, had agreed to a week of single parenthood so she could go see for herself that Kate was okay.

"I know it's last minute, but with the holiday Monday, it's one less day Pete has to jockey his schedule around the girls' school." Mary didn't want to give her too much time to think about it, and maybe realize that her little sister was mainly coming to check up on her.

The strategy apparently worked.

"I'd loved to have you!" Kate said without hesitation.

~~~~~~~~~~

Kate hadn't realized just how lonely she was until she'd heard her sister's voice. Looking forward to Mary's arrival helped her get through the next day. It started off rough and seemed to grow worse with each session.

Her three o'clock client was Jim Lincoln. One of his alters, a twelve-year-old boy named Sammy, was currently very depressed. She had been able to extract a promise from Sammy that if he felt the urge to harm himself, he would call her first.

She held back her sigh of relief until Jim was totally out the door of the outer office.

At least her last session would probably be an easy one. Cheryl Crofton was doing quite well lately, although Kate reminded herself to watch for signs of white knight syndrome regarding Rob.

Cheryl arrived a few minutes late and was dressed much more provocatively than usual. Despite the fact that her belly now had a significant bulge to it, she was poured into a snug knit top that revealed considerable cleavage, and maternity Capri pants that accented muscular calves. Again, she was wearing three-inch heels.

Seeing the appraising look in Kate's eyes, she grinned and sashayed around the outer office. "You like?"

"Wow," Kate said. "That's quite an outfit. But how *do* you walk in those heels?" She was concerned that Cheryl was going to fall and hurt the baby if she insisted on continuing to wear such footwear.

"Aw, I'm used to 'em." Cheryl snapped the gum in her mouth. Kate had never seen her chew gum before.

She ushered the client into the office. "You certainly seem to be in a good mood today."

"Oh, yeah," Cheryl said, dropping onto the loveseat. "But I can't wait to get this brat out of my body, so I can do some serious partying. This not being able to drink really sucks."

Kate struggled to keep her alarm from showing. Was that resentment in Cheryl's voice, under the joking banter?

So much for this being an easy session.

As she settled into her own chair, she decided to come back to the issue, after she'd had a few minutes to ponder the woman's apparent change in attitude toward motherhood.

"Have you heard any more from Frank?"

Cheryl's face morphed into a mask of rage. "No, that lying son of a bitch! Last time he called he said he was gonna send me some money but he hasn't called since. That was weeks ago. I tried callin' him and his phone's been disconnected."

This time Kate didn't bother to hide her shock. "You gave him your address? Cheryl, the idea was to keep him from knowing where you are."

"Oh, don't worry. He knows not to mess with me no more. I told him I had a gun and I'd shoot his sorry ass if he ever came near me again!"

The session continued along those lines, with Cheryl ranting about what she would do to Frank or any other man who ever messed with her again, and Kate trying to calm her down. Finally Kate said, "Look, these assholes, as you call them, aren't worth going to jail for."

Cheryl narrowed her eyes at her. "I thought you wanted me to stand up for myself?"

"I do, and if someone's actually attacking you, by all means protect yourself. But it's not okay to shoot some shmuck just because he makes a pass at you. You need to stand up for yourself verbally and only use a violent response as a last resort. Otherwise you're no better than Frank."

In a softer voice, she added, "Look, it's totally understandable that you're pissed at Frank, and men in general. And it's a good thing that you're letting that anger out." She pointed to Cheryl's belly. "But I don't want that baby growing up in foster care because his mom's in jail."

The client gave her a dirty look, then subsided into a pout. Kate managed to hide her surprise at this out-of-character behavior. Cheryl wasn't highly educated but she was an intelligent woman. She usually listened to reason.

After a moment, the pout shifted to a sly smile. "You really think this outfit is sexy?"

"About as sexy as it gets." Kate smiled back.

After a few more minutes of Cheryl switching from angry to almost flirtatious, she finally seemed to settle down. As the session was coming to an end, she looked down at her outfit, confusion on her face. "Don't know what I was thinking when I got dressed this morning. This outfit's a bit over the top."

Kate caught herself as her mouth was about to drop open. She stood up and ushered her client to the door.

"See ya next time," Cheryl said over her shoulder, clicking away on her ridiculously high heels.

Kate flopped back down into her desk chair. She was trying to process what had just happened. Could Cheryl have multiple personalities?

Maybe I'm imagining things, because she came in right after Jim today.

No, there was definitely something going on here. Kate shook her head, then made a note in the file to keep an eye out for additional signs of D.I.D. It was a diagnosis with serious implications, not one to be made in haste.

As she locked up the file, Kate shook her head again to clear it of client issues. She had places to go and sisters to see!

Driving to the airport, she experienced something she hadn't felt in quite awhile–a light, bubbly feeling in her chest, something akin to happiness.

She'd warned Mary that she would have to go to work next week, having already missed too much time with her clients. She'd even had to schedule Jim and another potentially suicidal client on Monday, Memorial Day. She wasn't sure either one would make it through a three-day weekend.

Mary had assured her that she could easily occupy her days with shopping and visits with childhood friends. She'd pointed out that stay-at-home moms rarely got vacations from their jobs. She was looking forward to some alone time and being able to shop without squabbling kids along.

~~~~~~~~~~

They had a delightful weekend, staying up late, drinking wine and chatting. Mary was regaling her sister with stories of her nieces until she caught the wistful look in Kate's eye. She changed the subject.

At breakfast Monday morning, Kate handed her a set of keys. "I hope it starts. It hasn't been driven in awhile."

With a jolt, Mary realized the keys were to Ed's Saturn. She faked a nonchalance she didn't feel. "Whatever. If it doesn't start, I'll laze around the house and we'll deal with it this afternoon."

Kate gave her a hug and left for work.

The Saturn's engine turned right over, then coughed and died. On the second try, it stayed running. Mary backed it carefully out of the garage and headed for Towson Town Center to check out the Memorial Day sales.

Two hours later, she returned with a bag of new clothes. Kate wasn't due home for another hour so she decided to take a nap. She'd come east to check on her sister, yes, but she had every intention of enjoying her vacation from motherhood while she was here.

She had no idea how much time had passed when she was awakened by the faint ding-dong of a doorbell. Groggy, she shuffled into the living room and over to the front door. She couldn't see out the peephole that Ed had apparently installed at Kate's eye level.

She tried standing on tiptoes. All she could see was the distorted image of one of the posts holding up the porch roof. The doorbell rang again.

This is ridiculous.

Mary unlocked and opened the door. There was no one there. She stepped closer to the screen door. Then she heard a truck engine roar in the distance.

The UPS guy! They never wait for you. Just ring the bell and take off.

She opened the screen door. Looking down in search of a package, she stepped out onto the porch. And fell into darkness.

CHAPTER EIGHT

Kate caught herself humming to the tune on the radio as she drove home.

Wow, I didn't think I'd ever hum again. Guess I'm gonna be all right, Eddie.

She imagined him saying, in his soft baritone, *Well of course you are, my love.* She smiled to herself.

The smile faded as she turned the corner onto her block. The street was clogged with emergency vehicles and bystanders. The latter were staring in the direction of her house.

Heart pounding, she parked haphazardly, jumped out of the car and raced toward the crowd. She elbowed her way through it without bothering to excuse herself.

A cop stepped in front of her, his hand in the air, palm out.

"I live here," she said breathlessly.

He let her go and turned to hold back the surge of neighbors craning to witness the next scene in the unfolding drama.

At the bottom of the steps, Kate looked up at the half dozen people on her porch and froze. In the middle of the group was her sister, strapped to a gurney, her head covered in blood.

Kate reeled, grabbing for the railing. "Is she okay?" she cried out.

One of the paramedics glanced up without answering.

"I'm her sister," she managed to push past the lump in her throat.

The paramedic glanced up again from the bandage he was wrapping around Mary's head. "She's unconscious, but she's breathing. Gotta get her to the hospital. Docs will be able to tell you more." His eyes dropped back to the task of securing the bandage.

"Comin' through, lady." His partner, who looked like a football linebacker, started down the steps backwards, lifting up his end of the gurney to keep the patient as level as possible.

Kate jumped back and collided with another cop. He tried to block her way as she started toward the ambulance. "We got some questions, ma'am."

"I have to go with my sister." She dodged past him.

The ambulance ride to the hospital was the scariest eight minutes of Kate's life. The siren screamed outside. Equipment beeped inside. Mary lay pale and still. The paramedic looked bored. Kate wasn't sure how to interpret that.

At the hospital, she was stopped by a firm but friendly hand on her arm as she tried to follow the gurney into the treatment room. A nurse, about Mary's height with *café au lait* skin, gave her a sympathetic smile. "You can't go in there. She's in good hands. Come with me, please. I need to get some information."

Kate turned to comply and almost collided with the same young cop, who'd apparently followed the ambulance to the hospital. "Still got those questions, ma'am."

"In a minute." Kate stepped around him and went to the ER counter. The nurse asked Kate about Mary's identity, health history, marital status and insurance. Kate answered as best she could.

The nurse nodded at the chairs. "Have a seat. The doctor will be out to tell you how she's doing as soon as he can." Her voice was gentle.

Kate glanced at the no-cell-phones sign on the wall and headed for the door. The cop stepped in front of her but she brushed past him, her fingers already punching Rob's number into her phone.

It went to voicemail. "Something's happened to my sister. We're at GBMC, in the ER. Cops have questions. Please come." She heard the shakiness in her voice and took a deep breath as she disconnected.

Gotta get the voice a lot calmer than that.

She punched in her sister's home number in California, and got voicemail again. "Pete, there's been an accident."

Better, not quite normal but not borderline hysterical either.

"Mary's going to be okay," she lied. "We're at GBMC, uh, Greater Baltimore Medical Center on Charles Street. The doctors are taking a look at her. Let's see, I can't leave my cell phone on inside there and I don't know the number of the ER nurses' station, but you can call information in Baltimore for it. Call when you get this and I should know more by then. Bye."

She disconnected and let out her breath. Turning around, she jumped. The cop was standing right behind her.

"You gotta stop doing that. I know, I know, you've got questions. Come on." She marched back inside and headed for some chairs far from the other people waiting in the ER. She didn't want to discuss her business in front of curious strangers.

He asked the obvious–who was Mary, why was she at Kate's house, did she have any enemies–writing the answers in his little notepad.

Kate pointed to the pad. "They must buy those by the gross for you all. Every time I see a police officer, he or she is scribbling in one of them."

He gave her an odd look.

Oookay, said the rational side of her mind to the semi-hysterical side, *probably shouldn't be admitting that I've been hanging around cops who needed to write down things about me.*

"Do you know what happened?" she asked the officer.

"Still investigating." Then in response to her glare, he added, "Probably burglars. There's been a rash of break-ins around Towson lately, during the day while people are at work. Might have seen you leave. Didn't realize you had a house guest."

"Were there any signs of a break-in?"

"None that I saw," the officer said. "Neighbor spotted your sister lying on the porch. Went up to investigate. Called it in when she saw the blood."

Kate clenched her teeth. She was trying hard not to think about the blood. She reminded herself that head wounds bleed profusely. It didn't necessarily mean the injury was severe.

"How would she have ended up on the porch if someone broke in?"

The cop shrugged. "Burglars might've rung the doorbell, to make sure no one was home. She came to the door. They panicked. Hit her with something."

Kate was debating whether to fill him in on a different theory when Rob came through the ER doors. He spotted Kate and barreled across the room. Grabbing her by the shoulders, he lifted her out of her chair. "Are you okay?"

"Yeah." She struggled to breath as he enveloped her in a bear hug.

"My voicemail garbled your message," Rob said into her hair. "All I heard was 'something's happened' and then 'GBMC.' You sounded terrified."

"That's 'cause I am." Kate pulled back to look up at his face.

The cop cleared his throat. "Your husband?"

"No, a friend. Could we have a moment? Don't go away." She led Rob out of earshot and quickly filled him in, including her temptation to tell this cop the whole story and maybe get someone with a new perspective involved in the case.

Rob shook his head. "That's not what will happen. This kid'll write it all down and turn it over to the detective who's already working the burglaries. Then that detective will come question us and we'll repeat the whole miserable story all over again. He or she will compare notes with Phillips but they won't get involved in Ed's case. It's more likely that the investigation into Mary's attack would be turned over to Phillips."

"Crap!" Kate said.

"Let me deal with the officer. I'll tell him to have the detective contact me. Be right back," Rob said.

Kate flopped down in one of the chairs around the perimeter of the waiting room.

A few minutes later, Rob came over and sat down beside her. "You okay? You seem a little too calm."

"Clinical detachment. I can sit on my feelings when I have to. I was trying not to lose it in front of the cop."

"Well, he's gone now so feel free to lose it whenever you want."

"Urge has passed for the moment, but I'm sure it will come back at some point."

Rob took her hand. She put her head back against the wall, closing her eyes. "Thanks for coming."

"That's what friends are for," he said.

They sat–her eyes closed, her hand gently encased in Rob's, her stomach tied in knots–for what seemed an eternity.

The swish of an automatic door opening. Kate opened one eye. The ER doctor was at the nurses' station. The nurse was pointing in their direction. He headed their way.

Kate jumped out of her chair, startling Rob. He followed as she rushed over to meet the doctor halfway across the room. "Is she awake? Is she going to be okay?"

"Hopefully to the second question. No to the first," the doctor answered. "Sit down, please." They all sat in the nearest chairs. "Your sister's still unconscious. Whoever hit her, with whatever, got her on the top of her head. That's good news and bad news. The top of the skull is pretty thick. We did a CAT scan and there are only a couple of hairline fractures. No signs of bleeding or swelling in the brain."

Knowing there was an unspoken *yet* at the end of that last sentence, Kate prompted, "And the bad news?" She understood the brain well enough to suspect what was coming.

"That's the part of the brain where some pretty important stuff is. Sensory and motor control centers, memory, upper level reasoning, even our personalities are centered in the frontal and parietal lobes." The doctor's voice was gentle but matter-of-fact. "It's hard to tell at this point if there's any permanent damage. She's being admitted and will be going up to intensive care soon. It's on the third floor. The chief neurologist is on his way in. He might be able to tell you more after he examines her."

He paused. "It would be good if you went in to see her as much as the ICU allows. A lot of research indicates there's still some level of awareness in people who are unconscious. Talking to her, holding her hand, may help bring her around."

Kate nodded and was thanking the doctor when the nurse called over, "Mrs. Huntington, your brother-in-law's on the phone."

Kate ran over and grabbed the receiver the nurse was holding up. "We're not allowed to release information over the phone," the nurse whispered. "But *you* can tell him what's going on. I can't have my line tied up though."

Kate nodded. "Pete, she's okay," she lied into the phone. "Are you home? Good, I'll call you right back on my cell."

She handed the phone to the nurse. "Thanks."

She turned toward the outside doors. Rob was already in front of them, triggering the automatic opener.

Standing on the sidewalk next to her, Rob was impressed with how well Kate handled the conversation with her brother-in-law. She lied through her teeth when necessary to keep him from panicking, but still managed to convey the need for him to get there as quickly as possible. She finally disconnected.

"He's calling his mom to come watch the girls and he'll get on the first plane he can. Tonight hopefully." She dropped her phone into her purse.

"You sounded quite calm," Rob said.

"Lots of practice. Unfortunately, it's a skill I'm only able to apply sporadically in my personal life. Right now, I'm calm. I make no promises about the future…. The doctor wasn't telling the whole truth, by the way."

"What do you mean?" he asked.

"If she was hit hard enough to produce even hairline fractures, and she's still out cold, that's not a good sign. As the doc implied, she may have memory loss, personality changes. She may end up with the IQ of a monkey. She may be paralyzed…."

And with that, Kate burst into tears. He gathered her up in his arms.

"What was I thinking?" She sobbed against his shirtfront. "How could I let her come here knowing somebody's trying to kill me?"

He held her, searching for something helpful to say. He opted not to voice the first thing that came to mind. It was understandable that she wasn't thinking straight right now. She'd just lost her husband.

"This situation isn't exactly something we're used to dealing with." Not exactly brilliant but it was the best he could come up with.

Her sobs subsided. He stepped back to fish out his handkerchief and handed it to her. "It's also possible that Mary will wake up in an hour or two with nothing worse than a bad concussion."

Kate nodded slightly, then wiped her eyes and blew her nose.

He almost laughed at her expression as she looked ruefully at the make-up and other disgusting things now smeared on his handkerchief.

"You really don't want this back, do you?" she said.

"No, I think not."

She stuffed the handkerchief in her purse.

"Let's go find the ICU," he suggested.

"Oh, my God, I've got to call my folks, and my brothers!" Kate fumbled in her purse for her phone.

He turned her around toward the doors and snatched the phone from her hand before she could protest. "You find the ICU. I'll make the calls. I'll be up in a little bit. I need to call Liz, too, and let her know why I'm not there to wait on her hand and foot."

At Kate's guilt-stricken expression, he said, "Stop it. Samantha's home today. That was my feeble attempt at a joke about her Highness, the Queen."

"Humph. If I know Liz, she's hating every minute of being waited on."

"Got that right. Thought she was gonna bite my hand off when I brought her coffee this morning. At this point, grouchy is winning out over gratitude most of the time. But the doctor said in a few more days she can ditch the wheelchair and hobble around on crutches. There'll be no stopping her then."

Kate actually smiled a little at whatever mental image that had conjured up… probably of Liz knocking over her throne with her crutches and beating it into matchsticks.

He made a shooing gesture, and Kate headed back into the hospital.

Deciding he needed some moral support himself, he called his Lizzie first.

CHAPTER NINE

While Kate sat in the ICU holding her sister's limp hand and talking to her, the family was once again converging on Towson.

After filling Liz in, Rob had called the elder O'Donnells at their retirement condo in St. Augustine. They'd immediately headed for the Jacksonville airport. When he called Jack's number in Chicago, his girlfriend answered. Jack wasn't home but she promised to track him down and get him on the next available flight.

Then Rob called Michael's home number. Phyllis answered. He told her what had happened, then where to find the spare key to Kate's house hidden in a fake rock by the front porch steps.

"Uh, Phyllis, hang onto that key for now." Having a key where just anybody could find it probably wasn't a great idea at this point.

~~~~~~~~

Phyllis dispatched Michael to once again make the airport runs, while she headed for Towson.

Retrieving the key, she walked up onto the porch. The sight of the rusty-red blood soaking into the floorboards hit her like a fist in the gut.

How could anyone do this to dear, sweet Mary?

Pulling herself together, Phyllis stepped over the still sticky puddle and unlocked the door. She went in search of fresh sheets and started making up beds everywhere she could, including the sofas in the living room and study. There would be no driving back and forth to Silver Spring this time. Everyone would want to be near the hospital.

She knew she should try to clean up the blood on the porch before her in-laws got there, but she wasn't sure her stomach was up to the task. She found an old throw rug in the laundry room on the back of the house and put it over the stain.

Her eyes stinging, she untied the remnant of yellow crime scene tape still attached to the porch railing.

~~~~~~~~~

Two long days went by with no change in Mary's condition. Rob stopped by the hospital as often as he could. The family was taking turns, two or three at the hospital at a time, the others going back to Kate's house to get some sleep.

Her parents and siblings seemed to be buying Kate's stoic facade, but he knew better. She normally had a voracious appetite. Watching her pick at the carryout food offerings he brought to the hospital told him a lot.

Wednesday evening, he walked into the ICU waiting area. Kate was alone. She shifted forward in her chair, nose in the air, sniffing.

"Oh, you wonderful man!" she said when she spotted the grease-stained bags in his hand.

He held out one of them. She grabbed it and pulled out a Big Mac and fries. Spreading out the feast on her lap, she dug in.

Hope sprang up in his chest. "Any change?"

Her face sobered. She shook her head, her mouth full of food.

Crap! No improvement in Mary's condition. Just Kate's appetite adjusting to the new normal.

He sank down on the chair next to her. "Is your family sticking to the two-by-two rule?" On Monday evening, he'd taken her aside and pointed out that none of them were safe on their own. So far, whoever was doing this hadn't gone after anyone who was with another person. Kate had brought up the one exception, when the jackass had shot at him and Shelley. But Rob wasn't sure the shooter had realized they were together. He'd been standing to one side, holding the door open as Shelley came out, when the biker rode into the path of the first bullet.

Kate swallowed a bite of her burger. "Yeah, but it's been tricky at times. I don't want to tell them everything that's been going on. They're already worried sick about Mary."

Rob thought a certain amount of worry was in order for the eldest O'Donnell daughter as well, but he kept his mouth shut. Not his family, not his call.

Kate paused in her attack on her food. "I've been trying to convince myself that you and I are the only ones in danger, and Mary was just mistaken for me. But Liz was attacked first, so apparently family members aren't exempt from whatever vendetta somebody has against us."

"This guy, he's got to be related to a mutual case," Rob said. "I've got my staff working on identifying those cases we were both involved in. Once Mary's out of the woods," he didn't want to think about any other outcome, "we'll have to try to figure out which one."

"We keep saying *he*, but maybe it's a she. A woman, no matter what her weapon, would be less likely to tackle two people at once."

"True. But would a woman be carrying around that much rage?"

"Oh, yeah. Quite possible," Kate said. "Just because this level of aggression is much more common in men, doesn't mean it can't happen in women. Close to one percent of females have antisocial personality disorder."

Rob shuddered. "As in one out of every hundred women would be capable of doing this? That's a scary statistic."

"Then you don't want to know the percentage of men," she said. "Hey wait, what about Liz and the girls? How are you keeping them safe?"

He took a deep breath. *Here we go.*

"Not to worry, that's taken care of."

"How so?" came the garbled response as she resumed eating.

"I've hired bodyguards." He said it as nonchalantly as he might say he'd gotten extra pickles on his sandwich.

Kate's mouth fell open, which wasn't a pretty sight since she'd just shoved several fries into it.

"One goes with me everywhere, one stays at the house with Liz." He ignored her expression as he took a bite of his own burger, with extra pickles.

A few seconds went by while he chewed, and Kate digested the concept of bodyguards. Finally she asked, "What about the girls?"

"Shelley's staying in Maine for summer classes. I've tried and tried to think of a way to keep Sam safe without disrupting her life. Couldn't find one. She'd be too vulnerable at school. And she's so rebellious right now, whatever restrictions I put on her, she'd probably ignore when I wasn't looking."

"If this weren't so serious, I'd laugh at the mental image that just popped into my mind, of Samantha climbing out her bedroom window. So what are you going to do?"

"I wouldn't put it past her, and that mental image isn't the least bit funny to a father, even under normal circumstances." Despite his words, he felt his mouth quirk up on one end. "She pitched a fit but I packed her off to her grandmother's in Ohio for the duration. Mom's going to home school her for the rest of the school year."

Kate chewed on more fries. "You think they're far enough away?"

"I hope so. It's the best I can think of. Why were you so surprised about the guards?" He intentionally brought up the subject again. "I'm not giving this jackass any more opportunities to hurt the people I love."

"It must be costing you a fortune."

"It is, but worth every penny. At least Liz can get around now so we don't need the aide anymore. … Uh, I hired a guard for you as well." Taking advantage of Kate's shocked silence, he quickly added, "I'm paying for it. I know the mortgage insurance paid off your house, but you've got car payments now."

She opened her mouth to protest. He cut her off, his voice soft, "I can afford it, Kate. I count you among the people I love."

He couldn't help but grin at the expression on her face. "I do believe I've rendered you speechless."

She gave him a half smile back and opened her mouth again.

A shout came from the inner sanctum of the ICU. Kate jumped up, the remnants of her dinner sliding from her lap. She raced toward the door. Rob plopped his food on the empty chair beside him and followed her.

In Mary's room, Jack and Kate were hugging and jumping up and down. "She opened her eyes! She opened her eyes!" Jack shouted.

They ignored the nurse who was trying to quiet them, but instantly shut up when a weak voice from the bed said, "Would you two eejits keep it down. I'm tryin' to sleep here."

Rob got a quick glimpse of Mary's pale, bruised face, eyes closed again but a faint smile on her lips, before the nurse hustled them out of the room.

~~~~~~~

An hour later, the chief neurologist, who'd gone home and had to be called back in, came out of the ICU to talk to the family now gathered in the waiting area. The doctor reminded Kate of an elderly gnome–a head shorter than herself with wisps of white hair sticking out in all directions.

"This is a very good sign," he said.

Pete looked like a little boy who needed to go to the bathroom. He was rocking from one foot to the other, wanting to hear what the doctor had to say but desperate to see his now conscious wife.

"Go on back and sit with your wife, son. I'll fill you in later."

Pete raced for the door as the doctor turned back to the rest of them. "She seemed to understand me when I told her she was in the hospital and I was her doctor. There are no obvious signs of long-term damage but we'll have to wait and see how her memory is, et cetera, as she continues to recover."

The doctor looked around at their still worried faces, then added, "She'll live, folks, but she's not out of the woods in terms of other possible complications."

Kate let out a pent-up breath. Muscles that had been tense for days started to loosen.

"She knew who Kate and I were," Jack said. "She called us idiots."

The doctor's expression said he wasn't convinced this meant Mary had recognized them. The nurse probably told him they'd been acting like idiots at the time.

"Any signs of paralysis?" Kate asked.

"Doesn't seem to be. She was able to squeeze my hand and wiggle her toes. Her reflexes are normal. I'll run some other tests in the morning. You folks should go home now. I'd rather you not go in to visit again until morning. You did your jobs brilliantly. You called her back to us. Now she needs sleep, Mother Nature's best healer."

"Please, doctor," Kate's mother said, her eyes shiny with unshed tears. "I…," she looked up at her husband beside her, "…we need to see our baby for ourselves, for just a minute. Please."

The doctor hesitated only a second. "I understand, but keep it short. Send her husband out and I'll tell him what I just told all of you."

As their parents went through the ICU door, by unspoken agreement, the O'Donnell siblings and Phyllis put their arms around each other in a circle. They leaned forward, eyes closed, foreheads almost touching.

Tears of relief were streaming down Kate's face. *Thank you, Lord!*

She felt Rob's big hand on her back. "I'll call you tomorrow," he whispered as he slipped past her.

CHAPTER TEN

Sitting in her sister's hospital room with her family on Friday afternoon, Kate knew she had a problem. And she needed to solve it soon because the patient was making rapid progress.

The tests the doctor had run the day before had shown that Mary's reasoning abilities were intact. Jack had decided to verify this for himself. "If two trains leave Philadelphia at the same time, one doing sixty miles an hour and the other a hundred miles an hour, how long will it take each of them to reach Baltimore which is two hundred and twenty miles away?"

Mary's response had reassured Kate that her personality hadn't changed a bit. "You've gotta be kidding, you eejit. I've got a killer headache here and you want me to do math in my head!"

Mary's long-term memory also seemed fine, but she had no recall of the day she was attacked and only vaguely remembered visiting with Kate that weekend. Her last clear memory was of her sister greeting her at the airport. Kate had to keep reassuring their parents that this was normal with severe concussions. Mary might never retrieve all of those memories, especially for the day of the attack.

There was no paralysis but Mary was having coordination problems. It was a little dangerous to let her reach for her own water glass. And if she did manage to get it to her face without spilling it, she couldn't get the straw to go into her mouth. The doctor had expressed optimism, however, that she would re-learn how to coordinate her movements, with the help of some physical therapy.

Jack had flown back to his job and girlfriend that morning. Pete and her parents were sharing Ed's car between them and tended to come to the hospital together, so Kate wasn't too worried about their safety.

Besides her father was no dummy. With his daughter's attacker still at large, Dan O'Donnell was sticking close to his wife's side. And the last two mornings, he'd stood on the porch as Kate had walked to her car and driven off to work. She'd felt like she was ten years old again, when her father would watch the corner bus stop from the front window of their house until his daughters were picked up for school.

What Dad didn't know, and she wasn't going to tell him if she could help it, was that a very tall, muscular guy with the unlikely nickname of Skip was now discreetly guarding her, following her every time she left the house.

Mary's gnome of a doctor bustled into the room. He had a big smile on his face. Kate suspected she'd just run out of time.

"Well, young lady," he said to her sister, "you're doing so well, another day or two, and you can probably go home." He put up his hand at the look of glee on Pete's face. "Not to California, just to your sister-in-law's house. It's going to be some time yet before your wife is up to traveling."

As the family all started talking at once, Kate stood and moved over next to the doctor. She whispered, "Doctor, could I speak to you for a moment?"

Kate walked a good fifty feet away from Mary's room before stopping. "Unfortunately, my sister isn't safe at my house," she began the opening she'd been rehearsing in her head. "There have been several attacks against me, my friend Rob Franklin, and our family members in the last couple months."

The doctor raised his bushy white eyebrows at her.

Despite her mental rehearsals, the next part did not come out smoothly. "My husband... he was mur... " She swallowed hard. "Killed by this maniac six weeks ago." A tear trickled from the corner of her eye. She ignored it. "Rob and I think Mary was attacked because the killer thought she was me."

The doctor was frowning. "The police didn't say anything about this when they questioned me regarding your sister's injuries."

Kate shrugged. "The police have been less than helpful. The guy investigating my husband's case, well, let's just say he's not the most competent detective out there. I know Mary's not in the best shape to travel. But she won't be safe unless we get her out of Maryland. And I don't want my family to know all this. They think the attacks on my husband and sister are unrelated. I need to get them away from me so they're safe. If they knew what was going on, they'd never leave."

The doctor again raised an eyebrow. "Maybe some of them *should* stay to protect you."

Kate sighed. How could she begin to explain to a stranger the jumble of feelings that she'd barely sorted out in her own mind? Of course she was afraid for herself. But the feelings of guilt and terror that someone else she loved could be harmed because of her, those feelings were much stronger.

"Thank you for your concern, Doctor." She tried for a reassuring smile but wasn't sure she'd pulled it off. "I've got a bodyguard. And my friend and I are going to try to figure out who's doing this."

The doctor thought for a moment, then nodded. "Come with me." He headed back down the hall.

Once in Mary's room, he said, "I think your sister must be sick of having you hanging around, young lady. She's convinced me to let you go home, *all the way home*, to California."

Pete cheered. Mary tried to give her husband a high five, but kept missing his hand. She giggled.

Kate smiled. *When things have settled down, I'm going to relive this moment and savor that giggle.*

"So here's what we're going to do," the doctor was saying. "Tomorrow we're going to get you on your feet so you can try out those legs of yours. If all goes well, in two or three days I think you can go home. But you can't fly. The changes in cabin pressure wouldn't be good for that noggin of yours. Hmm, I'd prefer you go by ambulance but that would be expensive."

He turned to Pete. "Young man, can you rent a station wagon or van, something that has seats that fold flat so your wife can lay down in the back?" Pete nodded enthusiastically.

"Thank you!" Kate whispered to the doctor as he swept past her.

"You're welcome," he whispered back and bustled down the hall.

~~~~~~~~

Monday morning, Kate was awakened by the doorbell. Her alarm would have gone off in fifteen minutes anyway, because this was the day that Mary and Pete were starting for home. But who was ringing her doorbell at seven-fifteen in the morning?

She grabbed her robe and raced down the stairs. When she looked through the peephole, the face she saw made her stomach clench. She groaned out loud.

Phillips hit the bell again.

She yanked open the door and pushed the screen door out, forcing him to back up. Pulling the inside door closed behind her, she stepped out onto the porch. "Do you mind, Phillips? The sun's barely up yet and I've got house guests."

"Oh, yeah, Franklin and who else? You into orgies now? And it's Detective Phillips to you."

"You really are disgusting, *Detective* Phillips. My parents and brother-in-law are here, as if it's any of your business."

"Everything you do is my business, lady. You're a murder suspect."

"Why don't you say it a little louder so all the neighbors can hear? And give my parents a heart attack while you're at it." Kate realized her fists were clenched. She willed them to uncurl.

Phillips actually had the decency to look sheepish, but he didn't apologize. "I have some more questions for you."

"You mean you have the same questions for me, *again*. I don't have time for this. My family is leaving this morning and I have to see them off. If Mr. Franklin is available, we can come to the station later." Spending part of her morning at the police station was not what she wanted to do, but she had to get Phillips off her porch before her family came looking for her and saw him.

"I don't need to talk to Franklin right now, just you."

"*Mister* Franklin is my attorney, and he has advised me not to talk to you again unless he's there."

"Oh, got something to hide?"

Kate gritted her teeth and reined in her temper. She had to get rid of him. "Look, Detective, give me a break here. Let me get my family on their way and I'll be at the station by ten-thirty." She didn't have clients scheduled until that afternoon.

The inside door swung open. Her father, in his bathrobe, stepped into the doorway, a baseball bat clutched in his hands.

"It's okay, Dad! Mr. Phillips is a neighbor. And he's about to leave. Sorry, Mr. Phillips, but I don't have any flour." She knew she was babbling but couldn't seem to stop herself. "I'm not much of a cook so I don't have stuff like that on hand."

Phillips gave them both a hard look. "Later," he said, and left.

As Kate turned back to her father, he lowered the bat and raised an eyebrow at her. "Funny thing. That fella's the spittin' image of the copper who was askin' questions 'bout Ed a couple a months ago."

Kate couldn't think of a thing to say. She'd forgotten how hard it was to fool her old man.

"Humph. Guess I'll be gettin' meself dressed." As he walked away, he said back over his shoulder, "Mac's comin' to see us off. Said he'd be here 'bout eight."

Pete had managed to rent a camper, complete with tiny bathroom and kitchenette. Mary wouldn't have to leave it until they reached their home. The doctor had approved. Her parents were going along to help Pete care for the patient on the road.

By the time Mac arrived, Kate was showered and dressed. Pete and her father had left in the Saturn to pick up the camper. Her mother was in the kitchen, still in her robe, making breakfast. Kate took the spatula out of her hand and tried to shoo her off to get dressed. Her mother gave her a skeptical look.

"Oh, come on, Ma. Even I can make scrambled eggs and toast."

"Don't worry, Aunt B," Mac said, reverting to his childhood name for Kate's mother, "I'll keep an eye on her."

Kate turned on him, swinging the spatula in mock battle. Mac just grinned as he helped himself to a cup of coffee.

Once her mother was out of earshot, she said, "Hey, Mac, do you have to be at the restaurant this evening?"

"Funny you should ask," Mac replied. "Got things covered there for awhile. Dan called me last night. Once they get Mary home, he's plannin' on leavin' your ma out there. But he's comin' back. Asked me to camp out on your couch 'til then."

Kate had to smile. Her old man was definitely nobody's fool.

But how to stop him from coming back? She'd have to give that some thought. At least she had a few days to come up with something.

"This evening I want to have a strategy session. A war council, if you will–you, me and Rob."

Mac nodded and the subject was dropped as they heard footsteps heading toward the kitchen.

Getting Mary and her retinue on their way went smoothly from there. After breakfast, Pete loaded luggage into the camper while

Kate stocked the tiny refrigerator and playhouse-sized cabinets with supplies.

Pete and her folks piled into the camper. Mac and Kate followed in his Hummer. Only Kate knew there was a third vehicle in their little caravan. Her bodyguard was dutifully tagging along behind.

At the hospital, Pete pulled the camper right up to the front doors. Mary was brought out in a wheelchair pushed by an aide. Her gnome of a doctor trailed behind. Kate doubted he normally escorted patients to their vehicles, but maybe he wanted to personally supervise this rather unorthodox discharge.

Kate hugged her sister gently. Then she and her mother exchanged a hug while Pete and the aide helped Mary into the camper.

The doctor handed her mother a clear bag of pill bottles, then leaned into the back of the camper. "I've gone over everything with your mama so I'll turn you over to her now," he said to Mary.

Bridget shyly said, "Thank you, Doctor, thank you so much." Despite the fact that she was a couple inches taller and quite a few pounds heavier than the doctor, the elderly gentleman gallantly took her elbow to assist her up the three little steps into the camper.

Pete closed the door, then grabbed the doctor's hand. He pumped it so hard Kate was afraid he'd give the little man whiplash. Eyes glossy with unshed tears, Pete said, "Thanks for everything, Doc!"

"Just try not to rattle her brains too much on the road, son."

The doctor pointed at Kate. "You, young lady! You be careful."

"I will," she replied, but before she could say anything else, the doctor quickly shook her father's hand and bustled off.

"He didn't give *me* a chance to thank him," she protested.

Her father gave her a sharp look. "Not endin' up a patient in his hospital I expect'll be thanks enough, lass." He turned and lumbered up to the passenger door of the camper's cab.

Pete gave Kate a hug, shook hands with Mac and headed for the driver's door. Kate walked to her father's open window. He reached out and stroked the side of her face, then cupped her cheek. She leaned into the palm of his big hand.

"Don't worry, Dad," she said softly. "I'll be careful."

"Yer a good lass, Kathleen." As Pete started the engine, her father patted her on the head, then retracted his arm inside the window. The camper pulled slowly away.

Once again Kate felt like she was ten years old. "I love you, Daddy!" she called out.

"I love you, too, Katie girl," drifted back to her.

CHAPTER ELEVEN

The meeting with Detective Phillips did not go so smoothly.

He was furious when he heard that Mary was on her way home. "You sent your sister back to California without telling me?"

Kate sat back in her chair. They were seated in a stark conference room. More likely an interrogation room, she thought as she struggled to tamp down her own anger. "I seem to recall saying something just a few hours ago about seeing my family off. What the hell did you think I was talking about?"

"I thought you meant your parents. The doc said your sister wouldn't be able to travel for at least a couple more weeks, and you turn around and sneak her out of the state."

"I didn't sneak her anywhere. It wasn't safe for her to be in Maryland."

Rob started to say something but the detective cut him off. "I needed to re-interview her."

"Why?" Kate asked. "She doesn't remember anything from the day she was attacked."

"And isn't that convenient," Phillips said.

"No, it's not at all convenient. It's retrograde amnesia, which is not unusual after a brain injury. It's documented in her medical records."

"Detective Phillips," Rob said, "I'm not familiar with any statute that requires a crime victim to obtain permission from the police before returning to his or her home once released from the hospital."

Phillips glared at Rob, then turned back to her. "Mrs. Huntington, I'm gonna have to *insist* you give me the names of your clients whose relatives might be out to get you."

"And I'm going to have to refuse to do that. I'm bound by rules of confidentiality. I *cannot* just give you my clients' names."

"You'll have to–"

"She can't, Detective," Rob said. "The rules of confidentiality for mental health professionals are more stringent than those for lawyers or doctors. She can't even admit that someone *is* her client."

"Well. I can't exactly do my job, now can I, if I can't even get the names of the suspects?"

"Look, Detective," Kate was trying her best for a conciliatory tone, "Rob and I are going to go back through our mutual cases to see if there's anybody related to one of them that might have a major grudge against us."

"Anyone you come up with, you give me their names and let me do my job!" Phillips ordered.

Kate resisted the temptation to point out that if he'd been doing his job in the first place, her sister might not have ended up in the hospital.

Out in the parking lot, Kate's ride was waiting. Mac leaned against the front fender of his Hummer, arms folded across his chest. He nodded toward Rob's car several rows over, where Lou, Rob's bodyguard, was sitting. "He your hired muscle? Not real subtle."

"Made him, huh?" Rob said.

"Made both of 'em. Only 'cause I know what to look for. Most people don't. That one's good. Discreet." He pointed with his chin toward Skip's dark blue Explorer. "Truck parked where it ain't obvious, but he can pull out quick if need be." He paused. "Did a tour at Fort Meade, when I was Special Forces. Worked for Langley awhile too."

To Marylanders, Fort Meade was shorthand for the National Security Agency, and Langley, Virginia was where the CIA's main offices were located. Mac was letting Rob know that he had experience with covert operations.

"That was quite some time ago though," Kate said.

"Kinda like ridin' a bike, sweet pea. Not somethin' ya forget. Where we havin' this war council tonight?"

"Liz wants in on this so it has to be at my house," Rob said.

"I'll get us some carryout after work," Kate offered. "We should be there about six."

That evening, they found Liz–in shorts and a polo shirt that matched her green eyes–propped up in the corner of the Franklins' family room sofa. Her legs were stretched out along its length. The cast on her right thigh had been replaced with a bright red brace. The lacings on it made it look like she was wearing a corset on her leg. Her left ankle and foot were now ensconced in a walking cast, the outer layer of which was a navy blue canvas boot with velcro straps. It was twice the size of regular footwear.

Kate was relieved to see that, despite the brace and ugly boot, she looked good. The bruises were gone from her face and her short, strawberry blonde hair had regained its luster.

"Mac, you devil! Come over here and give me a kiss," Liz said in her booming voice, so incongruous coming from her petite body.

Mac grinned and went over to give her a peck on the cheek. They all took seats and the war council was convened.

An hour later they'd polished off the Chinese carryout and had the beginnings of a plan. Skip would continue shadowing Kate during the day, so Mac could check on his restaurant. He would take over in the evenings, sleeping on her living room sofa, his Glock within easy reach.

Rob and Kate would start digging through their files. Once they had some likely suspects identified, Mac would track them down to see what they had been up to lately.

Liz had pointed out that she could handle any computer research needed. She admitted to having some limited skills as a hacker.

Rob looked at her, appalled.

"They're rusty. Haven't used them in years," Liz hastily added. "But desperate times call for desperate measures."

Mac confessed to having a small arsenal in the back of his truck, *most* of it legally registered. Wednesday afternoon he would take Kate to his favorite spot, in the rural northern part of the county, for some target practice. She wasn't enthusiastic about learning to shoot a gun, but Mac was adamant.

"Once we have the suspects narrowed down," she said, "maybe we can figure out how to lure the killer out–"

"Too dangerous, sweet pea."

She stifled a surge of irritation. "Mac, I can't turn names over to the police until we're fairly sure the person is the killer, and we can't go on like this forever. Rob can't afford the bodyguards. You've got a business to run. And I'm not willing to live in constant fear indefinitely."

"She's got a point," Liz said.

"Okay, first task, hit the case files." Rob pushed up from his chair. He leaned down to kiss his wife as he walked past the sofa.

"Want to join us for target practice Wednesday, Liz?" Mac asked.

Liz waved in the general direction of her big blue foot and the crutches propped against the end of the sofa. "I don't think I'm mobile enough yet to be stomping around in the woods. But I'll take a rain check. The idea of knowing how to blow away someone who's threatening you and yours has some appeal."

Rob gave her another shocked look. "No matter how many years you're married to 'em, don't ever think you know 'em," he muttered to Mac.

"Wouldn't know. Never could never get a marriage to stick all that long." Mac had been married twice, for about fifteen minutes each time.

~~~~~~~~~~

The afternoon sun was sinking toward the horizon as Mac drove Kate home on Wednesday. She was trying to sort out the jumble of emotions that was making her stomach churn and her head hurt.

Discouragement was definitely in there. Her target practice session hadn't gone well. With the pistol Mac had initially given her–a .38 snub nose he'd called it–she had hit absolutely nothing. Not even the *trees* to which he'd tacked the paper targets with human outlines on them. Reconsidering, Mac had produced a long-barreled revolver that looked like something out of the Old West.

"Thirty-two. Lighter. Easier to aim. Still enough stoppin' power," he muttered. "Good weapon for a girl."

Kate had been offended by his sexist remark, until she discovered she couldn't hit anything with that gun either. After three hours of practice, she had at least been consistently hitting the tree, several feet *above* the target.

Mac's disgusted growl, *Squeeze the damn trigger, don't jerk it,* was still echoing in her head.

This was on top of the frustrating sessions looking through case files on Monday and Tuesday evenings. She and Rob had discovered they had more shared cases than they'd first assumed, and it was taking far too long to go over them. They'd only gotten through the first third of the alphabet.

After rehashing the details of each case, they'd only eliminated two cases where there would be no reason for anyone to hold a grudge. The compulsive spender who'd turned to shoplifting when she ran out of money and the prominent businessman caught indulging in some recreational marijuana use were both grateful when Rob had gotten them off with no jail time. Kate had provided the counseling required by the court as part of their probation. But in every other case, someone had ended up unhappy. When things get to the point where a lawyer is required, somebody is likely to be the loser.

And now she had this other issue. As they drove down York Road, she pointed to a Walgreen's sign. "Can you pull in there? I need to get something."

"Sure." Mac swung his truck into the parking lot.

"Uh, what I need, it's personal. I'll be okay if I go in alone."

"No way, sweet pea. Too dangerous. But I'll stay up front. Keep an eye on the truck, while you shop."

Inside, she quickly found what she needed and took it to the pharmacy counter in the back of the store to pay for it. She stuffed the semi-transparent bag into her purse before heading up to where Mac was standing, his gaze moving back and forth from her to his Hummer out in the parking lot.

~~~~~~~~~

The doorbell rang. A shiver of fear ran through Rob's belly as he glanced at his watch. Nine-thirty. Rather late for legitimate callers.

Lou had nudged the curtain aside on the window in the front door and was looking out. Rob peered over his shoulder.

At the sight of Kate's pale face, he shoved Lou unceremoniously aside and yanked open the door. "Where's Mac?"

"I asked him to wait in the truck."

Rob pulled her inside and closed the door. "What's the matter?"

"Where's Liz?" Kate asked. She had a deer-in-the-headlights look on her face.

"In bed. What's the matter?" he demanded again.

"I'm pregnant."

Rob sat down abruptly. He landed on the overstuffed arm of the chair behind him and slid down into its seat. His mind stalled. He stared up at her for a beat, then pulled her down onto the ottoman in front of him.

Noting that Lou had made himself scarce, he asked, "This is a good thing, right?" Based on the expression on her face, he wasn't totally sure that it was.

"It's the most wonderful thing in the world…."

"But…?"

"I was scared enough before, now I'm terrified! Rob, this is a piece of Eddie. The last piece of him left on this planet. And someone is trying to kill me. I *have* to protect this baby!"

"How far along are you?" he asked, more to buy time than anything else. His brain was still trying to wrap itself around all this.

"About two and a half months, I think. My periods have never been all that regular." Kate blushed a little.

He felt heat creeping up his own cheeks. There were some things opposite-sex friends didn't discuss, no matter how close they were.

"When I missed the last two," she said, "I just assumed it was due to stress. But then I started noticing other signs, so I bought a test kit on the way home from target practice. It was positive."

Rob didn't need to ask what other signs. His wife had been pregnant twice. Nausea, weight gain, mood swings–although he doubted Kate could differentiate, at this point, between hormonal mood swings and the legitimate emotional roller coaster her life had become lately.

"Any morning sickness?"

Kate shook her head. "Just a little nausea occasionally. Mostly I'm ravenous all the time."

Rob grinned. "Of course *your* child would have a hearty appetite."

She returned his smile but it didn't completely make it to her eyes.

Liz's worried voice drifted down from the upstairs bedroom. "Rob, is that Kate? Is something wrong?"

"Come on." He stood up and pulled Kate to her feet. "Let's tell Lizzie!"

"Yes, it's Kate," he called up the stairs, "and she has some news."

CHAPTER TWELVE

Rob was having trouble concentrating on the tasks that he absolutely needed to get done before he and Kate could tackle the files again. His thoughts kept wandering to their investigation. So far, they'd only identified two major suspects. In each case–one involving domestic violence and the other child abuse–he and Kate had contributed to the abuser's incarceration. He'd given his files for those cases to Liz so she could do computer searches on the two felons.

Rob had just dragged his mind back to the document he was supposed to be reviewing when his cell phone rang. Sighing, he answered it.

"Got some info for you." There was a note of glee in Liz's voice.

"You're enjoying this way too much, hon."

A low chuckle. "Okay, first scumbag. Paul Connolly, wife beater. Arrested five years ago. With you and Kate propping up her backbone, wife refused to drop the charges. One year sentence, two years probation."

He could hear papers rustling. "Got out after six months for good behavior. I tracked down the wife. She's remarried now, lives in Massachusetts. Says she hasn't heard from the ex-con, ex-husband– but no doubt still an S.O.B.–in years. Has no idea where he is."

"Hmm, a possibility, but five years is a long time to wait for revenge," Rob said.

"Other scumbag's a better bet. Thomas Hunter, child abuser. Another joke of a sentence. Four years for molesting his five-year-old stepdaughter. Got out after two and a half for good behavior. What is it with this good behavior crap? If these guys knew how to behave, they wouldn't be in jail!"

Rob grinned at his wife's editorial on the legal system, but said nothing. Not a good idea to encourage her too much. "And?"

"Aaand, you know how these sexual abusers are supposed to register their addresses whenever they move? Well, he did, for the first year. Five months ago he disappeared and the police haven't been able to find him."

Rob tapped an index finger against his lips. "I seem to recall he was a wimpy little dude. Somehow I don't see him as a killer."

Liz snorted. "Hey, you never know what a couple years as some bruiser's bitch might've done to the man's already twisted psyche."

He held the phone away from his ear and stared at it. His wife almost never cussed. Trying to make light of it, he said, "You may need to wash your mouth out with soap after this conversation, hon."

"Hey, just calls 'em as I sees 'em, Big Guy." Then her voice lost the playful edge. "Seriously, Rob, whoever's doing this, we need to get him, and soon. He's tearing our lives apart. The girls can't come home. We've got mountains masquerading as men camped out in our living room. Can't afford to feed them, much less pay them much longer. This has got to end!"

He sighed. "I hear you, darling. Kate and I are going to keep slogging through the files tonight."

"And I'll keep trying to locate these two. See ya later. Love you."

"Love you, too." Rob disconnected, then mumbled, "And you're startin' to scare me a little, Lizzie."

~~~~~~~~~

By eight-thirty that evening, Kate was done in.

She'd spent most of last night staring at the ceiling trying to digest the idea that she was pregnant. When she'd come downstairs this morning, Mac had greeted her with, "Girl, I've seen dishwater looked better'n you." She hadn't even had the energy to come up with a snappy retort.

She and Rob had now gotten through the M's, and they'd identified a couple more serious suspects. But they'd only eliminated one more case as having no grudge potential.

"That's half the alphabet, at least," Rob said, sitting back in his chair. "Let's call it a night."

Kate leaned back in her own chair and put her feet up on the corner of his desk. She blew stray curls out of her face. *Gotta find time to get a haircut… Yeah, right.*

Out loud she said, "When it comes to last names, all letters are not created equal. I've got two file drawers of R's and three of S's, compared to one or less of most other letters."

"Ugh!" was Rob's only reply.

"Maybe instead of trying to eliminate cases, we should make three piles: strong possibilities, possibilities and unlikelies."

"Okay, until we know what he's been up to, Hunter goes in the strong possibilities pile. What about Connolly? Five years is a long time to hold a grudge."

"True, but he threatened to kill his wife when he got out. Somewhere along the way, he may have switched that anger onto us for 'putting ideas in her little head.'" She made quotation marks in the air. "That's how these guys think. They can't believe the woman might actually have it in her to stand up for herself."

"He's a pretty nasty guy," Rob said. "It's possible he got into trouble again and ended up back in jail."

Kate nodded. "And he may be out now and is finally able to seek his revenge."

"I'll get Liz to look through the court records in nearby states."

"She'll be thrilled. By the way, Mac made one of his cryptic comments this morning, implying that we're underutilizing his skills. I think he's itching to play private detective."

"We could send him off to locate these guys," Rob said.

"What about Phillips? What do we tell him, and when?"

Rob leaned forward and put his elbows on his desk. "I've been giving that some thought. Goes against the grain for me, as an officer of the court, to keep things from the police, but I don't think we should give him a name until we're pretty damn sure that person is the killer. Maybe not even until we have some solid evidence. If we figure out who it is, turn the name over to Phillips and then he screws up the investigation, this bastard could go underground and we'd never know when he would surface and strike again."

Kate shuddered at that thought. "Maybe we should go over Phillips' head. Complain to his superiors about him."

"I've been thinking about that as well," Rob said. "If we weren't his prime suspects, I certainly could, as the attorney of the grieving widow, object to the shoddy handling of the case. And then it might be reassigned to a different detective. But going to his boss under these circumstances would just–"

"Come across as protesting too much and would probably be dismissed," Kate finished his sentence. She frowned, then shrugged tired shoulders.

Getting up, she headed for the door. "You gonna heft that box back down to my office for me, Mr. Macho?" He'd scolded her earlier for carrying heavy boxes in her condition.

After returning Kate's files to her office in the counseling center, they came back out into the hall. "Hey, Lou, where are you?" Rob called out.

"Yo, Mr. F. Youse done?" echoed up the central stairway from the ground floor.

A loud metallic clang came from behind them. Kate and Rob spun around. A clattering sound echoed beyond the fire door at the end of the hall.

"To your right, Lou!" Rob yelled. "Somebody's running down the fire stairs. Stop them!" He grabbed Kate's hand and pulled her toward the central, open staircase. As they rushed down to the first floor, they could hear Lou's heavy footsteps pounding in the lower hallway.

Kate took a deep breath, trying to calm her racing heart. Her eyes darted around, looking for anything suspicious.

After a couple minutes, Lou came jogging back. "Lost him, Mr. F. He got through the exit door 'fore I got there. Pitch black outside. Couldn't see nothin'. Did find this though." He held up a small rubber doorstop.

"Well, that explains how he got into a locked building," Rob said. "Must've stuck that in the door earlier today to keep it ajar. Those stairwell exit doors lock automatically from the outside so the guard may not bother to check them when he locks up."

He waved off the small group of the law firm staff who'd been working late and were now gathered at the top of the stairs.

All of them now hypervigilant, Lou and Rob escorted Kate out to her car. She noticed they waited until she was pulling out of the parking lot, Skip's Explorer trailing behind, before they left.

Despite her exhaustion, Kate once again did not sleep well. Spooked by the fact that the killer had been in their building tonight while they'd been going over files, she tossed and turned, struggling with whether or not she should keep working. She certainly didn't want to jeopardize this baby, Eddie's child!

But her clients depended on her. For many of them she was their lifeline to sanity. What the hell would she even tell them? It's one thing to be out a few days or weeks because your husband died, or your sister's in the hospital. But she couldn't tell them she was taking an indefinite leave of absence because somebody was trying to murder her. Wouldn't exactly be good for their fragile psyches.

Especially old Mr. Phelps with his paranoid personality disorder. She finally had him half convinced that the world *wasn't* out to get him. Now she's gonna tell him she can't meet with him for the foreseeable future because some person, identity unknown, was trying to kill her? Yeah, not!

Kate lay on her back, exhausted. "Oh, Eddie, what am I going to do?" she said to the ceiling.

She was startled when her husband's soft baritone echoed in her head. *After me, your work's been your life. Without that, what would you have?*

Her eyes welled up. Eddie had always understood how important her work was to her, much more so than his was to him. He enjoyed playing with numbers, and especially enjoyed being paid good money for it. But her work was her passion. He'd respected that, despite the fact that she made less than half what he did in income.

As the tears broke loose and trickled down her cheeks, Kate knew her decision was made. And the father of her baby agreed.

She finally drifted off around two-thirty in the morning.

Less than four hours later, an explosion ripped her from a sound sleep.

CHAPTER THIRTEEN

Kate grabbed her robe and bolted down the stairs. At the bottom, she froze, staring across the living room. The big bay window Eddie had spent an entire weekend installing two years ago was gone.

"Get down!" Mac shouted.

Kate ducked down behind an armchair. She put a hand over her pounding heart. Her stomach grumbled, then heaved.

Dear God! Bad time for morning sickness.

She swallowed, willing her digestive system to calm down. Then she peeked out.

The dim, gray light of early dawn was seeping around the edges of the drapes on the other windows and through the hole where the bay window had been. Mac stood with his back against the wall beside the gaping hole. He wore nothing but briefs and was holding the biggest handgun Kate had ever seen.

She realized the urge to ask if he always carried a Glock in his jockey shorts was the product of incipient hysteria. Instead, she called across the room, "What happened?"

"Got up, headin' for the bathroom. Window blew behind me. One second sooner, my butt would've been full of buckshot." Mac flopped onto his stomach and belly-crawled across the floor toward her.

As he got closer, Kate's heart skipped a beat. "Your back!" she gasped and started to stand up.

"Get down!"

He reached the chair and crouched beside her. "Glass. Don't feel like it went deep. Probably saw my shadow on the curtain. Thought it was you."

She looked at his back more closely. There were a dozen or so cuts, but none of them were bleeding heavily.

After they'd been hunkered down for several minutes, she asked, "What are we waiting for?"

"Sirens. Neighbors should've called 911."

After another couple minutes, he grumbled, "Takin' their good ole sweet time. What's the matter with these cops anyway?"

"Budget cuts," Kate guessed. She suspected that was why Phillips was usually accompanied by Officer Hernandez, instead of another detective. Cheaper to have each detective partnered with a uniform so they could work more cases with fewer detectives. Either that or even his fellow detectives found Phillips so obnoxious they refused to work with him.

After another minute, Kate slithered out from behind the chair. Mac made a grab for her but she slipped past him. Staying low, she headed down the hall to the master bedroom and bath. She needed something to clean up Mac's back. Maybe he didn't mind that he was dripping blood on her rug, but she did. And she needed clothes. She could now hear sirens in the distance and she wasn't dealing with the police in her bathrobe if she could help it.

Once again police cars, their lights flashing, were providing entertainment for Kate's neighbors.

Inside, an officer was asking questions, scribbling in the obligatory notepad, while Kate, now in jeans and a shirt, was trying to clean up Mac's back. "You need an ambulance, sir?" the cop asked.

Mac shook his head at the same time that Kate nodded. Mac pointed his chin at her. "Nurse Nancy here'll do."

"I know you won't go to the hospital," she said. "But some of these cuts still have glass in them. That's beyond my nursing skills. Yes, we need paramedics."

Mac scowled as the cop spoke into his portable radio. "They're on the way, ma'am."

Rob and Phillips arrived at the same time. They stood on her front walk glaring at each other for a long moment.

"Looks like the shoot-out at the OK corral," Mac muttered, watching them from the open doorway. He was now wearing jeans, the Glock having mysteriously disappeared when the sirens were first detected.

"Get back in here, you eejit!" Kate hissed. "This guy may be crazy enough to try again, even *with* cops all over the place."

"You're right, sweet pea. Probably long gone but shouldn't take no chances. Hey, Rob," he yelled. "Get your butt in here! You're a target, too."

Phillips broke the staring contest off and made an after-you gesture. Rob walked ahead of him up the porch steps.

Once inside, the detective announced, "Well, folks, I think some police protection is in order here."

"I've hired private bodyguards–"

"You can save your money now, Franklin. The taxpayer's taking over."

"I was about to say that we'll take all the protection we can get."

"You got a bodyguard on *her* too, Franklin?" Phillips sneered, cocking his head in Kate's direction.

"Oh, come on, Phillips, I thought we'd gotten past that," Rob said through gritted teeth.

The detective ignored him. He was staring at Mac. "What are you doing here?"

"I'm a friend of the family," Mac growled back at him. "One of *her* bodyguards."

"Down, boy," Kate muttered out of the side of her mouth. She was fairly certain Rob wasn't going to deck Phillips, but she wasn't so sure about Mac. Especially now that a paramedic was trying to get him to stand still while she fished slivers of glass out of his back.

"Mac Reilly, Detective Phillips," she said.

"Pleasure ain't mine," Mac growled.

"Charmed. You feed him raw meat, Mrs. Huntington?"

Rob stepped between Mac and Phillips. "Do you and your officers have any more questions, Detective?"

"You all got any different answers yet?"

"No," Kate answered him.

"Then my officers will be canvassing the neighbors. Looking for clues. You know, doing our jobs," Phillips said. Turning away, he yelled, "Hernandez, get in here! New assignment."

An hour later, Kate stood in the middle of her living room rummaging through her briefcase for her schedule book. The crime scene technicians, who'd been removing buckshot from the walls and examining the splintered window frame, had finally left. Only she, Mac, Rob and Officer Hernandez remained.

Kate had no intention of stopping work completely but she knew she wouldn't be doing her clients justice today. She was too keyed up and yet sleep-deprived. Finding the book, she flipped through the pages. Good, no one she was supposed to see today was in crisis. She was a little concerned about Cheryl, but there was a hole in her schedule Monday. Maybe she could come in then.

Grabbing the phone, she punched in the center's number. As it rang in her ear, she said to the room in general, "War council. Kitchen. Ten minutes." She heard the brusqueness in her voice.

I've been hanging around Mac too much.

After working out the re-juggling of her schedule with Pauline, she took Officer Hernandez aside. "Look, I know you're supposed to stick close to me, but we have some confidential things to discuss. Would you mind sitting out on the porch. It's very pleasant out there this time of year."

The officer, a short but sturdy-looking young woman, held her gaze for a moment. There was a hint of suspicion in her chocolate-brown eyes. "Sure," she finally said. Kate waited until she was out the door, then went over and locked it.

As they took seats around the big oak table in her kitchen, Rob said, "Liz isn't going to be happy about not being included."

"Call her on your cell. Put it on speaker," Mac said. "Poor man's conference call."

Rob did as suggested, and Kate leaned in the direction of the cell. "Liz, can you hear us?"

"Sure can," Liz's disembodied voice boomed from the center of the table.

"Did Rob fill you in on what's happened here this morning?"

"Yes. Sounds like this guy's getting bolder."

"Or more desperate," Mac said.

"Or both," Kate said. "And we've got another problem as well. My father told Mac he's flying back here once they get Mary home. I talked to Pete yesterday. They were in Colorado. I do *not* want my father coming back here and becoming another target."

"You could lie," Liz said. "Tell him the burglars have been caught."

"Or we could let him come," Rob said. "We could use his help. Can he shoot a gun?"

Mac dipped his head in a half nod. "Yup."

Kate glared at both of them. She opened her mouth but Rob cut her off. "Look, I'm the father of two daughters, one who's almost grown and one who thinks she is. I understand the importance of stepping back and not interfering in your child's life. But if someone was threatening one of my girls, even if she was seventy years old and I was in my nineties, wild horses couldn't keep me away!"

"He's got a point, Kate," Liz said quietly. "It's what parents do, try to protect their children from harm."

Her stomach chose that moment to gurgle and heave. She swallowed hard and eyed the box of saltines sitting on the counter. But she didn't dare go get them. She didn't want Mac figuring out she was pregnant. He would tell her father, and then there was no way he would stay away.

Rob was still talking, discussing who would be guarding whom. "I'll put Skip on duty 24/7 for now. Mac, we need you to start investigating suspects. We've got two guys for you to track down. Liz found a lead on one of them, some unpaid parking tickets in Pennsylvania."

"I got mug shots of him, and the other scumbag, too," Liz said from the phone.

"Can you clean them up so they don't look like mug shots?" Rob asked. "People may not admit to knowing someone who's obviously a criminal."

"Sure. A little strategic cropping should do the trick."

"Good. Now back to the security set-up. Phillips has one officer on Kate and one on me. I'm going to ask him to put them both on Kate, one inside and one out."

Kate's stomach heaved again, then knotted. Afraid to open her mouth for fear she'd throw up, she shook her head vigorously.

Rob held up his hand. "Hear me out. If you think about it, all the incidents, except for the first two, have been directed at you. Either he's decided he wants you worse–"

"Or he wants her out of the way first," Liz finished.

"It's not just that you're at greater risk," Rob said, "but if we have more people on you, we might catch this guy in the act next time he tries something."

You're slick, buster. You knew that argument would get me.

Out loud, she said, "Okay, as long as Lou doesn't let you out of his sight."

"Amen to that!" came from the cell phone. "How about both Lou and Ben on 24/7 instead of alternating nights, like they have been?"

"Good idea, " Rob said. "They can take turns, one catching some sleep on the sofa, while the other patrols outside. This guy may decide to set fire to one of our houses."

"Maybe Kate should stay with us for the duration?" Liz said.

"I think that's too risky," Kate said. "With all his targets under one roof, he'd really be tempted to set fire to the house."

Mac had been too quiet. She suspected he was chewing on the idea that she was the primary target. Now he turned to her. "Sweet pea, you ain't leavin'–"

"Stop right there!" Her voice was louder than she'd intended. She lowered it but kept the tone firm. "I have seriously considered taking a leave of absence. There is no argument any of you can offer that I haven't already had with myself. The answer is no. After today, I'm not staying home from work. My life, my decision, period!"

After several seconds of silence, she turned to Rob. "I've cleared my schedule for the day. What's yours look like?"

"Not a damn thing on it that's more important than catching this bastard."

"Good. Only problem is, we need my files and I already told Pauline I wouldn't be in this morning."

"We'll figure something out. Let's go." Rob stood up.

"Need some plywood. For that hole," Mac said. "Liz, be there 'bout noon for those pics. That work?"

"Works for me," said the disembodied voice from the table.

They all jumped when another voice behind them said, "Where we going?" Officer Hernandez was standing in the kitchen doorway.

"How'd you get in here?" Kate asked.

"Through the hole, used to be a window. Heard raised voices," the officer said in a clipped, matter-of-fact voice.

Kate hid a grin and glanced at Mac. *These two need to get together.*

At their office building, they went up the fire stairs nearest Rob's office to avoid crossing paths with Pauline or Sally. Kate stopped outside the law firm's door. "I think I know how to do this. Rob, go check out the center's waiting room. If Pauline's at her desk, tell her you're looking for me."

A few minutes later, Rob returned. "One client waiting. Pauline's not at her desk."

Kate nodded and turned to head down the hall. She caught movement out of the corner of her eye and looked back. Officer Hernandez had apparently started to follow her. Rob had his hand on the officer's arm and was shaking his head.

Good. The only thing that would be harder to explain than her presence when she was supposed to be home asleep would be a uniformed police officer trailing after her.

Once in her office, Kate consulted the list of mutual cases Fran had put together. She hastily jammed the N's and O's into one of the boxes she'd been using to transport files to Rob's office. She peeked out her door. Still no Pauline. She grabbed the box and race-walked across the outer office. In the hall, Rob took the box from her and they hustled back to his office.

They set Officer Hernandez up with a stack of magazines in the sitting area at the far end of the room. She sat, ignoring the magazines, her face a neutral mask.

Cop training or natural personality? Kate suspected some of both.

Rob was pulling files out of his cabinet. He brought them over to the desk. "Don't know if this would be any easier if we'd ever gotten around to computerizing my old files."

She chuckled as Rob, the technophobe, glared at his dark monitor lurking on the end of his desk. "Sometimes old-fashioned paper and ink are best. In my case, I'd worry about hackers getting confidential information."

By noon they'd gotten through the R's. They'd been slowed down some by the necessity for subterfuge. Each time they finished a box, they had to wait for Pauline to leave her desk. Then Kate would slip into her office to grab another load of files. They also had to keep their voices down so Officer Hernandez couldn't hear them.

They were taking a break, waiting for Fran to bring them sandwiches from the deli across the street, when Kate's cell phone rang. It was Mac.

"Board on the window. Got the pics from Liz," he said without preamble. "Rob there? Don't have his cell number."

"Yeah, he's here, but first… Uh, hold on." She turned toward the other end of the room. She knew Officer Hernandez hadn't gone to the bathroom all morning. Even when she'd gone herself, the cop had stood outside her stall on guard. It had been rather embarrassing to have her tinkling monitored. "Officer, why don't you take a restroom break?"

The cop just raised one eyebrow at a forty-five degree angle.

"Uh, this call's confidential. We'll lock the door behind you. Knock three times, then give us the password and we'll let you back in. Hmm, let's make the password…" She thought fast, trying to come up with something funny to keep things light.

Inspiration struck. She grinned and sang out, "Skipped *to the loo, my darling.*"

Officer Hernandez switched eyebrows. "How 'bout I just ID myself."

"That'll work."

Once Rob had locked the door behind the officer, Kate said into the phone, "Mac, we have to waltz down a fine line here. I'm bound by strict rules of confidentiality. These guys have the same last names as my clients, or their former last names, so you can't mention me or anything that implies one of their family members was in counseling when you're asking questions about them."

"Got it, sweet pea."

"Thanks so much for doing this. And please be careful! I don't have enough guilt left in me to handle another person I love getting hurt because of all this."

"I know how to take care of myself," Mac said without his usual growl.

Wow, a complete sentence.

She handed Rob her phone. "He needs your cell number."

Rob rattled that off, then ended the call with his own admonition. "Be careful."

There was one emphatic knock on the door followed by a muffled "Hernandez."

Gotta work on that girl's sense of humor.

By two-thirty, Kate's eyes were drooping. She either needed a change of scenery or a nap. "Let me try to get the rest of my files out of my office and then let's take all this back to my house. I need to get more comfortable."

And maybe indulge in a second cup of coffee. She'd been restricting herself to one a day, but today she might have to go up to the two-cup-per-day limit for pregnant women.

She'd retrieved one box of files and was going back for the last half of the W's–another popular first letter for last names–when she heard Pauline's voice behind her. "Hey, Kate, I thought you were taking the day off."

Kate turned around. "Well, I figured once I'd gotten some sleep, I might as well do something useful with the rest of the day." Her mind was scrambling. What useful thing could she be doing that would involve her standing in the center's reception area with an empty box in her hands? "Uh, um, I thought I'd pack up some of Eddie's stuff at home. I had a few empty boxes here that I thought I could use."

Pauline gave her a strange look, but she was literally saved by the bell when the phone rang. As the receptionist answered it, Kate slipped into her office. She grabbed the last empty box from the corner and put some of the remaining files in each of them. Taking one handle of each box, she dangled them at her sides, trying to make it look as if they were empty.

Fortunately Pauline was still on the phone, her eyes looking down at the scheduling book. "See you later," Kate mumbled as she rushed toward the outer door that a big hand was reaching around the corner to hold open for her.

Rob grabbed the boxes from her and they hustled down the hall. Once inside his office, the absurdity of the whole situation hit her. She flopped into a chair and started giggling.

Rob chuckled. "If we tried to sell this plot to a TV producer, it would be rejected flat."

"Maybe as a sitcom," Kate said, which set off a fresh round of giggles.

"Get it together, woman." He gave her a mock scowl. "Let's get this done."

Kate glanced at the cop's face. Was that a crack in the mask? She looked like Mr. Spock from Star Trek with her eyebrow cocked at forty-five degrees.

"Why are you so bent on keeping what we're doing from Pauline and Sally?" Rob asked as he started packing up his own files for their mutual cases.

"Sally's been very supportive, giving me time off and all. But the center is her life. I'm not sure she'd go along with all this, despite the fact that our lives are at risk." Kate dropped her voice. "She'd probably tell me to leave it to the police to handle."

"Obviously she hasn't met Phillips," Rob said quietly. He added at normal volume, "So it's a case of you better not ask because she might say no."

"Exactly, and then if we kept at it, I might lose my job." That was something she'd rather not contemplate. When all this was over, she'd have a child to support as well as herself.

Kate consolidated her files into two boxes. Most of Rob's for the same cases fit in a third box. The few that were left over, he stuffed in his briefcase. "My files are skinnier than your files," he said, in a nanny-nanny-boo-boo voice. Kate stuck out her tongue at him.

The officer's eyebrow went up again.

Rob stacked two boxes on top of each other and hefted them. He looked at the officer and nodded at the third box.

She shook her head. "Gotta keep my hands free, sir."

"Of course." Rob put his boxes back on the desk and grabbed Kate's hand as it snaked toward the other box. "Me, Tarzan, you, Jane. I'll send Lou up for that one."

He did let her carry his briefcase.

They filed down the fire stairs, Officer Hernandez in the lead. At the bottom, she opened the door and cautiously looked around. "All clear," she finally said and led the way again, scanning the parking lot.

While they waited for Lou to retrieve the third box, Kate started to get into the backseat of Rob's car.

"You should be with me, ma'am," Officer Hernandez said.

"Oh, goodie!" She clapped her hands together. "I've never ridden in a police car before. Can we put on the lights and siren?"

"No!" The officer's tone was emphatic, but her mouth twitched on one end. Then she rolled her eyes. Opening the passenger door of her cruiser, she said, "Ma'am?"

Kate grinned at her as she climbed in.

CHAPTER FOURTEEN

Rob decided to blow Skip's cover. He didn't want the police mistaking the bodyguard for the killer. That could have disastrous results. When they arrived at Kate's house, there was another police car sitting at the curb. Rob motioned Skip over and introduced him to both officers.

"Uh, sir," Skip said, once they were out of earshot of the police, "I thought I was supposed to keep a low profile. Try to catch this guy next time he tries something."

"Skip, my man, we're not going for subtle anymore." Contrary to what he'd told Kate, he was hoping the extra coverage would actually discourage any more attacks against her.

"You still willing to go 24/7?" he asked the bodyguard. He had to look up to make eye contact, an unusual experience for him. The man was a good three inches taller.

"No problem, sir."

"Good. There will be two cops and you on her at all times. At her office, the police will be in front of her building and inside with her. You stay on the back parking lot. Park next to her escort's cruiser. I wouldn't put it past this bastard to blow up a cop to get to her. When she's home, one officer will be out front and one inside. You're in the back alley. At night, I'm thinking it would be better to have the cops outside. How do you feel about sleeping on a sofa?"

"No problem, sir," came the answer again.

Rob nodded. "Police cruisers out front and in the alley should be a good deterrent. Make sure, if it's different officers, that they know you're one of the good guys."

"Always a good idea, sir."

Rob hated telling another man how to do his job, but he wasn't taking any chances with Kate's life. He wasn't sure how much brain power went along with the brawn in these guys. However, he was beginning to think Skip was several IQ points above the other two.

He put a hand on the big man's shoulder. "Don't tell your siblings." He nodded toward Lou still sitting in his car. "But you're my favorite."

Skip chuckled.

Good, he got the joke. Out loud, he said, "One other thing, Skip."

"Yes, sir?"

"I think Mrs. Huntington's too smart to do this, but… Well, let's just say she has an independent streak a mile wide. At some point it may temporarily overpower her brain, and she may try to slip off her tether."

Skip started to roll his eyes, then caught himself.

Rob suppressed a grin. He gave the big man a friendly slap on the shoulder, then wished he hadn't when his hand came away stinging from contact with rock-hard muscles.

"Last but not least," he said. "Be careful."

"Always, sir."

~~~~~~~~~~

Kate put the coffee on, then changed into sweats and her bedroom slippers. They spread their files out on her kitchen table.

Three hours later, they'd finally gotten through the alphabet, but there were way too many files in the possibilities pile. Kate swiped her out-of-control bangs out of her eyes. "This is hopeless. My kid'll be starting school by the time we investigate all these people." She heard the whine in her voice and stopped to take a deep breath.

"Uh, by the way, I'm not telling Mac or my father that I'm pregnant yet. They'll get that much more overprotective and insist I stop working."

"I'm not sure anything would qualify as *over*protective at this point," Rob said. "It's that important to you to keep working?"

"Have you stopped?" He didn't answer her. She continued, "We can't stop working completely. We've got too many people counting on us to help them. What if one of my clients committed suicide, or one of yours lost custody of their children, because we weren't there for them? We'd never forgive ourselves."

"Excellent argument, Kate. Sure you don't want to go to law school?"

She snorted. "No thanks. I like belonging to a *respected* profession. There's maybe one stupid therapist joke for every thousand sleazy lawyer jokes out there."

"True." Rob glanced at his watch. "Our brains are tired. Let's call it a day."

"Okay, but why don't we meet at your house tomorrow afternoon, when I'm finished with clients? I'm thinking we need to get Liz's take on these cases. Breaks the rules, but we've got to narrow them down some more."

"Good idea, and you can trust her to keep things to herself."

Kate grimaced. "I know. I still hate doing this, though. My confidentiality vows are almost as sacred as a priest's, but–"

"It's a matter of life or death," Rob finished for her.

"Yeah, ours."

After Rob left, Kate put the case files back in their boxes, then called Officer Hernandez into the kitchen. "Have a seat." She gestured toward the table. "Would you like something? Coffee, soda, water?"

"Water'd be good, ma'am." The officer remained standing, eyeing the double windows that faced the street.

"Don't worry. Nobody's getting onto that porch without us knowing it. Each board squeaks to a different note."

"More bullets I'm concerned about, ma'am. From across the street."

"Good point." The windows were screened only by semi-sheer curtains. Kate handed the officer a glass of ice water. "Let's go into the living room."

Officer Hernandez drew the drapes over the side and back windows. Fresh plywood now covered the front window. Kate turned on lamps, then gestured toward the sofa and chairs.

The officer perched on the edge of an armchair. "What time do you leave, ma'am, for work in the mornings?"

"Eight-fifteen, usually."

The officer nodded. "Just be two shifts, most days."

Kate raised an eyebrow in the air. "Twelve-hour shifts?"

"Used to long hours, ma'am."

"Officer Hernandez, is your first name *Officer* or do you have another name?"

The young woman blinked, then said, "Elena Rosa. Go by Rose."

"May I call you Rose? We're going to be spending a lot of time together so we might as well drop some of the formality. I'm Kate, and please stop calling me *ma'am*. You're making me feel old."

The officer seemed to ponder that for a moment. "Sure, ma'am…uh, Kate. You can call me Rose. Unless Detective Phillips is around."

Kate suddenly had a thought. "May I ask a personal question, Rose?"

"I suppose so, ma'am…Kate."

"Were you ever in the military?"

"Yes, m…Kate. Army."

"Thought so. The way you talk reminds me of my friend, Mac, the one with the glass in his back this morning." Had it just been that morning, felt like a week ago. "He was Special Forces."

The young woman's eyes lit with respect.

"Why did you get out, if you don't mind my asking?"

"Wouldn't let me be an MP. Said I was too *petite*." She spat out the last word. "Put me on a desk. Shuffling papers."

"Rose, I would *not* call you petite. You've met Liz, Rob's wife?" The officer nodded. "Liz is petite. I would call you *compact*."

"Compact. I like that!" She flashed the most beautiful smile Kate had ever seen. It was brief, but it lit up her face.

Kate smiled back. *Okay, enough chitchat to soften her up.*

"Rose, I need to ask a favor." The woman's right eyebrow did the Mr. Spock imitation.

"As you know, Rob and I are going through our files, trying to come up with suspects to turn over to Detective Phillips." No need to mention that they had no intentions of telling Phillips anything anytime soon. "But in the meantime, if you accidentally overhear a name, or other random information, I'd appreciate it if you'd keep it to yourself, and not share it with the detective, for confidentiality reasons."

Rose looked thoughtful for a moment, then nodded. "If it's not related to the investigation. Not my business. Nor his."

"Thanks."

Something flashed across the young woman's face, then the cop mask fell back into place.

What was it? Worry, confusion, regret? Kate wasn't sure, but something was going on behind those chocolate-brown eyes.

"So what would you like for dinner?" she asked.

"Not picky, m…Kate."

"Good, 'cause I'm a lousy cook." She stood up.

Rose stayed seated but squirmed a little on the edge of her chair. "Uh, can I ask you a personal question?"

"Sure."

"Sorry to bring up unhappiness, but your husband, he was killed just a couple months ago. And someone's trying to kill you and Mr. Franklin. But the two of you were joking around today?"

Kate sat back down. "Rose, my husband and I…" Grief clogged her throat. She swallowed, then continued, "We've been close friends with the Franklins for years. Rob and I are very comfortable with each other, and we both use humor to help us cope. It's got to get really bad before we stop joking around."

She paused for a moment, deciding how much to share. "And it was that bad for awhile. I didn't even smile much, from the time my husband was killed until my sister woke up. When she opened her eyes, I was just so relieved I couldn't help but laugh, actually shouted with joy." She smiled now at the memory. "That seemed to bring back my sense of humor, and I'm trying hard to hang onto it, 'cause I missed it."

But not anything like I miss my husband.

I miss you too, love, Eddie's soft baritone echoed in her head.

She wasn't about to tell this young woman that she'd also been feeling better ever since she started talking to her dead husband.

Rose looked thoughtful again. Then she nodded. "Sorry for being nosy."

"That's okay. I guess it does look pretty weird to see us cutting up, under the circumstances. Now, to the kitchen and let's forage."

"Kitchen's not safe. For you at least. Tell you what, I'll cook."

"Oh, what a relief. You're saving us both from food poisoning," Kate said, and was blessed with another brief smile.

The light was starting to fade from the sky outside the kitchen windows, but it was dangerous to turn on any lights. For the first time since she and Eddie had sacrificed the formal dining room in order to expand the kitchen, Kate missed having another place to eat. She set up tray tables in the living room.

Even working in semi-darkness, Rose whipped up the best omelette Kate had ever tasted. Over dinner, she broached the next topic. "Rose, there's another factor that adds to the pressure here. I'm pregnant, and I really don't want to lose this baby. He or she is all I have left of my husband." She stopped, blinking hard.

Rose paused in her chewing. Both her eyebrows were in the air. Kate suspected she was counting backwards in her head.

"I'm close to three months along. The baby must have been conceived shortly before…." This time she couldn't completely blink the tears away. She swiped at her cheeks with her fingers.

Rose's expression softened. She swallowed her food. "Congratulations."

"Thank you. Liz and Rob know about the baby, but I don't want to tell anybody else yet, especially my family. My dad may be arriving here soon, and I definitely don't want him to know. He and Mac, they'd want to lock me up in a steel vault until this guy's caught. So I'd appreciate it if you'd keep the news that I'm pregnant to yourself."

The young woman took another bite of food, chewed, swallowed, then nodded. "No problem."

~~~~~~~~~

As they finished their omelettes in silence, Rose was chewing on a decision as well. Of course she wouldn't say anything to Kate's friends or family about the baby. Not her news to announce. The question was whether or not she was going to share this little tidbit with Detective Phillips.

He still wasn't convinced that this woman and the lawyer weren't lovers. He'd even speculated that maybe they'd hired someone to throw the police off by faking more murder attempts, and the hired thug had attacked Kate's sister by mistake.

The timing of the pregnancy was awfully tight. Of course, this lady could have gotten pregnant by her lover before her husband's death. Indeed, that would be a major motivation to knock off their spouses.

But Rose was having a lot of trouble imagining Kate Huntington as a stone-cold killer, especially one who would put her own sister at risk.

Besides, Elena Rosa, she argued with herself, *you know Phillips is an ass!*

If she told him Kate was pregnant, he'd assume Franklin was the father and would gleefully start nailing the lids down on their coffins.

She didn't want either of these seemingly nice people railroaded into a murder conviction if they didn't do it.

She'd watched them interact all day, and she hadn't seen anything that looked or felt like flirtation–no lingering touches, no sultry looks when they thought she wasn't watching. No sexual energy between them at all. They acted more like a married couple who'd been together for years. As Kate had said, comfortable with each other.

It suddenly struck Rose that these two were more like brother and sister. In her large family, she was especially close to her brother Ricardo. These people, with their teasing and joking around, reminded her of Ricky and herself.

But then again, they could both be really good actors.

She caught herself as she was about to shake her head in frustration.

Bottom line–she wasn't telling Phillips anything just yet. She'd keep watching these two closely, especially around Mrs. Franklin. It would be interesting to see how she reacted to Kate.

And if I decide to tell him later, I don't have to let on how long I've known about it.

That cover-her-ass thought was the first time Rose had considered the impact that withholding information from a superior officer might have on her career. Now that she did contemplate it, she wasn't sure she cared.

As they stood and gathered up their plates, the doorbell rang. It was the big, buff bodyguard. He informed them that her replacement had arrived.

As she was about to leave, Kate put a hand on her arm. "Yet another favor."

Rose cocked an eyebrow at her.

"Tonight, before you go to bed, I'd like you to say 'Yes, Kate'… 'No, Kate'… 'Please, pass the salt, Kate' out loud about twenty or so times."

Rose grinned. "Goodnight, *Kate*."

CHAPTER FIFTEEN

Rose rang her charge's doorbell at eight on Saturday morning. The woman opened the door and just stood there, staring at her. Then she stepped back and mumbled, "Hang on a minute."

Rose walked in and closed the door behind her. Kate Huntington disappeared into a room off the living room.

She came back in a minute, carrying two large department store bags. She dropped them on the sofa. "Mary bought this stuff, the day she was hurt. It got left behind when they went home." Kate was rummaging through the bags.

"Here." She held up a loose-fitting white shirt and beige slacks. "These should fit you. Might have to roll up the pants legs some, make a cuff."

Confused, Rose lifted an eyebrow at her. "Ma'am...uh, Kate?"

"I can't have a uniformed officer sitting in the waiting room at the center."

"On duty. Gotta be in uniform."

"But you'll scare the clients."

Rose lifted an eyebrow again. "You got clients who've broken the law?"

"No, and if they did, I couldn't tell you. But the majority of our clients have been victimized in the past, some of them by authority figures. There are a multitude of interpretations, most of them bad, that they might put on the presence of a police officer. You would make them very uncomfortable, and it's important that a therapist's office and waiting room feel safe."

Rose paused to process that information.

Meanwhile the woman kept talking. "Maybe I could have Skip sit in the waiting area, and you stay out in the parking lot. Although a big guy like him would scare some of them worse than a cop hanging around."

"My orders are to stick with you." She'd get in as much trouble for being out in the parking lot as she would for being out of uniform, if Phillips found out. He'd ordered her to spy as well as protect. But maybe she could use that as her excuse for being in civvies if he happened to show up. She'd tell him that this woman wouldn't let her stay close by if she was in uniform.

Kate was shaking her head in frustration. "I've got to go in today. One of my clients, last time I talked to her, she was feeling suicidal. If she doesn't get her session today, she may not make it through the weekend. Crap, I don't see a solution to this. I've gotta go in, you've gotta go with me. And my boss is likely to send me home if I show up with a uniformed police officer in tow."

"Okay, I'll do it," Rose said. "Got some of my own clothes in my trunk. And my ankle holster."

"But you can't. You'll get in trouble."

She rolled her eyes. "Kate, you just talked me into it. And now you don't want me to do it?"

"Okay, how about this, you stay in uniform going to and from the center and change into the street clothes while we're there?"

Rose nodded. "That'll work."

And it did. The clients in the waiting room paid no attention to the compact woman who was pretending to read a magazine. She was just another client waiting for her counselor.

When Kate finished with clients at noon, they headed to the Franklins' house.

~~~~~~~~~

The sun streaming through the sliding glass door in the Franklins' family room drew Kate to that side of the room. She closed her eyes and reveled in its warmth on her cheeks. The light dimmed.

She opened her eyes. Rose had stepped between her and the door and was firmly pulling the curtains closed across it. Kate stuck her tongue out at the silky, black bun on the back of the officer's head, even though she understood her motivation. That glass surface exposed her charges to the outside world.

Liz encouraged Rose to load her plate with food before joining the bodyguards out in the living room. On the big table to one side of the room sat a platter of sandwiches and a bowl of potato salad. Next to the obligatory jar of pickle slices for Rob, there was a bottle Kate suspected was meant for her.

Liz was telling Rob how good it had been to get out of the house that morning to run a few errands, and yes, she was careful, and yes, Ben's a very vigilant bodyguard. She looked over at Kate examining the prenatal vitamins and broke off.

"I took the liberty of getting those for you. I figured you probably hadn't gotten in to see your doctor yet. I saw those when we went to the pharmacy to get Ben some cough medicine."

Feeling vaguely guilty, Kate said, "It hadn't even crossed my mind to schedule an appointment yet, with all the craziness."

"Would you like me to call the obstetrician who delivered the girls and make an appointment for you? He's getting up there in years but I think he's still in practice."

"That would be a huge help, Liz."

"I'll call first thing Monday morning." Liz turned back to her husband. "And speaking of Ben, with all the joint people power we have here right now, can we send him home? He's been hacking and coughing for a couple days. He needs to get some rest, and as run down as we are from all this stress, I'm afraid we're going to catch whatever he has."

Rob leaned down to kiss the top of his wife's head. "Okay, Mother, I'll take care of it." He headed for the living room, as a fit of intense coughing from that direction proved Liz's point.

Kate and Liz sat down at the table. "Liz, I trust your discretion but I've got to say this out loud to appease my own conscience. Up to now, I've only bent the rules. Now we're about to break them, so nothing we discuss goes beyond this room."

Liz nodded.

Rob returned and took a seat. "Mac called this morning," he told them. "He's eliminated Connolly. Guy got himself killed a few months ago in a bar fight."

Liz snorted. "I think being dead qualifies him as an unlikely suspect."

Rob's mouth quirked up on one end. "Mac's in Morgantown, West Virginia now, where Hunter was last registered as a sex offender. He's gonna call in later."

Three hours later, the sandwiches were seriously depleted and they'd rehashed a couple dozen cases from the possibilities pile. With Liz's fresh perspective they'd eliminated quite a few and had added three files to the strong possibilities pile.

After a short break, they were halfway into the next case when Kate's cell phone rang. It was Pete. They were home. Mary was exhausted but otherwise fine.

"Wow, you made good time the last couple days," Kate said.

"Yeah, we'd been taking it slow but once we were close to home, Mary insisted we keep pushing on. Hey, your dad wants to talk to you."

"Sure… Hi, Dad, everything's okay here."

Rob wiggled his fingers in a gimme gesture. "Let me talk to him, Kate."

She ignored him. "We have police protection now," she said into the phone, "until they catch whoever attacked Mary." She was trying to avoid flat out lying to her father, but she wasn't above stretching the truth in order to convince him she was safe. She wanted him to stay in California or go back to Florida–any place far, far away from her.

"Kate! Give me the phone."

"Hold on, Dad. I'm at Rob and Liz's, and Rob is trying to ask me something." She put her thumb carefully over the tiny mouthpiece of her cell and glared at Rob.

Rob glared right back. "I thought we'd settled this."

Her stomach clenched. She gritted her teeth. "My father, my decision."

"No, Kate. Your father is an adult. His life, *his* decision. And we could use his help."

"You still there, Katie girl?" her father's gruff voice came from the phone.

"Yeah, Dad, hold on." Emotions collided inside her head. Her chest tightened. She hated fighting with Rob, and maybe he was right. But the thought of her father coming back, getting hurt, or worse, because of her….

Rob again gestured for her to give him the phone.

"Hang on, Dad. Rob wants to talk to you," she managed to get past the fear clogging her throat.

"You smirk and you're dead meat," she muttered as she handed Rob the phone.

"Not a smirking matter…Hi, Dan." Rob paused, listening. "Good, great to hear Mary's doing okay. We've got things under control here, for now. But the police aren't doing much as far as we can tell, other than providing some protection."

A faint rumble emanated from the cell phone.

"They've got two officers with her all the time, and I've hired private bodyguards as well. But we could use your help, if you're still inclined to come back here."

More rumbling.

"Monday's soon enough if you can't get a flight tomorrow, and I promise to do everything humanly possible, and then some, to keep her safe." Rob handed the phone back to her, muttering under his breath, "Even if she is the most stubborn, annoying woman sometimes."

She ignored him as she said goodbye to her father. "Okay, see you soon. I love you too, Daddy." She disconnected and turned to Rob. "I hope you know what you're doing. If anything happens to him…." Her throat closed completely. Tears sprang into her eyes.

"Damn!" She threw back her head. "I *hate* being so weepy!" she yelled at the ceiling. Tears streamed down her cheeks.

Rob was around the table in a second, kneeling next to her chair. He tried to wrap his arms around her but she fended him off. He put a big hand on either side of her face and made her look at him. "Kate, I'm sorry. But we do need him, and it *is* his decision."

The worry and pain in his eyes were her undoing. "Oh, Rob, I'm just so scared!" she sobbed as she let him gather her into his arms.

~~~~~~~~~

Kate's yelling had brought Rose to the doorway to investigate. She stopped at the sight of these supposed friends holding each other, then took a couple steps into the room. A second later, she was nearly bowled over by Mrs. Franklin flailing around the table on her crutches, headed toward Kate and her husband.

Thinking she was about to referee a catfight, Rose took another step closer.

But apparently that wasn't the wife's agenda. Mrs. Franklin awkwardly lowered herself onto her knees on the other side of Kate's chair. She wrapped her arms around the woman Phillips was so convinced was the *other* woman.

Kate dropped her head onto the wife's shoulder and sobbed harder. Mr. Franklin leaned back on his heels but kept one big hand on Kate, rubbing little circles in the middle of her shaking back. He swiped at his own eyes with his other hand.

Rose stood still, taking in the scene.

As Kate's crying shifted to exhausted whimpers, Mrs. Franklin snapped her fingers in her husband's direction.

He produced his handkerchief and handed it to Kate. "You're going to owe me a crate of these, dear, before we're done." Then he leaned over and kissed her gently on the temple.

Rose nodded her head. She stepped up to the table. "May I join you?"

All three of them looked as if a Martian had suddenly appeared before them.

"Not the hug fest," Rose clarified, with a slight smile at their comical expressions. "May I join the war council?"

The uncomprehending stares continued.

"Look, I know you all don't know me, so you've got no reason to trust me. But I don't lie... Well, sometimes I don't tell the whole truth to Detective Phillips," she felt compelled to add, thus proving her point. "I want to help. It's my *duty* to help you. I joined the police force to pursue justice, not do whatever the hell Phillips is doing and *calling* it police work."

She heard the derision in her voice and wondered if she was giving away too much to these strangers. But the righteous indignation, that had been building for months, would no longer be silenced. "We're supposed to *protect and serve* people like you, not force you to track down killers on your own!"

They all stared at her for several more seconds. Again she stifled a smile at their expressions. They seemed to be having difficulty digesting the idea that a police officer believed their version of reality and shared their poor opinion of her superior.

Then a grin slowly spread across Kate's face. "Wow, not only complete sentences but complex ones."

Rose gave her a small smile back. "I mostly tend to do the clipped sentences when I'm in police mode. They prefer rookies like me to be seen, but heard as little as possible. So am I in?"

Kate held her hand up in a stop gesture, then glanced at the Franklins.

"Sounds sincere to me," the wife said, as she struggled to get up off her knees while encumbered by leg brace and walking cast. Her husband quickly moved around the table to help her.

"Rob?" Kate asked.

Franklin put his hands under his wife's arms and lifted her to her feet, but his eyes were on Rose. His face was a neutral mask. "Up to you, Kate," he finally said.

Kate broke into a grin again and gestured to an empty chair. "You're in, Rosie."

Rose raised her own hand in the stop gesture. "Let's add *Rosie* to the list of things we do *not* call Rose. Only *mi padre* gets away with calling me that."

She sat down, her holster clunking against the chair, and the Franklins resumed their seats.

Kate looked at the gooey wad of cloth in her hand, then dropped it into her purse. "One of these days when I actually have time to do laundry again, I'll get that back to you," she said to Franklin.

He smiled at her, then turned to Rose. "What have you and Phillips found out in your investigation?"

Rose wasn't sure if he was testing her or not, but it didn't matter. If she was in, she was in all the way. Her actions weren't as impulsive as they might seem to these folks. She'd been seriously considering requesting a transfer for some time, had even contemplated resigning from the force.

"Wait, I have another question first," Kate said.

Rose cocked an eyebrow at her. Kate snickered. "You don't even realize you do that, do you?"

"Do what?"

"Never mind. My question is are you married, and with or without benefit of matrimony, do you have any children?"

Franklin frowned at Kate.

"Objection overruled, Counselor," she said. "The witness may answer the question."

"No and no," Rose said.

"Good, so if we get you killed, we're not leaving anyone widowed or orphaned."

"Well, I've got parents and siblings who'd probably be a little upset. But I don't think I'm at any more risk than I am as your police protection."

"Kate!" Franklin's voice had a hint of exasperation in it again. "She's an autonomous adult. As is your father and everyone else involved in this."

"Okay, okay, just assessing the risk of collateral damage. Back to Rob's question, Rose. What does Phillips know that we don't?"

"Actually he probably knows a lot less. He's been so convinced you two are the perps, he hasn't really pursued anything else. Just done the standard stuff, canvassing for witnesses around the crime scenes, analyzing the physical evidence. We don't have any other leads that I know of, other than your client idea. Conflicting descriptions of the vehicle that hit Mrs. Franklin. A wood splinter from your sister's head wound."

Kate winced.

"And a partial footprint in the yard across the street yesterday morning. Sneaker. Could be either a man's or woman's, but too small to be Mr. Franklin's."

"For cryin' out loud, they're Rob and Liz," Kate said. "If we're gonna get you killed or fired, we should all definitely be on a first-name basis."

"Okay, okay. Anyway," Rose gave an exaggerated sweep of her eyes around the table, "Kate, Rob and Liz, none of that does us any good until we have a suspect."

Franklin shook his head. "I can't believe Phillips is still hung up on his Kate-and-I-are-lovers theory. He can't be that dumb. You don't get promoted to detective by being stupid."

"Overblown ego unwilling to admit he's wrong," Kate speculated.

"And he's lazy," Rose said. "I've seen him do this before. Jumps on the most likely explanation. Either so the case will be ruled an accident and go away, or he goes after whatever suspect will give him a quick solve." She had other reservations about his ethics as well, that she wasn't willing to voice since she had no proof.

"Thanks, Rose," Franklin said. "And I do appreciate what you're risking by throwing in with us."

"Thank you, Mr. Franklin."

"'No, Rob'… 'Yes, Rob'… 'Please pass the salt, Rob,'" Kate said.

Rose grinned at her.

Franklin…Rob was staring at her, his mouth hanging open. Why did men always act weird when she smiled?

He saw her watching him and snapped his mouth shut. "Welcome aboard, Rose."

CHAPTER SIXTEEN

Sunday morning dawned hot and sunny. It was only early June but Maryland's oppressive summer humidity was already settling in.

Kate had suffered another restless night. She'd finally fallen soundly asleep just as the sun was rising. At nine-thirty, she was still in her bathrobe when the phone rang. Checking caller ID, she answered it and said, "Hey there, when are we going to work on the files today?"

"Uh, a little later," Rob said, hesitation in his voice. "I got a call from your father. He managed to get a flight early this morning. I'm heading over to pick him up at BWI."

Kate fought down nausea, not sure how much was morning sickness and how much fear. Her mind scrambled for more arguments, but she knew it was too late. Her father was here, and he wasn't going to leave until the killer was behind bars.

Maybe one more tactic. "I thought we might send Dad to help Mac investigate our suspects."

A couple beats of silence, then Rob said in a gentle voice, "He wouldn't necessarily be any safer, sweetheart, just because he's not around you."

Kate didn't respond, even though she knew he was right.

"Let's sort out assignments once we're all together," he continued. "Liz has been complaining about being cooped up in the house so much. I'll swing by and get her and we'll come to your house. Be about one, okay?"

"Okay. See you then." Kate disconnected. She took in a deep breath to loosen the tightness in her chest. It came out on a shudder as a horrible thought struck her.

If anything did happen to her father, she'd probably lose her best friends in the process. The relationship might not survive Rob's guilt and her anger.

Rose was off duty, but she'd said she wanted in on today's war council. She arrived early.

When Kate answered the door, she tried not to stare. The "civvies" Rose was wearing today showed off her figure to much better advantage than her uniform did. Sturdy had morphed into voluptuous. Her peach-colored knit top exposed a touch of cleavage and complemented her light beige skin tone. Despite the heat, she was wearing jeans. Kate detected a slight bulge at her right ankle. The young woman was armed.

Rose stepped inside the door and looked over at her replacement for the day. The young man was standing at parade rest in the middle of the living room. She turned back to Kate, her eyebrow doing its Mr. Spock imitation.

"I'm working on it," Kate whispered. "Have a seat." Rose nodded and headed for an armchair.

Kate motioned Officer Trudow over and resumed their discussion. It took considerable persuasion to finally convince him to stay out on the porch while her company was there. She clinched the argument by pointing out that two of her visitors, her father and her friend Rob Franklin, were big men. "Officer, nobody's getting past them."

She refrained from mentioning that the young woman who'd just arrived was an off duty police officer. Trudow didn't seem to recognize Rose and it might not be good for her career if he figured out who she was.

Unfortunately, Kate failed to restrain her mouth sufficiently in other areas. "Besides, I can't live in a fish bowl all the time, having every conversation overheard by strangers."

It was a perfectly reasonable statement, but the officer narrowed his eyes at her.

Kate realized she'd said too much. Mentally, she acknowledged that her brother Jack was right; she did sometimes suffer from foot *in* mouth disease.

Officer Trudow, his boyish face making him look younger than he probably was, finally nodded. He went out the front door and stood at parade rest on the porch.

A few minutes later, the doorbell rang. Peering through the peephole, Kate saw a reddish gold aura as the afternoon sun backlit the top of Liz's head. Rob was climbing the porch steps, carrying a plastic grocery bag. Her father and Lou trailed behind him.

She opened the door just as Officer Trudow stepped over to block Rob's way.

"It's okay, Officer. These are the friends I mentioned."

He hesitated a beat, then nodded and moved back.

Rob gave Lou instructions to stay on the porch with the officer while Kate held the screen door open for Liz.

"Where's Ben?" Kate asked as Liz hobbled past on her crutches.

Rob tilted his head toward his wife. "She took one look at him this morning, and insisted he go down to that walk-in clinic near us. Turns out he's got pneumonia." He glanced in Kate's direction but didn't quite make eye contact.

Holding up the bag he was carrying, he added, "Liz made sandwiches. You got any pickles? We forgot to bring some, and it's been hours since my last fix." Despite the joke about his pickle addiction, there was tension under the surface in his voice.

Kate decided it was time to be a gracious loser. "You and your pickles." She rolled her eyes.

His tense face relaxed.

After she'd hugged her father and introduced him to Rose, everyone settled down in the living room, balancing plates of food on their laps or whatever flat surface was available. For a little while, they ate in silence.

When Rob put his plate aside, Kate asked, "So do you have a game plan, Chief?"

He nodded, then turned to her father. "Dan, once we've identified more suspects, I may put you on the investigating team with Mac. Hopefully by then, Ben will be better–"

"We could hire a private investigator," Dan interrupted. "I'll pitch in on the cost."

Rob opened his mouth to answer but Kate jumped in. "Dad, unfortunately we can't do that. The people we're investigating are connected to my former clients. I'm already breaking the rules of confidentiality by discussing them with you all. But there's no way I can give a private investigator clients' names or details of their cases. And without that information, he'd be flying blind."

"It would be nice if Kate still had her professional license and a career when this is all over," Liz said. "And I'm not sure a hired detective would do any better than Mac's doing."

"For the next day or two then," Rob said to Dan, "until we see what's happening with Ben, I'd like to have you at my house, as Liz's guard."

Tears sprang into Kate's eyes. She ignored them as she gave Rob a grateful smile. At this point, Liz was the least likely target, and yet she still needed protection.

Her father crossed beefy arms across his chest. "Gonna be a bodyguard, I'm with me daughter!"

Rob's mouth fell open. A red tide swept up his cheeks.

Kate scrambled for something to say to smooth the waters, but her mind was a blank.

Rob jumped up, his fists clenched at his sides. "You damn stubborn O'Donnells! You expect me to be the...the ringleader of this circus and then you fight me every step of the way!"

The room went perfectly still.

Rob turned and stomped down the hall. He paused, his back toward them. Then he pushed open the master bedroom door, went in and slammed the door behind him.

Something clicked in Kate's mind. Liz was struggling with her crutches, trying to get to her feet. Kate stood up. "Wait, Liz! I know I may be stepping over the line here, but let me talk to him, please." When Liz hesitated, she added, "You said it yesterday. We're all stressed out."

"Okay, you talk to him first...." Liz's voice trailed off. There was both worry and a fiery flash of anger in her eyes.

Kate went down the hall. She lifted a hand to knock on the bedroom door, then stopped herself. *It's my own damn bedroom.*

She opened the door and looked in, and almost laughed out loud at the sight of Rob's big frame crammed into her antique rocker. The seat was wide enough for him–since it was made to accommodate the voluminous skirts of nineteenth-century ladies–but the tops of his thighs were higher than the arms and his knees were sticking up in the air.

Kate stifled her laughter. This was not a moment for levity. "Mind if I come in?" Without waiting for permission, she walked over and sat down on the stool of her dressing table.

She studied Rob's face for a moment. There were new wrinkles around his eyes and bracketing his grimly-set mouth. And behind the anger in those eyes was bone-tired fatigue, and pain.

Her chest ached. She leaned across the space between them and picked up one of his big hands in both of hers. "My dear friend," she said softly, then stopped, at a loss for words to express how bad she felt for him in that moment.

Rob's face crumpled. He dropped his forehead onto their clasped hands. For a few minutes, his back shook silently. Kate laid her cheek, wet with her own tears, against the top of his head.

When he started squirming in the too-small chair to get to his handkerchief, Kate sat back and pulled tissues from the box on her dressing table. She handed them to him.

He wiped the wetness off his cheeks without looking at her.

"Are you okay?" she asked.

"I will be in a minute." His voice was gravelly. "Kate, I'm sorry! I had no right to blow up at you or your dad, after all you've been through."

"Stop." She held up a hand. "What I'm realizing is that we've been ignoring what *you've* been through. Yes, I've lost my husband, but you've lost a friend. And you're right. Slowly but surely, you've emerged as the leader of this motley crew. You've been trying to protect everyone from a killer."

He opened his mouth just as she snapped her fingers. "Oh, yeah, I almost forgot. And you've been trying to ward off a jackass policeman who's itching to arrest us both for murder. Gee, I can't imagine why you're stressed out!"

He gave her a weak grin. "Well when you put it that way."

"Rob, the kind of pressure you've been under lately, it would have a lesser man in a fetal position in the corner. You're a strong person, but you're still human. You have limits just like we all do."

"Kate, you do realize the same applies to you. You're strong but–"

"Hey, buster, no turning the tables. My turn to lecture, your turn to listen!"

That got a short chuckle out of him. "I'm all ears."

Kate softened her voice. "Let me ask you a question. How do you think you ended up as the leader here?"

Rob thought for a moment. Finally he shrugged, then grinned. "Because I'm the guy and you and Liz are girls."

Kate returned his grin. "You do like to live dangerously, don't you? Better not say that in front of Liz."

"You think I'm crazy! Okay, I give up. How did I end up the leader?"

"Several reasons. One already mentioned, you're strong. Two, as a lawyer, you're used to analyzing situations and developing strategies. Three, your two most frequent partners in crime, your wife and your friend, have not been at their best lately, one being on crutches and house-bound until recently, and the other being a bit under par emotionally."

Rob digested that for a moment, then said, "Kate, I realized something yesterday. You are my closest friend, after Liz. That's been the case for years, but it took all this... this crap we've been dealing with to make me appreciate that fact."

Kate's eyes brimmed with tears again. She leaned over and kissed him on the cheek. Then she sat back and dabbed at her eyes. "Okay, we're getting so mushy now, we sound like a soap opera."

"Don't try to break the mood just yet," Rob said softly. "I have one more thing to say. I love you, friend."

"I love you, too, you big lug," Kate managed to get out despite the oversized lump in her throat.

Rob smiled at her, then started to extricate himself from the rocker. "I owe some major apologies to your father, and to Rose, for losing it like that."

"Don't be too hard on yourself. On one level, Dad's reaction is certainly understandable. He came here to protect his daughter–"

"And schmuck that I am, I totally ignored that."

"Yeah, but my father... uh, he's not always a good team player. Your plan not only puts him at the least risk, and I thank you for that, but it also just plain makes sense. He's pushing seventy, not exactly the best candidate for hand-to-hand combat with a killer. But his presence will deter any attempts against Liz. It *is* the best allocation of our resources."

"I thought so," Rob said. "And *you* don't need the additional stress of worrying about him."

She gave him a small smile. "Let me talk to Dad."

~~~~~~~~

Back in the living room, everyone's expressions had both tension and curiosity in them, in varying proportions. Liz's eyes flicked from him to Kate and back again. Rob knew she was waiting for him to apologize, which he had every intention of doing.

"I'm sorry, Dan. I was totally out of line."

"S'okay. Yer weren't entirely wrong, now were ye?" Dan ducked his head a little, his ruddy cheeks a shade redder than normal.

Rob said to the room at large, "I'm sorry I lost my temper."

Kate turned to her father. "Dad, could I speak to you for a moment, in the bedroom?" Technically it was a question but her tone implied it was an order. Rob had seen that expression on her face before, when she was testifying in court and the opposing attorney was trying to twist her words. He suspected stubborn Dan O'Donnell was about to meet his match, in his own daughter.

When they came out of the bedroom a few minutes later, Dan seemed subdued but his mouth was set in a grim line. Rob felt for him. With Shelley, he had already discovered that dealing with a grown child isn't always easy.

As they resumed their seats, Kate said, "Folks, we're in a kind of war here. So I'm going to suggest we adopt a military model, with modifications. We all can give input, say whatever we like, until Rob, our captain, makes a decision based on that input...." Her voice trailed off as the corners of her mouth twisted downward.

Rob fought to hide a grin. He also knew *that* facial expression all too well. Ms. Independent had spoken without thinking it through and had painted herself into a corner.

Rose jumped in and finished her sentence. "Then we follow the captain's orders."

Everyone nodded, including Dan. Kate shrugged, then turned to Rob. "You okay with that?"

He nodded, no longer able to suppress the grin.

"Now don't you be letting it go to your head," Liz mock scolded.

"Oh, don't worry, hon. I *know* who's in charge when we get home."

Kate leaned in Rose's direction. Out of the corner of her mouth, she said, "Rob always gets the last word in arguments with Liz."

Rob looked at everyone's startled faces, then winked at Kate. Together, they said, "Yes, dear!"

CHAPTER SEVENTEEN

Kate gave her father and Rose the "we're breaking the rules of confidentiality so nothing you hear leaves this room" speech. Then they picked up where they'd left off the previous evening, going through the case files to try to narrow down the list of suspects.

By five-thirty, there were less than a dozen files left to discuss. Several had been added to the unlikelies pile, but only three to the strong possibilities. One was a case Liz had been on the fence about initially. The suspect was the physically abusive father of one of Kate's former clients. He had sued for grandparent visitation rights, testifying that he was only violent in the past when he drank. Now he was sober, he'd claimed, and going to AA meetings. When Rob produced two bartenders who testified to the man's *current* drinking habits, the judge had ruled against the grandfather.

Liz was on the fence only because the man would now be in his eighties.

"Heard of old killers," Rose said. "He sounds capable of murder to me."

Kate was inclined to agree. This particular old man was as nasty as they came. "Something could've happened in his life lately that set him off, maybe a diagnosis of terminal illness. The only attack that's required any strength was the one on Mary. An old man would assume he was strong enough to beat up a woman with a two-by-four or a baseball bat. Heck, Dad was ready to take on Phillips last week with a bat." She grinned at her father.

"How'd I miss that?" Rob asked.

"Twas the morning we set out to take our Mary home. And you, lass, should have more respect for yer elders," Dan mock scolded Kate. "If that copper'd been 'bout to hurt me daughter, I'd have given him a good clatter."

The others chuckled as Kate breathed out a soft sigh of relief. Things were back on an even keel with her old man.

They were about to plunge into the next case, when Rob's cell phone rang. He listened for several moments, then said, "Okay. See you soon." He disconnected. "Mac's headed back. He spent the last two days looking for our child abuser. Couldn't even tease loose a thread to begin to unravel where the guy is."

"Somehow I don't think Mac said it quite that poetically," Liz said.

Rob grinned. "No, but that's the gist of what he said, via grunts and three-word sentences."

Kate frowned. "That doesn't bode well for the children in this guy's current vicinity, wherever it may be."

Rose did the Spock thing with her eyebrow.

Kate answered her non-verbal question. "When a sexual predator just forgets to register a new address, it shouldn't be that hard to track him down. If he disappears without a trace, it's more likely he intends to abuse again."

Liz grimaced. "So the question is do we think this guy's our culprit. Or has he gone underground so he can pursue his twisted habits?"

"Personally I think he's too much of a wuss to go after adults," Rob said. "That's why he picks on kids."

"I wouldn't assume that," Kate said. "Some abusers are attracted to kids because they're too immature to handle adult relationships. Those guys are usually pretty timid. But Hunter isn't in that category. He was married and according to his wife, they had a good sex life."

"Then why would he go after her daughter?" Liz asked.

"Different kind of urge. Sexual abuse is more about power and control. Abusers were almost always abused themselves as kids. Now they're trying to take back their sense of power by overpowering somebody else."

"Same as with rapists," Rose said.

Kate nodded. "Thank God only a fraction of abused children grow up to be abusers or rapists. But, having said all that, I'm thinking Hunter's not our guy."

Her father shook his head. "Please, forgive a befuddled old man, Katie, but I'm not quite sure which way yer drivin' that cart."

"Yeah, I'm a tad befuddled myself," Rob said.

"Sexual abusers are often a lot like drug addicts. They may rant and rave against those responsible for throwing their supposedly innocent hides in jail. But when they get out, they've only got one thing on their minds–"

"Getting their next fix," Rob finished for her. "I think we'll bump Hunter down to the possibilities pile for now. We can try again to locate him later, if other suspects don't pan out."

"Almost sounds like we know what we're doing, doesn't it?" Liz said in Rose's direction.

"Actually you all are making more sense than some detectives I know," Rose said with a flash of a grin.

For once, Kate's stomach wasn't the first to growl. Rose's and Liz's grumbled in two-part harmony.

"Uh, I haven't had time to grocery shop lately," Kate said. "And my bodyguard has a substantial appetite. My larder's rather bare."

Her father lumbered to his feet. "I'll go git us some dinner."

"Thanks, Dan," Rob said. "There's a Burger King not far from here. Take Lou with you. He knows where it is."

"He should be stayin' here with Katie an' you. I can juggle me a few bags of burgers."

Rob stood up. "I'm sending him to guard you. You're a potential target too." Dan opened his mouth but Rob raised his hand. "Both your daughter and my wife have extracted a promise that no male ego's to get in the way of keeping ourselves safe."

"Why can't one of them boys go git the food then?"

Kate narrowed her eyes at her father. *Damn! Here we go again.*

"Because they're not errand boys," Rob answered him, frustration creeping into his voice. "But going along to guard you *is* their job."

Dan opened his mouth again.

Kate jumped to her feet. "Dad, just take Lou and go get the damn dinner! And if you say, 'Watch your mouth, lass,' I will not be responsible for my actions."

Her father turned to her, his eyes wide. He blinked, then crossed himself.

Despite her fury, Kate almost laughed. No doubt he was praying that his blasphemous daughter not be struck by lightning.

Finally he lumbered over to the front door. The living room was silent until they heard Dan's heavy footsteps going down the porch steps.

Then Kate turned and glared at Rob. "*You* wanted him here!"

He held his hands up in a guilty-as-charged gesture.

Kate hadn't even noticed that Rose had stood up, but suddenly her compact body was between them. "Folks, arguing amongst yourselves is counter-productive, and you're giving me a headache. I get enough of those dealing with my so-called superiors."

Kate looked down into the young woman's face for a beat as her anger dissipated. Rose was right.

"I'm sorry," she said to Rob. "It's not your fault my father's a stubborn Irishman."

"Is there any other kind of Irishman?" Liz quipped.

Kate chuckled as she flopped back down on the sofa next to her.

Rose flashed another quick grin. "Gotta use the john." She headed for the hall powder room.

"Rose," Kate called after her.

The young woman turned back around.

"Thank you for reminding us we need cool heads, not hot tempers, and feel free to do so again, as needed." She shot her an impish grin. "'Cause I do so love it when we shock you into using complete sentences."

Rose gave her a full-blown smile, then headed down the hall again.

"Kate…"

She turned back toward Rob. He had resumed his seat and was staring at his hands on his knees. Slowly he brought his gaze up to meet hers. "I'm sorry."

She cocked her head to one side. "About what?"

"Liz pointed out last night that I might have… that maybe I was too much the heavy-handed lawyer, and pushed you too hard, about your father joining us."

"It doesn't matter. I could've lied to Dad, told him everything was fine, and he would've come back here anyway."

Rob's brown eyes were still muddy with emotion. "But I should've been more… I don't want you…"

Kate stared at him. She'd never known this man to be at a loss for words.

"I don't want all this...." His voice trailed off again.

Understanding dawned. He'd had the same dreadful thought that she'd had this morning. "None of this is going to come between us. We won't let it." Then she echoed his words from earlier. "I love you, friend."

Liz leaned toward her and stage-whispered, "Psstt, you better stop saying that in front of his wife. She might get suspicious."

Rob threw his head back and roared. Kate snorted, then laughed out loud when she saw Liz's mischievous grin.

From the doorway, Rose said, "Glad to see you all are back to normal."

Her father returned with Whoppers for everyone. Liz, a bit of a health nut, grimaced but then shrugged. Rob opened his sandwich and squinted at its contents.

Kate laughed.

"I'll get the pickles," Rose offered.

As they ate, they forged ahead with the files, determined to finish them that evening. It was after seven when they were finally done. They now had ten top suspects in what had gotten shortened somewhere along the way from strong possibilities to the likelies pile. The possibilities pile had been honed down to twenty-eight. Still a lot to deal with if they ended up having to investigate them all, but more manageable than the huge stack they'd started with.

Kate began putting her unlikely files in a box to return to her office. Rob was saying, "Let's call it a night–" when he was interrupted by raised voices from outside.

Her heart racing, Kate jumped up and followed Rob to the front door. He opened it cautiously. She ducked down to see under his arm.

In the gathering dusk of the summer evening, Mac was standing on the sidewalk in front of the porch, looking even more unkempt than usual after several days of living in his vehicle. Officer Trudow was barring his way at the top of the steps. The other officer had exited his car. His gun was out of the holster, held down along the side of his leg as he quickly moved up the sidewalk behind Mac.

Mac's face was brick red under his tan. He growled something at Trudow.

"Don't move, mister!" Trudow barked. His hand was on his gun butt. "Put your hands on your head."

Kate's stomach knotted. She felt the blood drain out of her face. Mac would be armed, and whatever he was carrying may or may not be registered.

"Stop right there, Officers!" she yelled.

In the same instant, Rob shouted, "He's a friend of the family."

The other officer returned his pistol to its holster. But Trudow's hand still rested on his gun. He sucked in air and puffed out his chest. "I *asked* to see your identification, sir."

Ah shit! This young buck was determined to have the last word, and she knew Mac would respond in kind.

She ducked around Rob and stomped out onto the porch. "We have vouched for this man and he is coming into *my house* right now! You're here to protect me, *not* run my life."

After a beat, Trudow, stone-faced, stepped aside.

Mac came up the steps, glowered at Trudow, then followed Kate into the house. Rob closed and locked the door.

Kate rushed to the hall bathroom and threw up.

Rose appeared in the open doorway. "You okay?"

Kate rinsed her mouth out at the sink. "I will be, as soon as I kill that little Irishman."

When she marched back into the living room, Mac innocently asked, "You okay, sweet pea?"

"Don't you *sweet pea* me, Mac Reilly! Do you realize how close you just came to getting shot? *Machismo* makes for lousy body armor."

"Cop has an attitude problem. Kept tellin' me to leave," Mac grumbled.

"Great so you get into a pissing match with him, when you are no doubt carrying an *unregistered, concealed* weapon."

Rose's eyebrows were doing the tango across her forehead, but she kept quiet.

Mac stuck his chin out defiantly, saying nothing, but his hand moved to his jeans pocket, confirming her suspicion.

After an awkward pause, he tilted his head in Rose's direction. "Who's she?"

Still steaming, Kate was trying to decide whether to allow the change of subject when Rob answered, "You probably don't recognize her out of uniform. She's one of Kate's police protection team, but she's thrown her lot in with us to help with the investigation. Rose Hernandez, meet Mac Reilly."

"Welcome to the Baker Street Irregulars," Mac said.

Rose's eyebrow went up again.

"Sherlock Holmes," Liz prompted.

"Not much time for recreational reading." Rose turned back to Mac. "Kate said you were Special Forces, sir." Her back straightened and her shoulders went back. "I was infantry. Six years."

With a jolt, Kate realized she was standing at attention. "Sheez, Rose, will you *pe-leeze* cut the *sir* crap. And if you salute him, I swear I'm gonna…." Too late, she caught herself. Still jittery with residual adrenaline, she was pointing her left-over anger in the wrong direction.

Rose did the eyebrow thing. "You're gonna do what, Kate?" Her tone was innocent, too innocent. And there was a glint in her eyes.

Kate couldn't read her expression. Her throat tightened a little. Had she pissed the young woman off? In a lame effort to turn her outburst into a joke, she said, "I don't know, maybe turn you over my knee."

Mac glanced at Rose's compact, muscular body, then looked at her. His grin said loud and clear that Kate hadn't fared well in the comparison of their physiques.

The corner of Rose's mouth twitched.

"You and what army," they said at exactly the same moment.

Rose broke out her glorious smile.

Mac's mouth fell open as his "sweet p…" trailed off.

Kate stared at his gaga expression. Eyes that normally sparkled with mischief or were hard, blue ice had melted into puddles of soft aqua.

She glanced quickly at Rose. A pink tinge crept up the young woman's cheeks.

Wow, can I call it or what?

A bubble of laughter threatened to escape. "Would you all excuse me for a moment?"

She raced into the kitchen and danced across the room, pumping her fist in the air.

Rose came around the corner. "Kate, it's not safe in… What the hell?"

"Charlie horse." Kate hopped on one foot, faking a cramp.

A streetlight snapped on outside, casting a shadow against the semi-sheer curtains.

The shadow moved.

CHAPTER EIGHTEEN

Rose's hand swooped down, in a much-practiced motion, to retrieve her gun from its ankle holster. She grabbed Kate by one arm and shoved her toward the kitchen doorway. "Get out of here. Now!"

Mac came around the corner and hauled Kate out of the room, just as a porch floorboard squeaked loudly.

Rose aimed at the window. "Police! Don't move!"

The shadow jerked.

"I *said* don't move!"

The shadow froze. "It's me, Officer Trudow," a male voice yelled.

"Don't move!"

"No, ma'am! I mean, yes, ma'am." The voice ended with a squeak.

Keeping her aim on the shadow, Rose reached over and shoved the curtains aside. She unlocked the window, then slid it up. All she could see was a dark blue shirtsleeve to her right. It was most likely Trudow, but she wasn't taking any chances.

"Arms out to your sides. Turn around slow."

The blue-shirted figure turned slowly and Trudow's face, pale except for two red blotches on his cheeks, came into view.

"Rookie," Rose muttered as she leaned down to return her gun to its holster.

She instantly regretted the comment when Trudow's flush spread. He lowered his arms. "And just who are you, ma'am?" he demanded.

She'd been about to apologize, but his tone pissed her off. Instead she slammed the window shut and locked it again.

Mac had slipped back around the corner. "Sweet," he whispered.

Rose stifled a grin and pretended she hadn't heard him.

They'd no sooner returned to the living room then there was a sharp rap on the front door. "Mrs. Huntington, open the door! I need to speak with that woman."

Trudow apparently wasn't going to let things stand as they were. Rose really couldn't blame him. He'd just been doing his job, standing guard on the porch.

Rob was headed toward the door. She slipped in front of him. There were advantages to being compact. "Have an idea. Let me handle it, sir."

Trudow banged again. "Open up, ma'am."

Kate called out, "I'm coming, Officer." Grabbing Rob's arm, she whispered, "Let her. It's her career at stake."

"So much for being in charge," Rob muttered.

Rose opened the door and Trudow marched in. "Keep your hands where I can see them, ma'am," he barked. "Now *who* are you?"

"Friend of the family," she said in as pleasant a tone as she could muster. She raised an eyebrow at him and cocked her head toward the hallway leading to the master bedroom.

Trudow missed the cue. He glared down at her. "I need to see some identification."

He'd dropped the *ma'am*, she noted. She turned toward him so that her back was to the rest of the room. "I'll be happy to show you ID, Officer." Her voice was sweet, but she gave Trudow a hard look and jabbed her chin several times toward the hall.

Trudow's eyes shifted toward confusion, then he gave her a slight nod.

Finally, the light's come on in his attic.

"Uh, Mrs. Huntington," the officer said, "is there someplace I can, uh, question this woman in private?"

Kate stepped forward and pointed down the hall. "You can use my bedroom, Officer."

Rose hoped Trudow didn't pick up on the suppressed snicker in her voice. She shot Kate a repressive look. Kate stifled a chuckle by disguising it as a cough.

Glad somebody's having fun here.

Fortunately, Trudow didn't seem to notice Kate's amusement. He made an after-you gesture to Rose, and she led the way to the bedroom.

Her idea worked. When she'd finished her explanation, Trudow nodded. She opened the bedroom door, and he followed her back to the living room.

The others were all staring expectantly in her direction.

"Thank you, ma'am, for your cooperation," Trudow said. For a moment, he looked like he was going to salute her. She narrowed her eyes at him. He nodded slightly and then went out the front door.

Rose locked the door behind him and pivoted to lean against it. Letting out a breath, she was mentally congratulating herself as she took a step back toward the living room. Suddenly she was stumbling forward, trying to catch her balance. She twisted around and landed hard on her rump.

Her cheeks burning, she glared at the offending tangle of entranceway rug that she'd tripped over. A male hand was thrust in front of her. She looked up.

"Well done, Ro…." Mac Reilly's voice trailed off when he saw her face. He snatched his hand back as if he'd been burned, then turned and stomped across the room.

What the hell's wrong with him? She pushed herself to a stand and brushed off her sore butt.

The others were all talking at once. "Everybody, plant your buns!" Liz barked from the sofa. "Rose, spill it. What'd you tell him?" They all resumed their seats.

Mentally shaking off her embarrassment, she said, "I told him the truth, just not the whole truth. That I'd also been assigned to protect Kate, and I was hanging out with you all on my day off. 'Detective Phillips did fill you in, didn't he?' I asked him. And the young fool admitted that he was told to spy on you, just like I was. So I let him assume I'd befriended you to find out what you were up to."

Grinning, Liz said, "For someone who told us roughly twenty-four hours ago that you never lie, that was one fine job of lying you did."

Rose shook her head slightly. "Trudow was easy, but he's bound to tell Phillips what I said, so now he'll be grilling me about what I've found out." Then she grinned at Liz. "And I think I prefer to call it *acting*."

"Well, yer a fine actress, lass," Dan rumbled, which elicited a chorus of chuckles.

"I have a suggestion, Rose," Kate said. "Just keep telling him we won't let you in the room when we're discussing cases, because of confidentiality, but you're working on getting us to trust you. And, if you get caught wearing civvies while you're on duty, you can use that as your excuse."

"Good idea." Rose flashed another grin in her direction.

It faded abruptly when she realized Rob was giving her a hard look. Her stomach knotted. The others grew quiet as they also caught his expression.

"Who are you really acting with, Rose?" His voice was low and hard.

She met his gaze while deciding how much to say. "I'm going to ask for a transfer, once this case is over. And if I don't get it, I'll probably resign from the force." She hesitated. How far could she trust these people she'd only known a few days?

Probably further than she could her superiors. She took a deep breath, then let it out. "Not only is Phillips an ass, but I'm pretty sure he takes bribes. Can't prove it though. I have no loyalty to him, and very little to BCPD at this point."

Rob's look did not soften. The others were silently watching, heads swiveling back and forth. Tension hung in the air.

"She's telling the truth, Rob," Kate said.

He flicked his eyes in her direction, then back to Rose's face. "You willing to bet your freedom on that?"

"Yes," Kate said. "You and I both know what to look for when someone's lying. She's telling the truth."

Rose stood perfectly still, her gaze locked on his. "I just stepped over the blue line, Rob. If I were still a loyal cop, would I have said that about my superior officer? And to civilians yet."

"Maybe, if you were *acting* in order to gain our trust."

Kate cleared her throat.

Rose held up a hand in her direction without breaking eye contact with Rob. "I can walk away from this, sir, if you want me to. I'll go stand on the porch with Trudow. Put in my transfer request tomorrow."

It wasn't what she wanted to do, but she'd do it.

Rob's stern expression finally relaxed. "I'm sorry. I–"

Rose cut him off. "No need to apologize, *Captain*. You don't know me, got no reason to trust me." She smiled at him, then turned toward Kate.

But Kate wasn't looking her way. She was watching Mac.

And Mac was staring at *her*, with that same mushy expression he'd had earlier when she'd smiled. Rose resisted the temptation to roll her eyes.

~~~~~~~~

Sunday night, Kate finally got a good night's sleep. Her sister was home, the tension with Rob was resolved, her father had a relatively safe assignment and she was getting used to having a virtual stranger camped out on her living room sofa.

It was actually comforting having a giant between her and the outside world while she slept. And despite his size, Skip was good at making himself unobtrusive. By the time she came downstairs each morning, he'd already eaten a bowl of cereal and was filling his thermos from the pot of coffee he'd made. He'd wish her a good morning, then take up his position outside until she was ready to leave the house.

This morning, he'd announced that they were out of cereal and had offered to cook pancakes for both of them. As she was mopping up syrup with the last fluffy bite, her phone rang.

"Hey," Rob said when she picked up, "with all the hoopla last night, we never discussed where we're going from here. Do we need to meet tonight, or shall I send Mac off to track down some of our suspects?"

"Yeah, let's meet tonight," she said. "I've got a couple thoughts about some other suspects percolating in my head. I'd like to discuss them with everyone."

"Anybody I know?"

"In one case, yes, but it's complicated. I'd rather spell it out for the whole crew tonight."

"I do so love a mysterious woman," Rob said with a slight chuckle. "Does seven sound okay to you? I'd like to stay at the office for a little while. This stuff has been so distracting that I'm getting way behind on my paperwork. The stacks on my desk are threatening to fall over and bury me."

"Sure, that's fine," Kate said.

"I'll put out the word. You okay with coming to our house? That'll save me some time."

"Fine by me."

It was a hellish day.

Kate's depressed client had made it through the weekend, but just barely. Kate asked her some questions to assess the current level of suicide risk and wasn't totally reassured by the answers. With the woman still in her office, she called the psychiatrist to whom the center referred clients. She managed to arrange an emergency appointment for that afternoon.

"Carol, it'll take awhile for antidepressants to start to work. You're going to have to hang on for a bit and have faith that you *will* start to feel better in time. Can you do that?"

"I'll try. I don't want to let you down, Kate."

Normally she'd confront such a statement and point out that Carol should be doing so for her own sake. But when a client was suicidal, you used whatever worked, including dependency and guilt.

As Kate ushered Carol out of her office, she motioned to Jim Lincoln to come in. She had run over time so there would be no break in between sessions.

As Jim walked past her, he said, "So how's the hottest counselor in town doing?"

Kate sighed inwardly. Out loud, she said, "Hi, Steve."

At four o'clock, Cheryl Crofton arrived. Kate breathed a tentative sigh of relief when she saw her client was wearing her normal attire–a loose-fitting top and stretch jeans.

Her relief was short lived. Cheryl exchanged pleasantries while walking into the office, but then she turned ugly. She was furious about the cancellation on Friday.

Halfway through Kate's apology, she went off into a ten-minute tirade that ranged from blasting her son-of-a-bitch husband to the customers at work who gave lousy tips, then on to the "fuckin' court system."

Both the level of anger and the amount of cussing were unusual for this woman. When she'd wound down a bit, Kate said, "You sound pretty pissed at the world–"

"Damn right, we're pissed."

Uh, oh! The *we* was not good.

"Did anything happen, besides me having to cancel Friday, to make you so angry?"

"Yeah, that fuckin' bitch who's supposed to be my *best* friend, she asked if it would be okay if she invited Frank over for dinner. Can you believe that?"

"Uh, this is the same Frank you were calling an S.O.B. a minute ago? The one you're divorcing?"

"Yeah, well, he may be an S.O.B. but he's my S.O.B."

Damn! Competition for her worthless husband was making him seem attractive again.

"Cheryl, I'd like you to stop and take a deep breath, and think this through for a minute. This is the guy you're divorcing because he beat the crap out of you. And your friend, who's been there for you through thick and thin, is *asking* you first before doing anything. She knows there's a line there she shouldn't cross without making sure you're okay with it. She's still being a good friend."

Cheryl sat back in her chair. The angry expression dissolved into bewilderment. "I'm sorry, I spaced there for a minute. What were we talking about?"

Inwardly Kate groaned, while out loud she tried to maintain a neutral voice. "Sue asked if it was okay to invite Frank over for dinner."

"Oh, yeah. How could she be interested in him, after all I've told her about the way he is? If she hooks up with him, he's gonna start beating on her eventually, just like he did me."

Twenty minutes later, as the session was coming to an end, the woman looked down at her clothes. "Fuck, this is one *uugggly* outfit!"

Shit, shit, shit! Kate plastered on a fake smile as she ushered whoever the hell was currently in control of Cheryl's body out of her office.

Her suspicions had been confirmed, which was disturbing on so many levels. Last thing in the world she needed was another D.I.D. case.

And they now had another murder suspect.

~~~~~~~

On the way to Rob's that evening, Rose told Kate she'd radioed the dispatcher to send her replacement directly to the Franklins'. When they pulled up across the street, Rose groaned.

Kate followed her line of vision to the profile of the officer sitting in a cruiser in front of the house. "What's the matter?"

"Jackson. He's got a serious attitude problem."

"How so?"

"Let's just say he's one of the reasons I've been having a lot of 'I wanted to be a police officer, why?' thoughts lately."

"I never realized there were so many bad cops," Kate said.

"There aren't." Rose's tone was bristly. "Most are good people, and they care about the job. But those who don't..."

"Stick out like a sore thumb," Kate finished for her.

Rose nodded. "Let's get this charade over with. Then I'll drive around the block and come to the back slider." They got out and Rose escorted her to the door, carrying the boxes of files.

Kate joined the others in the family room. Mugs and a carafe of coffee sat in the middle of the table.

"Decaf," Liz announced just as there was a light tapping on the sliding glass door. Rob went over to let Rose in.

The young woman caught Kate's eye and rolled her own. Apparently Jackson had been true to form.

Rose sat down at the table. "You all mind if I get comfortable?" Unbuckling her belt with its police accouterments dangling from it, she placed it on the floor next to her chair, her holstered gun on top. Then she unbuttoned the top button of her uniform shirt.

Kate watched Mac's face out of the corner of her eye. Big helping of starry-eyed, well seasoned with lust.

Rose must have also caught his expression before he could mask it. The pink tinge was back in her cheeks.

Mac nodded toward the belt on the floor and growled, "Gonna forget that."

"Nope. Good memory," Rose said.

"Gun don't do no good on the floor."

Rose just lifted an eyebrow.

"I better check the house. Make sure the perpetrator hasn't slipped past the *po-lice*." He exaggerated the last word in a derisive tone.

Uh, oh! He's resisting love's pull. After two failed marriages, Kate really couldn't blame him. But tonight was not the night to give Rose a hard time.

The young woman just shrugged. "I'll take the upstairs." She demonstrated how quickly she could retrieve her gun, then headed for the stairs.

When they were both out of earshot, Liz said, "What's with Mac? I thought he and Rose hit it off okay yesterday."

"Reaction formation," Kate said.

"What's that?" Rob asked.

"Guy likes girl. Guy doesn't want to admit he likes girl. Guy pretends, even to himself, that he can't stand girl."

"Why wouldn't he want to admit he likes her?" Rob asked.

"Two reasons–the Mrs. Reillys one and two."

Rob bopped his forehead with the heel of his hand. "Duh!"

Rose came back around the corner a few minutes later. Mac followed behind her, his gaze latched onto the silky bun at the nape of her neck.

Her bun, not her butt, so it isn't just lust.

The two of them sat back down at the table.

Kate cleared her throat. Time to get serious. "I've got two current cases that I think need to be added to our suspects. Since Rose may have heard me call these clients by name in the waiting room, I'm using fake names for them." She'd intentionally picked names with the same beginning sounds, in case she slipped and started to say the real name.

"Joe has dissociative identity disorder, what used to be called multiple personality disorder. Many therapists still call these folks 'multiples,' since saying 'so-and-so who has dissociative identity disorder' is a mouthful." She was stalling as she sorted out how much they needed to know about Jim Lincoln. She liked Jim and felt like she was ratting him out. She even liked Steve. He was just an insecure kid. Then she remembered that said insecure kid might be her husband's killer.

She forged ahead. "Joe has several alter personalities. One of those alters… Wait, let me back up. Joe is probably homosexual, but he's very conflicted about that. So his psyche has developed an alter that's quite heterosexual and macho. And that macho alter, whom we shall call Stan, flirts with me."

"Flirts, or tries to seduce?" Rob asked.

"Somewhere in between. It's very likely, since I've been working with Joe for over a year, that he's seen me with Rob, maybe on our way out to lunch. He may have assumed we were a romantic couple, in which case Stan might see Rob as his competition."

"I flirt with lots of women," Mac said, watching Rose out of the corner of his eye. "Don't mean I'm gonna knock off their boyfriends."

Rose just lifted an eyebrow.

Kate said, "Good point, Mac. But with multiples…Well, the host alter is usually fairly mature, but–"

"What's a host alter, Katie?" her father asked.

"Sorry. The host alter is the one who maintains the person's original identity, goes by their given name. That alter is often, but not always, more grown up than the others, has a maturity level at least close to the person's chronological age. But the other alters are almost always around the age they were when they were created, so they may be five years old, or ten or sixteen."

"How are they created?" Rose asked.

"Ho, boy. The short explanation is that these folks have horribly abusive childhoods. A new personality forms during or right after a traumatic event, to help the child deal with that event. Each alter only remembers some of the abuse, which actually helps the child cope. If their personality wasn't fragmented into alters, they wouldn't be able to handle that much trauma. It'd be too overwhelming.

"So back to Ji… uh, Joe, or rather Stan. He's a fifteen-year-old boy, with horrible stuff in his history, so he's even less sane than a normal teenager. There may be an obsessive crush on me hiding behind the flirting, and he could very well be unstable enough to try to take out his competition."

"That would explain going after Ed and shooting at me. But why would he try to run Liz down?" Rob asked.

"The hit-and-run could have been a coincidence," Liz said. "And he might've been aiming at Mac the other morning, thinking he was Kate's new boyfriend."

"What about the attack on Mary?" Dan asked.

"Assuming that attack was meant for me, he may have developed a…" Kate hesitated, then carefully avoided eye contact with the others as she finished the sentence. "A, uh, reaction formation." She heard an aborted snort coming from Liz's direction.

Rose's eyebrow went up, as Mac asked, "What's that?"

To Kate's left, her father turned a chuckle into a fake cough. She fought back the giggles trying to escape her throat. "Loves me but he's convinced himself he hates me," she answered when she could trust her voice again.

Rob was wearing his court face, but one end of his mouth was twitching. "How serious a suspect do you think he is?"

"I think he should go near the top of the possibilities–"

"I just had a terrible thought," Liz said. "Maybe when he hit Mary, his intention had been to knock you out, Kate, and kidnap you."

That stifled Kate's urge to laugh. Her mind ran wild, visualizing Jim Lincoln, or rather Steve, holding her captive and….

"That's a possibility we should keep in mind," Rob said, his expression now grim.

"This guy, Stan, or whoever our perp is, might have realized after he hit her that he had the wrong sister," Rose said.

"Or he freaked when he saw the blood," Mac said.

Kate nodded. "If it is Ste…Stan, then the sight of all that blood could've caused him to switch, and Joe or another alter came out and took off."

"Switching, is that when they shift from one personality to another?" Rose asked.

"Yeah, sorry. I keep forgetting and slipping into psychobabble."

"I think Joe/Stan should go in the likelies for now," Rob said.

"I couldn't bring home the files since these are active cases so I wrote this." She held up a sheet of paper on which she'd written: *JOE–has D.I.D. STAN–MACHO ALTER, 15-yrs-old, may have crush on Kate, taking out competition.*

The others nodded their approval. Kate placed the Joe sheet in the front of the box of files at her feet, then pulled out another sheet and put it on the table face down.

"The other current client we will call Shirley, and she's pregnant."

Rob's mouth fell open.

Kate gave him a small smile. "I've only just begun to shock you. I believe that Shirley is also a multiple."

Rob sat back in his chair. "Whoa!"

"Rob is Shirley's divorce lawyer," Kate told the others. "Her husband beat her, and she put up with it until she found out she was pregnant. Then she knew she had to get out. I won't go into the reasons I suspect she's a multiple but she has an alter who's angry enough to be physically aggressive. Often the alters hold different emotions, again to avoid the overwhelm of all the intense feelings together. One alter will experience most of the fear, another the sadness and yet another the rage about all the horrible stuff they endured as a child.

"Contrary to Hollywood's portrayal of them, multiples are almost never dangerous, except to themselves if the sad alter becomes suicidal. But the problem is that each alter lacks the normal range of emotions. The feelings can't counter-balance each other like they do, at least most of the time, in the rest of us. So the angry alter can *sometimes* become dangerous, because that alter may not feel the fear of repercussions that would keep them from acting on the anger. It's pure rage with little or nothing reining it in… in a personality that can be any age, from toddler to adult."

There was silence as everyone digested that.

"What about the husband?" Rose asked.

"He's a possibility, but my sense of him based on what Shirley's told me is that he's fairly passive with everyone but her. Many batterers are aggressive in general but a subgroup are the exact opposite. They bow and scrape with everybody else, build up a lot of resentment, then come home and take it out on their women. I think that…Fred falls into that category."

Rob was nodding his head. "I had a settlement conference with them. Not much hope of settling out of court, but you gotta try. Crof…uh, Fred was very self-effacing, to the point where it was embarrassing. Of course he tried to convince me that his wife was over-reacting. Women can be so hysterical and all that B.S. Assuming I'm going to drop the case on his say-so."

"Because he's the man so of course you're going to believe him over her," Kate said.

"Right. That attitude's not unusual in domestic violence cases. But his reaction when it became obvious that I *didn't* believe him and I wasn't going to drop the case–*that* was a bit unusual. Most guys turn ugly at that point. Couple times, we've had to call the police. But this guy kept right on kissing up."

"I think Fred should go in the possibilities," Kate said. "But I'm more worried about Shirley, or rather one of her alters. She's said some things recently that indicate she's developed a crush on Rob, because he's the white knight who's rescuing her."

Rob digested that idea for a moment. "Okay, I'll buy that maybe Ch…Shirley's developed a slight crush on me. But she's fallen hard enough to be willing to kill off her competition?" His expression skeptical, he looked down at his expanding midriff, then spread his arms and shrugged ruefully. "I'm no Brad Pitt, and I'm almost two decades older than her."

"Rob, you're a powerful man, who's also kind and sympathetic," Kate said. "You're the perfect good daddy in the eyes of a woman who's been mistreated by every man in her life, starting with her father. And it's not just that you're saving her from her husband. Abused children often develop powerful fantasies about being rescued from their predicaments. For boys, it's more likely to be some Rambo-type hero who comes in, guns blazing, to rescue them. For girls, a Prince Charming who will fall in love with them and take them away to live happily ever after."

"No doubt, that's why those fairy tales became so popular to begin with," Liz said.

"Okay, assuming Shirley thinks she's in love with me," Rob said. "That would explain the attack on Liz. But why go after me? Or *you*, Kate?"

"The attack on you and Shelley fits least well, but she looks a lot like her mother. It was reported on the news that Liz was still alive. Shirley may have been following you and thought Shelley was Liz."

"But wouldn't she realize that Liz would still be laid up, so soon after the accident?" Rose asked.

"Maybe not. Each alter is out–as in they have control of the body–some of the time. So their awareness of the passage of time is often not good, especially when they're decompensating."

Confused looks at the psychobabble. "Becoming less stable," she clarified.

"But why then would she turn her anger on you?" Rob asked.

"I found out she was around…" Kate paused to pick her words carefully. She didn't want to betray Rob's confidence. "That Tuesday evening you were in my office, decompressing a bit. Remember the noise we heard outside my door?" He nodded. "It was her. Ostensibly looking for her lost keys, which were in the bottom of her purse all along. She was my last client that evening. Now I'm wondering if she saw you headed for my office and intentionally eavesdropped. And thought she was witnessing something other than a friendly hug."

"So then you became another rival," Liz said.

Kate nodded. "I'm inclined to put her in the likelies pile." The others agreed. She placed the Shirley sheet in that section of her files.

"So what do you want to do about Shirley and Joe at this point?" Rob asked her.

"I'm not sure. I need to give that some thought. Maybe I'll be able to find out more about these alters next time I see them."

"Okay." Rob turned to Mac. "In the meantime, we need to track down the grandfather who lost the visitation suit. Here's the most recent address Liz could find for him. You ever heard of that town?"

"Yeah. Wide place in the road. Near Hagerstown."

Rob turned to his wife. "Tomorrow, can you find out what's been happening with the daughter and grandkids the last few years?"

Liz nodded, stifling a yawn.

"I don't think we need to meet tomorrow night," Rob said, "unless one of you comes up with something interesting. Kate has clients in the evening and I've got a major backlog of paperwork at the office."

While saying their goodnights, Liz slipped Kate a piece of paper.

Lou walked Kate to the police cruiser out front. As Officer Jackson pulled away from the curb, she unfolded the paper.

By the glow of a streetlight, she was able to make out a doctor's name and appointment time, for that Wednesday. She was impressed Liz had gotten her in so quickly, but then again not many people said no to Liz when she wanted them to say yes.

Hopefully the killer would behave between now and then, so she could keep the appointment. With a sinking feeling in her gut, she realized it had been almost four days since the last attack.

He, or she, was overdue to strike again.

CHAPTER NINETEEN

Tuesday morning, Rob looked at his desk and groaned.

Gotta get on top of this paperwork.

He felt like he was losing control over his job, and right now he needed to feel in control of *something*.

Buried in the mountain somewhere were at least two motions that needed to be filed today. So, first task was to prioritize.

Forty minutes later he had two piles, organized in order of importance. In pile one were documents for his own cases, prepared by his paralegal, Beth Samuels, based on his instructions. The second pile were for cases being handled by associate lawyers in the firm, that for one reason or another needed his input or review. Most of those were prepared by their newest hire, Tim Williams, whose future with the firm was questionable.

Rob relaxed a bit. He had a handle on the task. Now he just needed to get it done.

He plowed through the top third of pile one in a little over an hour, making only minor corrections. After buzzing Beth to come get them, he sighed and picked up the most pressing of those prepared by Williams.

Halfway through the document, Rob was trying to decide if he should just rewrite it himself, which would probably take less time than trying to edit it. He opted for scrawling REWRITE over the entire page. Obviously, this one wasn't getting filed today.

His cell phone chirped. He tossed the brief across his desk so hard it slid off the edge and into his trash can. Deciding that was where it belonged, he answered his phone. "Franklin."

"Got a bead on Grandpa," Mac said. "Watchin' the bastard as we speak. Should know more by tonight."

"Good. You want to report in later, say about nine-fifteen?"

"Will do."

Rob disconnected and called Liz. She reported that she too had some interesting information about Grandpa. Eyeing the stacks of paperwork, Rob said, "Save it to tell everyone tonight. Can you call Kate and ask her to come over at nine for a short war council? ... Thanks. Love you."

Sighing, he got up to fish the damn document out of the trash can, and went back to figuring out what the devil this young man thought he was saying.

The next thing he knew, his stomach was growling. He looked at his watch. *How'd it get to be twelve-thirty already?*

He buzzed his assistant to come into his office. Handing her the document he'd considered trashing earlier, he said, "Fran, three things. Take this to Beth and ask her to redo it. It needs to be filed tomorrow."

Fran frowned down at the front page, covered with Rob's scribbles and REWRITE slashed across it. "Beth did *this*?"

"No. Tim."

Fran rolled her eyes.

"I need Beth to fix it. Tell her I owe her, big time."

"And two and three?" Fran asked.

"Take these back to Tim and tell him to rewrite them according to my notations." He handed her a stack of papers. "And, would you mind getting me a sandwich from the deli?"

"No, problem. Ham and cheese on rye, extra pickles?"

"You know me too well, Fran."

After a quick trip to the men's room, Rob got back to work. When Fran brought in his sandwich and a soda, he barely paused long enough to mumble a thank you.

About an hour later, Fran stuck her head in his door again. He looked up and she came in.

"The correspondence you dictated last night is done. I took the liberty of signing and initialing them for you. You want any of these?" She waved pink message slips at him.

He jumped back in mock horror as if they were snakes. "Hell, no."

Fran laughed. "Nothing that can't wait until tomorrow. I passed some on to associates."

"What would I do without you?"

"Learn to type?" She looked meaningfully at his dark monitor on the far end of his desk. It was an ongoing but friendly battle between them. She was trying to drag him into the twenty-first century, but at least once a month the damn computer would eat something he was working on. Fran would have to figure out what random key he'd accidentally hit that had sent his half-written document to some dark corner of the hard drive.

"You need anything else before I go?"

Shocked, Rob looked at his watch. Ten after five. Where the hell had the afternoon gone? "No. Have a good evening."

Three more hours before he'd have to head home for the war council. He wasn't sure his eyes or temper would hold out that long, but he'd keep at it for awhile. Just to be on the safe side though, since he kept losing track of time, he pulled out his cell to call Lou.

He hated spending money to have Lou babysit his car, but he didn't want to end up like Ed. Tears sprang into his eyes. He swiped at them with his fingers. The grief kept doing that to him, blind-siding him when he least expected it.

It took him a moment to realize Lou wasn't answering. The damn phone had turned itself off. He pushed the power button. It flashed *low battery*, then turned off again. He stifled the temptation to throw it across the room. A quick rummage through his briefcase confirmed he had left his charger at home.

Picking up his desk phone, he dialed Lou's cell.

"Yo, that you, Mr. F?"

"Yeah, Lou. I'm still working, but I keep getting into stuff and losing track of time. Can you call this number at eight… No, that won't work." The receptionist would switch the phones over to voicemail when she left at six.

Wait! Skip'll be down there waiting for Kate. He can watch the car.

"Ya there, Mr. F?"

"Yes, I was just thinking this through. My cell phone battery's dead. So if I'm not downstairs by a few minutes of eight, run upstairs and get me."

"It safe for you to be up there after hours, Mr. F?"

"This is a law firm. There's always somebody working late. And Mrs. Huntington and her police officer are down the hall. But I think I will lock my office door now that my assistant's gone for the day."

Not that the flimsy lock would stop anybody, but no one could take him by surprise if they had to break the door down first.

"Okay, Mr. F. I'll come an' get ya by eight."

"Thanks, Lou."

Rob got up and locked his door, then sat back down and picked up the next document in pile two.

Great. Another Williams masterpiece. But it didn't need to be filed until Friday. He gleefully scrawled REWRITE on it and grabbed another document.

Hopefully he could get through most of these tonight. Tomorrow's schedule was packed with meetings and court. And everything he was sending back for re-write would have to be reviewed again later in the week.

Aaargh, being stalked by a killer really messes with your workload!

~~~~~~~~~

At seven-forty, Kate glanced quickly at the clock. Mr. Phelps would get upset with her if he caught her doing it. He was being particularly difficult tonight–very resistant, along with his normal paranoia. He kept changing the subject. It was getting on Kate's nerves, but the last thing you could express to a paranoid client was anger.

Wonder if it's a full moon tonight.

She once again brought up the issue they'd been discussing. He changed the subject, again.

Hell with it. Go with the resistance.

"You seem to be easily distracted tonight, Mr. Phelps. I'm wondering if we should stop a bit early?" She was sure he would accuse her of trying to cheat him out of his full hour. Then she'd gently point out that *he* was the one wasting his hour.

But he surprised her. "Yeah, I got a lot of stuff running around in my head tonight."

She wasn't about to start the pulling-teeth process of getting him to tell her what that stuff was, with–another quick glance at the clock–only fifteen minutes left in the session. Just about the point where she'd get him to open up, they'd be out of time.

Instead, she said, "Well, why don't you work on sorting those things out and, if you're still in mental overload next time, maybe I can help you get those thoughts organized." One had to word things so very carefully with a paranoid client. Why had she let Pauline schedule him for last thing on a Tuesday night when her brain was tired?

Mr. Phelps looked at her suspiciously, trying to figure out if she was trying to pry into his head. Finally, he said, "Okay." Kate walked him to the door.

He frowned at Rose, sitting in the waiting room. "I thought *I* was your last client."

Kate smiled. "You are. She's a friend. We're going out for a late dinner."

"Well, okay then." He nodded at Rose and shuffled out the door.

Kate motioned Rose into her office. "Hang on one second." She made a quick note in Mr. Phelps' file to watch for signs of dementia.

Yeah, and how the hell are you going to broach that topic? Oh by the way, Mr. Phelps, could you possibly be going senile?

As she locked up his file, she told Rose a war council had been called for nine o'clock. They'd need to hurry, since she wanted to stop at her house first to get her files.

In the restroom, as Rose quickly changed into her uniform, she told Kate about her encounter with Phillips that morning. Trudow had indeed told him that Rose was carrying her spying assignment beyond the time she was on duty. "Phillips actually commended me on my initiative. Didn't know he knew such a big word."

Kate snorted in response, then checked her watch. Seven-fifty-three. She relaxed a bit. They should have enough time.

~~~~~~~~~

Down the hall, Rob was working away. He quickly reviewed three documents prepared by other associates, then braced himself to tackle another gem from Williams.

Halfway into it, he glanced at his watch.

Eight-twenty-five!

He jumped up and started stuffing the document he'd been working on into his briefcase.

Where the hell is Lou? He probably fell asleep.

Rob opened his door and was greeted by silence. Where was everybody? Usually there were at least several people working late, preparing for court the next day or getting caught up on the perpetual paperwork.

The silence was making him nervous. Hypervigilant, he crossed the reception area. Opening the outer door cautiously, he stuck his head out just far enough to look up and down the hall. All clear. He took a step.

Searing pain in his back. His thoughts scrambled, he fell forward, limbs and muscles twitching. A sharp stab in his shoulder.

His mind cleared as a numbing sensation spread through his body. His last conscious thought was that he should've called Lou from his office phone to come get him.

CHAPTER TWENTY

Despite getting away from the office early, everything went downhill from there. At the house, Rose had to go through the process of checking the property. She carried the files out to her cruiser, then walked Kate to her replacement's car and officially turned over her charge.

It was Officer Jackson again, the one Rose said had an attitude problem, although he'd seemed okay to her last night.

But tonight she realized what Rose had meant. When she told Jackson she was going to her friends' house for the evening, he informed her that he was her protection, not her chauffeur. Standing next to his cruiser, she gave him the you're-not-here-to-run-my-life speech. It had no impact.

Tamping down her anger, she weighed her options. She could take her own car, and force this guy to follow her, or she could ride with Skip. The latter was probably safer.

Her cell phone rang in her purse. She ignored it as she turned toward Skip's Explorer down the block.

Jackson moved around the car to block her way. She glared at him. "Touch me and I'll have your badge!" She took a step to dodge past him.

"Okay, get in the cruiser." He stomped back to the driver's door.

Once they were under way, Kate checked her phone. The missed call had been Liz. She hit the button to return the call. "Sorry I'm running late. I'll be there in—"

"Rob's not home yet!" Liz's voice was frantic.

Worry shot through her. Her stomach clenched, then did a somersault. She put her hand on her abdomen, willing her body to settle down. She didn't dare ask questions with Officer Obnoxious listening in. "My evening police guard is bringing me over," she said into the phone so Liz would know why she couldn't talk. "Be there in a few minutes."

At the Franklins, she opened her door before the car had completely stopped. "Wait out here," she ordered.

It was probably the wrong thing to say to a male cop with an attitude problem.

"Hell I will, lady." Jackson opened his door and got out.

Kate gritted her teeth. She didn't have time for this. She had to find out what was going on. She glared at him over the car roof. "There are bodyguards inside. I'll be fine."

The cop seemed unimpressed. He slammed his door.

"You follow me and I'll…." she wasn't quite sure how to finish the threat. The thought crossed her mind that she could shoot the asshole with the pistol Mac had insisted she carry in her purse.

Maybe it's not a good idea for me to be armed after all.

She turned and marched toward the house. Jackson followed. When she reached the door, it opened and Liz yanked her inside, then closed the door in the officer's face.

Kate turned the lock. "Is he here yet?" she asked, praying he'd just been delayed at the office.

"No!"

They heard a tapping noise in the family room, followed by a faint, "It's Rose." Kate hurried into the room but her father was already opening the door.

"Saw you arguing," Rose said to Kate, then leaned down to put the boxes of files on the floor. "That guy's the biggest…." Her voice trailed off when she turned around and got a good look at their faces.

"Rob's not home. He should've been here an hour ago," Kate told her.

"Not good." For the first time since Kate had met her, the young woman looked scared.

"Okay, ladies, everybody sit down and take a deep breath," Dan said.

Sitting down sounded good. Kate's knees were about to give out. She wasn't sure about the deep breath though. Her chest felt like it was in a vise. She pushed aside the horrible images popping into her mind, of Rob lying bleeding somewhere.

Kate was the only one who had followed her father's advice. Liz continued to hobble around in circles on her ugly blue boot. Lord knew where her crutches were.

She spotted one of them, sticking up from the corner of the sofa. It looked like Liz had thrown it across the room, embedding it between the cushions.

Dan said, "Calm down now. Tis a bit soon to panic."

"Men," Rose muttered under her breath.

Kate knew what she meant. Her father fell into that category of old-fashioned males who tried to reassure women by downplaying the severity of the situation, not realizing they were insulting the woman's intelligence. A killer was chasing them, and one of them was not where he was supposed to be. It was *most definitely* time to panic.

She couldn't let her father take charge. Rob had said she was strong. Now she had to be, for his sake.

She stood up and grabbed Liz's arm as she hobbled past. "You've called his cell?"

"A hundred times. Goes right to voicemail."

"And Lou's?"

"Rings a few times, then goes to voicemail."

"Do you have Fran's home number?" Liz nodded.

"Go call her. Find out when she left the office and if Rob was still there." Kate grabbed the crutch out of its sofa-cushion holster and thrust it at her. "Dad, go with Liz and help her."

For a second, he looked rebellious. Then the don't-mess-with-me look she gave him must have changed his mind. He helped Liz hobble toward the kitchen.

Deep breath, Kate told herself. Nope, her chest was still too tight.

She turned to Rose but the young woman was a step ahead of her. She already had her cell phone out and was punching 911. "This is Officer Hernandez. I have reason to believe that a man is in serious danger or has come to bodily harm at..."

Kate yanked her own phone from her purse and walked a few feet away, punching the speed dial number for Skip. "Rob's missing!" she said without preamble. "Come around back to the family room door. There's an asshole cop out front—"

"You mean the one who's yakking on his cell?" Skip said in a disgusted voice. "Be right there."

The Franklins' house line rang. Kate grabbed it.

"Rob?" Mac's voice.

"He's missing! Have you heard from him?"

"Not since this morning. Been tryin' his cell. Goes to voicemail."

"Same here. We haven't been able to reach his bodyguard either. How far away are you?"

"Hagerstown. Hour an' a half."

Kate knew it was at least a two-hour drive. "Be careful, Mac. We need you *here*, not dead! And there's a cop out front who makes Trudow look sweet. No pissing matches. Sneak around back to the family room and knock."

"Be there soon. Don't *you* take any chances, Kate."

Kate opted to interpret the ensuing silence as Mac having disconnected, even though she knew he was still on the line, waiting for her promise to be careful. At the moment, that was not a promise she was willing to make. She disconnected.

Two taps on the slider had Kate starting toward it, but Rose, cell phone at her ear, stepped in front of her. "Should be Skip," Kate whispered.

Rose handed Kate her phone. "Anyone comes on the line, ask them to hold for me." She pulled her gun and flattened herself against the wall beside the slider. Nudging the drape aside, she looked out. Then she unlocked the door and Skip slipped in, relocking it behind him.

Rose retrieved her cell phone just in time. "I'm Officer Hernandez, working a related case…" She turned and walked away.

Liz hobbled back into the room, crutch on one side, Dan on the other. "Secretary left a wee bit after five," he said. "Rob was still there workin'."

"Thanks, Dad. You holding up okay?" she said to Liz, who nodded mutely.

"Let's sit down and re-group," Kate said.

Rose glanced their way as they were helping Liz get settled on the sofa. Into her phone, she said, "Secretary saw him last, little after five, in his office." Then she disconnected and walked over to them.

"I have some information." Rose's voice was all professional cop, but she was pale and Kate saw the shadow of fear in her eyes.

She was actually heartened by the fear. If there was still reason to fear, there was still reason to hope.

"When I called dispatch, they already had units at Rob's firm. Somebody'd knocked a paralegal over the head. When she came to, she called 911. They patched me through to the scene."

Rose took a deep breath, then plunged on. "Officers searched the building. Found Lou in a stairwell. Out cold but breathing. Paramedics didn't find any lumps on his head. They think he might've been drugged. No sign of Rob. His cell phone was on his desk. Battery's dead. Found his briefcase in the hall. Suit jacket on the floor of the elevator."

Kate's heart pounded. The horrible images were back.

"I gave them Rob's description," Rose said. "Told them there was good reason to believe he'd been kidnapped from that location and they should handle the crime scene accordingly."

"How'd they know it was Lou?" Skip asked.

"Wallet was in his pocket."

"Did they search outside the building?"

"Doing that now, best they can in the dark."

Kate tried the deep breath again, with moderate success. "Any detective on the scene yet?"

"No, and Phillips will probably catch it. Related case."

"Shit!" Kate said. It was a sign of the times that her father didn't chastise her.

"Should we call Phillips?" Liz asked.

Rose's eyebrow shot up, eloquently echoing Kate's thought. *Why the hell would we want to do that?*

"Maybe he knows more than the officers on the scene," Liz said.

"Possible but I doubt it." Rose glanced at her watch. "He's probably just now getting there."

Kate thought she knew the answer to the next question but she wanted Rose's professional take on it. "Why do you think he was kidnapped?" For Liz's sake, and her own, she did not add *instead of killed.*

"Because he's not there. This guy hasn't taken the time to hide his victims before, he's just hit and run." She glanced down at Liz's boot. "Sometimes literally. And he left Lou lying in the stairwell. Young man in another office was also knocked out. Said he'd been

Tasered first. From behind. Neither he nor the paralegal saw who hit them."

Kate put two and two together. "So if this bastard has switched from shotguns to stun guns, he probably wanted to take Rob alive."

There was a loud knock on the front door. They all jumped up and raced toward the living room. Liz almost tripped over her crutch. Skip swept her up in his arms like she was a feather.

Rose yelled, "Wait!"

The stampeding herd came to a halt. Skip put Liz down on her feet and stepped in between her and the door.

Rose plastered herself against the wall, gun drawn, and twitched aside the curtain over the window in the door. She grimaced. "Don't have to call Phillips. He's here."

"Shit!" Dan said.

Holstering her gun, Rose opened the door. Phillips started into a parody of surprise that Officer Hernandez was still there when she should be off duty.

Both Liz and Kate rushed forward. Liz grabbed the back of a chair for support. "Where's my husband? Is he okay?"

Phillips looked at Kate. A smirk started to spread across his face.

She made a chopping motion with her hand. "None of your crap! Yes or no question–have you or haven't you found Mr. Franklin?"

"No."

"Any leads?"

"Officers are still processing the scene."

Yeah, and why aren't you there, asshole?

"I have some questions for you and Mrs. Franklin."

Kate glanced at Liz. She was on the verge of collapse. Kate wasn't going to let Phillips push her over the edge. "Well, being the wife of an attorney, Mrs. Franklin feels strongly about having a lawyer present, and she's very distraught." She wrapped her arms around Liz. "Play along with me," she whispered in her ear.

Liz collapsed against her, shaking as if she were crying. Or maybe she was crying. Kate couldn't tell. She knew her own act was as phony as a three-dollar bill, but she didn't care whether Phillips believed her. She just wanted to force him to leave Liz alone.

Phillips said, "I thought she was so damn anxious for us to find her husband."

Kate ignored him. "Dad, could you take Liz upstairs to lie down, please." Her father took Liz's arm and helped her toward the stairs.

They'd won that round. Phillips couldn't question someone once they had asked for an attorney, until that attorney was present. Kate hoped he didn't try to force the issue by threatening to take Liz to the police station. She'd shoot him and shove his corpse into a closet before she'd let that happen.

But Phillips had a different agenda. "Slick." The smirk was back. "Get the distraught widow out of the room so she won't say anything that might incriminate you."

"She's not a widow yet, Detective. We're operating under the assumption that Mr. Franklin's been kidnapped, not killed."

"You're right. I mis-spoke. Don't have a body. And *I'm* not even convinced he's been kidnapped. Way I see it, Franklin's pulled a disappearing act, after knocking out his own bodyguard. You wait a little while, hoping we assume he's dead, then you disappear, too. Go join him on some tropical island and live happily ever after."

Kate reined in her anger. "You have a lively imagination, Detective. Unless you have some concrete questions to ask, how about you go find Mr. Franklin and leave us alone."

"Oh, I have no intentions of looking for Franklin, not for forty-eight hours at least."

Her mouth fell open. Rose was standing behind Phillips. Her face mirrored Kate's.

"His bodyguard and two people in his office were knocked unconscious," Kate yelled, "and you're not going to investigate it as a kidnapping?"

"Nope, from where I'm standing he's a missing person. Now when the bodyguard wakes up and fingers his boss, then I'll have to track Franklin down to arrest him for assault. But until then, hey, a grown man has the right to take off without telling anybody where he's going. Hell, maybe he's tired of *you* now as well, and he's gone off with some other little chippy."

Kate snapped. She charged at Phillips through a red haze.

Skip grabbed her, pulling her back in a restraining bear hug. Rose stepped between them and Phillips. "No, Kate!"

"Officer, arrest that woman for assaulting a police officer." Phillips' voice was seething.

Rose froze, her back to him. "Sir, I'm not sure we can make that charge stick."

"Cuff her, Officer."

Kate had stopped squirming, but Skip was still holding onto her.

Rose looked at them, her eyes wide, her jaw clenched. Then she took a deep breath, and the cop mask fell into place. She turned around to Phillips. "Sir, could I speak to you for a moment, privately?"

She herded him over toward the door. The police officer and detective had a hushed but somewhat animated conversation.

Then Phillips came back over and said to Kate, "No problem, ma'am. Of course you're upset. I'll be going now and let you all get some rest."

Skip released Kate, as Rose opened the door for the detective and he left.

Kate stared at Rose. "How'd you do that?"

"Pointed out you've got lawyer friends who'd probably sue for false arrest. Also convinced him I could get more info out of you than he could, now that I've got your trust. So he assumed that's why I stood up for you, to strengthen your trust."

"You're brilliant!" Kate said.

Rose flashed a quick grin, then her face sobered again. "He was bluffing. He knows he can't dismiss Rob's disappearance as a missing person. He was trying to provoke you. Get you to say something incriminating. Probably assumed you went after him 'cause of the *chippy* remark. He'll think that was jealousy."

Kate ground her teeth. "Actually what tipped me over the edge was the insinuation that Rob had grown tired of Liz."

"The man's a bloody eejit!" her father said, as he helped Liz down the stairs. Somewhere along the way the remaining crutch had gotten lost.

"Actually, he's not dumb," Kate said. "But he is a bully who enjoys intimidating people. Probably why he became a cop in the first place, for the power trip."

Rose nodded. "That's my take on him."

Liz gave a slight shake of her head. "I gotta tell you, Kate, you need to take acting lessons from Rose here. You're terrible." She sounded almost like her normal self.

"I take it you heard everything."

"Clear as a bell, from the top of the stairs. I had to stand on the top step to keep your daddy from coming to your rescue. I figured even as big as Skip here is, he could only hold back one O'Donnell at a time."

As they returned to their seats in the family room, Kate said, "Since I don't have much confidence in the police at this point, I think we should look for Rob ourselves. Tonight."

"Starting at the office building, I assume." Rose said. "Who do you want where, Kate?"

Kate silently thanked her for the implication that she was their new captain. She suspected Rose did it quite purposefully. She was beginning to think Rose did most things quite purposefully.

"I'd like you and Skip to get started right away. Make concentric circles moving away from the building, looking for any sign of where Rob might have been taken."

"Might still be some people around on the street. We can ask if they've seen anything suspicious," Skip said.

"Yeah, like a big man being forced into a car, or if he was Tasered or drugged like the others, the kidnapper might've pretended he was helping a drunk buddy," Kate said. "Might even be holding him nearby. It'd be hard to move a big man like Rob, unconscious, especially if our culprit is Ch…Shirley."

Skip looked confused but she didn't want to take the time to fill him in on the potential suspects.

He'd caught the gender of the name, though. "Taser could point to a woman. Ms. Franklin here could take down a giant with a Taser."

Rose nodded agreement.

"When Mac gets here," Kate said. "I'll send him to join you."

She wasn't quite sure how to present the other vague plan that was forming in the back of her head. But first she needed to get her father out of the room. "I just had a terrible thought. Maybe this guy's thinking he'll sneak in here while we're distracted. Skip, Dad, would you please go check out the house thoroughly?"

The men nodded and left the room.

Kate turned back to the other women. "I have this half-baked idea and I need you two to help me flesh it out. I'm thinking the killer may have kidnapped Rob to lure me to him, or her."

"Same thing occurred to me," Rose said.

"So I want to switch that around and use myself as bait to get the killer to lead us to Rob."

"You're right. It's a half-baked idea," Liz said. "You're not going out there, for a variety of reasons, the first one being the bun in your oven."

"Please hear me out. I don't want to lose the baby, but... he or she is still just an idea, the idea that someday it'll exist and then I'll love it. But Rob's real, and we've got to get him back safe." Tears stung her eyes. She had to do this. Even the thought of losing Eddie's baby wasn't enough to stop her. She could *not* sit back and wait while others searched for Rob.

"Kate, dear," Liz said, "I appreciate your bravery, but has it occurred to you that the killer's *only* reason for keeping Rob alive is to get you? Once he has you, then he'll kill my husband."

Kate sat frozen, stunned, as Rose nodded her agreement.

She felt her face crumple. The pressure in her chest threatened to explode.

No! I can't fall apart. There's no time for that now.

She tried to take a deep breath. The vise was back. Her voice shook as she said, "No, Liz, I hadn't thought of that."

Rose cocked an eyebrow at Liz. "You're not going out there either. If you do, we'll have to spend time guarding you instead of searching for Rob. Not to mention the whole leg brace, boot and crutches issue."

Liz just blinked at her.

"Neither one of you is going," Rose drove home her point. "Having to protect you would just slow us down."

"Amen to that, lass!" Kate's father said as he and Skip re-entered the room.

"Sorry, Mr. O'Donnell. Same argument applies to you. You would be a target too, as bait to get to Kate."

He opened his mouth but Kate headed him off. "She's right, Dad. You're with Liz and me, as our guard. Rose, Skip, go! Go find him!"

They hurried to the sliding glass door and slipped out into the darkness. Her father closed and locked the slider behind them.

Kate swiped the tears off her face with her sleeve.

"Now what do *we* do?" Liz said from beside her on the sofa.

Sighing, Kate reached over and took her hand. "We sit and wait."

While others search for our guy.

CHAPTER TWENTY-ONE

Rob woke in a dimly lit room. His alarm clock was silent.

Did I oversleep?

His brain sent signals to his neck muscles to turn and look at the clock. Nothing happened.

Maybe it's Saturday.

But why did his head hurt? Actually quite a few parts of his body hurt.

Cold. Need to pull the covers up.

His brain sent signals down his arm. But his hand just flopped around, and felt bare skin and coarse chest hair.

This time the neural impulses sent to his neck were obeyed, and he was able to lift his head for a moment. It fell back down with a thud, sending a jolt of pain through his skull.

Must've been one hell of a frat party last night.

He was lying on some kind of narrow cot, naked from the waist up and wearing dress pants, no shoes or socks.

Wait a minute!

He didn't go to frat parties anymore. Hadn't in years. He was married. Had kids. Shelley's and Samantha's faces swam in his mind's eye.

My God, where the hell am I? Liz'll be frantic.

He made a concerted effort to sit up. More pain, few other results. Another brief glimpse of hairy chest and gray pinstriped slacks. No belt. Okay, one more piece of information. A more lucid part of his mind realized that if he was this slow figuring out what was going on, he was going to die of old age first.

Die… something about death. Ed's death. Car blew up.

More fragments of memory drifted through his mind. Mac called. Working late. Fran brought him a ham sandwich. No, she brought the sandwich and then he was working late. Empty reception area. Throwing his cell phone across his office.

No, he'd only thought about doing that. Phone died. Couldn't call Lou. Have to get to a meeting… some kind of council. Kate's on the council.

Why are we on the same council?

He tried to think what he and Kate had in common that would put them on the same council. Had some clients in common.

That's it!

They were looking for clients they had in common.

The final wisps of fog cleared.

Holy shit! I've been kidnapped by the killer!

His brain commanded his body to jump up and run. His body tried to obey. He could feel his legs twitch. His torso raised up partway and flopped around. Then he fell off the cot onto his face.

Excruciating pain in his head. His right eye was squished against a hard surface.

After a moment, he opened his left eye. The hard surface was a concrete floor. He tried to roll his eyeball around to the left to see more. His head swam. He closed the eye.

Okay, message to neck muscles. Pull up from the floor and turn head. Rest side of head on floor… There, that's better.

He opened his eyes. It took his brain a moment to focus them both on the same spot–a dusty soup can, about eight feet away on a metal shelf. White, concrete block wall behind it.

Good. Okay, let's try the eye thing again.

He rolled his eyes to the left, saw something. Then a wave of dizziness forced him to close his eyes. But he had an image in his mind.

Boards. Wide, rough, wooden boards. Side by side. Other boards, running along them, every few feet, at right angles to the flat boards.

Joists.

Another part of his mind had provided the word, but he couldn't connect the dots.

Joists, joists…What are joists? Floor joists!

He'd been looking up at the underside of a floor. He was in a basement.

Hallelujah, maybe I'll get out of here before I'm ninety.

Eyes still closed, he had a short debate with himself. Should he try to move again or open his eyes first? Move first, so he was in a position to see more. Then open the eyes.

After several moments of concentration, he managed to get enough neural impulses going down the correct pathways to flop over onto his back. Knives of pain shot through various parts of his body. His skull throbbed.

He lay still, praying for the pain to end. Eventually it subsided. He opened his eyes. Cement wall to his left, cot against it, small window near the top. On the adjacent wall, shelves, dusty cans. Floorboard ceiling.

He couldn't see the other side of the room without turning his head. But his head hurt like hell and would hurt worse if he moved it. He was getting tired of pain.

Just move the eyes instead.

He rolled his eyes toward the right. Nothing but the floorboards above. He tried to roll them a bit further. The basement room spun, then blurred into darkness.

~~~~~~~~~~

Kate woke to the sound of soft snoring. Her legs were covered by a throw that usually resided on the back of the Franklins' family room sofa. Her father had also tucked part of it around Liz, who was curled up on the sofa beside her.

Another gentle snore. Near the slider, her father was sitting in a recliner that was *not* tilted back. But despite keeping the chair upright, he was sound asleep. Mac's long-barreled revolver, that Kate had given him, was resting in his lap.

There was a soft knock on the front door, then a faint voice. "Officer Hernandez, reporting for duty."

Kate gently slid out from under the blanket, trying not to wake Liz. She glanced at her watch as she headed for the door. Ten of seven. Remembering Rose's routine from the night before, Kate stood to the side of the front door and twitched the curtain aside to make sure it was Rose.

She opened the door and took in the young woman's disheveled uniform. Her throat closed. A wave of jumbled emotions swept over her. The only one she could identify was gratitude.

Rose turned around from locking the door and looked up into her face.

"Did you find him?"

Rose shook her head.

Kate struggled not to burst into tears.

After a moment, she said, "Are you going to get in trouble for reporting to duty looking..." She paused, unable to think of a diplomatic way to say that Rose looked like she'd been dragged through a sewer.

Rose smirked a little. "I think we've got an I-won't-tell-if-you-don't situation. Caught Jackson sleeping. Rapped on his window. Jerk jumped out of his skin."

"What did he say when he got a good look at you?"

"He leered at me and asked if I wanted to party with *him* tonight. Thought I'd been out on the town, I guess, and never made it home to change."

"Ick!"

"Yeah! I told him, when donkeys fly. Now I need a shower for two reasons."

"Where's the other officer?"

"In his cruiser further down the street. But we're vulnerable in the back of the house, without Skip or Lou."

Kate leaned closer and whispered, "And my father's not good at staying up all night at his age."

"I heard that, lass. I was just restin' me eyes." Dan was helping Liz around the corner. Her crutches were still missing in action. The haunted look in her eyes said she'd realized that if Rose had found her husband, she and Kate wouldn't be chatting quietly in the living room.

But Rose answered the unasked question anyway. "No, we didn't find him, but I did find something else interesting. Can we sit down?"

"Be with you in a minute, ladies. I think I'll check the house."

Kate muttered, "In case there were intruders while he was resting his eyes."

"I heard that, lass," her father called back over his shoulder as he headed for the stairs.

They moved into the family room, and Rose sank into a chair. "Found a big wheelbarrow, flipped over, in some tall grass at the back edge of the parking lot. Officers must have missed it in the dark last night. It was probably swiped from the construction site down the street. Used a stick to lift up one side. Grubby piece of cloth under it.

I'm thinking that if Rob was unconscious, the wheelbarrow may have been used to get him away from the building. I need to call Phillips and tell him about it, so he can send the crime scene techs out. But my brain's too tired to think of an explanation for how I discovered it."

"You could say you drove past the building this morning," Kate said. "Play the eager beaver rookie trying to impress the detective by checking out the scene on your own time. And while you're at it, pump him for anything the police have learned."

As Rose got out her phone, she gave Kate a tired smile. "You may not be a good actress, but you're great at writing the screenplay."

Kate attempted to return the smile without total success. She suspected it looked more like a grimace.

She walked across the room to use her own phone. There was no way she was going to try to see clients today. She left a message on the center's voicemail, asking Pauline to reschedule her appointments for that day. Then she added, "On second thought, I think I need to clear my schedule for the next few days. Tell them I have the flu. Thanks."

Rose was still on her phone. "Yes, sir... No, sir... Will do. Thank you, sir." She disconnected, then mimicked sticking her finger down her throat and gagging.

Kate managed a brief smile this time.

Before Rose could say anything, they heard tapping on the slider. "It's me, Skip."

Rose went over to twitch the drapes back and then let him in.

"Sorry, Kate. I was starting to walk into things," he said. "Figured I should report in and then get an hour or two of sleep."

"Of course." If the searcher wasn't offering news, they probably didn't have any, but she asked anyway. "Find anything?"

Skip shook his head. "Afraid not."

Liz sent him off to the kitchen to forage for food. When her father returned from checking the house, Kate motioned them into seats and nodded to Rose.

"Lou's awake, finally. His doc was apparently getting worried 'cause he was out so long. Took them several tests to figure out what drug had been used on him. It was an animal tranquilizer, for horses and cows. Unfortunately, Lou doesn't have a clue what happened. Said Rob called him and asked him to come up to the office and get him if he wasn't down by eight. Last thing Lou remembers is heading inside to do that, and being hit by a stun gun from behind."

Rose's jaw clenched. "But Detective Asshole's trying to get him to say it was Rob who stunned him. Said he's going to 'take another crack at the *retard*' when the doc thinks he's rested enough. Soon as this is over, I'm getting out of there, before I kill that man!"

"Gotta wonder how he's managed to survive this long," Skip drawled as he leaned against the doorjamb, sandwich in one hand, glass of water in the other. "Kinda surprised nobody's taken him out before now."

Validation from someone who'd only met Phillips once seemed to calm Rose down. She nodded sharply. "Lazy bastard's sending an officer down to check out the wheelbarrow, but he didn't sound too interested. Once the lab gets hold of it, maybe they'll find prints on it. No prints were on the briefcase but Rob's and his admin assistant's. She identified the suit jacket as his."

"Where's Mac?" Dan asked.

"I called him when I needed to head back here. He hadn't found anything. Told him we should come back and check in. He just growled and hung up." The last part was accompanied by an eye roll.

"Liz, call Mac and tell him to get his butt back here," Kate said. He wouldn't give Liz any grief. "You all need rest and refueling, and then we'll think about what to do next. And check on Ben, please, Liz. We may need him soon."

She turned back to Rose. "Thank you! Now get yourself one of those." She pointed at the remnants of sandwich in Skip's hand. "And there's a bedroom and bath down the hall next to the stairs. Shower and nap time."

"Can't sleep. I'm on duty."

"Rose, I don't have the energy to argue. We'll resist the temptation to tell your boss. Now go!" After another moment of hesitation, Rose went.

"Skip, I know you need rest too, but I have a couple questions for you first. You want another sandwich?"

"Good idea."

As they headed for the kitchen, they passed Rose, carrying an apple. "Too tired to make a sandwich," she mumbled, shuffling toward the back hall.

Kate sat down at the kitchen table as Skip got out bread and lunch meat. "Want one?" he asked.

Her stomach growling answered for her and Skip flashed her a quick grin. He constructed two huge sandwiches with meat, cheese, and tomato. Kate was grateful he didn't get out Rob's jar of pickles. She wasn't sure she could hold it together if he did.

He handed her a plate. She ate a bite of her sandwich, then asked, "How well do you know Lou?"

Skip grimaced. "Not that well. We don't hang out together outside of work."

"You don't like him?" She took another bite, realizing she was hungrier than she'd thought.

"It's not that… It just kinda bothers me that he reinforces the stereotype, you know, if you got muscles, then you can't have brains. Not that he can help it. He's not the brightest bulb on the Christmas tree. And he's from New Jersey yet, to complete the stereotype. 'Hey, what's youse guys doin' over dere?'" Skip mimicked Lou's accent.

Kate produced a faint smile.

"That sounds horrible, doesn't it? It's not the guy's fault."

"But working with him makes it harder to get people to realize you *do* have brains," Kate said.

Skip nodded.

"Do you think Lou's bulb is dim enough he'd get confused, if someone's trying to convince him something happened that didn't?"

Skip paused for a moment, thinking. "Doubt it. He's very honest, and loyal. And not really stupid so much as literal. Subtleties tend to go over his head. He's not going to say Mr. Franklin did something that didn't happen."

"First names all around, Skip. Less time consuming."

"Right, Kate. Lou's not going to get it if Phillips just hints around. And if he gets too blatant, Lou might take a swing at the jerk for insulting his boss."

"Phillips does seem to have that effect on people," Kate said. "By the way, I never thanked you for saving me from getting arrested."

"No problem." Skip flashed her a grin, then took another big bite out of his sandwich. They ate in companionable silence for a few moments.

"So how'd a big guy like you end up with the nickname Skip?" Kate asked, then quickly added, "Sorry, I'm being nosy." Her natural curiosity about people, that made her good at her job, sometimes got her in trouble socially.

Brushing slightly too long, brown hair back off his forehead, Skip replied, "No need to apologize. I get that question a lot. My full name is Reginald William Canfield, the third. Gramps was Reggie, my daddy was Bill, and my mother hated the nickname Trey. I guess when I was just a little babe, Skippy didn't seem like such a bad idea."

Kate swallowed her last bite of sandwich. "Okay, *Skippy–*"

"Now if you're gonna use that information against me, you need to keep in mind I'm a lot bigger'n you," he drawled, hazel eyes twinkling.

Kate grinned. "I'll bet you had more than your share of schoolyard brawls over your name."

"Oh yeah!"

She realized that for the last few minutes she'd forgotten to be tense. "Okay, you need some sack time, but Rose was pointing out we're getting stretched a bit thin. Can you get comfortable enough to sleep on the recliner in the family room? To cover that side of the house."

"I could probably sleep on a rock pile about now. But I wake up fast and hit the ground running, if need be. Adrenaline is a wonderful thing."

"Okay, we'll get everybody a bit refreshed and then…"

"Do you have a plan for what to do from here?"

Kate shook her head. "Best plan I can come up with right now is you all sleep while I pray."

CHAPTER TWENTY-TWO

Rob woke up on a cool floor. It only took him a moment to remember what had happened. He carefully lifted his head and looked around. His body was functioning better, his muscles actually listening to his brain.

The light from the window was brighter, midday maybe. Which meant he'd been here for at least a night and part of the next day. Liz would be frantic. He saw her in his mind's eye, and then Kate looking over her shoulder, both of their faces twisted with worry.

Tears sprang to his eyes as a wave of loneliness swept over him. He felt a pain in his heart and a knot in his stomach that had nothing to do with the gnawing hunger he'd noted a moment ago. Now he understood why it was called home-*sickness*.

Gotta get a grip or I'll never get out of here alive.

His head still hurt, but not as bad. His back stung but most of the rest of the pain had subsided. His stomach felt like there was a rat in it bent on escape by chewing its way through his abdominal wall. And he was extremely thirsty.

He sat up slowly and pulled himself awkwardly up onto the side of the cot. His head spun but only for a few seconds. He looked across the room. About twelve feet away was another wall, a door in the middle of it. Where the doorknob should be, there was a deadbolt lock, the kind that has to be opened with a key.

After a moment, he was able to coordinate the signals from his brain to his muscles in order to stand up and stagger over to the door. He knocked on its wood surface. Solid. Noticing a peephole, he ducked down a little and looked into it, but saw nothing. Then he realized he was on the wrong side of it.

It was there so his captor could look in at him.

The window.

He turned around slowly and studied it from across the room. At the top of the wall, just below the floorboard ceiling, it was about two feet wide and maybe nine inches high. Too small an opening to climb through even if he could get up there.

Could he break it? Yell to get somebody's attention outside? Seemed doubtful. The window looked like the ones he remembered from his grandmother's basement. A big block of glass the same thickness as a cement block, set into the wall to let light in but keep burglars out.

Rob looked down and noticed two objects on the floor, several feet from the door–an empty, metal bucket and a big china bowl next to it. A faint whiff of chicken emanated from the greasy liquid in the bowl, stirring up the rat in his stomach.

As it registered what the bucket was for, Rob realized he very much needed to utilize it. He did so.

Then he picked up the bowl. Shuffling carefully over to the cot, he sat down slowly. He didn't want to spill one precious drop. He raised the bowl to his lips and cool broth slid down his parched throat. Tilting the bowl up further, he used his fingers to shovel noodles and little bits of chicken into his mouth. It was cheap, canned soup, but it tasted wonderful. The rat in his stomach settled down.

When the bowl was empty he put it on the floor next to the cot, then leaned his head back against the wall to rest for a moment.

~~~~~~~~~~

Kate woke with a start, her father shaking her shoulder.

"Katie girl," he whispered. "Wake up, lass. I have me an–"

Skip sprang to his feet, pearl-handled pistol in his hand. When he saw there was no threat, the gun disappeared under his shirttail, tucked into his waistband at the small of his back.

Kate attempted to rub the grit from her eyes. "What time is it?"

"Almost eleven," her father said.

She glanced over at Liz. She was slumped at the opposite end of the sofa, but she was awake.

"I have me an idea, Katie–" Dan was interrupted again by tapping on the sliding glass door.

After checking to verify who it was, Skip let Mac in.

Rose came around the corner, silky, black hair hanging loose, still damp from the shower. The exhaustion in her face had been downgraded to just plain tired. Her uniform looked even worse for wear, since she now had slept in it.

Kate gestured everyone into seats and nodded to her father.

"Rosie lass," he began. Rose winced but didn't say anything. "I bin thinkin' 'bout what you said, that the killer might find me a tasty bit of bait. Couldn't we be turnin' the tables on the bastard now and use meself to draw him out?"

Kate started to protest but was shocked into silence by a glare from Liz.

Rob's voice echoed, *He's an adult, Kate. His choice.*

Great, now I've got two men talking to me in my head. Maybe she really was going crazy.

She decided to wait for Rose's input. As a trained police officer, she was better qualified to assess the suggestion. Kate prayed she would find a fatal flaw in it.

Rose thought about it while she methodically twisted her hair into a tight bun. "Might work," she finally said. "Go back to the area around the building. Killer may be waiting there expecting Kate to show up for work, or to look for Rob herself. You show a picture of Rob to passers-by." Her eyes swept over Mac and Skip. "We hang back, keep a sharp eye on him."

Skip and Mac were nodding.

Kate opened her mouth but Mac cut her off. "We ain't gonna let nothin' happen to Uncle Dan, sweet pea." His voice was uncharacteristically gentle.

She opened her mouth again, then abruptly closed it when a realization struck her. She hated it when they were overprotective of her, but here she was trying to keep her father from taking risks, a man who had survived sixty-eight years on this planet without her supervision.

As she was processing this disconcerting thought, Rose was saying, "Heck, we might even get lucky and someone will have seen something useful."

"Okay," Kate conceded defeat. "Dad shows Rob's picture around. Skip and Rose follow." She held up her hand as Mac started to protest. "They've had some rest. You haven't, and you look it."

She knew Mac would never agree to being excluded from the operation, and she wanted him there to help protect her father. But he was someone who stood out in a crowd when he *hadn't* been awake for over twenty-four hours. "I was going to suggest that you watch from a parked car. Pretend you're waiting for your wife or something."

"That's a good idea," Liz said. "Three people following Dan around on foot would be a bit obvious."

"How's Ben doing?" Kate asked her.

"He's on the mend. Said he could come back to work whenever we need him."

"Good, call him and get him over here. He can be our guard. Mac, you got something in your arsenal that Dad can carry? My gun's too big to put in his pocket."

Mac nodded.

"Rose, go get your civvies from your trunk. Mac, wait a few minutes–we don't want a parade attracting the attention of the officer outside–then get Dad a gun. Everybody reconvene in the kitchen in fifteen minutes. Scrambled eggs and toast all around, and no cracks about my cooking."

~~~~~~~~~

They were finishing their meal when a sharp rap on the front door made them all jump. They rushed into the living room, hoping for news of Rob.

Skip beat Rose to the door. He did the twitch-the-curtain routine, then opened the door.

Rose recognized the black officer on the porch. Calvin Young had his back to them, his eyes on the man standing on the sidewalk.

Ben, the bodyguard she'd met briefly on Saturday, was built like a grizzly bear, with dark hair and a beard to complete the image. He had a huge bottle of cough syrup tucked under his arm and was carefully holding his hands where the officer could see them.

Rose stayed well back, peering around Dan's large frame, since she was now out of uniform while on duty. She'd gone through the academy with Calvin Young. She'd always liked him, and her respect for him went up another notch as she watched him handle the situation.

His gun was in his hand, extended down along his leg, his finger hovering near but not on the trigger. "Mrs. Huntington, this guy says he's one of your private bodyguards reporting for duty?"

"That he is, Officer," Kate said.

"Sorry for the inconvenience, sir." Calvin holstered his gun.

"No problem, Officer. Reassuring to know you're on the job." Ben's voice rumbled with phlegm.

Rose and Skip exchanged a look. She nodded and he headed for the door. Since his replacement had arrived with such fanfare, he could walk right out the front. One less person who had to sneak out the back and risk drawing Calvin's attention.

Skip froze in the doorway. "Uh, oh, the press has arrived for their feeding frenzy." He stepped back so the rest of them could see.

News vans from most of the local stations were pulling into every available parking space near the house.

"I'll do my best to keep them at bay, ma'am," Calvin said quietly.

Kate thanked the officer. Skip left ,and she closed the door behind him.

The Franklins' landline rang. Kate raced into the family room and grabbed the portable out of its charger. She listened for a moment, then her face hardened. "No comment." She disconnected.

It immediately rang again. They dared not ignore it since it could be the kidnapper or Rob calling. As Rose followed Mac out through the back slider, she heard Kate say, "No comment. We need to keep this line open."

Twenty minutes later they were in position to begin what Skip had dubbed Operation Bait and Switch.

Dan walked up and down the sidewalk in front of Kate and Rob's office building, stopping people to show them a snapshot of Rob and asking in a booming voice if they'd seen the lad, who was a friend of his daughter's.

Skip and Rose followed at a distance on either side of the street, posing as just another shopper or office worker on a break. Their eyes constantly scanned the people near Dan. Mac sat in a parked car at one end of the block pretending to read a paper while his gaze never left Dan.

As Rose had coached him to do, Dan periodically went into the small park across from the building and asked anyone there to look at his picture. Then he sat down on a bench and hung his head down in apparent frustration and fatigue, the perfect inattentive target. Skip would disappear into the nearby bushes while Rose pretended to be strolling across the park, some distance away but on an angle where she could watch Dan out of her peripheral vision.

~~~~~~~~~~

Kate hung up on a reporter.

"Should we tell the media what's going on?" Liz asked, desperation in her voice. "Maybe go on TV and plead that the kidnapper let Rob go?"

Kate sat down beside her on the sofa. "I'm not sure that would do much good—"

The phone rang again. Yet another reporter. This one was a bit pushier than most. Before she'd finished her line, he said, "But the public has a right to know how the wife is holding up."

She was about to lash back with an angry retort when the phone beeped in her hand and then went dead.

Kate stifled the bubble of laughter in her chest, afraid it could all too easily turn into hysteria. She leaned over and put the phone back in its base. At least they would get a few minutes' reprieve while it recharged.

The doorbell rang. She got up to answer it, Ben following her. She stood back and nudged the curtain aside to peek out. Ben nodded in approval.

Officer Young was standing on the porch again, gun holstered but his hand on its butt. A rotund middle-aged man in an expensive business suit was standing at the bottom of the steps. Kate opened the door.

"Ma'am, his ID checks out. He said he's—"

"I know. He's Mr. Franklin's law partner. Hello, John. Come on in. Thanks, Officer Young."

John Bennett waited until she'd closed and locked the door, then he took both of her hands in his. "How's everybody holding up, Kate?"

"About as well as can be expected. Liz is in the family room." She led the way.

"I'll check the rest of the house," Ben said. Kate gave him a grateful smile.

Rob's partner sat down on the sofa next to Liz and patted her hand. "Bill and I are horrified by this, Liz. If there's anything we can do for you, let us know."

Liz nodded mutely.

Kate sat down in the recliner Ben had vacated. "Have you talked to the police, John? Do they have any leads?"

Bennett grimaced.

Apparently he's talked to Phillips.

"Yes, I've met with the detective in charge and I'm..." he glanced sideways at Liz, "...a little concerned."

"You don't have to mince words with us," Liz said. "We've been dealing with the man for weeks. He's a horse's patoot."

"Don't hold back now, Liz," Bennett gently teased his partner's wife. "Tell us how you really feel."

Liz managed a tiny smile.

"Okay, make that a lot concerned," Bennett said, his face now grim. "I know Dave Phillips, slightly at least. His son and my grandson are on the same Little League team. He and the boy's mother are divorced but he never misses a game. He's always struck me as a devoted father. So I was a bit surprised this morning when he interviewed me about Rob's disappearance. He didn't come across as very competent. Seemed to just be going through the motions."

"Did he say anything about his pet theory regarding my husband's death?" Kate asked.

"No."

She didn't even try to keep the sarcasm out of her voice. "He thinks Rob and I are lovers and Liz's hit-and-run was our attempt to get rid of her, but we were more successful with...." She turned her head away as tears sprang into her eyes.

John Bennett leaned forward to pat her hand, resting on her knee. "Ah, now the things Bill was spluttering about after his interview with Phillips make more sense. Apparently the detective was a bit more careful with what he said to me, maybe because we're acquaintances. But Bill said he was implying that Rob might have disappeared on purpose. Phillips told Bill to call him immediately if Rob contacted us to send him money."

Kate had also met Bill Stockton, the law firm's most senior partner, at social gatherings at the Franklins. He was in his mid-seventies and very old-fashioned, with a strong sense of honor. The insinuation that his law partner was an adulterer and murderer who'd skipped town would have made him absolutely apoplectic.

"Is there anything we can do to get Phillips pulled from the case, John?" she asked.

"I was giving that some thought on the way over here. I'm a defense attorney so the police don't exactly see me as their friend, but still I am not without influence in this town. I think I'll find out who his superior officer is and have a little chat with him, or her."

"That would be extremely helpful." Kate smiled at him.

"I just had another thought," Bennett said. "One of the few times Phillips and I have ever talked at any length was at one of the kids' games. We were standing on the sidelines during a lull in the action and somehow he got to talking about his divorce. Seemed really bitter toward his wife, and her lawyer. I opted not to tell him that I was a lawyer myself. He was rather shocked when he walked into my office this morning and recognized me."

"That would explain a lot," Kate said.

The phone rang. She answered it and went through her spiel. She'd no sooner returned it to its base then it rang again.

Bennett reached over and snatched it up. He listened just long enough to determine it was a reporter and then snapped, "Leave these poor people alone, you bloodsucker." He punched the end button. "I miss the good old days when you could bang a receiver down in someone's ear."

"Funny," Kate said, "I had that same thought the first time I talked to Phillips."

Bennett let out a short chuckle.

"John, do you think there's any way we can use the media coverage," Liz asked, "to help us find out what's happened to Rob?"

He sat back and gave that some thought. "Maybe. Let me talk to Phillips' supervisor first and see where that gets us. But if the police aren't going to work all that hard to track Rob down, maybe we could set up a hotline at the office and ask the public to call in if they know anything."

Liz's face brightened some. "That would be great."

Bennett patted her hand again and stood up. "I'll let you know what I find out."

"Thanks for coming by, John."

"I'll see you out." Kate got up and followed Bennett to the door. "John," she said quietly, once they were there, "I'm a little concerned about the media coverage. Whoever's doing this has made several attempts against me since Eddie's death. We think they kidnapped Rob to use him as bait to get to me." She dropped her voice even lower. "I'm afraid if the press makes too much noise about this, it may spook the killer and he'll decide to get rid of Rob and run."

"Dear God, I hadn't thought of that!" Bennett hooked the curtain aside with a pudgy finger and looked out at the small crowd of reporters on the sidewalk. "I think I'll have a little press conference here, as Liz's lawyer, and see if I can get these clowns to go away."

"How are you going to do that?" Kate asked.

"Tell them I'll keep them informed if, and only if, they go away and leave Liz alone. I'll get their names and contact information. Then if we decide to do the hotline, I'll be able to get in touch with them."

"Good idea." Kate took his hand. "Thank you so much, John."

After John Bennett's impromptu press conference, the calls from reporters tapered off.

A little before one o'clock, the phone rang for the first time in almost an hour. It was Bennett. "I just got back from meeting with a Lieutenant Cody in the homicide division," he told Kate.

"What'd he say?"

"Not much. He listened to my complaints about how Phillips has been handling the case, both your husband's death and now Rob's disappearance. Then he said he'd look into it."

"Did it seem like he was taking you seriously?"

"Hard to tell. He was pretty stone-faced. Cops don't like it when you complain about their brothers in blue. But my gut sense is that he's a good cop and he'll at least be keeping a closer eye on what Phillips is doing."

"Thanks, John." She disconnected and repeated the conversation to Liz.

Shortly after two, the phone rang again. This time it was Rose. She reported that she was sitting on a bench across the park from Dan. "No luck so far."

Kate told her about John Bennett's hotline idea and her own concerns about the media coverage.

"Worth keeping in mind, but I'm with you. It could spook the perp," Rose said. "I think we're going to move our operation around to the street behind your building. See if any of the people who come and go there on a regular basis have seen anything in the back parking lot that might be helpful."

Kate agreed with that plan.

~~~~~~~~~~~

They continued Operation Bait and Switch all afternoon, back and forth between the crowded sidewalks on either side of the building, with periodic stops in the park.

At six, when the evening rush hour of pedestrians was thinning, Rose strolled nonchalantly toward Dan's bench. She watched him out of her peripheral vision. He genuinely looked tired and depressed now.

Without breaking her stride or looking directly at him, she whispered, "You want to keep going?"

"Aye, lass," he said softly.

As she strolled on, she passed Skip coming the other way, hands in his pockets whistling tunelessly under his breath. They made eye contact for a second and Rose nodded as if she were just being pleasantly friendly to a stranger.

They finally had to stop when the summer sun had set and the growing dusk made it too dangerous to continue.

Back in Skip's truck, she called the Franklins' house phone. When Kate answered, Rose said, "No luck. We're coming in."

Silence, then a soft sob from the other end.

Rose's throat tightened. She disconnected.

CHAPTER TWENTY-THREE

Early Thursday morning, the occupants of the Franklins' house were startled awake by banging on the front door. Ben got to the living room first and went through the twitch-the-curtain routine. "Some guy in a suit. How'd he get past the officer on the street?"

Kate had a bad feeling. Rose stepped over to the other side of the door and moved the curtain aside. Her expression confirmed Kate's suspicion.

"Brace yourselves." Rose unlocked and opened the door.

Ben put his hand on his pistol. Kate caught the gesture and quickly said, "*Detective* Phillips, any news?"

Ben dropped his hand, letting his loose shirttail fall over his holster.

Kate said a quick silent prayer. *Dear God, please get us through this without somebody shooting this ass.* She doubted they'd be able to convince a judge it was justifiable homicide, even though it would be.

Phillips had one hand behind his back and a fake smile on his face. "Officer Hernandez, I'm impressed by your dedication that you would stay–"

Kate cut in, saving Rose from having to *act*. "Phillips, yes or no question. Have you found Mr. Franklin?"

"No, but we do have an interesting new development." Phillips pulled his hand out from behind his back. In it was a large, clear evidence bag.

Kate leaned forward and squinted at the green piece of silky fabric inside. It was a man's necktie, still loosely knotted in a big loop. On it was a pattern. Tiny, black scales of justice. She gasped.

Liz blanched and swayed on her feet. Skip caught her. Sweeping her up in his arms, he carried her to the living room sofa.

Kate turned back to the detective in time to catch the hint of a smirk on his face. Through gritted teeth, she said, "Phillips, whatever snide crack you're thinking, keep it to yourself, or someone in this room might just kill you."

"Is that a threat against an officer of the law, Mrs. Huntington?"

"No, it's a warning. Our nerves are strung out to their limit. It would not be wise to pluck them right now."

Phillips looked around at the tight faces of the men in the room. His Adam's apple bobbed in his throat.

Kate hid a smirk of her own.

He made an after-you gesture toward the armchairs at either end of the sofa. Kate took the one nearest Liz. She reached for her friend's hand and they hung onto each other.

Phillips took the other chair. Dangling the evidence bag in his hand, he said, "Do you recognize this tie, Mrs. Franklin?"

Tears were streaming down Liz's face. With obvious effort, she pulled herself together to answer him. Her voice was a raspy whisper. "Yes, it was a Father's Day gift...a few years ago, from the girls."

Kate had a flash of insight about why women *do* sometimes fall apart in a crisis, when they can't do anything but wait and worry. She filed it away for future contemplation and focused on Phillips.

"Went by your house this morning, Mrs. Huntington," he was saying. "This was hanging from your front door knob. It's got blood on it. What's your husband's blood type, Mrs. Franklin?"

Kate heard Liz choke on a sob. Fury was keeping her own horror and anguish at bay, for the moment at least. She flashed back to Rob's words from a few weeks ago. Something about wrapping his hands around this man's throat and squeezing until his eyes bulged out. She now shared the desire.

"O negative," Liz finally managed to whisper.

"Fairly rare," Phillips said. "Lab'll tell us if this is a match." He reached into his inside jacket pocket and pulled out another, smaller evidence bag with a piece of paper in it.

"This was pinned to the tie. Shall I read it to you?" He held up the clear bag. "It says, 'You come to me now, Bitch. When and where I say. Alone. Or he dies!'"

Liz gasped, tightening her grip on Kate's hand.

The room went fuzzy and tilted for a second. Kate closed her eyes and prayed she wouldn't faint.

Phillips was waiting for their reactions. When neither woman commented, he asked, "Any thoughts about who this might be from?"

Kate pulled herself together and stated the obvious. "From the kidnapper, of course. But it doesn't tell us much."

"Any other thoughts?"

No one said anything. They had thoughts but none they particularly wished to discuss in front of Phillips.

"This wasn't on your door when you left this morning, Mrs. Huntington?" he asked after a moment.

"I haven't been home since Tuesday evening," Kate said.

Phillips looked at the two big men standing behind her chair. "And your names are?"

"Skip Canfield. Ben Johnson," Skip answered for both of them. "Tanner Security and Investigations." His tone was calm, but Kate thought she detected an edge to it.

Phillips took out a notepad and wrote down their names.

He stood up. "Well, just wanted to keep you all informed. Let me know right away if the *alleged* kidnapper tries to contact you?"

Rose said, "I'll walk you out, sir."

~~~~~~~~~~

When they were by the door, Phillips asked in a low voice, "Has *she* had an opportunity to slip out and plant this?" He waved the evidence bag with the tie in it.

Rose pretended to give the idea some thought, then shook her head. "Somebody's been with her all the time, either me or her bodyguard."

"Yeah, but Franklin's paying him. He could be in on the whole thing."

"Sir," Rose whispered in her best differential tone, "would you let me know right away what the lab finds on the tie and note, and on the wheelbarrow. I'm betting one of *their* fingerprints will be on them." She pointed her chin toward the others.

Then she had another horrible thought.

She felt everyone's eyes on her as she conferred with Phillips a few more minutes by the door. Then she sketched him a small salute and opened the door for him. It was all she could do to contain her fury and play the deferential junior officer until he was out of the house.

She turned to the others. "I can't believe that man! He's convinced the note's a fake. Thinks one of you planted it."

She repeated the first part of her exchange with Phillips.

"Once again I must commend your acting skills, Rose," Liz said, sounding almost normal.

"Thanks. I'm hoping that'll spur him to get the tie and note to the lab. He should've done that right away, and taken pictures of them to show you all, instead of carrying them around in his damn pocket!"

She paused and, for the first time in days, a full-blown, dazzling smile spread across her face. "When this is over, I might just be able to get that man fired."

Skip's and Ben's mouths dropped open.

Mac glared at them, growling under his breath. Rose gave him a sharp look, one eyebrow in the air. He quickly looked away.

"Any ideas about the note?" Kate asked.

"Wait, there's more," Rose said. "It occurred to me Phillips might not be following procedure in other areas either, so I asked how the canvassing for witnesses was going. He said he wasn't wasting manpower on a fake kidnapping. So here's my thought, Kate. The note says to me that the perp's watching your house. I think we should move Operation Bait and Switch to your neighborhood and do our own canvassing. See if anyone saw anybody hanging around your house."

"Can I say something?" Skip asked.

"Of course," Kate said.

"Is it time to dump the idea of trying to get the perp to go after Dan. Just split up and do as much canvassing as possible."

"How about Mac stays with Dan," Liz said. "And Rose and Skip canvas on their own."

Rose nodded. Mac was so scruffy-looking, probably nobody would open their door for him, but if he hung back while Dan rang the bell and did the talking. Should work.

Kate seemed to hesitate. Then she said, "Okay, but you both stay close enough that you can get there quick if Mac and Dad need help. Everyone, synchronize your cell phones."

They all gave her a blank look. "Make sure you have everyone else's number in there, on speed dial. Dad doesn't have a cell phone so I'll give him mine. Put Liz's landline on speed dial as well. That's how you'll contact us."

Everybody exchanged numbers and punched buttons on their phones for a few minutes. Skip earned a few tension-breaking chuckles when he quipped, "Sorry, Mom, you're not my number one gal anymore."

"Skip, there's something you need to know," Kate said. "One of our suspects is a woman who's about five months pregnant. But you can't assume she'll be protective of her baby. There's a part of her that doesn't want the child. And if she comes after Dad, that means she's a killer and she has Rob."

She paused and looked around the room. "Are you all capable of doing what it takes to bring her down?"

Good question, Kate! Rose silently chastised herself for not thinking to ask it.

Total silence reigned for a moment.

"Dad?"

"I'd hate to hurt the babe, Katie, but if this is the person who has Rob and who took…" Dan stopped. Tears pooled in his eyes. He cleared his throat. "If she's who took *our* Eddie from us…." He turned his head away and swiped at his face with his shirtsleeve.

Rose looked down at the floor. She swallowed the lump in her own throat.

"Mac?" Kate said.

"I wasn't finished, lass. Even if it means I'll burn in hell for killin' an innocent babe, I'll not let this woman go loose to harm one hair on yer head. And I wanna see that strappin' lad of yours comin' back through that door, Liz."

After a beat, Mac said quietly, "'Bout says it all, Uncle Dan."

"Amen," Rose whispered.

"I'm not fond of the idea of tackling a pregnant woman," Skip said, "but if she's got Rob and has killed before, then we've got to stop her, bottom line."

Kate nodded. "All right, troops, let's do it."

~~~~~~~~

Liz had suggested the men rummage through Rob's closet and find some fresh clothing, so the people they approached would actually talk to them. She sent Rose to Shelley's closet.

Kate insisted everyone grab something from the kitchen that would serve as breakfast. Then one at a time, they slipped out the back slider.

Once they were all gone, the house was suddenly too quiet. Kate sat down at the family room table and prayed silently, *Dear God, keep him alive and help us find him.*

She glanced at Liz, who had hobbled over to the sofa. She was curled into a semi-fetal position, the leg brace forcing her to keep that leg straight. With her eyes closed, she looked almost like a sleeping child, if you ignored the haggard look on her face.

Ben was sitting in the recliner, back straight, handgun in his lap, alertly watching the sliding glass door. From the tilt of his head, Kate knew he was listening for sounds in the rest of the house as well.

She was trying to sort out the flash of insight she'd had earlier, but her brain was too tired to think. She crossed her arms on the table and rested her head on them, planning to get up in a minute and get herself something to eat.

~~~~~~~~~

Rob woke with a foggy head and a fuzzy tongue. It tasted like a platoon had marched across it, in muddy boots.

There was a fair amount of light coming through the little window. Daytime, but Rob had no idea anymore *what* day it was. The rat in his stomach had invited his extended family over to join the party.

He was sitting on the cot, leaning against the wall. Twice he thought, *I'm going to move now.* Nothing happened. His body once again was not responding to his brain.

His mind wandered to the discussion about Cheryl.

When was that?

Felt like over a week ago. Now her image swam into his mind's eye. A somewhat hard face, aged beyond her years, with bleached blond hair fluffed around it.

Couldn't be her. How could a woman, even one as big as her, drag around his dead weight? But then another mental image of Cheryl popped up, tall and robust in her waitress uniform, carrying heavy trays of thick china plates across a busy diner. She was no weakling, and she was smart. She was quite capable of figuring out some way to transport his inert body. No, it was not beyond the realm of possibility that his captor was Cheryl.

He thought about the peephole in the door, imagined Cheryl looking through it, watching him while he slept. Only the image in his mind wasn't the face he'd seen when they'd met to discuss her case–worried but determined. Now her expression was twisted, diabolical.

He lifted a hand to scratch an itch. It was not a very coordinated movement. His hand flopped around before finding its target. When fingers connected with bare skin and chest hair, he imagined that twisted part of Cheryl watching him now, staring through the peephole at his naked chest.

He felt exposed and shuddered with disgust. His cheeks grew hot with embarrassment. No more than that… It was a feeling he'd never felt before. He couldn't even come up with a word for it.

He fought the feelings, but his head was so fuzzy.

Why is my head fuzzy?

He tried to focus on that question. The feelings subsided some.

Good, think about that instead. Why… wait, what am I supposed to be thinking about? Oh yeah, why is my head so fuzzy?

His mind flashed to the china bowl.

The soup!

He'd been drugged again.

Then he noticed the bowl had been moved. It was now back by the bucket, near the door. His captor had been in the room while he slept. He shuddered again at the thought of Cheryl–that diabolical version of her–coming that close to him while he was out cold.

Maybe even touching me!

Another wave of emotion washed over him–helplessness, fear, and again the feeling he couldn't name.

And guilt. About what he wasn't sure. He just had this vague feeling that he'd done something, or failed to do something, that got him into this mess. He tried to figure out what that something was, then stopped himself. What he needed to figure out was how to get *out* of this mess.

There was a faint smell of beef in the air. His stomach growled and rolled over at the same time. He fought down nausea. There was no way he was going to eat or drink anything provided by his captor again. The rats in his stomach protested vehemently.

Got to get to the door. See if there's a way to get through it. He managed to stumble to his feet and stagger across the room. The door seemed sturdy, but he still might be able to break it down.

But how?

While he was thinking about that, might as well get the necessities out of the way. He opened his fly. It took a moment for a thin stream of urine to begin to flow into the bucket. Was he getting dehydrated?

He turned around too quickly and his head swam. *Gotta remember to move slow.*

His eyes fell on the cot. Maybe he could use it as a battering ram. Moving carefully back across the room, he tried to pick it up. It was heavier than he'd thought. He could only lift it a couple inches off the floor. Okay, using the entire cot as a battering ram wasn't going to work.

But if the thing was so damned heavy, maybe he could break loose a piece of it and use that instead. He slowly lowered himself to his knees and managed to tip the cot onto its side. No wonder it was so heavy, it was made of thick metal pipes.

The surface of the pipes was mostly rust. He pulled and tugged on all the joints, but they were welded together. He yanked on the pipes some more, sweat now stinging his eyes.

His right thumb connected with a sharp edge. A searing pain, and a small gush of blood erupted from the middle of the sensitive pad. *Shit!*

He sucked on the thumb. Couldn't afford to lose even a drop of moisture. Then he wrapped his other hand around it to apply pressure. After a few minutes, the bleeding had stopped, but the thumb hurt like hell.

With his other hand he shoved the cot in frustration. It only moved an inch.

"Can't give up," he said out loud, but his mouth was so dry it came out "ka-gib-uh."

A corner of the thin, grimy mattress was sticking out from beneath the side of the cot. Rob stared at the inviting triangle. He slowly stretched his sweaty body out on the cool floor, laying his throbbing head down on that corner of mattress.

Just need to rest awhile and think about what to do next.

CHAPTER TWENTY-FOUR

Kate startled awake when the phone jangled across the room. Liz struggled to sit up on the sofa and grabbed the portable from its charger on the end table. Kate raced over. Shoulders sagging, Liz passed the phone to her.

It was Rose calling in to say no luck so far. "We've covered the residential area near your house. I'm thinking we should head back over to the businesses in and near your building and talk to their staff. Someone might have been working late and saw something Tuesday night."

Kate agreed to the plan, then glanced at her watch as she hung up the phone. She'd slept for over two hours in that uncomfortable position, head on her arms at the table. Rolling her stiff neck, she shot a worried glance at Liz, already curled up on the sofa again. At least the press calls yesterday had given them something to do.

Kate headed for the kitchen and her delayed breakfast. She opened the refrigerator and stared into it, but her mind was pondering how both she and Liz were using sleep to escape. She knew she did that when she was depressed. She'd slept over fourteen hours a day the first two weeks after Eddie's death. But she'd never realized that she used the same defense mechanism when she was scared.

It hit her with a jolt that she'd never before been this scared for this long–not even when Mary was lying unconscious in the hospital. That had been more an intense gnawing anxiety. This was constant terror.

Kate closed the refrigerator and started to sit down at the kitchen table to digest that idea. She caught herself. Best not to sit down again to *think*.

Instead she leaned against the edge of the counter to sort out her thoughts. She was becoming increasingly worried about Liz.

Whenever there was something to focus on, something to do, she would rally and seem almost her normal self. But as soon as they were back to sit-and-wait mode, she would slide into a much more fragile state. And *fragile* was not a word Kate would have ever applied to Liz before Tuesday night.

She went back into the family room and sat down in the recliner. Ben was making a circuit of the house, checking for any signs of intruders.

"I had an interesting insight earlier today, and you know how I am," Kate said. "I sometimes need to process things out loud."

Liz swung her feet to the floor and sat up on the sofa. She gave Kate a sharp look.

"Okay, and I love to analyze everything to death. Occupational hazard, I'm afraid. So here's my insight. You know how some men, more traditional ones like my father especially, tend to assume women are going to fall apart emotionally in a crisis, so they try to protect us."

Liz nodded.

"What occurred to me earlier is that when the men try to protect us by not letting us do anything physically dangerous, they unintentionally make it more likely that we'll fall apart emotionally. When we're forced to wait and can't do anything, one, we have nothing to distract us, and two, we feel helpless. And that's the worst feeling for human beings to cope with. We can't stand not being able to *do* something. It's crazy-making. Is this making sense?"

"Yes. You're trying to tell me that if I don't come out of my stupor and do something, I'm going to go crazy," Liz replied.

Kate gave her a small smile. "Well, yeah, that's partly why I brought it up. But I also wanted a sounding board. I'm not saying it's the guys' fault. They've been raised that way. But it's a vicious cycle. He's protective, she can't do anything, she falls apart emotionally, and then he says to himself," she lowered her voice to a mock gruff tone, "'See, I was right to protect the little woman.'"

That actually got a faint smile out of Liz. "You notice Dan hasn't objected to Rose being out there in harm's way, but he probably would be if she weren't a cop."

"Yeah, it's okay for her to take risks when she's in uniform but not when she's in civvies would sound silly even to my father's ears." Kate chuckled. "Besides, I think he's a bit intimidated by Rose.

Short, reserved and voluptuous does not fit his stereotype of a female cop."

Liz snorted. "So what shall we do with ourselves to stay sane?"

Kate looked around the room, hoping for inspiration. Her eyes landed on the boxes Rose had put against the wall near the door Tuesday night. "The files. Let's go through them again, check out the suspects on your computer. Maybe we'll find something that jumps out as a big motive."

"Sounds good."

Kate dragged the boxes over to the table and pulled the likelies files out of one of them. She held up the top file. "We never did get Mac's report on Grandpa."

"Ah, speaking of a big motive," Liz said. "I found a newspaper article about his oldest granddaughter. She was killed in a boating accident last summer. He could be thinking he was cheated out of those last few years with her."

Kate nodded. "We'll put him aside for now though, until we get Mac's report. Let's take a look at these others."

She hesitated, then sighed and handed the Shirley sheet to Liz. "You might as well start with her. Her real name is Cheryl Crofton. Husband's name is Frank. See what you can dig up on them. I'm going to make us some sandwiches and then read through the likelies files again."

It was after three before Liz pushed back from her computer desk. She swivelled her chair around toward the table where Kate was reading files.

"Got something?"

"Not much really, after all that digging," Liz said. "They're both pretty broke. Routine deposits every Friday, no large withdrawals or big checks written. Only thing the least bit interesting is that the deposits stopped in the husband's account about two months ago. Could be he's cashing his paychecks instead of depositing them, thinking he can hide his assets from Rob's audit when it comes time for the property settlement."

"Or he could've lost his job," Kate said.

"The only other thing I found were the police reports for the domestic disturbance calls. There were forty-two of them total."

"Good heavens, they've only been married a little over two years. That's almost two a month."

"And the police would've only been called when it got really bad," Liz added.

"Yeah, there would've been a honeymoon period between each blow-up." At Liz's puzzled look, Kate added, "Guy beats the crap out of his wife, then feels at least somewhat remorseful and worries she'll leave him, so he tries to make it up to her, brings her gifts, promises to never do it again."

"And she believes him?"

"At first she does. He's back to being the guy she fell in love with, so she convinces herself it was all an aberration and it won't happen again. Then the tension starts to build up until he blows again."

"Doesn't she ever catch on that he *is* going to keep doing it?" Liz asked.

"Eventually, but by that time she's so beaten down and scared of him she's afraid to try to leave. Anything interesting in the police reports?"

"I just skimmed most of them, but there are a couple things. Some mention the wife going after the husband physically once the police arrived. One time, she had him up against the outside wall of the house, waving a kitchen knife in his face."

"Hmm, Cheryl never said anything about fighting back. But then she probably wouldn't if it was another alter who was doing that. She might not even remember it." Kate paused. "That confirms that the angry alter is capable of violence. But the thing I'm having trouble getting past at this point... Cheryl's a strong woman, but could she drag Rob around unconscious? Of course she might have knocked everybody else out and then forced him to go with her at gunpoint."

She wished she could take the words back when Liz cringed.

But then Liz straightened her shoulders and took a deep breath. "She could have an accomplice."

"Possibly. None of Cheryl's friends that I know of would be likely to join her in a crime spree. But sometimes the other alters have friends, or even romantic partners, that the host alter doesn't know about."

Liz nodded. "Other interesting thing about the police reports is that they confirm your assessment of the husband. The officers couch it in cop-eze but several of them imply that he's a wimpy dude who was trying to kiss up to them."

Kate thought for a moment. "Print out those reports for me. I'll read through them more thoroughly, in case there's anything else helpful in them. And then see if you can find out what these guys have been up to." She handed over several files she'd finished reading.

She sat down on the sofa with the police reports. After awhile, they began to blur together into one long, sad story of domestic violence repeated over and over again.

By dusk, when the troops came back to base, Kate had found nothing else useful in those reports, but Liz had found addresses for two of their suspects and had eliminated two others who were either in jail or dead.

~~~~~~~~~~

Liz laid out the makings for sandwiches on the family room table. Everyone gathered around and started constructing their dinners. Rose nodded to Skip that he should give his report first.

"Found a man who was cutting across the back parking lot of the office building Tuesday night," Skip said. "He saw a big vehicle toward the back of the lot. Somebody was stuffing a large bulky object into the back of it. But it was too dark back there for him to make out any details. He thought maybe it was something the guy had stolen so he decided not to get too nosy. Just put his head down and kept walking fast."

"But he thought it was a man?" Dan asked.

Skip shook his head. "When I pressed him on that, he admitted he couldn't really tell if it was a man or woman. He mainly saw shadows and movement."

"Don't really tell us nothin' new," Mac grumbled.

Rose silently agreed. It only confirmed what they'd already suspected.

They all settled into seats, balancing plates on their laps. She gave them her report. "Talked to Beth Samuels, Rob's paralegal. She thought she smelled beer Tuesday night, when she was standing by a printer out in the common area. Said she was wondering if Tim Williams was having a solitary pity party in his office. Next thing she knew she woke up on the floor with a bad headache. According to the firm's grapevine, Williams' days there are numbered. He was the lawyer who said he'd been Tasered before he was knocked out."

"Could he have faked that?" Kate asked.

Rose had already had that same thought. "It's possible. I left a message for the officer I talked to Tuesday night. We'll see what he remembers about the guy's injuries. Might have to track down the paramedics who were there."

"If Rob was about to fire him," Kate said, "that might give Williams a motive to harm him. Wouldn't explain the attacks against me, or the note, but…"

"We have to follow all leads," Skip finished for her.

Rose's cell phone buzzed in her pocket. She put aside her half-eaten sandwich and answered it. It was the officer who'd been on the scene Tuesday night. What he had to say did not surprise her.

She disconnected. "Williams refused treatment, so we got nothing but his say-so that he was hurt."

"He could have knocked out Beth and Lou," Kate said. "Then overpowered Rob and stashed him somewhere, maybe in his vehicle. Then came back inside and faked his own injuries."

"Still don't explain why he'd go after you, sweet pea," Mac said. "And all this started two, three months ago."

Liz picked up on his train of thought. "It's unlikely he would have been given notice that long ago that he was going to be fired."

"Unless he was put on probation about then," Skip said.

"I can call Fran," Liz said. "Find out what she knows about all that."

Kate nodded. "And do a background check on him. Maybe he'll turn out to have some connection to one of our other suspects."

Kate remained on the sofa as most of the others trudged off to bed. Rose felt bad for her. Fatigue and worry had etched new lines in the woman's face.

Skip went to the table and made another sandwich. He carried it over and offered half to Kate. She shook her head. He sat down in the recliner.

Rose decided to check in with Phillips. She got his voicemail and left a kiss-up message. Then she called the lab directly, hoping they would give a lowly rookie the results on the note and wheelbarrow. In case Phillips had already gotten the report, she told the lab tech she was calling on behalf of the detective, to clarify the results. The tech bought it.

She listened, then disconnected and went over to sit next to Kate on the sofa.

"No prints on the wheelbarrow, tie or note. On the wheelbarrow, that's significant. It should be covered with prints from the construction workers. Somebody wiped it down. Cloth under it was part of a torn dress shirt."

Kate nodded. "So that was how they got Rob away from the building. Maybe dragged him partway, to where they'd stashed the wheelbarrow, and his shirt got torn. Then they used the wheelbarrow to get him to their vehicle in the back of the parking lot. Doesn't make sense though, that they wiped the prints but left the shirt?"

"Perp may have left it on purpose, like the tie," Skip said. "To show us they have Rob."

Kate thanked Rose for the information, then got up and headed for bed.

Rose watched her slumped shoulders go around the corner. She was glad she hadn't told Kate the lab tech's exact words. He had said *shredded*, not *torn*.

"Blood on the shirt?" Skip asked, keeping his voice low.

Rose nodded. "O negative. Same with the tie."

"If it's Williams, the kidnapping could be a ruse to make it look like it's tied to the other attacks. In which case, Rob's already dead."

Rose pressed her lips together and nodded again.

~~~~~~~~~~

Rob woke shivering on the floor, a cramp in his gut.

Oh, great. Now I'm getting sick.

He'd been scared all along, since the moment he'd realized he'd been kidnapped, but now it really hit him.

I'm gonna die in this basement!

Heart pounding, he struggled to fight down the terror. He had to find a way out of here.

He carefully got to his feet and shuffled to the door in the fading light. There was a plastic water bottle sitting next to the bowl of soup. Leaning against the bowl was a piece of paper with *EAT* written on it.

Guess Cheryl doesn't like it that her boy toy might prefer starvation to being her captive.

He looked longingly down at the water bottle. His mouth was so dry, it felt like he'd been chewing on cotton balls. Then he averted his eyes from the bottle and concentrated on examining the door again.

Although it was solid, the frame looked flimsy. Maybe he could use a brace from the shelves as a makeshift crowbar and break up the doorframe enough to pry the door open.

He felt his way over to the shelves in the growing darkness. They covered most of the wall and were probably once filled with a frugal homemaker's stock of canned and dry goods. Now they held just a few dusty cans. He started tugging on the thin metal braces between each shelf and the metal uprights, looking for one that might be loose.

The room was soon completely dark and he was debating whether to keep working when a flash of light streaked across the top of the wall.

What was that?

A moment later, the light appeared again, swung in an arc over his head, and then was gone, leaving the room even blacker until his eyes readjusted.

Headlights!

The lights from passing cars were shining through the little window.

He grabbed a brace as the next car went by, then tugged and pulled on it in the dark until another set of headlights showed him where the next brace was. It was slow going.

As the room returned to inky darkness after a flash of light, he banged his sore thumb against a bolt on the shelves. Pain shot up his arm. He put the thumb in his mouth and tasted the metallic saltiness of blood. With nothing else to press against the wound, he once again wrapped his other hand tightly around the thumb to stop the bleeding.

Afraid of doing himself further injury in the dark, he decided he might as well get some rest. But the thought of his captor coming in while he slept made him shudder.

Inspiration struck. He waited for the next set of headlights to show him where the metal bucket and bowl were. Then he placed the bucket on top of the bowl so that someone opening the door would knock it over. The noise should wake him up.

His spirits brightened a little. Even as weak as he was, with enough adrenaline pumping and the element of surprise, he just might be able to overpower his captor.

Wrestling the cot upright, he sat down on it. Best not to lie down. In such a small space, his captor would be on him before he'd be able to get up. He leaned his sore back carefully against the cement wall.

He was jolted awake again by a cramp in his gut. Doubled over on the cot, he gritted his teeth until it started to ease.

Eventually he was able to sit up. The bucket was where he'd put it, on top of the bowl. Light was filtering through the window. Morning, or daytime at least. His captor had not returned last night.

He tried to stand and almost fell on his face. Once again, his muscles weren't responding well to neural impulses. That didn't make sense. He hadn't been drugged in at least twenty-four hours.

He managed to get himself upright. Moving carefully, he made his way over to use the bucket. A thin trickle of dark yellow urine was all he could produce.

Not good. When your body stops making urine, you are seriously dehydrated. Was that why his muscles weren't behaving themselves? He looked longingly down at the water bottle.

Wait! If the cap's still sealed then it's probably safe to drink.

He picked up the bottle and gently turned the cap. It came right off. The little plastic ring gave no resistance since it had already been broken free of the cap.

Shit!

For one moment of excruciating temptation he held that open bottle of tainted water. He could almost feel the wetness sliding over his dry tongue and down his parched throat.

If he drank it, he would be totally helpless. The killer could do whatever he wanted to him.

Or whatever she wants....

He shuddered. "No!" he roared and threw the bottle across the room. It rolled under the cot, most of its contents spilling out on the floor.

Okay, I've got to get out of here. Now!

He stumbled over to the shelves and frantically went over them again. He found a bolt that was a little loose. Awkwardly, he struggled to unscrew it with his left hand. It took awhile but he finally got it out, freeing one end of the brace. He bent the brace back and forth repeatedly, stopping a few times to rest. Eventually the metal snapped at the other end.

Eureka!

If he couldn't get the door open, he might pretend he was asleep and, when his captor came in, use this as a weapon. With a Plan A and a Plan B, he felt better.

Back at the door, he attempted to jimmy the lock with the makeshift tool. No success. He jammed the metal strip between the door and frame. Working it around in the narrow space, he tried to get some leverage against the frame. He listened for a cracking noise that meant the weak wood was starting to give.

It didn't happen. He paused to catch his breath, then tried again. Nothing.

He kept at it for five, ten minutes at a time, stopping when his starved and thirsty muscles began to quiver. Then he would rest and try again. At one point, he thought he felt the wood beginning to give. He renewed his efforts.

The strip of metal broke, one half still between the door and its frame, the other stubby, useless end in his hand. He leaned his forehead against the doorjamb. He didn't even have the energy to swear.

Stumbling back over to the cot, he laid down. The cramping in his abdomen was now a constant companion. He turned over on his stomach, hoping to find a position that would ease the pain in his gut. His left hand dangled off the side of the cot and connected with the plastic bottle lying on the floor.

Despair and temptation joined forces. Lifting the bottle carefully, he rolled over and poured the few remaining tablespoons of liquid into his dry mouth.

Sighing, he stared at the ceiling, his mind empty. Eventually he drifted off to sleep, wondering if he would wake up again.

CHAPTER TWENTY-FIVE

When Kate woke up in Shelley's bed on Saturday morning, she wasn't sure if it *was* Saturday. She sure hoped it was because she'd only had Pauline reschedule her clients until the end of this week, or last week if they had somehow managed to slip into the next week. Okay, now she was *really* confused.

She realized she didn't really give a damn if a client was sitting at the center waiting for her. Sally and Pauline would just have to deal with it. Her priority was finding Rob.

A wave of fear washed over her. She stared at the ceiling, her heart thudding in her chest. It had been more than three days. With every passing minute the chances of finding him alive diminished. Fear morphed to terror. Adrenaline shot through her system, making her want to jump out of bed and run around the room, screaming.

She made herself take a deep breath. Running and screaming wouldn't help. She needed to think. She started mentally reviewing everything they'd tried so far. Was there something they'd missed?

The Williams lead. Fran had confirmed that he'd been on probation for almost three months, but at the times when most of the earlier incidents had occurred, he'd been working. On Memorial Day, when Mary was attacked, he'd been at a family reunion in Ocean City, on the opposite side of the Chesapeake Bay. Rose and Skip had spent part of the previous day verifying those alibis, and a computer search had revealed a mundane life with no apparent connections to their other suspects. The young lawyer had been bumped down their suspect list.

Yesterday afternoon, after checking Kate's house for new notes from the kidnapper, Rose and the others had extended their canvassing to a five-block radius around the office building, hoping to stumble on someone who had seen something helpful. They hadn't.

The previous day she'd finished re-reading the likelies files while Liz probed cyberspace for information on their top suspects. They'd downgraded a couple cases and eliminated a few others. The likelies pile was now down to six cases, and they had current addresses on all but one of them. He was one of their strongest suspects. She intended to send Mac out today to track him down.

By process of elimination, Cheryl had risen toward the top of the suspect list. With Lou recovered enough to return to duty, she'd assigned Ben–the only one of them whom Cheryl wasn't likely to recognize–to tail her.

Kate had toyed with the idea of calling Cheryl to see if she could probe a bit, under the guise of checking on her client while she was out sick. But she'd decided against it. If one of Cheryl's alters was the perpetrator, such a call might alert that alter to their suspicions and spook her, which could have disastrous repercussions. Surveillance was the better way to go. So far, however, Cheryl had only gone back and forth between work and home.

Grandpa had been bumped down the list a bit for now. Mac had been watching him water his garden, ten miles beyond Hagerstown, around the time Rob was kidnapped. Skip had pointed out that the old man could have hired someone to do his dirty work while he stayed home to establish an alibi. Liz was going to do some digging today to see if he had the means to hire a hit man.

Rumbling in her stomach was followed by a wave of mild nausea. Better feed the baby in her belly soon or she would be sick. She dressed quickly and went downstairs to gather everyone for a war council over breakfast.

Liz had risen early and had already been at her computer for a couple hours. While they fueled up on the bagels and fruit she'd laid out on the table, she filled them in on Grandpa's finances. "He's living on Social Security and regular withdrawals from a savings account. But I found another account, at a bank near where his daughter lives. It was opened thirteen years ago in his and the granddaughters' names."

"A college fund maybe," Kate said.

"Probably. Over the years he added money to it until it totaled almost ten thousand dollars. After the oldest granddaughter's death, he closed the account and transferred eight thousand into his regular savings account. It's still there. But I found no trace of the other two thousand dollars."

"You can hire muscle on the street for a couple grand," Skip said. "But it's not enough for a professional hit man, someone who actually knows what they're doing."

"This guy's a control freak," Kate said. "I don't see him hiring some lowlifes on the street and then staying home, trusting them to do the job right. He'd be there supervising. However, he's got a strong motive, so I think we'll keep him at the bottom of the likelies pile for now."

"Is it time to try John's hotline idea?" Liz asked.

Kate wasn't sure. She turned to Rose.

"Maybe," the young woman said. "It's been long enough now that the perp would be feeling more confident. Going to the press to ask people to call with info would likely be seen as an act of desperation."

Kate grimaced. *That's because it is.*

"I agree," Skip said. "Perp's probably congratulating himself, or herself, that they've gotten away with it. They'd see Rob's partner setting up the hotline as a sign that we've lost all confidence in the police."

This time Kate gave voice to her thought. "Because we have."

"I'll call John and set it up." Liz got up from the table, her breakfast half eaten.

"Ask their staff to call here with anything that sounds promising," Kate said. "If we agree it's worth pursuing, we'll pass the lead on to you all in the field."

Rose and Skip both nodded.

When the others had finished their breakfast, Kate sent them off to the closets again for fresh clothes. Mac returned in a few minutes wearing a shirt two sizes too big. Kate handed him a sheet of paper. "Here's all Liz could find on this guy. See if you can track him down?" She gave Mac a quick summary of the case.

Richard Wagner was a sexual abuser who'd gone to prison a few years ago, but was now out on parole. When Kate's client had gotten up the nerve to turn in her former high-school softball coach for molesting her, Rob had met with her to give her an idea of what would happen when she testified in court. Then he'd gone with her to meet with the police.

After the press got wind of the case, several other young women had also come forward with similar stories. Nonetheless, Wagner had blamed all his problems on the "damn shrink" who'd supposedly planted ideas in his former star player's head, and the "shyster lawyer" who'd encouraged her to report him. He had vowed vengeance on them for ruining his life.

"I'm on it." Mac headed for the slider, as the others returned in fresh clothes that more or less fit them.

"Rose, we've got addresses on Lennox and Marshall," Kate said. "Maybe you and Skip should check them out this morning."

Rose thought for a moment. "They weren't super strong suspects as I recall, were they?"

"No. I actually considered bumping them down to the possibilities pile."

"Then let's save them for this afternoon. First, I want to check your house, see if the kidnapper's left any more notes. Then I think we should canvas around your office building again. Workaholics who're in their offices on a Saturday morning might have been working late on Tuesday. I also want to talk again with any of Rob's staff who're in today. Sometimes people remember something later that turns out to be significant."

Skip nodded his agreement. "Somebody else may have seen something in the parking lot or around the building Tuesday. I'd love to get a lead on that vehicle."

That sounded like a long shot to Kate, but she didn't say anything.

Skip guessed her thoughts. "You'd be surprised how stupid criminals are. This bozo may very well be driving his own truck or van, with his own plates on it, and his address is listed big as you please down at the MVA."

Rose's eyes lit up. She turned to him. "You were you on the job, weren't you?"

"Eleven years. State trooper."

The tightness in Kate's chest—a constant companion for the last few days—loosened a bit. With two trained police officers looking for clues, there was a glimmer of hope that they might just find Rob, before it was too late.

"Mr. O'Donnell," Rose said, "it would really be better if you stayed here today. Skip and I can move faster on our own."

He opened his mouth, then seemed to reconsider. After a beat, he said, "Maybe I could go help Ben. Keep me eye on this Shirley gal so he can get a bit a rest?"

Kate turned to Rose. "Should be okay," the latter said. "If you stay in the car with Ben. I'll take you over and swing by for you later."

Kate had a short internal debate. She'd been toying with putting her father on guard duty today here at the house and sending Lou to watch Grandpa. But Ben hadn't had any relief in over twenty-four hours and Cheryl was one of their strongest suspects. If he fell asleep and she got away from him, Rob could end up dead because they'd missed that opportunity to follow her to him.

Suddenly the burden of command weighed heavy. "Okay," she finally said. "Be careful."

After they left, Kate sat down hard in a chair at the table, struggling to keep the fear at bay. A wrong decision could cost her dearest friend his life. He would be wiped off the face of the earth–as Eddie had been–lost to her and his family forever. She fought the urge to sob hysterically, to shriek at the ceiling. She was afraid if she started, she would never stop.

Liz was watching her from across the table, concern in her eyes. Kate struggled to pull herself together. She had to *do* something.

She had planned to spend today re-reading the possibilities files, to make sure nothing had been overlooked. But first she pulled the sheet labeled *Joe* from one of the boxes under the table. "Liz, can you find out if this guy has any arrests or complaints against him for violence?" She gave her Jim's real name and some background information on him.

"This could take awhile. Rose could probably get the info in minutes, but I'll have to go into the police records in all the counties and Baltimore City." Then Liz shrugged. "It's not like I've got anything better to do at the moment." She pushed up from the table and hobbled across the room to her computer.

That can't be good for her healing bones.

Physical action had more appeal than reading right now, so she set out to find Liz's crutches. She was only able to locate one of them, behind the family room sofa.

As she leaned it against the computer desk, Liz murmured, "Thanks," then went back to scrolling down her screen.

After bumping several files down to the unlikelies pile, Kate's eyes were starting to cross from reading. Deciding to check on the troops, she went over and dropped onto the sofa. The phone rang just as she reached for it.

It was Fran. "Got something that sounds promising, or at least should probably be checked out. This woman wouldn't give her name, but she said she saw a guy who looked like Rob down in Mt. Vernon, walking with another man, near the monument."

"Okay, I'll pass that on. Has that been the only call?" Kate hoped she'd managed to keep the disappointment out of her voice.

"Heck, no. Phones have been ringing fairly steady the last half hour, since the noon news. But most are totally off the wall. Either so vague or so crazy, they aren't helpful. Like the guy who said he saw Rob being abducted by an alien spaceship Wednesday morning, from a field in Carroll County."

Kate snorted, then asked, "How vague is vague?"

"Very, as in they don't really know anything. They just want to be part of the excitement and feel important."

"Got it. Thanks for doing this, Fran."

"No thanks necessary. I adore Rob…." Fran cleared her throat. "I'm glad I can do something to help, and so is the rest of the staff. Pauline's here, too, answering phones."

"Tell them…" Kate's own throat closed. Her eyes stung. "Tell them that they're all wonderful people," she finally managed to get out.

"I will. Hang in there, Kate." Fran disconnected.

She took a moment to collect herself, then she called Rose.

"No note at your house," Rose said, "or any other sign that the perp's been around there. Only one neighbor reported seeing anyone. Short, stocky guy in a suit knocked on your door earlier this morning."

"Phillips."

"Yup. I'm at Rob's firm now."

"Go see Fran. She's got a lead for you from the hotline."

Kate disconnected, then called her own cell number. Her father answered and whispered that Shirley was at work. They were in the diner parking lot, and Ben was having a wee nap in the backseat of the car.

As she disconnected, Liz said, "Nada on your guy. No complaints or arrests."

"Thanks." Kate took the Joe sheet to put it in the possibilities section of the box. Then she carried several files over to Liz. "See what you can find on these guys."

Kate went back to reading files.

Two hours later, she had passed along several potential leads from the hotline to Rose and Skip, and she and Liz had narrowed the possibilities pile down to ten cases. Liz had tracked down current addresses for them.

Kate dropped the last file she'd been reading into the box at her feet and sat back in her chair. She had no idea what to do next.

Why hasn't the kidnapper contacted us again? What if Rob's already dead and his body's hidden somewhere, the killer long gone?

Kate struggled to push that thought, and its attendant array of overwhelming feelings, out of her mind.

Liz broke into her reverie. "Now what do we do with ourselves?"

Kate glanced at her watch. It was only a little after two. She shrugged. "I'm fresh out of ideas."

"How about a jigsaw puzzle," Liz said. "Samantha has a bunch of them. That would keep us occupied for awhile."

"Beats staring at the walls."

And conjuring up horrible scenarios.

Twenty minutes later the phone rang. Kate got there first since a glare from her caused Liz to stop and grab her crutch. It was Fran with another lead. A bit of a long shot but probably worth pursuing. She called Rose and gave her the information.

Kate and Liz spent the next few hours alternating between trying to focus on the puzzle and answering the phone. Kate had brought the portable over to the table. Most of the calls were from Fran. Kate passed the more plausible of the possible Rob sightings on to Rose or Skip.

One call was from John Bennett. He had been calling or stopping by at least once a day to check on them. He too expressed gratitude that they were able to do something to help.

Kate thanked him, then went back to filling holes in the picture of a running horse evolving on the table.

~~~~~~~~~

Gray light filtered through the window.

Rob's head ached. He drifted in and out until a cramp ripped through his gut. When the pain finally eased, he told himself he should get up and do something. But he had no idea what. He'd tried everything he could think of.

His body felt so heavy. His brain was numb. Images swam into his mind's eye. Liz's face crumpled in grief, his daughters holding each other and sobbing. Kate with that same stunned look she'd had the day Ed died.

He told himself he owed it to them to keep trying to escape. Still he didn't move.

Something about Kate was nagging at the edges of his tired brain. He closed his eyes, praying for sleep, or better still… His eyes flew open.

Kate!

The killer was keeping him alive as bait to lure her to him. If he didn't get out of here, she could end up dead.

He pushed himself up to a sitting position on the edge of the cot. The room was spinning. He focused on the doorknob, or rather the deadbolt where the doorknob should be. After a few minutes, the spinning slowed and his vision cleared.

A surge of determination had him up and stumbling across the room. Where had the metal shelf bracket gone? Then he remembered it had broken off. He saw half of it on the floor. Leaning over to pick it up, he almost nose-dived into the smelly bucket.

More carefully, he crouched down and retrieved the strip of metal, then managed to get upright again. He tried to work it into the crack between the door and frame. It was too short. His thumb throbbed with renewed intensity.

His forearm against the door, he hung his head and stared at the floor for a moment. His eyes stung, but there was no moisture for tears. He beat his other fist feebly on the wall next to the door, once, twice, in slow motion.

Rage at his captor exploded in his chest. He swung his arm back and slammed his fist against the wall.

The fist went through it, all the way up to his shoulder.

He froze, stunned, his mind trying to process what had just happened.

Slowly he pulled his arm back out and looked through the hole. Dim light, gray walls. The rest of the basement. At the far end was another glass block window and three cement steps leading up to old-fashioned basement doors, the kind that push upward.

He wasted only a second berating himself for not checking out the wall sooner. What could he use to break through it?

The bucket!

He picked it up and put both fists inside, oblivious to the urine that spilled down the front of him. He rammed the bottom of the bucket against the wall. Wallboard broke loose and fell away.

Within a few minutes, he had knocked out a sizeable hole between the two-by-fours that served as studs for the poorly-constructed wall. He squeezed through it, then stumbled across the basement and scrambled on hands and knees up the steps below the doors.

He stood up carefully. Now was not the time to lose his balance and end up unconscious on the basement floor. A metal latch on the doors held them firmly together. Praying they weren't locked from the outside, he opened the latch and pushed. The doors moved upward a bit and a sliver of grayish light shone between them.

Thank you, God!

He shoved with both hands on one of the doors. It flipped open, clanging against the ground outside. Rob scrambled out.

Shielding his eyes until they adjusted to the light, he tried to figure out what time of day it was. The overcast sky gave him little to go on. It could be any time from morning to dusk.

What the hell was he doing standing here? He needed to get away.

He staggered out into an alley and down it to a street. It was lined with red brick row houses, their marble stoops grayish-white in the gloomy light.

Baltimore City, his mind registered. The city was well known for such neighborhoods of solid working folks.

He lurched toward some people on the sidewalk down the block, but as he approached, they averted their eyes and moved out of his path. He reached out to the nearest one.

The man jumped back.

Rob staggered forward. "Please help me!" But the sounds coming out of his dry mouth were "iz el mm."

The pedestrians gave the shirtless, incoherent man, reeking of urine and sweat, a wide berth.

~~~~~~~~~~

Just before six, the phone rang again.

"Found the bozo," Mac said. "Didn't try too hard to cover his tracks. He's in Pennsylvania. Runnin' a summer camp."

Restless, Kate got up and paced across the room. "He must have charmed them so they didn't check his credentials very carefully."

"It's over two hours, here to Towson. Be hard for this guy to be watchin' you and Rob. He's been at work every day. Camp counselors say he's breathin' down their necks all the time."

"So Wagner's probably not our perp." Kate dropped down onto the sofa. "How about calling in an anonymous tip regarding his whereabouts, then come on back."

"Will do. See ya in a bit."

The phone rang the second after Kate disconnected. She jumped a little.

It was Fran. "Calls are beginning to taper off. Hopefully it's been a slow news day and they'll run John's press conference appeal again tonight. But I've got one lead that sounds promising." She gave Kate the information.

Kate called Rose with the lead, then dropped the phone on the sofa as she picked up the TV remote from the end table. Liz joined her. They waited impatiently through the six o'clock news for coverage of the press conference.

Luck was not with them. The Baltimore metropolitan area had had its usual violence-prone Saturday. The litany of gory homicides and other crimes pushed Rob's disappearance to the end of the program. There was no footage of the press conference, only a few seconds of Rob's picture as the anchorwoman asked anyone who had any information to call the number on their screen.

Discouraged, Kate and Liz got up off the sofa and went back to their puzzle.

~~~~~~~~~~

Rose and Skip drove to West Baltimore in Skip's Explorer. This was the most promising lead they'd received so far from the hotline. A man answering Rob's description had been seen staggering down Monroe Street, mumbling incoherently. The woman who'd called it in had said that at first she'd assumed he was a homeless drunk, but then she'd remembered the story from the noon news.

Skip parked his truck. They got out and started knocking on doors, dragging people away from their suppers to shake their heads at the photo of Rob.

~~~~~~~~~~~

Rob stumbled down yet another street, trying to tell those he encountered who he was and what had happened. But his words came out as nonsense syllables, and everyone veered away from him.

A cramp in his gut forced him to sit, doubled over, on one of the small marble porches. As the cramp was easing, the overcast sky opened up. Rob raised his face blissfully to the cooling rain, then leaned back and opened his mouth to catch the raindrops.

A sound behind him. He twisted around. A woman, in house dress and curlers, was looking out at him through her screen door.

Rob reached out a hand to her as he tried to stand up.

She screamed.

The world tilted. He sprawled across the gleaming marble.

If the woman had said, "There's a man lying unconscious on my front stoop," the dispatcher would have sent an ambulance as well as the police. But when she said, "There's a drunk passed out on my front stoop," the dispatcher relayed the message to the beat cop.

The beat cop arrived, saw what he expected to see and radioed for the prisoner transport wagon. When the van pulled up, the driver got out and helped the beat cop lift and shove the semi-conscious man into the back of it.

"He's a big un," the driver grunted. He closed and locked the door.

"Can't have been on the streets too long," the beat cop said. "He's still got a good bit of flesh on him. Usually these guys are pretty scrawny, and they're wearing layers of old clothes, not half naked."

"Might not be homeless. Maybe he had a fight with the missus, went out and got stinkin' drunk, and then couldn't find his way home."

"Gonna be tough for him to explain to her how he lost his shirt and shoes." They both laughed.

"Well, he's gonna have to sleep it off in the drunk tank tonight," the driver said as he climbed back into the van. He drove away in the gathering dusk.

CHAPTER TWENTY-SIX

When the troops finally returned to base, Kate was plugging the last pieces into the puzzle of the running horse while Liz hobbled around the kitchen, laying out a platter of cold chicken and salads. Mac arrived a few minutes after the others.

Kate asked Lou to eat in the kitchen. Everyone else filled their plates and settled into seats in the family room.

Rose and Skip gave their reports. All the potential Rob sightings had been a bust. But Skip had found a woman who'd seen a pick-up truck Tuesday afternoon, in the back of the parking lot behind Kate's building. And fortunately she had taken note of the license plate. "It stuck in her mind," Skip said, "because she'd thought it odd that an old truck would have a plate that said ROYZTOY. Unfortunately, she didn't notice the make, just that it was a dark color and rusty."

"I ran the plate. Perp's not too bright." Rose shook her head. "Swiped a vanity plate off a BMW sports car."

Skip grinned at Kate. "Told ya criminals are dumb."

She wasn't sure whether she found that reassuring or frightening. Dumb people were more likely to panic.

Liz hobbled over to her computer. "Give me the full names of our top suspects, Kate. I'll check the MVA records. See if any of them owns an old truck."

After carrying those files to her, Kate informed the others, "We've now got the likelies down to four, including Shirley."

"Stopped by Lennox's address this afternoon," Rose said. "Nobody home. But a neighbor confirmed he still lives there. We were headed for Marshall's place when you called about the homeless dude downtown."

Kate looked at their tired faces and hesitated. Every minute counted, but they'd been going full-tilt for days and then taking turns on guard duty at night. Shrugging to loosen the tension in her shoulders, she said, "Tomorrow I want to put these other three under surveillance. Anything else before we–"

"I'll take one of 'em tonight, Kate," Mac said.

Kate looked at the tough little man, debating.

"I'm okay, sweet pea."

Kate reached into the file box to retrieve the address of James Marshall, another batterer whose wife had refused to drop the charges against him. Marshall had convinced the judge he'd seen the error of his ways and would get counseling. He'd gotten off with probation and a stern warning from the judge to stay away from his wife. He'd made it into the likelies pile because that trial had occurred just one week before a truck tried to run Liz over.

As Mac headed for the slider, Skip echoed Kate's earlier thoughts. "I wonder why the kidnapper hasn't tried to contact us again."

"Maybe the dumbass can't think how to set up a meet, without setting himself up to get caught," Rose said.

"Could be," Kate said, "or if it's Shirley, the personality that's behind all this may be a kid or teenager who isn't savvy enough to figure out how to do that."

The same would apply to Jim, she realized. Maybe she'd been too hasty bumping him out of the likelies. Fifteen-year-old Steve might be at a loss as to how to proceed at this point.

Skip was looking confused. "Is the pregnant woman schizophrenic?"

"Yes and no," Kate said. "That's a common misconception. Schizophrenia's a totally different disorder from multiple personalities. Schizophrenics are out of touch with reality, talk to themselves, hear voices. But, yes, I believe Shirley has multiple personalities."

Skip nodded.

"Anything else before we call it a night?" Kate asked.

"I'm a little concerned that the perp hasn't tried anything in awhile," Rose said. "If he or she has figured out that this is our base... Calvin Young's on duty out front tonight but I'm thinking somebody needs to be out back."

Skip said, "I was thinking the same thing. Flip ya for the first shift."

Rose nodded.

"None of our top four owns a truck," Liz reported from the computer desk.

"Check Jim," Kate said. "I mean Joe. Oh, you know who the hell I mean."

A soft chuckle from Liz as she turned back to her computer.

"Truck's probably stolen. I'll check the auto theft reports tomorrow," Rose said.

"Nope," Liz said, "Jim/Joe drives a Mazda. No truck in his name."

She grabbed her crutch and struggled to her feet. "I figure we've got enough food left to feed this crew through breakfast," she said to Kate. "Tomorrow somebody needs to go shopping."

~~~~~~~~~

Rose and Skip walked over to the slider. As he was digging a quarter out of his pocket, Rose said in a low growl, "That bastard Phillips! If he'd had the area canvassed first thing Wednesday morning, we would've had that lead on the truck and could've put out an APB before the bozo had time to ditch it or change the tags again."

"Is there any way to get an APB out now?" Skip also kept his voice low.

"Have to give that some thought. Might just go over his head to the lieutenant."

He frowned. He knew how police hierarchies worked. A rookie going over a detective's head would not be well received. "More likely to get yourself in trouble than him."

Rose shrugged. "Not sure I care at this point, if it means we get Rob back safe."

"Call it, Rose." He flipped the quarter in the air.

Skip lost the toss.

~~~~~~~~~

Early Sunday morning, when the other drunks were waking up–some clamoring to be let out 'cause they didn't do nothin' wrong, just had a few beers on a Saturday night, and the others holding their heads and telling the first bunch to shut up–the big guy with no shirt or shoes was still out cold.

The guard was getting nervous. The guy could be in a diabetic coma or something, even if he didn't have a medical alert bracelet.

Might have lost that the same place he lost half his clothes. So the guard called for a paramedic to check the guy out.

The paramedics quickly realized the man was seriously dehydrated. They wrestled him onto their gurney and hustled him out the door of the jail to the waiting ambulance.

The emergency room at St. Agnes Hospital was having a slow morning–the residents had even been able to snatch a couple hours of sleep after a busy Saturday night. Dr. Abbott took his time while examining the dehydrated John Doe. As the nurse adjusted the IV, the young resident started at the top of the guy's head and worked down. Face kind of bruised up but no signs of head injury. Filthy dirty, stank of urine and sweat, but no injuries on his chest or stomach. Abbott had the nurse help roll the man onto his side. His left shoulder and that side of his back were covered with scabbed over scratches that looked to be a few days old. There was some gravel or dirt in some of them that needed cleaning out.

The nurse had moved down to clean the fresh cuts and scraps on the guy's feet. Abbott started examining the man's arms. When he got to the swollen thumb, he stopped. The wound was showing signs of infection.

But it wasn't safe to give the man a tetanus shot and antibiotics without knowing his history. In his weakened state, an allergic reaction could be fatal. But also in his weakened state, the infection could send him into septic shock.

~~~~~~~~~

Abbott's supervisor, Dr. Walters, concurred with the resident's concerns.

"Should we ask the police to try to find out who he is?" Abbott asked.

That would normally be the procedure, but Amy Walters suspected that identifying a John Doe from the drunk tank who had an infected thumb would not rate as a high priority with the overworked police force. She thought for a moment.

"Yes, call missing persons. But I've got another idea, as well." She picked up the phone on the ER desk and dialed the home number of her friend who worked in the hospital's public relations office.

"Cindy, it's Amy. Sorry to bother you so early, but we've got a John Doe in the ER who's in bad shape. We need to identify him before we can treat him properly. Do you think you could get the TV stations to put out a bulletin with his picture? We might get lucky. And it would be some good exposure for the hospital too–going above and beyond to make sure every patient gets the care they need, et cetera... Thanks, you're a love! I owe you a lunch."

Cindy chuckled on the other end of the line. "Amy dear, for dragging me in there on a Sunday, you owe me a week's worth of lunches."

Dr. Walters grinned as she hung up the phone.

She stared for a moment at the unconscious man's gaunt, bruised face, covered with several days' worth of beard growth. She couldn't shake the nagging feeling that she'd seen this guy before. But where? At one of the college functions her professor husband dragged her to periodically? Or had he been a patient here before?

She shook her head and turned to the resident. "Let's take a chance on the tetanus. Not too many people are allergic to that. But we'll hold off on the antibiotics for awhile. Get him admitted, get his back cleaned up, and keep a close eye on that thumb for now. Actually I want him in the ICU. We need to watch him for renal failure."

Abbott's eyes went wide. "Dr. Walters," he said, in a with-all-due-respect-ma'am voice, "is it likely there's someone out there who cares about a homeless dude and will recognize him on TV?"

She resisted the urge to scowl at the resident. "This guy's got plenty of muscle, some middle-aged fat and no tan. And he came in wearing nothing but dress slacks. Who knows how he got into this state, but I doubt he's homeless."

She hid her smile until she was out of sight.

That'll teach you to question your elders, you young whippersnapper.

~~~~~~~~~~

When Kate came downstairs Sunday morning, the others were already gathered around the big table in the family room for breakfast. Her stomach growled at the sight and smell of eggs and bacon. The next moment she was fighting down nausea.

Does Rob have anything to eat this morning? Is he even still alive to feel hunger?

She swallowed hard, blinking back tears, as she sat down at the table.

A familiar ring tone sounded, coming from her father's pocket. He took it out and answered, while the others held their breath.

"It's Mac." He handed the phone to her.

"First thing this mornin'," Mac said, with his usual lack of preamble, "this guy comes out with a woman. Couple a kids. All dressed up. Followed 'em to a church few blocks away."

"What's she look like?"

He described the woman.

"Sounds like the wife," Kate said. "She dropped out of therapy shortly after the trial. Come on back and get some breakfast."

She told the others the gist of Mac's report.

"So either the wife caved and took him back," Liz said, "or he *is* getting counseling and they're doing okay."

"Most likely the former," Kate said. "But either way, he's got his family back so he's unlikely to still be harboring a grudge against Rob and me."

Everyone nodded and reapplied themselves to their breakfast. With the grumbling in her stomach threatening to erupt into full-blown morning sickness, Kate picked at her food. She caught Skip looking her way and tried to give him a reassuring smile. He didn't look reassured.

Rose sat back and patted her stomach. "Liz, I want to be *you* when I grow up." Dan chuckled.

Kate pushed away her half-empty plate. "Lou, you're going to be with Liz and me again today."

"Sure thing, Miss Kate." She'd encouraged him to call her Kate but Lou had resisted. He'd come up with Miss Kate instead.

"We need to discuss some things that are confidential so since you won't need to know them…" Lou was still looking expectantly at her. Skip was right. No subtleties here, totally literal. "I'm afraid I have to banish you to the kitchen again."

"Okay, Miss Kate." Lou scooped a second helping of eggs onto his plate, then stood up. "Anybody 'sides Skip want more bacon?"

"Leave some for Mac," Kate said. The others shook their heads.

Lou eyeballed the bacon, meticulously separated out one third of the remaining slices to put on his plate, and then headed for the kitchen.

Kate winked at Skip. He flashed her a grin, then nudged her plate back in front of her. She gave him a small smile and took a bite of toast.

They'd begun to sort out surveillance assignments, when her father's pocket beeped. "It keeps makin' that noise, Katie, but when I answer it, nobody's there."

"That means there's a message."

He dug out the phone and handed it to her. The others waited anxiously as she retrieved the message.

Ben's deep voice rumbled in her ear. Excitement bubbled in her chest. Punching the number to replay the message, she grabbed her napkin. "I need a pen."

Rose quickly produced one, and Kate jotted an address down on the napkin, then handed her phone back to her father.

"Ben followed Ch...uh, Shirley...oh, screw it, her real name's Cheryl. He followed her to a house in Baltimore last night. She went in with a bag of groceries and a six pack of water bottles and came out a little while later empty-handed."

"Could be where she has Rob stashed," Skip said, as they heard tapping on the slider. He got up to let Mac in.

"Rose, should we call Phillips with the address or check it out ourselves first?" Kate asked.

"I vote for checking it out ourselves," Skip said from across the room. "Phillips may blow it and get Rob caught up in a hostage situation."

"So how do we find out if Rob's there without doing that ourselves?" Rose said.

"What's goin' on?" Mac asked. Before anyone could respond, Kate's cell phone rang again.

Dan answered it. A confused expression on his face, he held the phone out to his daughter. "'Tis someone called Pauline who's yellin' to turn on the TV."

Kate grabbed the phone. Pauline was still talking, "...and I could've sworn it was Rob."

"Start over, Pauline!" Kate's heart was in her throat. She pointed in the direction of the TV, and Skip crossed the room in two long strides to turn it on. He hit mute and started scanning through the channels–a golf tournament, commercials, a religious program, more commercials.

"I was watching to see if they'd have anything on again about Mr. Bennett's press conference, and then I saw a picture that looked like it could be Rob," Pauline repeated. "Some kind of special report."

Kate jumped to her feet. "Did they say where he is?"

"St. Agnes Hospital. Said he was unidentified, and they needed to know who he was to give him the treatment he needs."

"Pauline, you're an angel!" Kate punched end and then 411. "Baltimore, Maryland," she said to the automated voice, then "St. Agnes Hospital." While the computer looked up the number, she quickly filled the others in on what Pauline had said.

Liz started crying. Dan put his arm around her shoulders.

Kate punched the required button for directory assistance to dial the hospital. "You had a picture on TV a minute ago. We might know who it is… She's transferring me to public relations," Kate informed the group. "Yes, can you e-mail a copy of the picture you just had on TV to us. We think we know who it is."

Kate thrust her phone at Liz. "Give her your e-mail address." Rose was already at the computer across the room, hitting the power button.

Liz gave the woman her e-mail address while Dan helped her hobble to the computer desk. They clustered around as she opened her e-mail. After a moment that seemed like a year, a new message popped up. Liz clicked on it, then the attachment.

Kate dropped to her knees beside Liz's chair and stared at Rob's bruised and stubbled face on the monitor. She'd never seen anything so beautiful. Relief washed through her, leaving her lightheaded and giddy.

Liz turned on her chair and collapsed into her arms. They clung to each other, crying and laughing.

Rose grabbed up Kate's phone from the computer desk. "We know him. What do you need to know?…Liz, is he allergic to antibiotics or tetanus shots?"

Liz straightened up in her chair. "No. No allergies." She swiped at her wet cheeks with her fingers.

"No allergies. His name is Robert Franklin," Rose said into the phone. "I'll have his wife there in fifteen minutes."

"St. Agnes is all the way 'round on Wilkens Avenue," Mac growled at her. "Can't get there in fifteen minutes."

Rose flashed him a big smile. "With siren and lights, I can."

CHAPTER TWENTY-SEVEN

True to her word, Rose got Kate and Liz to St. Agnes Hospital in fourteen and a half minutes. Leaving Lou to guard the house, the men had piled into Skip's Explorer. With flashers and liberal use of his horn, he was able to keep up in the light Sunday morning traffic on the Baltimore Beltway.

Kate charged up to the information desk in the hospital lobby. "The John Doe who was on TV? Where is he?"

"Adult Intensive Care, second floor, turn right when you get off the elevator."

Impatiently they all waited for the elevator, Kate and Liz squeezing each other's hands. Kate's stomach was tied in knots. Intensive care did not sound good.

On the second floor they followed the signs and surged into the ICU waiting room. Different hospital, but Kate still had an uncomfortable moment of *deja vu.*

Liz hobbled quickly to the nurse's window, which was being slid open by a large African-American nurse. "Robert Franklin. How is he?" Liz demanded. "I'm his wife."

"And these people are?" the nurse asked in a tone that said she wasn't giving out any information until she knew who was who.

Kate jumped in. "All family or close friends. I'm his sister."

"Is he okay?" Liz yelled at the nurse.

A tall, thin woman in a white coat, with a cap of short gray hair, came through the door into the waiting area. There were laugh lines around her brown eyes, but at the moment they had a no-nonsense glint in them. She strode briskly across the room.

~~~~~~~~~

"Dr. Amy Walters." She offered her hand to the woman yelling at the nurse. "Mrs. Franklin, I presume."

The woman grabbed her hand and hung on. "Doctor, how is he?"

"He's not out of the woods yet, but I think he'll be okay. Everybody sit." She wasn't hung up on who heard what. These people cared about this man or they wouldn't be here, relief and anxiety in equal portions on their faces.

They all quickly found chairs clustered around her. "He's very dehydrated but he doesn't seem to have any serious injuries, other than some scrapes on his shoulder and side and an infected thumb. Which was why we were anxious to make sure he wasn't allergic to antibiotics. But we've got those into his system now, and we've given him a tetanus shot.

"Mrs. Franklin, I need you to give the nurse his medical history and then you can go in to see him. Don't be frightened by his appearance. He looks pretty rough, but other than a few concerns about repercussions from the dehydration, I'm relatively confident he'll be okay. And if he opens his eyes and doesn't seem to recognize you or speaks and you can't understand him, don't worry. Dehydration can cause delirium, but once we get enough fluids into him, his head should clear." She wasn't quite as confident as she sounded but no point in scaring these folks any more than necessary.

As Mrs. Franklin hobbled back to the nurse's window, the doctor eyed the leg brace, crutch and walking cast.

"Car accident," one of the other women said.

"And you are?"

"Kate Huntington. Actually I lied to the nurse and said I was Rob's sister, to get her to tell us how he was. We're not related." Tears pooled in the woman's eyes. "He's just a very close friend."

"No *just* about it, young lady. I've got several friends I'm closer to than my siblings."

Ms. Huntington blinked away the tears. "Please be honest, doctor. How confident are you that the delirium will be temporary?"

Amy Walters leaned back in her seat and took a deep breath. Some people dealt better with the truth; others would prefer you lie, even when they asked you to be honest. She looked into this woman's eyes and saw anxiety but also strength. Softening her voice a bit, she said, "On a scale of 1 to10, about a 7. We don't know how long he's been without fluids. When did he go missing?"

"Tuesday evening. He was working late and never came home."

"Would he have had dinner or at least something to drink during the evening?"

"Maybe, but probably not." The woman's eyes shifted. She wasn't telling her the whole story.

The doctor went fishing. "Where could he have been all this time that he wouldn't have had access to water? When he came into the ER, he didn't have any signs of exposure other than the dehydration."

Ms. Huntington countered with a question of her own. "How did he get here?"

"He was brought in by ambulance. He'd been mistaken for a homeless drunk and spent the night in jail. When he didn't wake up this morning, the guard called for the paramedics."

"What precinct, ma'am?" the young Hispanic woman spoke up for the first time.

Odd question.

The doctor shook her head. "Don't know, but it'll be in his chart."

Ms. Huntington asked, "What other complications of dehydration are you concerned about?"

"Main concern is whether his kidneys will start functioning again on their own once he has enough fluid in him. He's catheterized and the nurses will be watching carefully for those first critical drops of urine."

"What happens if the lad's kidneys don't start up on their own?" The older man had a slight Irish brogue.

"Dialysis to get the toxins out of his blood." She was hoping no one would ask what came after that. Mr. Franklin could end up needing a kidney transplant.

She eyed the big, buff guy. He gave her a slight nod. Something was up with this crew. She was curious but she also needed to know anything that might be relevant to her patient's care. Again she asked, "Do you have any idea what happened to him?"

Ms. Huntington said nothing for a long moment, then she took a deep breath. "Someone has made several attempts on Mr. Franklin's life and my own, and against some of our family members. He was kidnapped by this person, who was going to use him as bait to lure me away from my friends and bodyguard."

Ah, buff guy.

The doctor started to push up from her chair. "Then I should be calling the police."

Ms. Huntington's eyes went wide. "No need!" She gestured toward the Hispanic woman. "This is Officer Hernandez. She's... uh, working undercover to try to catch the perpetrator."

The officer pulled out her badge.

Dr. Walters examined it, then gave the young woman's rumpled clothing a skeptical look. She still wasn't getting the whole story, but she had other patients to see to.

"Okay, Officer." She stood up and moved briskly towards the door. "We'll let you know when he's awake and coherent."

~~~~~~~~~~

Kate thanked the departing doctor's back. Realizing her cell phone had been left behind at the house, she borrowed Rose's phone to call John Bennett and let him know his partner had been found.

"Hallelujah!" he shouted, then said he would spread the good news. Kate held back the information about potential repercussions from dehydration. Soon enough to share those grim possibilities if they became reality.

Returning the phone to Rose, Kate flopped back in her seat. The adrenaline, that had been drenching her system for the past five days, was now draining away. She leaned her head back against the waiting room wall and closed her eyes. Her father, sitting beside her, took her hand in his and followed suit.

An hour later, Liz was shaking her awake. A big smile split her tear-stained face. "Kate, you can go in to see your *brother* now. The nurse just told me there's a little urine in his bag, and it looks normal."

Dan grinned. "Now isn't that the best news we've been hearin' in a long time?"

Kate followed the plump nurse down the corridor in the ICU. The nurse gestured toward one of the small rooms. As Kate went past her, she put a big hand on her shoulder and said, "Talk to him, honey. It'll help bring him 'round."

Kate resisted the temptation to tell her she was an old pro at talking to unconscious people.

She sat in the chair next to the bed and wrapped her two hands around Rob's big, inert paw. "Rob, dear heart, please come back to us...." Her throat closed. Tears broke loose and rolled down her cheeks. The thought that he might not make it, or that he might be permanently brain-damaged, was unbearable.

She swallowed hard and tried again. "Rob, you're safe now. You're at St. Agnes Hospital. Liz is here. Actually everybody's here. But we need our fearless leader back."

She paused trying to think of something else to say. "Come on now, you're scaring Lizzie and she's already been through enough."

She looked down at the big hand she was holding–the hand that had reached out for hers so many times in the last few weeks, to comfort his grieving friend.

When she looked up at his face again, she jumped. Big, beautiful, brown eyes were looking back at her. He mumbled something. It sounded like he had marbles in his mouth, but there was intelligence in those eyes.

"Don't try to talk until your mouth gets re-lubricated," Kate said, smiling and choking a little again, this time on tears of relief. "You're safe now and there's a very competent lady doc taking care of you. I know how you like strong women."

A faint smile. He closed his eyes again.

She sat there for a few more minutes, holding his hand and saying a silent prayer of thanksgiving.

She told the nurse on her way out that Rob had opened his eyes.

The woman said, "That's a good sign, honey. You go tell Miz Franklin her man's trying real hard to make his way back to her."

In the waiting room, Kate told the others that Rob seemed to be coming around. Liz's face lit up, and she rushed back to sit with him again.

When the others' cheers subsided, Kate asked Rose to help her get coffee for everyone. They found some vending machines down the hall in a small lounge area.

"Come sit for a minute," Kate said. "We need to sort something out." They sat down on the not-very-comfortable chairs. "We really should be calling Phillips at this point, but I'm afraid he'll come storming in here and stress Rob out before he's strong enough to deal with the jerk–"

"And you might just kill him if he did that."

Kate smiled at her. "I'm confident you'd stop me."

"Don't be. Might help you at this point." Rose paused, her expression thoughtful. Then she said, "Best bet's to wait. See what Rob can tell us about his kidnapper."

"But I can't think of a way you can justify to Phillips why you didn't call him right away."

"Yeah, I don't think I can stretch the I'm-trying-to-convince-them-I'm-on-their-side routine quite that far. Can't say I'm too worked up about it though. Not sure I want to work for a department that gives a gold badge to someone like him."

"He probably puts on a good show for his superiors," Kate said, "and maybe he was a good cop *until* he got promoted to detective. Now he thinks he's got enough power, he can do whatever he wants. But sometimes that's the very thing that brings men like him down. They get so arrogant they make mistakes, or piss off the wrong people."

"He's certainly made mistakes but so far he hasn't pissed off the brass. He kisses up to them."

"Come on, let's get some bad coffee to take back to the troops." Kate stood up. "Wait, I've got it!" She turned back toward Rose. "If Phillips tries to get you fired, I'll threaten to sue the department for harassment, which would definitely piss off his superiors and bring his mistakes to their attention."

"Might work."

Kate grinned. "Heck, I might even lie and tell him Rob is friends with the police chief, just to see the expression on his face."

Rose grinned back at her. "It's *acting*, Kate, not lying."

Several hours later, Rob was awake enough to take some water by mouth. Doctor Walters came out to the waiting area. "Okay, folks, here's where we are," she said in her brisk tone. "He's awake and reasonably coherent, knows who he is and gets it that he's in the hospital. His kidneys don't seem to need a jumpstart. All excellent progress."

Both Kate and Liz blew out air at the same time. Liz gave her a lopsided smile, then reached over and squeezed her hand.

The doctor was looking at Rose. "As a matter of fact, he's in good enough shape to move him out of the ICU, but I want a guard on his door, Officer. I do not take kindly to my patients being attacked."

Rose nodded. "I'll take care of it."

Once Rob was settled in his new room–a private one since putting him in with someone else would put that other patient at risk–Rose asked to speak to Kate and Liz in the hall. Her chocolate brown eyes moved from one to the other of them. "I need to question Rob about what happened, and I'm thinking he's gonna need some support to get through it. But I'm concerned he'll leave things out that he thinks might upset you, Liz, if you're in the room."

Liz narrowed her eyes. "He might not tell the whole truth in front of Kate either."

"Maybe, maybe not," Kate said. "He tries to look out for me but he feels responsible for you, because you're his wife."

Liz snorted and started to shake her head, then stopped.

Kate met her gaze. "I know, but he can't help it. It's how men were raised in our generation."

"Actually for once I can relate," Liz said, " because I'm feeling pretty protective of him at the moment."

Kate nodded, realizing she felt the same way. It was only natural, when you believed someone you loved was physically or emotionally vulnerable. In that light, men being protective of women didn't seem quite so unreasonable. She tucked that thought away to mull over later.

"Look, let's both sit in while Rose talks to him. We'll point out that he needs to tell us everything, and probe some if we think he's holding back."

Rose asked questions at first, taking notes in her pad, but after awhile Rob just told the story, with only occasional prompting. His speech was a bit garbled. Kate or Liz had to translate some of his answers for Rose, like parents with a toddler whom no one can understand except those who know the child well.

Forty minutes later they had the gist of it and Rob kept drifting off. Rose nodded, and Liz gave his hand one last squeeze.

Kate leaned over and kissed his forehead. "You rest now, dear heart."

Keeping their voices low out in the hall, they summarized for the others what Rob had told them.

"Do you think he left anything out?" Skip asked.

"Probably," Kate said, "but I think more about what he was feeling rather than what happened."

"So the lad thinks Cheryl was who took him?" Dan asked.

"He does, Dad, but his thinking may have been clouded, by those feelings as well as by hunger and thirst."

"He never actually saw or heard anything that identifies his captor," Rose said. "But nothing he told us rules out a woman either."

"It sounded like he was imagining it could be Cheryl and then started assuming it was her," Kate said. "The line between imagined events and what really happened can get blurry, especially when one's mind is impaired. We still need to check out that house, but now that we know there was indeed some shifting of his unconscious body required, that makes a woman a bit less likely in my book."

Skip cocked his head to one side. "We've been assuming Rob's shirt got torn and his back scraped up because he was dragged, but here's another possibility. Maybe Cheryl brought the wheelbarrow into the building. It would fit in the elevator. How big a woman is she?"

"She's a couple inches taller than me, and fairly muscular," Kate said.

"If she brought the wheelbarrow up next to Rob's body and leaned it over on its side, she could roll him into it and tip it up." Skip pantomimed those actions with an imaginary body and wheelbarrow.

"So how'd he get scraped up?" Rose asked.

"Maybe she lost control of her load at some point and he dumped out onto the pavement. Then she had to shove him around some to get him in position to roll him back into the wheelbarrow."

Rose nodded. "Shirt got torn up and bloody. Maybe ripped some more when she's struggling to transfer him into her vehicle. She uses it to wipe down the 'barrow and then tosses it underneath it so we know she's got him."

"She drives a car, according to Ben," Kate said.

"Easy enough to beg, borrow or steal a van or truck," Mac pointed out.

Kate nodded as she spotted Dr. Walters coming down the hall. "Call Phillips," she whispered to Rose, then stepped forward to intercept the doctor.

"Can I speak to you for a moment, Doctor?" Kate steered her away from the others, thinking the woman might be more willing to go along with what she was about to propose if there weren't any witnesses to their conversation.

Kate paused to choose her words carefully. "Doctor, the lead police detective on our case is not very competent, but he is quite arrogant. He hasn't handled the investigation very well so far. Now that Rob's awake, Detective Phillips will probably be showing up at any moment. So I have a favor to ask." She took a deep breath and then plunged ahead.

"Rob's in a fragile mental state right now, and that's not just a friend's opinion. I'm a psychotherapist. I'm very concerned that Phillips is going to come barging in here and create additional stress for Rob. And I'm not at all sure he can handle that right now."

"So you want me to stick around until this chap gets here," the doctor said.

"Yes, but that's not the entire favor." Kate took another deep breath. "I was hoping that you wouldn't let Detective Phillips in to see Rob, at least not tonight."

The doctor took a step back and gave her a sharp look. "You're asking me to obstruct justice?"

"No, ma'am, I'm asking you to protect your patient from one of the most obnoxious people on the planet!" Kate spat out.

So much for carefully chosen words.

"Besides," she added less vehemently, "Officer Hernandez has questioned Rob and she can tell the detective what he said."

She nervously watched the doctor's face as the older woman mulled it over.

~~~~~~~~

On the one hand, it was a rather outrageous request. But on the other hand, Amy Walters was impressed by Ms. Huntington, who was obviously accepted as the leader of this group, even by the men. And she considered herself a good judge of character.

She'd also interacted enough with the police in her professional life to know that while most were dedicated and competent, some were not.

Dr. Walters looked at her watch. Her husband of thirty years had long since learned to expect her when he saw her. She wasn't sure what she would do when the detective arrived but she was certainly sticking around to make sure he didn't upset her patient.

"I'm going down to the cafeteria and get a snack," she finally said. "Something tells me I don't want to face this gentleman with low blood sugar. Have the nurse page me if he shows up before I get back."

After buying an apple in the ground-floor cafeteria, Amy Walters went over to the bank of elevators. She punched the up button as she bit into the apple. One of the doors slid open. The only occupant of the elevator was a short, stocky man in a rumpled business suit. He was slouched against the back wall.

He eyed her white coat and stethoscope, then straightened up and threw his shoulders back. His chest puffed out a little.

The doctor stepped on, suppressing a smile at the man's sudden transformation. She observed elevator etiquette by turning to face the front and pretending she was alone. As she worked on the apple, she checked the guy out in her peripheral vision. *Built like a fireplug, touch of gray in his hair. Early to mid forties maybe.*

When the elevator reached her floor, the man, honoring neither age, gender nor who was closest to the door, rushed past her with a self-important air. The doctor's amusement shifted toward annoyance. The man paused, looking around, then headed briskly toward Mr. Franklin's room.

Damn! He's the police detective.

Down the hall, her patient's wife and her friends were lined up, touching shoulders—a human barricade in front of the door. It sounded like the wiry little guy was actually growling.

The detective raised his voice. "If you all don't move aside, I'm going to arrest you for obstruction of justice!"

Amy Walters inserted herself into the middle of the group. "Detective, please lower your voice. You're disturbing my patients. Shall we take this to my office?"

The detective glared at her. "Who are you, lady?"

Who the hell does he think I am, the janitor?

"I'm Mr. Franklin's doctor. Amanda Walters." She did not offer to shake the man's hand. "If you will follow me, we can discuss in private when you may see my patient, instead of yelling in a hospital hallway. Officer Hernandez, Ms. Huntington, please join us." She started to turn away.

"There's nothing to discuss. I need to interrogate this man."

Dr. Walters pivoted back around and stared at him for a beat. "Sir, I will call hospital security and have you forcibly removed from this hospital if you attempt to enter my patient's room without my permission. Now follow me!" She tossed her apple core in a trash can as she marched down the hall.

She glanced back. The detective's expression was not happy but he was following her. Ms. Huntington and the officer were trailing behind the man, staying well back.

In her office, the doctor settled intro her desk chair and gestured toward the cluster of visitor chairs in front of her desk. "Detective, ladies, have a seat."

Phillips remained standing, glaring at Ms. Huntington. "Why is she here?"

It was a good question. She realized she'd invited Ms. Huntington as the leader of this ragtag group of folks associated with her patient. "Because *I* asked her to join us, as Mr. Franklin's representative, if you will. It is my office, Detective. Please sit down."

Ms. Huntington left an empty chair between them as she and Phillips sat down. The officer stood near the door at parade rest.

"Detective, Mr. Franklin was in critical condition when he arrived in our ER. I understand your need for information in order to catch whoever kidnapped him. So when he regained consciousness and was relatively stable, I allowed your officer to question him." Watching this man's scowling face, she was more and more inclined to keep him away from her patient, at least for tonight. "He is now sleeping so it's unlikely you will be able to talk to him this evening. He needs to rest."

Still looking at her, Phillips barked, "Hernandez, report!"

The young woman took a step forward and opened her pad. "Mr. Franklin stated he was held since Tuesday evening in a storage room, in the basement of a row house somewhere in Baltimore City. He managed to escape, passed out on the street and woke up here in the hospital. He never saw his kidnapper."

"He give you an address?" Phillips snapped.

"No, sir. Just said the house was red brick, with a white marble stoop."

Phillips sat back and a smirk spread across his face. "How very convenient. There are only several thousand such houses in the Baltimore area. Did he happen to notice what street it was on?"

"No, sir. He said he felt a sense of urgency to get away quickly."

Phillips was still looking at the doctor rather than his subordinate. "So let me get this straight, Officer. This big man was taken by force by someone he never saw who managed to get him from Towson to somewhere in West Baltimore, locked him in a basement for several days, after which he miraculously escaped but can't tell us the location of the house where he was held."

Amy Walters shook her head slightly. It sounded like this guy didn't believe her patient had actually been kidnapped. "Detective, this man arrived in our emergency room unconscious and seriously dehydrated."

"Both of which can be faked."

She pursed her lips. "No, actually they can't. Any first-year resident can tell whether or not someone is unconscious. And the paramedics picked up right away that he was dehydrated. There are very obvious symptoms, especially when someone's been without fluids for as long as Mr. Franklin was."

"Or for as long as Mr. Franklin claims he was without fluids. Officer, did he have an explanation for why his kidnapper didn't bother to feed and water him?"

"The kidnapper left food and water in the room when he was asleep, sir. But the first time he ate the food, he passed out for quite awhile and realized it had been drugged. He was afraid to consume anything after that."

"And how did he escape?"

After the briefest of hesitations, the young officer said, "He was eventually able to break through a wall into the rest of the basement, and escape through the basement door to the street."

Amy Walters put her hands on her desk to push herself to a stand. "Detective, assuming my patient hasn't suffered any setbacks by morning, you may talk to him then."

"Not acceptable. I need to interrogate him tonight."

Startled, she dropped back into her chair. "That's the second time you've used the word *interrogate*. That implies Mr. Franklin is a suspect rather than a victim."

"That's because he *is* a suspect, in the murder of this woman's husband." Phillips pointed at Ms. Huntington. "And the two of them have been staging all kinds of scenes since then to make it appear someone's trying to kill them."

Ms. Huntington opened her mouth. The doctor held up a hand in her direction.

"So let *me* get this straight, Detective," Dr. Walters said. "You think this man staged his own kidnapping and went without food or water for almost five days, just to throw you off… after killing Mrs. Huntington's husband? Why would he do that in the first place?"

Phillips leaned forward. "Because the two of them, Franklin and her, are having an affair. And the man's wife is too stupid to see it."

Mrs. Huntington's eyes flashed with fury. She started to come up out of her chair. In an instant, Officer Hernandez was behind her, hands on her shoulders holding her down.

The doctor cocked an eyebrow in their direction, then turned her attention back to the detective. "My sense of Mrs. Franklin, sir, is that she's anything but stupid. And I repeat, you seriously believe this man deliberately allowed himself to become dangerously dehydrated?"

"Well, now we only have your word for it that he was that dehydrated, Doctor."

Okay, that does it!

Amy Walters stood up. Her voice low and even, she said, "I see. So I'm either incompetent or lying to cover for a couple of murderers. Sir, you are no longer welcome in my office and you cannot see my patient until tomorrow, if then. I will determine in the morning if he is strong enough to talk to you."

Phillips stood, put his hands on her desk and leaned within inches of her face. "I will be back tomorrow and if you try to stop me from seeing him then, I'll arrest you for obstruction of justice."

She didn't blink. She hadn't carved out a successful career in the still male-dominated medical field by allowing herself to be bullied. While maintaining eye contact with Phillips, she reached toward her phone and hit the button for the intercom–that went to an empty clerk's desk outside her office. "Carrie," she calmly bluffed. "Call security. I need three officers in my office stat."

She sat back down in her chair. "Would you care to wait, Detective, or would you prefer to show yourself out?"

Phillips stormed out, slamming the door behind him. She shook her head. "What an incredibly obnoxious little man!"

"Tends to be the common reaction to him, ma'am," the officer replied evenly.

The doctor suppressed a snort. Even his subordinates didn't like him. She turned to Mrs. Huntington. "He seriously thinks you and Mr. Franklin are having an affair, and set up a fake kidnapping, complete with very real dehydration, just to throw him off?"

Mrs. Huntington shrugged. "Actually at this point he probably realizes his theory is off base, which may be why he feels that much more compelled to defend it. He's made some serious blunders in the investigation, because he was so convinced we were the culprits. Now, I think he's getting desperate."

The doctor nodded. "And unfortunately it isn't hard for some people to believe that when a man and a woman are friends, there must be romance and sex involved as well."

Mrs. Huntington gave her a startled look.

"I've been a doctor for three decades, most of them at this hospital. Of course, I've developed some friendships amongst my colleagues, many of whom are male. Every so often, my husband receives a note or phone call informing him that his wife is having an affair. I am fortunate to be married to a trusting man who thinks these communications are amusing."

She looked at her watch and stood up. "And he is currently waiting patiently to have dinner with me. Ladies, I assume some of those big strapping fellows you have with you will be sticking around tonight to protect my patient from the kidnapper. I will send a hospital security officer up as well. His assignment will be to keep Detective Phillips out."

As she ushered them out of her office, she added, "Officer, I am prescribing a good night's sleep for Mrs. Huntington and Mrs. Franklin. Will you see that they follow doctor's orders, please?"

The police officer smiled for the first time. "Yes, ma'am."

Amy Walters blinked once at the brief but radiant transformation, then she smiled back at the young woman. "See you all in the morning."

CHAPTER TWENTY-EIGHT

Kate was awakened by Lou's voice calling up the stairs. "Yo, Miss Kate, Ben's on the phone for you."

She scrambled out of bed and pulled on her crumpled clothes. Smiling at the thought that today they could actually worry about mundane things like clean laundry and groceries, she bounded down the stairs.

Lou handed her his cell phone.

Wondering why Ben wasn't calling on the landline, Kate put the phone to her ear as she walked into the kitchen.

Liz was skeptically peering into her refrigerator. "How am I supposed to feed four people and one giant with five eggs?"

Kate shook her head in sympathy as she said into the phone, "Hey, Ben."

"Thank God Rob's okay. Lou told me yesterday that you were at the hospital, so I figured that's why you weren't answering your cell. Was Rob at that house?"

"What house?" She walked into the family room in search of her cell phone. She spotted it on the computer desk, where Rose had dropped it as they'd raced out the door yesterday.

"Didn't you get my messages?" Ben asked.

"Oh, yeah." She glanced over at the portable phone's base. It was empty. The phone was lying on the sofa.

"So was he at that house on Wilkens?"

She was headed back toward the kitchen, punching buttons on the portable phone and getting nothing but a low battery beep, when Ben's words finally registered. "Damn! Wilkens Avenue. I didn't even make the connection."

The excitement in her voice had Liz turning around, ignoring the sizzling pan on the stove.

"What kind of house was it?" Kate asked.

"Row house, red brick."

"What time was she there?"

"Hang on." Paper rustled as Ben checked his notepad. "She got there at eight-thirty-six, left at eight-fifty. Caught sight of her face in a streetlight. She looked pissed."

"Give me the house number again?" Kate jotted it down on Liz's grocery list lying on the table. "Good work, Ben. Rob was found on a street near St. Agnes, in that same area. You okay to stay on Cheryl today, or do you need to be relieved?"

Rose had walked into the kitchen. A questioning eyebrow was cocked in Kate's direction.

"I'm good," Ben said. "I've been dozing some at night. Her car's such a rattle-trap, she'd never get out of the parking lot without waking me up. She's in there now. I can see her moving around through her patio door."

"Stay with her then."

Kate disconnected, then turned to Liz and Rose. "Good thing Rob didn't stick around to look at street signs. That house Ben followed Cheryl to is on Wilkens Avenue and she was there right after dark Saturday night."

"What's the house number?" Rose asked.

"2345."

"That jives with the City cop's report. Rob was found about six blocks from there."

"You're way ahead of me, Rose. I was about to ask if you could get that information."

"That last hotline tip was legit after all," Rose was saying when they smelled something burning.

Liz whirled back toward the stove. "Crap! I just ruined four pieces of French toast and there was barely enough bread and eggs to begin with."

Rose looked in the pan. "Flip 'em over on their good side. Bet Lou'll eat 'em."

A few minutes later they were all sitting down to a large platter of French toast. When they'd demolished the upper layers and were down to the burnt pieces, Liz warned that they were charcoal on one side. Lou looked at the others. They all shook their heads. He scooped them onto his plate.

"Lou, would you mind finishing your breakfast in the kitchen?" Kate asked.

"No problem, Miss Kate." Grabbing the syrup bottle, he headed out of the room.

"Cheryl being at that house near where Rob was found definitely makes her our strongest suspect now," she said.

"But all we have on her is circumstantial evidence," Rose said.

"Right. I'm not comfortable giving her name to Phillips until we have something more concrete. I'll come back to her in a minute."

Kate stopped and thought about who was rested and who was not. There was a lot to do today, so deploying the troops was a bit complicated. "Dad, you and Lou will take Liz to the grocery store while—"

"Groceries can wait," Liz said. "I want to see my husband."

"I checked in with Mac and Skip while you were fixing breakfast," Kate said. "Everything's fine at the hospital. I can't wait to see him either. But there may not be a good opportunity to get food later, and we've gotta eat."

Liz frowned but she gave a slight nod of her head. "Okay. You were saying?"

"Rose, you got a fresh uniform back at your place?"

Rose nodded.

"Good, you and I will go get it, then swing by my house to pick up some clothes. Whoever gets back here first needs to check the place over since it will've been unattended for—"

"I'll stay and guard the house, Katie," her father said.

She stifled a sigh. "Dad, we've been over this. You're a potential target, so you can't be alone. Now where was I?… Oh, yeah. Rose, since you and Lou were on guard duty here last night, when we get back I want you to take a nap while—"

Rose opened her mouth.

Kate held up both hands, palms out. "If one more person interrupts…."

Rose closed her mouth.

Kate softened her tone. "I've got a good reason for wanting you rested, Rose. I'll get to that in a minute. Lou will take me and Liz to the hospital. We should be fine in Rob's room, with the police officer and hospital security guard on the door. The guys will come back here to get some rest. Dad, sit on Mac if you have to, but make sure he takes a nap." That mental image evoked several grins. "Then Lou can guard the house and–"

Liz raised her hand, as one would in school.

Kate chuckled. "Yes, Liz?"

"I'd prefer that Lou stay at the hospital. I'm not comfortable with trusting Rob's safety, and yours, to one police officer and a hospital rent-a-cop."

"Good point. Okay, we'll just have to check the house over again later."

"And what happens after they've all had a wee nap, Katie girl?"

"I'm going to send Mac to check out our other suspect, and Rose and Skip will bring you to the hospital to stay with us. Then… Rose, I hate to keep asking you to break the rules, but are you willing to go in uniform to that house on Wilkens, with Skip as your back-up? See who lives there. Find out what Cheryl was doing there. Maybe get into the basement and see if the set-up looks like what Rob described."

"Then we *would* have some concrete evidence!" Liz said.

Rose flashed a brief smile and nodded in agreement.

"Exactly," Kate said. "Let's do it, folks."

~~~~~~~~

As Rose drove along block after block of brick row houses, their white marble steps gleaming in the afternoon sun, she had to admit that Kate's enforced nap had done her a world of good. The fresh uniform helped considerably as well.

When they reached the 2300 block of Wilkens Avenue, Rose parked the cruiser. She and Skip walked up the sidewalk of number 2345. Skip stayed at the bottom of the steps, arms casually crossed, his right hand tucked under the sports jacket borrowed from Rob's closet and resting on the gun in his waistband holster.

Rose walked cautiously up onto the porch and rang the doorbell.

"Curtain twitched," Skip whispered.

One hand now on her own gun butt in her unsnapped holster, Rose rang the bell again.

The door opened a crack, a safety chain in place. Half of an elderly woman's face appeared an inch below Rose's chin. She looked down to make eye contact, a rather unusual experience for her unless she was dealing with children. "Ma'am, I'm Officer

Hernandez. We're investigating an incident that occurred in this neighborhood a couple days ago. May we come in?"

"Yer no cop. They don't 'llow no girls to be cops."

Skip stepped forward. "Afternoon, ma'am. We truly do hate to be a bother," he drawled. The occasional hint of the South in his voice had morphed into a thick Texas accent that sounded authentic to Rose. "It's real important though, ma'am, that we ask y'all a couple a questions."

The old woman's belligerent glare softened as she looked Skip over. "Well, young man, I can see *your* mama taught you manners. Okay, you can come in, but wipe your feet."

Cautiously they entered a small foyer that opened to the right into a spotless living room. To their left, a set of stairs led to the second floor.

"Watch the stairs," Rose whispered. Skip nodded. She moved into the living room, where the tiny old woman was settling herself onto the sofa. "Mind if I sit down, ma'am?"

"Ain't talkin' to you, girlie. Now this young man here, him I'll talk to." It looked like she was actually fluttering her eyelashes at Skip.

Rose exchanged a glance with him, then they quickly traded places. Skip sat down in the chair Rose had been denied.

"What's yer name, sonny?" the old lady asked.

"Uh, Detective James, ma'am."

Rose stifled a groan. They'd just stepped over the line from investigating a lead without authorization to a civilian impersonating a police officer.

"Ma'am, could I have your name please?" Skip asked.

"Elsie Burnett."

Yup, she's definitely batting her eyelashes.

"Miz Burnett, a young woman was reported comin' out of yer house night 'fore last, just after dark—"

"Weren't nobody comin' outta my door." The belligerent scowl was back. "Not one of my worthless kids comes to visit no more."

"I see. Well, ma'am, do ya happen to know a gal by the name of Cheryl Crofton?"

"Nope. Never heard of her. Hmm, got a niece named Cheryl, but her last name's Burnett. Saw her 'while back. Can't remember exactly when. What's been happenin' round here, young man?"

"I'm sorry, ma'am, but I'm 'fraid I'm not at liberty to tell ya that."

"Well, la-di-da! Not at liberty to tell me, huh? Well, then I don't feel like I'm at liberty to tell you nothin' neither."

"Well now, ma'am, I sure as heck would love to tell ya 'bout it, but that's not allowed in an ongoin' investigation. But I can tell ya this. We think some yahoo might've snuck into yer basement an' has been usin' it for criminal activity. Miz Burnett, with yer permission, we'd sure like to take a look down there."

The old woman grew wary. "I'm not too sure 'bout that. Maybe I should call the police station. Make sure you really are cops. Still don't believe they let no girls be cops, 'specially not a shorty like this one. Hell, she couldn't stop no bad guy."

Rose gritted her teeth, but she kept her voice neutral. "They've dropped the height restrictions, ma'am."

"Humph, well I think I'll just call anyways. What'd you say your name was, sonny?"

Skip looked confused for a beat. "Detective Jones, ma'am."

Rose winced. Wrong name. But the old lady didn't seem to notice.

Skip quickly continued, "Well now, ma'am, lemme ask ya this. Have ya been down in yer basement lately?"

"Hmm, lemme think. I was down there, musta been mornin' before last. Or was that last week? I go down there at least once a week or so and clean up. I clean this house from top to bottom every week." Mrs. Burnett beamed with pride.

"But ya might not've been down there since this Tuesday past?" Skip asked.

She stared at the ceiling for a minute, thinking. "Yeah, coulda been that long ago. Seems like it's 'bout time for another cleanin'."

"Ma'am, do you have a storage room in your basement?" Rose asked.

The woman narrowed her eyes at her from across the room. "Now why you askin' me that, girlie? You been snoopin' 'round here when I weren't home?"

Rose figured that was as close as they would get to an answer and this paranoid old lady wasn't going to let them into her basement. Time to get out of here. "No, ma'am. Thank you for your time."

She reached behind her to open the front door. Skip stood up.

The old lady ignored Rose as she struggled to her feet. She took a couple steps toward Skip. "Thank *you*, Detective, for comin' to see me." She laid a wrinkled hand on his arm. "Let's you and me ditch this girlie and go on back to my bedroom, dearie."

Rose opened the door wide. Skip ran.

~~~~~~~~

At the hospital, they had neither seen nor heard from Phillips, which was puzzling. But Kate had decided not to look a gift horse in the mouth. Other than a short visit from John Bennett, the morning had been quite uneventful. She and her father were walking toward the vending machines in the small lounge near Rob's room when she realized she was bored.

Wow, what a concept!

She was trying to select something vaguely nutritious from the snack machine when she spotted Dr. Walters headed toward them.

"So how's our patient doing this afternoon?" the doctor asked.

"Better. He's still dozing off and on, but each time he wakes up, he seems more like himself." Kate hoped the doctor would agree to let him go home today.

John had told her he'd had to make good on his promise and tell the press that Rob had been found. Of course they'd have discovered this soon enough anyway. By now, the killer could very well know where to find his escaped victim. It would be easier to keep Rob safe at home, where total strangers weren't wandering past his door. Any one of them, posing as a patient's visitor or hospital employee, could be the killer.

Or someone paid by the killer. Kate hadn't forgotten that Grandpa had an extra eight grand in his savings account, which probably *would* be enough to hire a professional hit man. She shuddered, then opened her mouth to broach the subject of Rob's release.

"Good," the doctor said. "Because I had a call a little while ago from a Lieutenant Cody. He wanted to know why I was denying his detectives access to a crucial witness in an ongoing investigation."

Aha! The mean lady doctor scared Detective Obnoxious so he went running to his boss.

"What did you tell him?"

"I told him I was only denying one particular detective access because he's an ass. And I had every reason to believe said ass would upset my patient and delay his recovery."

Her father snickered behind her.

Kate grinned at the doctor. "Wow! You said that?"

"Most definitely. I informed the lieutenant that I would be happy to let *him* interview my patient, but I would need to be present. He'll be here soon."

"Uh, excuse me, Doctor. I need to talk to Rob and Liz before he gets here."

Kate caught the frown on the doctor's face and realized she'd once again said too much. That had sounded like she wanted to be sure all their stories were straight.

But she'd have to deal with that later. Right now, she needed to ask Rob a question before the lieutenant arrived. She dashed back down the hall, her father following in her wake.

When Kate entered Rob's room, he was sitting up in bed, propped up against several pillows. He and Liz were laughing at some shared joke.

When he turned his smiling face toward Kate, she literally felt her heart swelling in her chest.

Another moment to savor later.

She quickly filled them in on her conversation with Dr. Walters, then told Rob about John Bennett's meeting with Cody to complain about Phillips. "Is this our chance to tell the lieutenant what Phillips has been doing, and not doing, and get him yanked off the case?"

"Absolutely not," Rob said. "At least not yet."

"Why not?" she and Liz said in unison.

"Because we'll likely run up against resistance if we directly criticize his man. Let's get a feel for this guy first. For now, we just answer the lieutenant's questions with the facts."

"Okay, glad I asked instead of just plunging in."

Liz was in the bedside chair, her crutch propped against the wall, and Kate was standing on the other side of Rob's bed when Lieutenant Cody entered the room. Dr. Walters followed him in and introduced him to Rob and Liz.

Kate took a step forward and extended her hand. "I'm Kate Huntington, Lieutenant."

Cody wrapped both of his hands around hers. "You have my deepest condolences, ma'am."

Disconcerted by the sympathy in his tone, Kate felt her eyes pooling with tears. She blinked them away, then whispered, "Thank you."

The lieutenant took out a small notepad and asked Rob to start at Tuesday evening, when he was working late.

Kate tried to hide her anxiety as she listened to him describe his captivity again. The lieutenant stopped him several times and asked for more details. She hoped the policeman realized that Rob's flat tone was his way of defending against his emotions.

His mind had apparently cleared enough to realize they still had no concrete evidence against Cheryl. He didn't mention her. But whenever he talked about the peephole or his captor coming into the room while he was drugged or sleeping, he would clench his jaw and close his eyes for a moment.

The second time this happened, she noticed he was also tightening his grip on his wife's hand. Liz was struggling not to react to these subtle signs of distress.

Kate's heart ached for both of them.

To hell with how it looks!

Stepping closer to the bed, she placed her hand on Rob's shoulder and squeezed gently, then left her hand resting there.

The next time Rob got to a rough spot in his story, she squeezed again. The pause was shorter and his grip on his wife's hand not quite so tight. Liz flashed her a small smile.

Lieutenant Cody was wearing his cop mask, but Kate suspected he was taking it all in. What would he make of the supposed *other* woman showing affection and support in front of the wife?

When Rob finished his story, the policeman said, "Mr. Franklin, we may have some more questions for you later. Thank you for your cooperation. Mrs. Huntington, may I speak with you for a moment outside?"

Rob became agitated. He tried to push himself more upright in the bed. "No, you may not. I'm her attorney and you cannot question her without me present."

Kate squeezed his shoulder more firmly as Dr. Walters stepped forward to intervene.

The lieutenant held up a hand. "No problem. I'll ask her my question here. Mrs. Huntington, what exactly is your relationship with Mr. Franklin?"

"*I* will answer that question, sir." Liz struggled to her feet, fire in her eyes. "Kate is my husband's *friend!* Kate is *my* friend! Her husband was my husband's friend, and my friend. Since when did they pass a law against friendship? Stop harassing us, and go find this madman!"

"Mrs. Franklin, I apologize for upsetting you. Actually friendship was the answer I was expecting, but I had to ask. Again, thank you all for your cooperation."

Dr. Walters said, "I'll see you out, Lieutenant."

Once the door had closed behind them, Liz sank back into her chair and covered her face with her hands. "Oh, hon, I'm sorry! I did exactly what you told us not to do."

"Actually, Lizzie," came Rob's tired voice from the bed. "You were perfect. Come here, hon." Liz moved into his arms and he somehow made room for her to stretch out next to him on the bed—leg brace, blue boot and all.

As Kate slipped quietly out of the room, her cell phone vibrated in her pocket.

She'd cheated today and left it on, anxious for the safety of the troops. Hurrying to the lounge area, where at least there were no signs actively prohibiting cell phones, she answered it.

She was relieved to hear the voice of the person she was most concerned about. "Senile old lady lives there. Wouldn't let us in the basement. Tell you more when we get back. Gotta get Skip to a men's room. Save my upholstery."

Then a snicker from Rose, Skip growled something in the background and Rose disconnected.

CHAPTER TWENTY-NINE

Kate sat down in the lounge area to get her thoughts organized. She'd called Pauline earlier to have her reschedule her Monday and Tuesday clients. She was hoping they could get Rob settled at home this afternoon, then make some decisions about how to proceed. Maybe she could have a day of relative normalcy tomorrow, before facing clients again on Wednesday.

When her neglected stomach rumbled, Kate selected a bag of peanuts from the vending machine. She crammed a handful into her mouth just as her cell phone vibrated again.

"Found the pervert," Mac said, with his usual lack of greeting.

Kate winced at the use of that word. She actually felt sorry in a way for this particular pervert. Ten months into therapy, Peter Lennox had admitted to Kate that he had sexually abused his niece in the past. When it came to child abuse, therapists were not only allowed to breach confidentiality, they were required to do so by law. Kate had no choice but to report him. Rob had tried to get him probation, since he was already in therapy trying to get himself straightened out. But a tough judge had given him the maximum sentence. Lennox had then turned nasty toward Kate for reporting him.

Liz had discovered he'd been paroled four months ago.

"He's in jail again," Mac said. "Been there since Friday. Violated parole. Cops caught him hangin' round a daycare center."

"Good job, Mac" came out as "Goo ja, Muc" as Kate tried to talk and chew at the same time. She swallowed, then said, "I'm going to ask the doctor to release Rob today. After we get him home, I'll see if Rose can get in to question Lennox."

"See ya in a bit, sweet pea."

It was not hard to convince Dr. Walters to release Rob sooner than she normally would. It had also occurred to her that the killer would now know where to find his escaped victim.

After the obligatory paperwork and wheelchair ride to the hospital's front door, they settled Rob and Liz in the backseat of Skip's Explorer. Kate and Rose followed in her cruiser, with the second officer bringing up the rear.

As they turned off Hillen Road onto Willow Way, they found a short row of stopped cars blocking their way. It took a moment to register that the emergency vehicles clogging the street further down the block were in front of the Franklin home.

Heart in her throat, Kate jumped out of the cruiser and ran up the sidewalk. She'd sent her father and Lou on ahead to check the house.

Rose caught up with her, then took the lead. As they reached the crowd of onlookers gathered at the police barrier, she used elbows and the power of her uniform to forge a path.

Kate was relieved to see Lou standing inside the barrier with a uniformed officer. She looked frantically around for her father. All she saw was yellow police tape strung along the sides of the yard and more officers urging people to stay back. Rose grabbed Kate's arm and lifted the tape, growling, "She's with me," at the officer who stepped into their path.

Heart pounding, Kate raced toward Lou. "Where's my father?"

"In there, Miss Kate."

Lou pointed in the direction of an ambulance, parked between two police cars. She willed her knees not to buckle, then ran toward it, and collided with her father as he stepped out of one of the police cars to intercept her.

"Tis okay, Katie girl." He caught her by the arms, keeping her from tumbling to the ground. "Settle down, lass."

"What happened?" she asked breathlessly.

But before her father could answer, a man in a suit stepped forward. "And you are, ma'am?"

"Tis me daughter," Dan answered him. "This here is Detective O'Brien, Katie. Fine young Irish lad."

Her father beamed at the forty-something detective, whose mouth twitched. But he managed to maintain his serious demeanor.

"Lou and me, we found somethin' out back."

"Bomb squad should be here soon, ma'am," the detective said.

Kate's mind reeled at the words *bomb squad*. Again, her knees wobbled. Suddenly remembering Rob and Liz, she whirled around. She didn't see them anywhere.

Guessing her thoughts, Rose whispered, "Skip probably made them stay in his truck."

Kate let out a pent-up breath and turned back to her father. "What did you find?"

"Lou found a rucksack under a bush. He was startin' to open it when I came 'round the corner. Told 'im to wait for the coppers."

A bomb squad van pulled up to the barricade, followed by two TV station vans.

Damn!

Last thing they needed now was another media frenzy and the press dogging their every move. Kate turned back to the detective. "Sir, can I ask a big favor? The owner of this house, Mr. Franklin, we were just bringing him home from the hospital. He's not up to dealing with the press. Could you downplay this as a suspected kids' prank?" She knew that would only delay the inevitable. They would connect the dots soon enough.

"And if you don't mind, I'm going to send him and his wife to my house until this all gets resolved. I'll give you my address so you can come by if you have any questions. My father and I are friends of the family. We'll stay here until the bomb squad's finished."

That must have sounded reasonable to the detective because he didn't hesitate. He gave her a slight nod, then turned to talk to the bomb squad.

Kate called Skip's cell phone to fill him in, asking him to take Rob and Liz to her house. "I'll send Lou back to you with the key. Rose checked the house quickly earlier but you and the other officer need to go over—"

"Don't worry, Kate. I'll take care of it," Skip said.

"Thank you."

A few tense minutes later, there was a rustling in the crowd. The bomb squad was coming around the corner of the house—four men covered in protective gear and carrying a large black metal box attached to two long poles. Each man was on the end of a pole, transporting the box as if it were a pharaoh on a royal litter.

As they loaded it carefully into the back of their van, the detective came back over to Kate and her father. "Box is just a precaution," he said in a low voice. "They've already disarmed it. My people are checking the rest of the property. With the owner's permission, I'd like to check inside."

Kate's mind flashed to the files and suspect lists lying around the family room. She glanced at her father.

"Me and Lou already searched inside, Katie."

She turned back to the detective. "Thank you for the offer but I don't think that will be necessary."

He gave her a suspicious look.

No wonder. Normal people don't search their friends' houses.

Her adrenaline dissipated, she was suddenly exhausted.

Rose stepped forward. "Let me fill you in, sir." She turned to Lou, who'd just returned from delivering Kate's keys. "Please take Mrs. Huntington and her father back to my car."

It was all Kate could do to keep from hugging her. "Thank you, uh...Officer Hernandez."

Thank God I don't have to tell the whole sorry story to yet another skeptical person.

It was almost six o'clock by the time Rose pulled the cruiser into the curb at Kate's house. They had gone through a fast food drive-thru to get burgers, since all the lovely groceries Liz had bought that morning were now at the house where they were not.

Liz had already settled Rob into bed in the master bedroom. Kate sent her father in to guard the napping patient. Even with two police cruisers sitting outside and Skip on the porch, she wasn't taking any chances.

"Gonna check in. See what I can find out about the bomb." Rose walked away from them to make the call.

"We left Lou guarding the house," Kate told Liz. "The bomb squad disarmed the bomb he found. I called Mac. He's on his way here. Do you think Rob will be up to having a war council later?"

"Maybe, after he's rested a bit." Her voice sounded worried.

Kate joined her on the sofa. "What's the matter?"

"I don't know. I'm probably being hypersensitive. After all, he's been through hell and he's still exhausted..."

"But?"

"He seems a little off, not really himself. But maybe I'm over-analyzing things."

"Liz, you know him better than anyone. If you think something's off, then it is. What's giving you that feeling?"

Liz thought for a moment. "I guess it's that he's too passive. When Skip said to stay in the truck, he just accepted it. And not the way he usually would when someone makes sense, where he'd think about it for a moment and then nod. He just sat there and waited, like we were stuck in traffic."

"Which definitely isn't like him. But it could be a temporary thing." Kate tried to sound reassuring as she patted Liz's hand, but she was worried herself now. It sounded like Rob was dissociating. She downplayed this some to Liz. "He may be spacing out a little because it's all too much. Let me know if you notice anything else that seems off, okay?"

"Okay. You too. Your eye is trained to pick up on this stuff better than mine."

Rose came back into the room. "Basic pipe bomb. Similar materials to the remnants they found in your car, Kate, after.... Anyway, pretty crude. Hooked up to a simple timing device. Set to go off at midnight."

Kate and Liz both gasped and grabbed for each other's hands. At midnight, they would have all been in the house.

"Lou's getting a bonus!" Liz said. "But how'd the killer know we were bringing Rob home today?"

Kate shook her head. "The assumption would be the doctors would keep him awhile longer. The perp may have been trying to take out the rest of us, so he or she'd have a clear shot at Rob when he got out of the hospital."

"Lieutenant authorized more protection," Rose said. "Two officers on you and two on Rob and Liz. Should be here soon."

"Wait a minute," Kate jumped up. "I haven't heard from Ben in awhile. He'll know if Cheryl's been hanging around your house." She pulled out her phone and dialed Ben's cell number.

After several rings, a groggy voice said, "Hello."

"Ben?"

No response.

After a few seconds, she said again, "Ben? Are you there?"

"Yeah. This Kate?" His voice sounded strange.

"Yes. Where are you?"

"That's what I'm trying to figure out. I think I'm in a hospital, in one of those little cubicles in an ER."

"Oh my God!" Kate sank back down onto the sofa, clutching the phone. "What happened?"

"Good question. Last thing I remember was seeing something moving around that lady's slider to her patio. Thought she might have spotted me watching her place and was trying to sneak out that way through the bushes. So I went to investigate."

"Are you okay?"

"Guess so. Got a big lump on the back of my head. One hell of a headache. But, don't worry, I've got a thick skull."

"What time did all this happen?" Kate asked.

"Just after three. I'll head back over to her place now."

"No. You stay put until the doctors have checked you over thoroughly. Then go to the Franklins' house. Lou's there by himself." Kate told him about the bomb. "Keep me posted on what the press is doing, will you?"

She was telling Liz and Rose what had happened to Ben when the doorbell rang. Kate went to answer it, Rose trailing after her. Kate groaned as she looked through the peephole. "Our extra protection is here. The good news is, one of them is Officer Young. The bad news is the other's Trudow."

"I'll talk to them." Rose opened the door and stepped out onto the porch, motioning for Skip to take her place inside.

Kate filled Skip in. "Not like Ben to let a woman get the better of him," he was saying when Rose came back inside.

Kate said, "Yeah, but he may have underestimated her *because* she's a woman."

"Timing's a little tight," Rose said. "But she could've gotten to the house and planted the bomb before your dad and Lou got there. All Phillips told Calvin and Trudow was the protection's been beefed up. So I took the liberty of telling them the lieutenant no longer buys Phillips' theory, and we're to assume there's a real threat out there."

"Do you really think the lieutenant believes us now?" Liz asked.

"Probably, but don't know for sure. But then neither does Trudow." Rose flashed a small grin.

"Anybody but Trudow," Kate said.

"May be a case of better the devil we know. He seems to think I outrank him. Guess that's something else he doesn't know, that I've only been on the job a few months longer than him."

Mac arrived, getting past Trudow with a minimum of growling and posturing back and forth. Kate's grumbling stomach reminded them that the burgers were getting cold.

As they started to eat, Rose said, "Seems to me our perp is doing that decomposing you were talking about the other day, Kate."

Kate grinned. "Decompensating, but decomposing isn't a bad way of describing it either. I agree. But you tell me your reasoning first, Rose."

"This attempt with the bomb wasn't very well thought out. And the method of attack keeps changing."

"But that's been the case all along," Liz said.

"Rob's escape might have made the killer more desperate," Kate said. "And the attack on Ben definitely points toward Cheryl. The changing *modus operandi* would fit with her. There may be several alters involved, and they each have their own preferred method of attack. I think it's time to set some kind of trap to see if she takes the bait."

"What bait we gonna use?" Mac asked.

Kate took a deep breath. At least her father was out of earshot, so she could deal with one protective male at a time. "I think it has to be me." Then she quickly added, "I know there's some risk involved, but we can't go on like this forever. We need to be more proactive, or eventually the killer's going to get to one of us again."

To her surprise, Mac didn't argue. He looked thoughtful for a moment. "Gonna need a surefire plan. We take this woman down before she gets anywhere near you."

Kate nodded. That sounded like an excellent idea to her.

"You're gonna need more shootin' practice, sweet pea."

She grimaced. "Why? I thought you just said I wasn't going to be the one to take her down."

"Just in case. You're gonna have that .32 on you. And you're gonna know how to use it."

Rose said, "Amen."

With another grimace, Kate shrugged her acceptance.

"Where do you shoot, Mac?" Rose asked.

"Out in the boonies. Northern part of the county. Took her once before. Lousy shot."

"Sounds good to me," Rose said.

Mac scowled at her. "Don't remember invitin' you."

Kate reached over and punched him in the shoulder. "Stop trying to stick her pigtails in the inkwell, Mac. She's coming."

Rose's eyebrow went up.

"*Anne of Green Gables*," Kate prompted.

"Girl, you gotta learn how to read." Mac's tone was derisive.

"I know how to read. Just don't have time."

"Important. Make time."

"Yeah, I'll get right on that, right after I save Kate's and Rob's lives!"

Liz interrupted their spat. "May I suggest we *all* get a good night's sleep and tomorrow morning we'll plan how to set this trap."

Kate groaned inside. So much for a day of normalcy. "I think you and Rob should stay here tonight," she said. "Hopefully the press will have lost interest by tomorrow."

"And tomorrow afternoon," Rose said, "we take you target practicing, Kate."

This time she groaned out loud.

CHAPTER THIRTY

As Kate had suspected it would be, the war council the next morning was long and intense.

She was relieved to see that, after a good night's sleep, Rob seemed more grounded.

Skip made pancakes for everyone. Over breakfast around her kitchen table, Kate summarized their investigations for Rob's benefit. "Recent events have made Cheryl our number one suspect," she concluded. "So I think we need to set a trap for her. She'll either step into it or not. And if she doesn't, then we can investigate the others some more."

Rob turned toward her. "I could work late again. See if we can lure her into taking another crack at me."

Behind his back, Liz was emphatically shaking her head. Kate wholeheartedly agreed. No way were they putting Rob at risk again. "Well, I don't know how realistic that would look. You're in the hospital, and just a few days later you're working overtime, and unguarded?"

Liz quickly added, "Cheryl would realize you aren't that stupid and might catch on that it's a trap."

"Besides," Rose said, "the perp hasn't repeated him…herself yet. Used the same kind of weapon a couple times. But not in quite the same way. Not sure she'd come after Rob again at the office."

"Could use meself again, to draw her out," Dan said.

Rose shook her head. "Actually, I'm not sure our perp even realizes you're related to Kate. After all the times we tossed you out there as bait, and never a bite."

In response to Rob's puzzled look, they told him about their efforts to find him, including trying to get the kidnapper to go after Dan.

By the time they had finished, Rob's eyes were shiny. Voice rough with emotion, he said, "I'm the luckiest man on earth to have you all for friends."

Rose rolled her eyes. Mac squirmed a little in his chair.

Kate hid a smile. *Yet another thing these two have in common–a low mush tolerance.*

Rose pursed her lips and looked right at her. Kate nodded slightly.

Rose gave her the necessary opening. "So how *are* we going to bait the trap?"

Kate took a deep breath. "Guess it's my turn to be the worm on the hook." She was praying her father wouldn't blow.

No such luck.

He jumped out of his chair. "No! Yer not doin' that!"

"Dad, calm down."

"The hell I'll calm down, Kathleen!"

Kate stood up. "Dad, listen. We *can't* continue to live like this. Rob and Liz can't even let their daughters come home. We've got to stop this woman. This is the only way."

Her father glared at her. "We almost lost Mary…." His voice broke.

"I know," she said softly, "but think about this. I can't visit Mary, or Ma, or my brothers, and they can't come to see me because it isn't safe." Her chest tightened. She fought back the tears stinging her eyes. "I've lost my husband, Dad, and I need my family…." She lost the battle. The tears came.

Her father reached out and crushed her against him in a bear hug. "Tis okay, Katie girl, tis goin' to be okay," he murmured.

She allowed herself the luxury of sobbing softly against his sturdy chest for a minute, then she pulled back and looked up into his face. "Dad, without Eddie, I'm not sure it's ever going to be totally okay for me. But if we can stop this woman, then I can get on with my life."

And raise your grandchild in safety, she thought but didn't dare say out loud.

"Okay, you win." He looked around at the others. "We'll bait this trap with me daughter, but we ain't lettin' nothin' happen to her!"

A chorus of "Amen."

Kate found a tissue and blew her nose. She and her father resumed their seats, then she laid out the beginnings of a plan that she'd come up with. "I think it needs to be at the office. That's the easiest place to set up the illusion that I'm alone while you all are actually nearby. And I'm scheduled to see Cheryl tomorrow so I can drop something into the conversation about how I have to work late the next couple nights to get caught up on paperwork after being out sick."

"But how do we explain the sudden lack of police protection and bodyguards?" Rob asked.

"Yeah, she's going to wonder why suddenly there aren't any police cars outside," Liz said. "And she may have caught on that Rose is one of your bodyguards. She'll wonder why she's gone."

"Could make a case that the protection's been switched to Rob," Rose said, "because of the kidnapping."

"Good idea," Kate said. "And I think I know how to convey that information. I'll call Pauline tonight and see if she's willing to do some acting while Cheryl's in the waiting room tomorrow. Pretend she's talking to a friend and is nervous because the protection's been pulled off of me."

"You think she'll go for that?" Rob asked.

"Probably. Pauline loves a little excitement now and again. The question is will she agree to not tell our boss. There's no way Sally would go along with setting a trap for one of our clients right there in the center."

"So assuming Pauline's cooperative, how do we arrange folks to keep you safe?" Liz asked.

It was decided that the bodyguards would watch the outside entrances from discrete hiding places. Rose would be in the center's ladies room, around the corner from Kate's office, and Mac would be in the law firm's reception area down the hall.

The tension rose again as both her father and Rob insisted on being part of the operation.

"Dad, just in case the perp does know you're my father, you need to stay here, for the same reasons Liz and I couldn't help look for Rob. Someone would have to be with you to protect you."

"I'll not be sittin' cozy back here while me daughter's in danger."

"Dan stays with Liz," Rob said, "but I'll be with Mac!"

Kate was pleased to see a spark of his old gumption coming back. Unfortunately they were going to have to snuff it out. "Rob, dear, it killed Liz and me to sit and wait while you were in danger. But we would've been an encumbrance rather than a help. The others wouldn't have been able to concentrate on finding you."

Rob's determined expression didn't changed.

Rose shook her head. "If either of you are there, then we can't focus on *keeping Kate safe.* We'd have to watch out for you as well."

"She's right," Mac grumbled, his tone implying that he hated to have to agree with her.

Dan and Rob slumped back in their seats in defeat. It was an argument they couldn't refute.

Liz took Rob's hand. "How do you feel about jigsaw puzzles, hon?"

~~~~~~~~~

In a clearing in the woods, Mac tacked a paper outline of a man to a tree, then worked with Kate on her stance and how to squeeze the trigger slowly. After a half hour of missing the target completely, she dropped her hands to her sides, pointing the gun at the ground as Mac had taught her. "This is hopeless."

Rose had been standing by, quietly watching. Now she stepped forward. "You're closing your eyes and flinching at the last minute, and then your hands jerk upward."

Kate tried several more times, but was still hitting well above the target.

"Mac, you got any tin cans in your truck?" Rose asked.

He snorted. "Yeah, but she's gonna be shootin' at a person, not a can of chili."

"I think that's the problem. So let's start her on cans. When she can actually shoot straight, then we get her used to human targets."

"Waste of time," Mac said.

But Kate nodded. "I think Rose is onto something. Get the cans, Mac."

Grumbling, he went to get the cans.

Sure enough, over the next hour, Kate's aim improved until she was hitting the cans three times out of four. Then Rose drew a tin can on one of the human outline targets, in the middle of the torso.

"Just focus on the can," she said.

"Just focus on the can," Mac mimicked in a high-pitched voice.

Kate blew. She whirled around toward him, remembering at the last second to point the gun at the ground. "Mac, cut it out! We're all tense enough without you sniping at Rose. If you can't act like an adult around her, we'll send you back to your restaurant!"

Mac glared at her, then stomped off toward his truck.

Kate was debating whether to follow him–to apologize or keep yelling, she wasn't sure which–when Rose quietly said, "Ignore him. If you try to talk to him right now, you're just gonna get male ego talking back."

Kate nodded, and focused on the drawing of the can on the target.

And hit it dead center. Despite her aversion to the whole concept of guns, a bubble of excitement rose in her chest. Hot damn, she was finally getting the hang of this.

She steadied her hands and squeezed the trigger. Dead center again. The third shot was slightly above the can, but still in the middle of the chest.

"Alright! You go, girl," Rose said. "Any one of those shots would stop somebody, or at least slow them down long enough to get off another shot. Now we're gonna practice that."

Kate practiced for another half hour, shooting two to three shots in rapid succession, until they were all in or near the can. She was feeling rather pleased with herself.

Rose drew on another target–a big round belly, and a tin can in the chest area, just above the belly.

Kate stared at it, frozen. Her vision blurred. For a moment, she thought she might faint.

Rose had stepped well back. Her expression grim, she nodded.

Kate lifted the pistol in shaking hands, then let it drop again. "My arms are too tired to do this anymore."

Mac had moved up behind them again. He shot Rose a look that Kate couldn't quite interpret.

Rose nodded slightly. "Okay, but you might want to try at least a few times. Otherwise, we'll have to come back tomorrow afternoon. Just focus on the can."

Kate grimaced. She aimed and pulled the trigger. The gun jerked up again.

Mac's voice came from behind her, unusually gentle. "Kate, look at the can and tell yourself, 'It's only a tin can.'"

After several more tries, she was able to shoot the picture of the can five times in a row fairly accurately.

Rose drew on another target. Big belly, no can this time. "Now pretend there's a picture of a tin can on her chest."

Kate steeled herself and pulled the trigger. It went a bit high, hitting the target's head.

"Middle of the chest, Kate," Mac said in the same strangely gentle voice.

They wouldn't let her stop until she'd put six holes in a row in the middle of the target's chest.

~~~~~~~~~

Wednesday, as Kate dressed for work, she tried to calm her nerves by reviewing the plan for baiting the trap. Pauline had willingly agreed to be part of the adventure. She would tell Cheryl that Kate was running a little behind schedule. Then, with the client listening, she'd fake the call to a friend to complain about the withdrawal of police protection. Kate was praying that Sally wouldn't come into the waiting area during this little charade.

She had far more confidence in Pauline's acting ability than she did in her own. Hopefully, she'd be able to get her scene over with at the beginning of the session, by dropping a comment about her need to work late into the casual, how-have-you-been chit chat as she ushered Cheryl into the office. With that behind her, she could then shift into therapist mode and get through the rest of the session.

Kate's first prayer was answered—Pauline's scene went off without a hitch and without Sally's knowledge—but the second prayer was not granted. When Kate stepped into the waiting area at five minutes after eleven, it was obvious that the personality seething in Cheryl's body was not in the mood for chit chat. Kate braced herself and led the way into her office.

She'd no sooner closed the office door than 'Cheryl' lit into her. "You've got a lot of nerve. First you cancel, *twice,* and now you keep us waiting. Well, you better not try to cut us short 'cause we're gettin' our time!"

Kate knew better than to offer the obvious defense, that she couldn't control being out sick. Such a defense when a client was angry about perceived abandonment just kept the confrontation going. Hard as it was, you had to swallow your pride, stay calm and try to get back into sync with the client.

"I understand that you're angry. I'd be upset too if I needed to talk to my therapist and couldn't get in to see–"

"What makes you think we needed you, bitch," the client interrupted in a deep snarl that sent a cold shiver down Kate's spine.

She struggled to keep her voice calm. "Okay, why did you *want* to see me? What's been happening?"

Cheryl sat back in her chair and her face subtly shifted. "I'm sorry, my mind drifted for a minute. What were we talking about?"

Kate breathed out a quiet sigh. "I was wondering how things are going for you? It's been awhile since we've been able to meet."

The young woman began filling her in on the events in her life over the last couple weeks. Kate almost fell off her chair when Cheryl started venting about visiting her great aunt, who had berated her for not coming around more often.

Kate quickly schooled her face into a neutral expression.

Did the kidnapping alter use the senile aunt's basement as a prison without the host alter's awareness?

"And to think I spent some of my hard-earned money to buy her groceries," Cheryl wound down.

Kate commiserated and was finally offered the opportunity she needed as the session ended. Cheryl wished her a good afternoon off.

She grimaced. "Not going to be much time off this week, I'm afraid. I'm so backed up with paperwork, I'm going to be here this afternoon and late tomorrow, and probably Friday evening as well." She could only hope that the possible perp alter was listening in.

Cheryl sympathized and said her farewells. Once she'd left, Kate collapsed into her chair in relief. She definitely was not meant for the stage. Her hand was shaking as she picked up her pen to jot some notes in the case file.

After trying to concentrate on paperwork for a few hours, she decided she'd stayed long enough on her first day back from supposedly being sick.

The others were using two-way radios provided by Mac, but Kate had decided against carrying one. She was afraid it would squawk at the wrong moment, when the perp was in earshot. Instead, she was relying on cell phone contact.

She called Rose and told her she was leaving.

Rose spread the word to the others. A few minutes later, Skip radioed that Kate was safely in her car and headed home.

According to plan, Rose donned a big hat and sunglasses and went out the front.

Lou, who'd been watching the building from Ed's Saturn, did a credible impersonation of a dutiful husband waiting for his wife. He got out and opened the passenger door for her.

She managed to hide her surprise when he landed a peck on her cheek.

Phase one of Let's Trap a Killer had been completed.

CHAPTER THIRTY-ONE

Kate wasn't surprised that she had trouble sleeping that night. She kept going over and over the plan in her head. She was finally drifting off when a new thought yanked her back from the edge of sleep.

Shooting at paper silhouettes of pregnant women was one thing. Shooting a real pregnant woman was another. Could she risk an innocent child to save herself? She was fairly sure she could not, even if she was being attacked by that unborn child's mother.

And the person she knew as Cheryl–a good woman who was trying to create a new life for herself and her child–that person would be just as dead as the murderous alter, if Kate or the others had to shoot to stop her.

"Oh, Eddie," she whispered into the darkness. "What am I going to do?" But this time there was no answering baritone. Either her conversations with her dead husband had truly been products of her grieving imagination, or he had no answer either.

Tears burned her eyes. A jumble of feelings welled up inside her chest, demanding release. She rolled over onto her stomach, buried her face in her pillow and let them escape.

A couple minutes into a good cry, she became aware of a subtle sensation, a fluttering in her stomach. She lay still. There it was again. Not the same as the anxiety that had been twisting in her gut a little while ago.

She felt it yet again. The slightest ripple of movement in her abdomen, made by a tiny fetus pressed against the mattress.

A new emotion welled up in her.

She had her answer. She couldn't kill to save herself, but to save her *own* baby? Yes, she could kill to protect this precious living piece of Eddie that was now quite real to her.

"I can do it for my baby," she whispered as she rolled over onto her back.

Our baby, love, came the soft baritone in her head.

~~~~~~~~~

At breakfast Thursday morning, Rob informed his wife that he was going into the office. She looked at him through narrowed eyes.

He covered her hand with his own on the kitchen table. "Hon, I'm not trying to set myself up as a target. I'm just feeling restless and I'm sure the paperwork on my desk has not miraculously disappeared. Besides my police escorts around the building will discourage Cheryl from trying anything during the day. We want her to strike after hours, when there are fewer people around. Less risk of someone getting caught in the crossfire."

Liz was still glaring at him. He added, "And the police coming and going with me confirms that they've been switched off of Kate."

Liz partially relented. "Half a day."

"We'll see how things go."

Officer Young drove him to the office, where Fran greeted him with tears and a big hug. Within minutes, his partners and the entire staff were crowding around him to express their relief and welcome him back.

Once the others had dispersed, Rob waved Fran into his office. He gingerly lowered his sore body into his desk chair. "I need you to do something for me."

"Of course, boss."

He wasn't so sure she'd be agreeable when she heard what it was.

"Once John and Bill have left for their court cases this afternoon, I want you to go around and tell everyone they are to go home at five sharp, no matter what they're working on."

Fran gave him a narrow-eyed look disturbingly reminiscent of his wife's.

"I can't explain now but it's important. Life and death important."

She crossed her arms. "You're not staying after five, are you?"

"No, I'm not." He honestly didn't think he'd make it that long.

Fran finally agreed to spread the word for him.

He spent the morning valiantly attacking the mountain of documents on his desk. By eleven, he was wishing humankind had never discovered how to mash wood pulp into paper. But if he concentrated hard enough on the paperwork he could ignore his sore thumb and feet. And the half-healed scratches on his back and shoulder that had now reached the itchy stage. The scabs caught on his shirt every time he moved.

By lunchtime, he had to admit his body was giving out on him. Fran brought him a sandwich from the deli. When she got a good look at his face, she said, "Boss, you've got to go home." He offered a feeble protest but she went right for the ultimate weapon. "Don't make me call your wife."

All he could do was pray that the police presence for at least half a day had discouraged Cheryl from striking until after hours.

By one-thirty, he was tucked into bed with a pain pill and a promise from Liz that she would wake him at five, so they could wait and worry together.

~~~~~~~~~

At five, everyone was in place. Not wanting Trudow's cruiser in the lot, Rose had convinced him to guard Kate's house, to discourage the delivery of any more bombs. She and Mac were inside the building and the bodyguards were hidden strategically around the outside, positioned so that, between the three of them, they could see all the entrances.

Liz had compiled a packet for each of them, with the physical descriptions, and where available, photos of their suspects, including those still on the possibilities list. If the bodyguards saw any of them entering the building, they were to call Kate's cell phone.

Then she would turn out the light, lock her office door and stand back against the wall, gun ready should the killer break down her door before the others could close in. Once Kate had been warned, the radios would be employed to alert everyone else and they would close the net.

Mac had wanted Kate to keep her door locked the whole time, but she felt that made her more vulnerable. If she couldn't see or hear what was going on in the outer office, she could be taken by surprise should someone slip past her protectors. The argument had been settled when Rob had agreed with her. The flimsy lock could easily be broken and her attacker would be inside her office before she could react. The outer door of the center would be locked, but its glass window made it a poor barrier as well.

At six o'clock, the rent-a-cop security guard made the rounds of the building's entrances, setting the locks so the doors could be opened only from the inside. A few minutes later, he came out the back door and left. Mac then went around and discreetly unlocked the doors again. There was a risk the easy access would make the perp suspicious, but the bodyguards needed to be able to get into the building quickly.

By seven, the setting sun was behind the building, casting the back parking lot in shadow. Now the light in Kate's window made it obvious hers was the only occupied office on the back of the building.

They had decided to keep the trap set until nine, a likely time that Kate might call it a night.

By eight-forty, nothing had happened, and Kate was a nervous wreck. She dreaded the thought that they would have to go through all this again tomorrow night. But another part of her was starting to feel relieved. Maybe the perp wasn't Cheryl after all.

Was that a noise out in the hall, or just her anxious imagination? She strained to hear in the silence of the deserted building.

Then she definitely heard several sounds at once–a scratching noise, a soft crack and distant rapid clicking.

Kate jumped out of her chair, barely catching the pistol as it started to tumble from her lap. She raced to the wall switch and doused the light. Then she stared at the door resting back against the office wall, on the *other* side of the doorway. No way was she crossing that open space to get to the door and close it.

Her cell phone began to vibrate, purring and dancing around on her desk.

A day late and a dollar short, guys!

A bubble of hysteria tried to escape from her throat. Her racing pulse made her ears ring.

She took a deep breath and backed away from the doorway, sliding her right shoulder along the wall to steady herself. She stretched her arms out in front of her as she had been taught, grasping the gun in both hands.

A figure stepped into the doorway, silhouetted against the light from the outer office. A distended belly hung across the threshold.

Her heart sank. She held her breath.

A roar and a flash of bright light. The back of her desk chair disintegrated.

She gasped.

The figure turned toward her. A low voice growled, "Got ya now, bitch!"

Kate clenched her jaw. She squeezed the trigger.

CHAPTER THIRTY-TWO

She sagged against the wall, trembling fingers fumbling for the light switch. Her gaze focused on the ghostly pale face of the woman she had just shot.

The ghost, still standing, looked down at the floor. "Frank, what the *hell* have you done?"

Kate shook her head, her mind stalled. She followed Cheryl's line of vision to a man lying in the doorway. Blood was spreading across the T-shirt stretched over his beer belly.

Relief washed through her. She caught movement in her peripheral vision. "Don't shoot!" She yanked Cheryl out of the doorway.

Rose and Mac converged on them, guns aimed at the man on the floor. Ignoring the blood, Rose cuffed the man's wrists together. Footsteps pounded up the stairs.

"Is he dead?" Cheryl asked in a tone that said she wasn't quite sure how she'd feel about the answer either way.

"No," Mac growled.

The bodyguards swarmed into the outer office. At the sight of Rose and Mac standing over a bleeding, handcuffed man, they raised their gun barrels toward the ceiling.

"Somebody call Rob and Liz," Kate said. Skip was already talking into his cell phone. She heard a trio of relieved shouts from ten feet away.

Cheryl looked again at her husband. She shook her head. "He called and said he was gonna take care of those, quote, 'people who were keepin' us apart.' Then he hung up. I remembered you were working late, and I got a *real bad* feeling." She tilted her head toward the empty reception desk. "I called but just got voicemail, so I hightailed it over here to warn you."

Her voice became child-like. "I was so scared he'd hurt you."

Kate wrapped her arms around her trembling client and whispered in her ear, "It's okay, honey. We're both safe now. He's never going to hurt either one of us again."

Mac had stepped around them to lean over and pick up the .32 lying on the floor.

Rose's quiet but firm voice stopped him. "Mac, don't touch that gun. Legal or not, it's evidence."

~~~~~~~~~~

Rob, Liz and Dan arrived a few minutes after the back-up officers and the ambulance Rose had called for. She was handcuffing the prisoner's wrist to the side bar of the paramedics' gurney, when Lieutenant Cody threaded his way through the now crowded room.

Rob took him aside and pointed out that the two women he needed to question were both pregnant and had just been through a harrowing experience. "I'm sure you don't want to be responsible for adding to their stress level right now."

The lieutenant got the hint. He took a short statement from Kate and Cheryl, then told Rob to bring them to the police station the next morning.

Detective Phillips arrived as Rob was asking Ben to escort Cheryl home. This time Rob was more direct. "Keep that man away from us, Lieutenant, or I *will* be filing a lawsuit against the police department tomorrow morning for harassment and dereliction of duty."

CHAPTER THIRTY-THREE

A good part of Friday was spent at the police station, being interviewed and then asked to wait while one of the others was questioned. Then everyone was interviewed again.

Lieutenant Cody conducted most of the interviews. Phillips was nowhere to be seen, much to Kate's relief. The lieutenant wanted them to start at the beginning with the hit-and-run.

Finally, their statements were being typed up to be signed.

At the end of her shift on Saturday, Rose stopped by the house. Kate called Mac and asked him to bring something over from the restaurant for their dinner. While feasting on spinach pie and Maryland crab soup, Rose filled them in.

The judge had denied Crofton bail, and he had been transferred to the county jail's infirmary that morning. Rose, as the arresting officer, was being allowed to be present during the interrogations. No one had ever caught on that she had failed to report everything to her commanding officer.

Crofton had been assigned a public defender, who was trying to keep him from talking. But the physical evidence the police had gathered–both from the truck he had borrowed from a friend and from the motel room where he'd been holed up–was damning.

Rose rattled off the list. Threads caught in a bolt on the truck's bumper matched the skirt Liz had been wearing when she was hit. A shotgun, syringes, and an almost empty bottle of animal tranquilizer were found in his room. The tool box in the back of the truck had contained a stun gun and a baseball bat with dried blood on it–Mary's blood type.

A few of Crofton's hairs were on the backpack in the Franklins' backyard. The bomb in the backpack was the same type used in Ed's murder, which unfortunately was the only link with that crime. However, the State's Attorney was planning to charge Crofton with first-degree murder anyway. The bombing fit the rest of the pattern.

"No jury's likely to believe that two murderers were stalking you at the same time, Kate," Rose said.

"Humph. They knew how annoyin' she can be, they might," Mac teased.

Kate shot him a mock glare. "The lesson here is never underestimate wimps. Apparently when he no longer had Cheryl as a punching bag, his anger built up enough to give him the gumption to come after us. He probably figured that, without our support, Cheryl would go back to him."

Her heart thumped in her chest as she braced herself for the next topic of conversation. "Dad, Mac, I've got some news." She took a deep breath. "I, uh, I'm pregnant."

The two men sat in stunned silence. The range of emotions crossing her father's face would have been comical if Kate hadn't been so afraid that anger would win out.

Finally he stood up and lumbered around the table. He pulled her out of her chair and engulfed her in a big hug. Mac let out a whoop so loud it rattled the windows.

The smile on Rose's face actually stuck around for more than a few seconds.

~~~~~~~~~

At twelve-thirty on Wednesday, Kate was sitting in Mac's Place, waiting for Rob. At Liz's insistence, he was only working half days while his body continued to recuperate from his ordeal. But Kate was concerned about how well his mind was healing.

He arrived and lowered himself carefully onto the bench across from her in the booth. "How you doing, Kate?"

"Pretty good, all things considered. How about yourself? And how's Liz?"

"She's good. Oh, this is for you." He handed her a slip of paper. "She took the liberty of rescheduling your doctor's appointment to next Wednesday."

"Wow. She got me in again that soon?"

"Yeah, they were resistant but she pointed out that kidnappings and attempted murder were damned good reasons for broken doctor's appointments."

"Well, thank her for me, and I will definitely keep this one."

He gave her a worried look. "So how are you really doing, Kate?"

She studied his drawn face, the dark circles under his eyes. He'd given her the opening she needed, but she would answer his question first, before turning the tables on him. "I know I should be angry, and I'm sure that feeling will surface eventually. But right now I'm mostly relieved, and also... I'm not even sure what to call it. It just sickens me that my work brought about Eddie's death."

Tears pooled in her eyes. She opted to ignore them. "I had a long talk with Sally Monday. I told her I wasn't willing to take any more domestic violence cases for awhile. And maybe never again."

As one of the pools broke loose, Rob dug out his handkerchief and handed it to her. Dabbing at her eyes, she managed a weak smile. "I think I have a whole washer load of these now."

He gave her a small smile back. "Is Sally going along with that?"

"Well, she's not happy about it. We decided that I wouldn't take on *any* new cases for now, since I'll be taking maternity leave in a few months. And I'm only going to work part time after the baby's born."

"Can you afford that?"

"Well, actually yes. It turns out Eddie and Paul Richardson took out partners' life insurance policies a few years ago. The insurance company sweetened the deal with a good price on personal policies, for a million dollars each."

Rob's mouth dropped open. "You didn't know about it?"

"No, and we'll never know now why Eddie didn't tell me. Although it fits with his personality, to quietly take care of things behind the scenes, without a fuss." Tears were leaking out of her eyes again.

"Yeah, that would be like him," Rob said in a soft voice, his own eyes shiny.

She wiped her cheeks with his handkerchief.

Rob sat back and let out a low whistle. "So you're a rich woman now. Damn, it's a good thing Phillips *is* so lazy. If he'd found out about that policy, he would've arrested you for sure."

"Paul didn't like the detective's attitude, so he neglected to mention the insurance policy. That's why he held off telling me about it as well, hoping the case would be solved quickly. He figured if it came out later, he'd just pretend it had slipped his mind."

The waitress appeared beside their booth. "Sorry about the wait, folks. What'll it be?" They ordered their usual crab cake sandwiches, with salad and fries respectively.

"So, how about yourself? How are *you* doing *really?*" Kate was watching his eyes. For a brief moment she had her answer, before the emotional shutters began to close. "Don't bother with the macho cover-up, bub." She pointed her thumb at her chest. "Closest friend here, who also happens to be a shrink."

He gave her a small grin, then his expression sobered. "Honestly, I haven't been sleeping all that well."

"Nightmares?"

"Yeah, almost every night. And the stuff I dream about, it doesn't make sense."

Before Kate could respond, he went on. "While I was there, in that basement..." He looked away. "I thought it was Cheryl who'd kidnapped me." He stared at the condiments at the end of the table.

"I felt... I don't even know what to call it. I think I felt some of what a woman would feel who's been kidnapped by a rapist. Maybe not as physically vulnerable. But the thought of her watching me through that peephole and coming in when I was passed out, it really...." Rob shuddered slightly as his voice trailed off.

Kate had never felt the feeling he was trying to name, but she'd heard it described all too often by her clients. There was no good word for it–that sense of being stripped bare, figuratively if not literally, and at the mercy of someone who sees you as an object to be used rather than another human being.

She wanted to tell him how normal it was that he'd felt that way, under the circumstances. But she caught herself. There were things a therapist could say that a friend, especially a female friend, could not. If he knew just how well she understood that dehumanizing feeling, he might never be able to look her in the eyes again.

He was staring down at the table. "It really creeped me out, for lack of a better way of putting it."

Then he looked up and his voice took on a frustrated edge. "But that wasn't what really happened. Her son-of-a-bitch husband was the kidnapper. Yet the stuff I'm dreaming, it's as if it had been Cheryl. That's totally crazy, isn't it?"

"Not at all." Kate reached for his hand resting on the table. "Emotions aren't always logical. You felt some intense feelings during a scary experience. The fact that some of your perceptions of that experience turned out to be inaccurate later, when you had more information, well, that's pretty much irrelevant to your emotions. It was what you experienced at the time, and the stress of that trauma is causing the nightmares."

Rob looked at her in disbelief. "Are you telling me I have PTSD?"

"Yes, and I'd be surprised if you didn't have at least some post-traumatic stress symptoms. You were kidnapped, and your life was in danger!"

His expression was now an odd mixture of relief, anxiety and embarrassment.

She squeezed his hand. "Rob, the definition of trauma is something so overwhelming that we can't process it emotionally at the time it happens. Even the strongest people may struggle with processing those emotions later. Indeed, stronger people are *more* likely to push aside their feelings so they can act to get themselves out of the bad situation. Which is exactly what you did. But those feelings don't just go away, not until we let ourselves feel them, so we can get them out of our systems. And telling ourselves it's over or that we shouldn't feel that way doesn't work."

The waitress chose that moment to bring their food. Kate let go of his hand to pick up her sandwich. She took a bite, but her eyes never left Rob's face as he digested what she'd said.

He busied himself with swiping her pickles to add to his own on his sandwich, which always made her wince. Seemed like the ruination of a good crab cake to her.

"I have another question about those feelings." He chewed on a French fry for a moment. "At the time, I felt... responsible, like I'd somehow caused it to happen. Because I didn't think to call Lou from the office phone, just went out there by myself, like a dunce–"

She intentionally interrupted him. "That's a very normal reaction. When something bad happens, we beat up on ourselves for some little thing we did or didn't do that we think might have changed the outcome."

"Yeah, that's it exactly. I was trying to figure out what I'd done to get myself into such a mess."

"Rob, it wasn't your fault!"

"Yeah, I know that up here." He touched his temple. "But I still felt that way, and kind of still do. It doesn't make sense."

Kate put her sandwich down. "Actually in a weird way, it does. We human beings can't stand to feel helpless. We'd rather blame ourselves, to give ourselves some sense of control, rather than acknowledge that there truly was nothing we could do about what happened."

"So by telling myself, if I'd just called Lou I wouldn't have been kidnapped, I'm..." He faltered, looking confused.

"... taking back some semblance of control," Kate said.

"'Cause it's better to feel guilty than helpless."

"Exactly. As awful as guilt feels, it trumps helpless every time."

"Okay, that makes sense 'cause I felt plenty helpless too, and that truly was an awful feeling." Rob finally picked up his sandwich and took a bite.

After a moment, he asked, "So how long am I likely to have these nightmares?"

"That's hard to say, but you don't have to just wait for them to go away." Kate pulled her wallet out of her purse and extracted the business card of a colleague–a card she had strategically placed there before leaving the office. "I strongly recommend that you see this lady a few times, to help you get through all this."

His face was skeptical as he read the card.

"Rob, trauma can cause all kinds of repercussions. It can undermine trust, affect our relationships."

His expression still said, *I'll think about it and get back to you.*

"This is my field." She heard the edge of anger in her voice and decided not to suppress it. "You expect me to listen to you when you give me legal advice, well you need to listen to me on this. You are one of the most mentally healthy people I've ever known. I do *not* want this bastard leaving any lasting scars on your psyche! Please, do this, for me, and for Liz and the girls, if not for yourself."

"Now that's playing dirty."

"Hey, I'm willing to play dirty if that's what it takes."

He raised his hands in surrender. "Okay, okay, I'll call her and make an appointment. I should know better than to resist when I'm dealing with the second most stubborn woman I've ever known."

Kate grinned. "Liz being the first, of course."

"First of what?" Rose asked as she dropped onto the bench next to Kate. She was wearing jeans and the peach knit top that made her skin glow.

"Rob's list of most stubborn women. Liz is first and I'm second."

"Can I be third?" Rose asked, a mischievous twinkle in her eye. "Stubborn women get things done."

Rob chuckled. "An astute observation, Rosie!"

She winced. "Never should've told you all I don't like Rosie. Now you're gonna use it against me every chance you get, aren't you?"

"Yeah, but we only tease people we like." Kate smiled at her.

"Not that I'm not delighted to see you, Rose, but what brings you here?" Rob asked.

Kate answered for her. "She's going shopping with me this afternoon, for maternity clothes. Everything's getting tight."

Rose winced again.

"Not big on shopping, huh?" Rob said.

"She made me feel sorry for her. Said Liz was too busy, getting caught up at work."

"You don't have to go!" Kate protested.

"Naw, I don't really mind."

The waitress came along to ask about dessert.

Kate ordered a brownie with vanilla ice cream.

I am eating for two, and I've been really good about avoiding caffeine lately, she rationalized to herself.

"Get something, Rose. It's on me. Payment for going shopping."

"Geez, Kate, first shopping, now chocolate desserts. You trying to turn me into a girlie girl?" But she did order a brownie, no ice cream.

"So anything new on the case?" Rob asked.

"Yeah, but you've got to pretend we never had this conversation." Rob and Kate both nodded.

"Bastard confessed this morning, so there won't be any trial."

Rob breathed an audible sigh of relief.

"Hallelujah!" Kate said. "Did he give any reason why he did it? Besides the obvious that he blamed us for the break-up of his marriage."

"Yeah, at first he was focused on you, Rob, 'cause you were handling Cheryl's case *pro bono*. His rationale for going after Liz was kind of confusing. Sounded like a combination of revenge–take away your wife since he saw you as taking away his–and he figured if he could distract you with a dead wife, get you out of the picture for awhile, the other lawyers at your firm wouldn't be willing to handle Cheryl's case for free. My sense is, also, that he was too chicken to take on a man directly, so he went after Liz instead. When that didn't work, he tried to shoot you from a distance. Didn't even realize your daughter was with you."

"Why'd he switch his focus onto Kate?" Rob asked.

"That happened when Cheryl told him Kate had advised her to change her phone number so he couldn't call her. He also got it in his head that her buying a gun was Kate's idea."

"Hardly. I never was too thrilled about her having that gun." She still wasn't, since she was more convinced than ever that Cheryl had D.I.D.

"How'd Crofton happen to be there Thursday night?" Rob asked. "Just coincidence that he stepped into our trap?"

"That's the question that led to his confessing. Umpteenth time he was asked why he was in the building, he said, 'Just hangin' around,' like he had before. But then he added, 'Once the bastard got away from me….' His lawyer tried to shush him up but it didn't take much longer to get him to admit he kidnapped you. Apparently after you escaped, he started hanging around the building, hiding in one of the stairwells, waiting for a chance to get at one of you. Once he started talking, he couldn't help bragging about the rest of it. Like he's some kind of master criminal."

Rose snorted. "Even admitted to hitting Ben on the head. That afternoon he'd gone over to Cheryl's place to try to talk to her. Saw Ben in his car near her apartment and thought he was her new boyfriend. Decided to hide in the bushes by her patio and spy on them."

"So that was the movement Ben saw," Kate said, "and when he went over to investigate, Crofton hit him with something."

"Yup. Flowerpot. And the day he hit Mary… We had the wrong perp but the right motive. He was planning to kidnap you, Kate. Use you to get to Rob. When he saw all the blood, he thought he'd killed you and he took off."

"That fucking bastard!" Rob shuddered. "Sorry, ladies."

Kate reached for his hand to steady them both. "Don't apologize on my behalf. That's pretty much my sentiment as well!"

Rose nodded her agreement.

"Did Phillips get all this out of him?" Kate asked.

Rose shook her head. "Lieutenant did the interrogations himself." Then she grinned rather maliciously. "Phillips is on suspension. Being investigated. Seems he found a note on your front door Saturday morning, before I checked your house. He took it to the lab and didn't bother to follow up on it. I didn't hear what the location was, but apparently it said for you to come to a certain spot at ten that night, alone, or Rob would be killed."

Kate gasped. "If you hadn't gotten away, Rob…."

"Who knows what Crofton would've done," Rose said. "And it was a big missed opportunity to catch the bastard at the meeting place. Before he had the chance to try to shoot you."

Rob's face was dark with anger. "So Phillips almost got us both killed."

Rose suddenly sat up even straighter than her normal posture. "What if Phillips was *hoping* you wouldn't be found, Rob? Then he could just let the case go cold. An unsolved case would do his career a lot less harm than having his pet theory proven wrong and all his blunders revealed."

"Especially since those blunders meant other crimes weren't prevented that could've been," Kate said.

"Like the attack on Mary," Rob said.

"And your kidnapping itself," Rose added. "If he'd been looking for other leads instead of being so focused on you two, the whole thing might've never gotten that far. This perp's no rocket scientist. We probably could've caught him if we'd actually been chasing him."

"I think I need to have a talk with Lieutenant Cody," Rob said through clenched teeth.

"Probably not necessary. I don't think Phillips is gonna be carrying that gold badge much longer. Gave the lieutenant my report about the other stuff he did, and didn't do. Like not canvassing after the kidnapping, and telling you all he was going to treat it as a missing person case."

Rob's jaw dropped. "He did what?"

"Yeah, that was our reaction at the time," Kate said. "He told us he wasn't even going to look for you for forty-eight hours."

"At which point Kate went after him. It was all Skip and I could do to keep her from getting arrested for assaulting a police officer."

Rob batted his eyelashes at Kate and said in a falsetto voice, "My hero!" They all chuckled.

The desserts arrived.

Kate took her first bite. Savoring the contrasts of hot and cold, rich chocolate and smooth vanilla, she closed her eyes.

When she opened them again, Rob was watching her with an indulgent smile.

"Have you given any thought to names for the baby?" he asked.

"How does Edwina Elizabeth Rosa Huntington sound?"

"Long." Rob gave her a teasing grin. "What, no Roberta?"

'Rosa' had just raised an eyebrow, but Kate saw the corners of her mouth twitching. Rose was pleased.

She swallowed another luscious spoonful of gooey chocolate. "Thought about Roberta, but she's going to hate me enough for Edwina. Going to call her Edie."

"Then why not Edith as the formal name?"

"That's my mother-in-law's name." Kate excavated another spoonful of ice cream and brownie.

"'Nough said. What if it's a boy?"

"Then you get second billing. Edward Robert Mathias Huntington."

Rob grinned at her as she slowly demolished the rest of her dessert. Meanwhile, Rose was pretending she wasn't really enjoying hers all that much. This was revealed as some of her acting when she smacked her lips after the last bite disappeared.

As they were getting up to leave, Mac appeared, *sans* greasy apron and wearing a clean, Army-green T-shirt. Kate suspected it was the spare he kept in his office, and that he had put it on for Rose's benefit.

Sure enough, after they'd exchanged pleasantries, Mac gruffly asked Rose if he could talk to her alone for a moment.

Kate hid her smile as she and Rob walked out into the summer heat. They exchanged a long hug, and he headed for his car.

Waiting for Rose, Kate savored the feeling of being able to stand on the sidewalk alone without fear.

When the young woman came out of the restaurant, Kate asked, "So what was that about? Did Mac apologize for being so obnoxious?"

"Not exactly." Rose flashed one of her beautiful smiles. "But he did ask me out."

~~~~~❈~~~~~

AUTHOR'S NOTES

If you enjoyed this book, please take a moment to leave a short review on Amazon and/or other retailers. Reviews help to sell books and sales help me keep the series going! You can readily find the links to these retailers at http://misteriopress.com/misterio-press-bookstore/.

Sign up for my newsletter at **http://kassandralamb.com**, then e-mail me to let me know you've done so, and I'll send you a **free e-copy** of any of the Kate Huntington books. My e-mail is **lambkassandra3@gmail.com**. Heck, go ahead and e-mail me just to say hi; I love hearing from readers!

We at *misterio press* take pride in producing the highest quality books we possibly can. All of our books are proofread multiple times by different sets of eyes. But proofreaders are human. If you found mistakes in this book, please e-mail me so I can correct them. Thanks!

This book was my first novel in a series that now has five other books in it. When I *finally* finished writing it, I gave it to friends and family to read. They all said they loved it, but some had a note of surprise in their voices. That told me they really meant it. They had read out of obligation but were pleasantly surprised that they truly liked the story! Let me express my gratitude again to all those people. You helped make this book and the Kate Huntington series possible. And a big thank you to the beta readers, editors and my fellow authors at *misterio press*, all of whom have helped me grow as a writer.

This book took over fifteen years to write. It's not unusual for first books to take awhile, but not usually *that* long. I started it in my mid-forties; then life kept getting in the way. When I retired from my practice as a psychotherapist, I finally had time to focus on my writing.

Once I thought the book was sufficiently polished, I braced myself to start looking for a literary agent. With that goal in mind, I went to a writers' conference in August, 2011. There, two life-changing events occurred.

First I attended a workshop on the relatively new (at the time) phenomenon of e-publishing. I'd only had my own e-reader for a few months at that point, and I was intrigued by the changes in the publishing world that e-books had precipitated.

Second, I met a woman who was to become a good friend and the co-founder of *misterio press*. To make a long story short, while the other writers at the end-of-conference cocktail party were schmoozing with the agents and publishers, Shannon Esposito and I sat at a table drinking the free wine and plotting our strategy. A little over a year later, *misterio press* was born. We are a small indie press dedicated to producing high-quality stories for mystery lovers, while also allowing our authors to retain artistic control and the profits from their hard work.

A few quick apologies. As the disclaimer at the beginning of the book says, all characters and events (including Kate's therapy cases) are figments of my imagination. When I pick a character's name, I research it to try to determine if anyone famous has that name. But I'm bound to hit on some people's real names at times. So if I've happened to use your name for a character, it was not intentional. Nonetheless, I apologize, especially if that character was a child molester or wife-beater!

Most of the places I mention are real, although the streets where Kate and the Franklins live are made up. Also I apologize if you happen to live or own a business located at 2345 Wilkens Avenue. This street name I could not fictionalize since anyone familiar with Baltimore would know St. Agnes Hospital is located there. And the Cheryl sighting had to be on that street in order to make the story work.

Also to make the story work, I have made it sound a lot easier to hack into people's finances than it actually is. Liz is indeed a hacker *extraordinaire*.

Also, apologies to the Baltimore County Police Department for the fictional Detective Phillips. I tried very hard to make him a more balanced human being, with some good as well as bad in him. But characters sometimes have a will of their own, and no matter what I did, he refused to be anything but obnoxious. As is said several times in the story, the majority of police officers are good people and dedicated professionals. But every barrel has the occasional rotten apple. I have met police officers who were as egotistical and lazy as Phillips is. Indeed, I've met a couple who were worse.

People often ask me if Kate is a fictitious version of myself. The answer is no, she is the person I wish I was. She is infinitely more patient than I am. But she is not without flaws, and the curve balls life throws at her are definitely challenging. I have totally enjoyed watching her and the other characters grow and change as the series has progressed.

There are now six books out in the series, plus a more light-hearted Christmas novella. I'm working on Book 7, and a second novella has started down the long path of editing and polishing. I have ideas for at least two more books, so I don't see the series ending any time soon.

And on that note, let me share with you a synopsis of Book 2 in the series.

ILL-TIMED ENTANGLEMENTS
A Kate Huntington Mystery:

Widowed while still pregnant with her daughter, Kate Huntington knows she'd never have made it through the last year without the support of her closest friends, Rob and Liz Franklin. So when Rob asks her to help his great aunt, Kate can hardly say no.

He's in the middle of a major child custody case, and his octogenarian aunt, a best-selling author of historical romances, has been accused of plagiarism. He asks Kate to accompany Aunt Betty to a meeting with her publishers and help her deal with the messy business.

But by the time Kate arrives at Betty Franklin's retirement community in Lancaster, PA, the situation has gotten a lot messier. Betty's accuser is dead, and the local police detective is giving off signals that he thinks Betty is the murderer.

Unfortunately, the pool of suspects is huge. Just about every resident at The Villages Retirement Center had a reason to dislike the victim. When Kate and her friends start asking questions, they begin having "accidental" brushes with death themselves. Somebody doesn't like them poking around in people's pasts. Meanwhile the elderly residents are continuing to die off, and not from old age.

As if things weren't complicated enough, Kate realizes her interest in romance may be coming back to life, despite the conversations she still has in her head with her dead husband. Two men ask her out in as many days. She tells them both no; it's still too soon after her beloved Eddie's death. But she's having trouble denying her growing attraction to one of them.

When Rob arrives, still in stress overload after his tough court case, he doesn't handle the budding romance well. Could he be *jealous?* As they attempt to narrow the field of suspects and stop a murderer, Kate begins to fear what this whole mess might end up costing her... a second chance at love, her friendship with Rob, the life of someone she holds dear, or maybe even her own.

ABOUT THE AUTHOR

Kassandra Lamb has never been able to decide which she loves more, psychology or writing. In college, she realized that writers need day jobs in order to eat, so she studied psychology. After a rewarding career as a psychotherapist and college professor, she is now retired and can pursue her passion for writing.

She spends most of her time in an alternate universe with her characters. The portal to this universe, aka her computer, is located in Florida, where her husband and dog catch occasional glimpses of her.

For part of each summer, Kass returns to her native Maryland, where the Kate Huntington series is based.

To read and see more about Kate Huntington you can go to **http://kassandralamb.com**. Be sure to sign up for the newsletter there to get a heads up about new releases, plus special offers and bonuses for subscribers. (Psst! If you e-mail Kass and let her know you've signed up, she'll send you a free e-copy of any Kate Huntington book!) Her e-mail is **lambkassandra3@gmail.com** and she loves hearing from readers! She's also on Facebook and Twitter, and she blogs about psychological topics and other random things at **http://misteriopress. com**.

Please check out these other great *misterio press* series:
Karma's A Bitch ~ **The Pet Psychic series**
by Shannon Esposito
The Metaphysical Detective ~ **The Riga Hayworth series**
by Kirsten Weiss
Dangerous and Unseemly ~ **The Concordia Wells series**
by K.B. Owen
Murder, Honey ~ **The Carol Sabala series**
by Vinnie Hansen
Maui Widow Waltz ~ **The Islands of Aloha series**
by JoAnn Bassett

Plus more at **http://misteriopress.com/misterio-press-bookstore**

Made in the USA
Monee, IL
22 May 2021

69232411R00173